A Village in the Fields

a novel

Patty Enrado

Eastwind Books of Berkeley

Berkeley, California

Published by
Eastwind Books of Berkeley
2066 University Avenue
Berkeley, California 94704
www.asiabookcenter.com

Published 2015

First Edition

Printed in the United States of America

For more information or to book an author event, contact www.pattyenrado.com
or www.asiabookcenter.com

Cover design by Melody Shah
Book design by Harvey Dong

Front cover photo: Filipino migrant workers at a Central California labor camp, circa 1960s. From the Lorraine Agtang private collection. Reprinted courtesy of Welga! Filipino American Labor Archives, University of California Library, Davis.

Back cover photo: Filipino migrant workers at Fukui Photo Studio in Stockton, California, circa 1930s. Reprinted courtesy of Welga! Filipino American Labor Archives, University of California Library, Davis.

Library of Congress Control Number: 2015940386
ISBN: 9780996351706 (hardcover)
ISBN: 9780996351713 (paperback)
ISBN: 9780996351720 (e-book)

10 9 8 7 6 5 4 3 2 1

For beginnings and endings, and endings and beginnings

In memory of my mother and father,
Conchita C. Enrado (1926–2012)
and
Henry E. Enrado (1907–1995)

Here is my tale for you

Sleep peacefully, for your labors are done, your pains
Are turned into tales and songs

— Carlos Bulosan, from "Now That You Are Still"

CHAPTER 1

Visitors

Agbayani Retirement Village

Delano, California, August 1997

The fever was relentless—like the hundred-degree heat that baked the brick-and-tile buildings of Agbayani Village. Fausto Empleo lay on his bed, the window wide open, the curtains still, the table fan unplugged. He didn't move, though his body pulsed with the chirping of crickets. The groundskeeper's dog barked, and Fausto imagined jackrabbits disappearing between the rows of vines. Dusk was spreading across the fields like the purple stain of a crushed Emperor grape. With the poles of Mylar ribbons stripped of their hard, silvery glint, the crows—their caws growing in strength—descended, stealing ripe berries as the shadows of the oleander bushes stretched across the grounds.

The heat lingered. Even as the world outside went black.

Fausto clapped his hands. On the third try, the nightstand lamp threw out a circle of light. His nurse, Arturo Esperanza, had given him the lamp weeks ago. There's a genie inside, Arturo had teased him every time Fausto clapped. But this time, he drew his arm across his face. He sucked in his breath and smelled burning wax and the faint trace of sulfur as if from a lit match. But he had no candles. When he lowered his arm, his room was studded with hundreds of tall, white tapers standing in pools of wax at the edge of his bed and on the windowsill, his desk, the top of the television set. The milky lava dripped from the plastic petals of the bouquet on his dresser, and rivulets ran across the linoleum. The flames merged into a constellation of blazing stars. He turned away, his face prickling from the heat.

He shut his eyes. "Well, God, are you calling me?" The wind-up clock on his desk ticked like a giant, tinny heart. "Because if you are," he said, struggling to unbutton his shirt, now cold and damp against his skin, "I'm *not* ready to go!"

Fausto opened his eyes. The candles were gone. He shook his head. Why did he say that? He was the last *manong* here—the last Filipino elder at the Village. The rest of his compatriots—all retired farm workers—

had passed away. He should be begging God to take him now, but that would mean he'd given up, and he couldn't admit to such a thing—not yet.

He clapped his hands and willed himself to sleep, but sleep came in fits. When he woke up, it was still dark outside. The lamp gave off a weak glow, sputtering like a trapped fly. The wind-up clock was stopped at 12:20. Before Fausto could raise his hands, the light went out. A second later the lamp came back on, only to be snuffed out in an instant. It threw out light again, but it soon dimmed and then the room went dark for good. Fausto drew the sheets to his chest, listening for a knock on the door. Didn't his mother tell him, as a child, never to answer a knock at night? It is an evil spirit come to get you, she had warned. If you say, "I am coming," the evil spirit will take you, and you will die. Though she had counseled him to be as silent as Death, he cried out now, thumping the left side of his chest, "I'm still alive, son-of-a-gun! You go get somebody else!"

Awake for the rest of the night, he watched the sun creep into his room, exposing his sweat-stained sheets. When the door creaked open, his shaking hands formed fists. But it was only Arturo, his square-bodied nurse, filling out the doorframe. Fausto pieced together Arturo's eyes, nose, and mouth as the nurse approached his bed. It was as if the rest of Arturo's face had sunk into a blanket of Central Valley fog.

Arturo pressed his hand against Fausto's forehead, blocking out the light. "*Ay buey!* Somebody put you in a freezer!"

"Did you bring candles last night?" Fausto called out as Arturo disappeared into the bathroom. He licked his cracked lips, the tip of his tongue tasting salt and copper.

Arturo returned with a bowl of water and sat on a chair by the bed. He pressed a steaming, wet towel against Fausto's forehead. "I didn't come here last night."

"There were hundreds of candles burning in my room." Fausto pointed to the floor, the empty windowsill. "And then an evil spirit tried to snatch me."

"*No te creo!*" Arturo's brow formed a thick line. He peeled off the towel and anchored the thermometer under Fausto's tongue. "Your fever gave you nightmares."

When the thermometer beeped, Fausto gave it to Arturo without looking at it. "My fever is gone," he proclaimed. "I'll live forever, eh?

Then you'll be sorry for promises you made when you were a little boy."

"When was I *ever* a little boy?" Arturo's hand, bulky as a boxing glove, sank into the mattress. The seams of his white uniform strained with every movement.

"You were a little baby." Fausto held up his hands, inches apart. "You were born so early your father was afraid you would disappear. Then he thought he fed you too much. I told him it's better to have more meat than just bones. He was trying to be a good father. When we visit his grave, I always tell him he *was* a good father. Being a big boy made you strong!" Fausto laughed, though it hurt the sides of his head.

Arturo smiled. "He was a good father. He taught me to keep promises. Even if you live to 110—another twenty-five years!—I'll still watch over you."

"Ai, you can't tell what will happen." Fausto lowered his voice as Arturo wrung out the towel and placed it across his temple. "I made many promises."

"Well I've got a new promise—to get you out of this room!" Arturo bounced the mattress springs as he stood up. "Staying in bed so long makes you *loco*, makes you think an evil spirit is after you. I'll come back when it cools down. We'll go outside tonight, okay?"

Fausto shrugged. Arturo knew that when Fausto couldn't sleep, he took walks. Otis, the groundskeeper's German shepherd, never left his side, though Fausto tried to shoo it away.

He wanted to be with the crickets in the cool air. He always ended up at the edge of the Village, facing the open field, the health clinic, the old union building just beyond. What stretched before him was a great darkness that could swallow him whole if he stepped too far. When the stars came out, he felt small. And yet, he felt close to the earth.

"You go see your patients in town now," Fausto answered. He was getting lightheaded again, but Arturo wouldn't leave until he ate his meal. Fausto stuffed crackers in his mouth, melted them with gulps of hot soup from a Thermos to satisfy Arturo, who lingered by the door until Fausto waved him away.

He wanted the spirit to return so he could prove that he wasn't afraid, give himself a reason to fight. But the spirit didn't come.

Five days passed, and in that time, Fausto's fever broke for good. But he was still having trouble sleeping. One night, he battled unsettled sleep. Was the pressure in his head from the heat, or did his fever return?

He wavered in the moment separating deep sleep and awakening. It was as if he wanted to sleep finally, to remain in that state, but something was pulling him back to wakefulness. With a gasp, he shook free and fell into the night.

———————

Fausto stood at the end of the covered walkway. Faint, pink light edged the Sierra foothills to the east. A feral cat sat licking its fur by the barbecue pit. How bold the cat was, with Otis digging a hole by the brick building! Fausto was a little unsteady, but he was walking without pain. He pinched his hand—the sting ran to his fingertips.

He lifted his arms, inspecting the long-sleeved black shirt and black trousers he didn't remember putting on. *"Bumbye*, it will get hot before noon, and I'll burn up," Fausto said to himself.

"Fausto! Fausto Empleo!"

The voice shook him. He didn't hear the crunch of gravel as a man walked onto the grounds and paused next to a slender cypress tree that towered above him. The man fanned himself with a straw hat as his gaze swept the lawn and the buildings.

"Benedicto," Fausto whispered. "Benny."

"Fausto!" the man cried out, facing in his direction.

Fausto thought of running to his room, but his legs wouldn't move, and within a few dizzying moments, the man stood before him. Fausto waved his arms and stamped his feet.

The man stumbled back, the corners of his smile turning down. "Fausto, it's me. After twenty-four years, this is how you greet me?"

"Ania iti impagarupmo nga aramidek?" Fausto demanded.

"I don't know what to expect from you." Benny shrugged. "I should have come sooner, but you know how stubborn I am. You're stubborn too."

Fausto had always been half a head taller than his cousin. Now Benny, shrunken with a curved back, reached only to his chin. Benny was always slender, but his clothes hung on him as if he were a wire hanger and nothing more. The skin on his hands and face were pale and soft as if he hadn't spent a harsh summer working in the fields in years. Fausto wanted to hug Benny, but twenty-four years were still between them.

"You son-of-a-gun!" Fausto tried to keep the edge in his voice.

The knife creases in Benny's forehead vanished, though the spidery fine wrinkles remained. He smiled again. *"Kumusta?* How are you? I know you have been sick, but you look good, still strong."

"Eh? How did you know?"

Benny walked up to the long, U-shaped building and touched the weathered bricks set crooked in the mortar. When he brushed up against the rose bushes along the wraparound walkway, the flowers barely shivered. He stepped across the saltillo tiles without making a sound and stood beneath the porch, held up by silvered wooden poles. The sun had crept across the walkway, but all the curtains were still drawn shut.

Benny leaned into a splintered pole. "You are the last manong at Agbayani."

"You know Ayong and Prudencio are gone?"

Benny laughed nervously. "You were always with them." He passed a hand over his face, an old habit of his. "But I only see you, eh?"

A tremor worked its way out from the center of Fausto's body. "I was always with you too!" He kicked the base of the pole. He shouldn't be disrespectful after so much time passing. Benny might turn around and leave; he could see his cousin's eyes wavering. *"Saan nga bali.* Never mind," he said. "You must be hungry, traveling so far. We'll pick vegetables, eh? You still like your tomatoes dipped in *bagoong?"*

Fausto drew Benny to the vegetable garden. They walked around the sow-thistle sprouting in bunches from cracks in the ground. Wild grasses rose up like yellow flames spreading across the field, threatening to break the line of cacti towering over them. They passed leafless, blackened trees. When Otis barked behind them, Benny gave a start.

"That's Otis," Fausto said. "He'll not hurt you—he'll see you are with me."

The German shepherd trotted out from behind the building when Fausto whistled. But once it caught sight of them, the hair on its back stood on end. Otis sniffed the air. He stared them down and growled.

"C'mon, Otis!" Fausto called out, but the dog slunk away. "Ha! When I go walking at night, I can't get rid of that dog. Always tripping me up. Son-of-a-gun!"

Benny turned and walked past the empty rabbit pens, cracked pellets of feces still littering the floorboards. He squeezed through the half-open gate of the vegetable garden's chicken-wire fence to inspect the tomato plants. Overripe tomatoes lay flattened as if melted on the rocky soil.

"Even our vegetables are old!" Fausto laughed and put his foot through a cobweb that stretched across brittle leaves.

"Fausto," Benny said, looking him in the eye. "What have you been doing with yourself all these years?"

Fausto worked his mouth open, but nothing came out.

"Nobody told me anything after we left," Benny said. "Nida finally told me you stopped going to the parties and dances. You even stayed away from Domingo's funeral! They said you did not want anyone seeing you, so everybody gave up."

Fausto struck a lone stick with his heel, splintering it in two. "Is that what everybody has been saying? Macario is saying the same thing?"

"Nobody kept you from returning to Terra Bella."

"Ai! You are all still punishing me!" Fausto cried out.

"Kanayon nga insaksakit ka. I was always on your side."

"Until you abandoned me." Fausto scattered the slivers of wood between them with a sweep of his shoe.

"You want to stay bitter? You want me to go away?" Benny flattened the crown of his straw hat on his head. But he didn't leave.

"Saan! No!" Fausto motioned Benny to follow him. "You come with me."

He led Benny to the empty field, stopping beside a Datsun station wagon that sat in a patch of nutsedge. Wide cracks in the car seats exposed brittle foam and cut a pathway from one end to the other. Wires stuck out of a hole where a radio had once been. Fausto placed his hands on the car hood, away from the crusted layers of pigeon droppings. "I take my walks and I stop here. I pretend I'm driving, going somewhere," he said. "Sometimes to our house in Terra Bella. Sometimes back home in the Philippines."

In his daydreams at Agbayani Village, he always made a grand entrance in his yacht-sized car at the plaza of their hometown of San Esteban, rolling down the tinted windows so his townmates could feel the blast of cold air from the air conditioner. He let them run their fingers across the buttery leather seats. "You have to be smart to drive one of these," he said to the barefoot boys, whose eyes were as bright as the lighted dials on the dashboard. As he drove off to give the car to his parents, he heard his townmates cry out, "Ai, Fausto has a beautiful wife and baby. How generous he is with his wealth. He did the right thing, going to America!"

"You *are* rich. We are all rich," Benny said. *"Nagasat tayo."*

"We?" Fausto said. "I'm not lucky. You are. You have Luz and Rogelio and BJ."

"You did the right thing for *you.* There was no other way."

"I believed in what we were fighting for." Fausto struck the car hood with his knuckles. "Things are different, Benny, here and in the fields. But I'm alone—I've been alone now for many months. And every day I'm reminded of what I gave up and lost."

"You did not lose everything." Benny pulled up his sleeve and glanced at his watch. "We'll be together again soon."

"Are we not together now? Are you leaving me again? You came all the way from Chicago and you're leaving already?" Fausto tried to focus on his cousin, who seemed to fade like the Sierra foothills in the glare of the morning light. They hadn't been together for more than a half-hour. It couldn't have been past eight in the morning, but Benny's watch read 2:20. Benny pulled the cuff of his shirt over his watch. Fausto wanted to grasp his shoulders to prove that his cousin was really there. Instead, he pinched the loose skin of his own arm. His nerves tingled.

"Rogelio is coming to see you," Benny blurted out.

"Rogelio?" Fausto shivered. "When is he coming? Why now? What will he tell me?"

"Adda kayatna nga ibaga kenka." Benny's voice was tense, as he said again, "He'll be here soon to tell you. God willing, you already know."

"He's going to tell me the truth!"

Benny's head dipped, exposing the thinning crown of gray hair. "You still believe that, after all these years." His voice was full of uneasy wonder.

"Is this why I'm still alive, Benny? To hear the truth?"

"You'll believe what Rogelio tells you."

As Benny wiped his brow, his cuff pulled away from his bony wrist. Fausto saw that the hands on his watch had not moved at all.

"Benedicto, are you really here?" Fausto whispered. Benny looked at him as if he didn't understand. *"Agpayso nga addaka ditoy?"* he repeated.

"I go now." Benny adjusted his hat and strode toward the entrance.

"Where are you going? You just arrived. Benny, come back!"

Benny was several feet away from him already. "Wait for Rogelio. Don't be afraid. We'll be together again soon." His voice bounced back like an echo.

"Why should I be afraid?" Fausto shouted. He hurried after Benny, amazed that his cousin's quick stride was putting great distance between them. "Wait for me!"

He reached the entrance of the Village, short of breath. A gust of wind swept across the land. The trunks of the palm trees in the open field leaned toward the ground. Palm fronds shivered. Dust stung his eyes. He searched the road, but saw only fine particles floating and settling all around him. Then the earth gave way beneath his feet.

———————

Fausto woke up on the wooden bench at the end of the walkway, his socks and shoes scattered at his feet, his clothes covered in dust. His forehead was cool, the back of his neck damp. If he'd had a fever last night, it was broken now. He had battled the evil spirit and won again. Maybe for good.

A car pulled into the driveway. The door opened and slammed shut. The crunch of gravel grew louder. Perhaps it was Rogelio.

"Hombrecito!" Arturo marched toward him, his fists swinging at his sides like dumbbells. *"Ay buey!* How long have you been out here?"

"Eh?" Fausto squinted in the sunlight.

"Who brought you here so early in the morning?" Arturo sat next to him, bending the wooden bench board. He touched Fausto's forehead. "You feel cool to me."

"My fever came back last night, but I have recovered for good now." He felt lightheaded in his happiness. "I saw Benny. That is what gave me strength to come outside. Everything is okay now. He'll return, and Rogelio is coming to see me."

"Your cousin from Chicago? His son?" Arturo's eyes watered.

"Benny came here, I tell you! I have to wait for him to return." Fausto leaned forward, facing the entrance to the Village. A silver tabby licked its paws near a cypress tree. He grinned, pointing. "See that cat? It means visitors are coming."

Arturo searched Fausto's eyes. Fausto stared back, unblinking.

"You help me to my room. Then you bring me two more chairs and a table." He swayed for a moment when Arturo pulled him up. The tiles were hard on the balls of his feet, making him wince with every step. His room, at the end of one side of the U-shaped building, seemed as far away as the clinic across the field.

"Hombrecito, no way you coulda' come out here by yourself," Arturo said. "Look at you—you can hardly walk. Who moved you?"

"*Saan nga bali!*" Fausto rapped his own head. He tried to think but couldn't remember. "Ai, it does not matter," he repeated.

The door to his room was flung wide open. The air inside was cool, as if the door had been open for some time, maybe all night. Fausto was still panting after Arturo helped him to the chair. He pointed in the direction of the dining hall. "You go get three plates with lots of rice and fried fish."

"Three?" Arturo was out of breath too. He leaned over Fausto.

"Benny told me I did not lose everything." Fausto rocked in his chair. "He said Rogelio would tell me. It's better to hear it from him. That's why I'm still here. My heart knew. I did not understand until Benny came."

Arturo took Fausto's wrist and felt for his pulse. "Hombrecito, you'll be okay."

A black moth scraped across his window. It bumped into the walls, spinning in circles, before flying out the door. Fausto's heart raced. The burning candles, the stopped clock, lights going on and off. Even though he had defied Death twice, the moth made it clear. It was a sign of death. Before Rogelio's arrival and Benny's return. After all these years, he would be cheated again, but this time with the finality of death.

"We'll go to the hospital." Arturo's voice echoed in his head.

"No," Fausto whispered. "Call St. Mary's. Bring Father Bersabel to me."

He grasped Arturo's hands and rested his face between his soft palms. Arturo's fingers cooled his skin. The moment before his head fell back and the world went black, the room spiraled below him, Arturo's hands like enormous wings lifting him up.

CHAPTER 2

What was left behind

Fausto woke up in his bed. The room was hazy, as if a dust storm had blown in through the window. When he breathed, he imagined specks being sucked into his nose and swirling in his lungs. He thought of when he picked table grapes decades ago—Muscat, Thompson, Ribier, Emperor, Calmeria—from July through September, from one vineyard to the next on Mr. Cuculich's acres of farmland. The farm workers wore scarves or bandanas, or wrapped and pinned T-shirts around their noses and mouths to keep from breathing dust. Some duct-taped the ends of their gloves to their long shirtsleeves and the tops of their boots to their jeans. Everybody wore straw hats or baseball caps. But it was useless. Late afternoons, when Fausto peeled away layers of clothes, dust clung to everything. It seeped through his outer clothes and dirtied his undershirt. Dust and sweat turned his white socks muddy brown. Even his teeth felt gritty. Fausto ran his tongue along his teeth, expecting grit.

"Fausto! Come home with me!" His wife, Marina, gripped his arm.

Nearby, a scratchy voice boomed from a bullhorn: "Your boss says we're Communists! They're trying to scare you. We're trying to bring justice to the fields!"

The picketers waving red-white-and-black signs and the grape packers at the roadside field station moved back and forth like an uneasy wave. Across the road, plainclothes policemen, sheriffs, and deputies in crew cuts and sunglasses leaned against patrol cars, arms folded against their chests, pistols in holsters bulging at their waists.

The picketers chanted the Spanish word for "strike": "*Huelga! Huelga!*"

"*Esquiroles!* Scabs! Come out of there!" a woman shouted, and held up a sign.

Grape pickers, who came from Mexico in buses supplied by the growers, swarmed the fields. The replacement workers—scabs, the strikers called them, while the Mexican strikers called them esquiroles—kept their heads down. But one sparred back.

"We need to feed our family! Take care of *your* family!" a man yelled.

Before anyone could respond, gunshots rang out. A woman screamed down the road, setting off sirens. The law enforcers ran toward the crowd where picket signs converged, their boots pounding against the blacktop. Fausto pushed Marina in the opposite direction. She fled without a word, abandoning the lunchbox she'd brought Fausto on the rocky soil. He caught a flash of her white blouse as she drove off in their Bel Air, but she did not offer him her face. Even as he told himself she'd be safer at home, his muscles tightened as he spun around and headed into the fields.

———————

Fausto clenched his teeth and dug his heels into the thin mattress as if that would stop the shouting. With Rogelio coming, he would have to relive his past, recount it to Rogelio because Rogelio would want to know his side of the story. Fausto owed him that, and much more. He squinted at the clock, its hands still stuck on 12:20. Stomach grumbling, he knew it was close to dinnertime, which meant Arturo would return soon. Earlier in the morning, instead of calling the *pinoy* priest, Arturo rushed him to the emergency room, where he was examined and released. Fausto hushed Arturo, who questioned the doctor's judgment. He didn't want to stay in the hospital. What if Rogelio were looking for him at that very moment? Under protest, Arturo brought him back to Agbayani Village, vowing to check up on Fausto morning and evening—and midday, if his schedule permitted.

Fausto didn't ask if Arturo avoided calling the priest because the nurse was just as superstitious as he was. Fausto didn't want the Evil Spirit to think Father Bersabel was giving him his last rites—a sure sign that he'd surrendered. Even if Fausto was only given a blessing, the priest's presence would draw the Evil Spirit to his door, outside his window, waiting. Fausto was not about to tempt anyone.

Something bumped up against his door, making Fausto bolt up in bed. The knob turned and Arturo burst in, clutching two grocery bags to his chest. Fausto looked past the nurse. He passed his hand over his face. Everything was okay. Arturo was here now—with nobody, nothing else behind him—and he had brought Fausto his lunch, which he laid out on a TV tray. While Fausto ate, Arturo weaved in and out of English and Spanish, first complaining about his Camaro having trouble starting in the heat wave and then declaring that the doctor had made a hasty decision.

"He didn't check the clouds in your eyes." Arturo unpacked cans of chicken soup and fruit in heavy syrup on Fausto's desk with a thud.

"Okay, Nurse Know-It-All! Why don't you trade places with that doctor? He sees I'm okay, I'm getting stronger." Fausto lowered his voice. "For Rogelio's sake."

"Hombrecito, that kind of thinking is gonna make you sicker!"

"He's coming, I tell you!" Fausto insisted. "Benny came just to tell me."

"Dios, me ayuda a ayudarle," Arturo mumbled.

Fausto rattled one of the TV-tray legs. "You say you want to help me? Then come here."

Arturo moved the tray away from the bed and sat down, his face shiny with sweat.

"How long are you staying tonight?"

"As long as you need me," Arturo responded. "I'll spend the night if you want me to."

"I want you to listen to my stories," Fausto said. "I want to get everything right before Rogelio comes."

Arturo looked down at his scuffed white shoes. "Don't," he said, in a soft voice.

"Ai, then go away!" Fausto thundered. He punched Arturo's massive shoulder, the flesh soft, but the bulk of it unyielding.

"I said I would stay." Arturo grabbed his fists. "You want to talk about the strikes?"

Fausto took a deep breath. He allowed Arturo to massage his fingers until they went limp. "Sure," he said slowly. "But you have to go back to when I was a boy in San Esteban."

"That far back?" Arturo rolled his eyes.

Fausto shook his hands free. "I was born in 1912. I came here in 1929."

"I guess I *will* be spending the night here." Arturo leaned against the headboard and crossed his arms, bunching up his white shirt. "Go on then, hombrecito."

Fausto blinked several times, suddenly speechless.

"You worked the land back home too, right?" Arturo coached him.

Fausto raised his chin to keep his lips from trembling. "My father owned several hectares of land. We planted rice, tobacco, and agave— *maguey.* We were not rich, but we were not poor! And I had an American education. I was not as ignorant as Pa said I was!"

"You were so full of promise, Fausto, but you were meant to work the land."

Fausto jerked his head in the direction of the open window. The curtains hung limp. He didn't say anything to Arturo; it was not Arturo's voice that had spoken to him.

———

When Fausto's father, Emiliano, began taking him to the rice fields to plant and harvest at the age of seven—the same age his father and grandfather had begun to work—Fausto knew he would not follow in their footsteps. He would not get up before the sun rose and ride the *carabao*—the plodding water buffalo—to the rice fields for the rest of his life. He would not harvest maguey and strip, wash, cure, and braid its fibers into rope and then haggle with agents over how many pesos could be paid for several kilos of maguey. Somehow, he would find a way to attend the American school in San Esteban. His uncles had allowed his older cousins—Macario, Caridad, Serapio, and Domingo—to go to school but only when they weren't needed in the fields. They fell back a few grades until Uncle Johnny, Macario's father, forced his son to quit for good, and Fausto's other cousins quit soon after.

Fausto couldn't hang around the schoolhouse after classes to catch the American teacher's attention because he came home from the fields after sundown, long after Miss Arnold had closed up the wooden building. He knew one of the students' mothers cleaned the schoolhouse on Saturdays. Fausto convinced his *lelang*, his grandmother, to stop by the schoolhouse on their way to the marketplace one Saturday and talked his way into polishing the floors for half of the four centavos the woman was earning. The musty odor gave him a coughing fit, but he rubbed the floors with petroleum-soaked banana leaves until the wood gleamed like the bow on Miss Arnold's hat. His lelang agreed to keep his job a secret; Fausto told her he wanted to replace their sickly farm animals with the money he was making. He hoped Miss Arnold would show up while he was working, but she never came.

No matter. When he finished cleaning, he opened up books stuffed on shelves that spanned the length of the room. He cut his fingertips along the edge of the pages, but he minded them less than the calluses on his palms. He copied the curves and lines from the books onto the slate board and stood back to admire his work before erasing all trace of white chalk. He stared at the colorful pictures tacked on the walls until his lelang returned and scolded him that his secret would be found out. The following week, he asked one of the girls from town who was a student to help him write a sign. The next Saturday morning, he left it at the entrance of the schoolhouse: "Floor cleaned by Fausto Empleo."

By the third Saturday, when nothing had happened, he realized he would have to introduce himself to Miss Arnold, without his mother's and his lelang's knowledge, at St. Stephen's, where the teacher and his family worshipped. After mass, he spied Miss Arnold greeting members of the congregation. The men craned their necks—she towered above them with a head piled high with brown hair—and saluted. "Good morning, Miss Arnold!" they said in lively voices. The women bowed and addressed her as *maestra*. She strode across the gravel walkway, her big feet marching in dusty brown boots. It was a warm day and yet she wore a wool suit—a long-sleeved jacket and a stiff skirt that puffed out— with a blouse that covered her neck to her chin. As she came closer, he saw wrinkles in her sunburnt face. Gray hairs poked out along her hairline like fine wire.

She would have walked by Fausto if he hadn't stepped into her path. "Miss Arnold, are your floors shiny enough?" He shifted his feet; his toes curled in shoes that didn't fit.

She studied his face for a moment before responding in Ilocano in a bright voice, "You must be Fausto Empleo! I see you leave your signature like an artist." She took his hand and shook it. She didn't seem to notice his calluses. Her own hands, as big as a man's, were covered with brown spots. "You look to be seven years old, ready for school. Why are you cleaning my floor and not attending my class?" She bent down, her eyes level with his. She slid her glasses to the tip of her slender nose. Her eyes were as clear as the sea off of San Esteban on a cloudless day. He couldn't stop staring.

"I have to help my pa with our land," he answered in English. Fausto stole a glance past Miss Arnold. Father Miguel, in his starched white cassock, was greeting his mother and lelang. "My pa says I'm a good worker in the fields."

"Oh, dear," she said in English, and held her cheek as if her tooth ached. "I'm sure you are a good worker, but you need to go to school! We teach industrial skills, not just reading and writing. The whole world is changing. You must realize we are living at a time of great progress. You can't be left behind. School is for everybody."

Fausto's head swam. While even the laborers were teaching

themselves English—American and English-speaking businessmen had flooded the islands since the Spaniards were driven out—what he knew was not enough. "I know about school," he said, looking past the yellow-flowered *gumamela* bushes and acacia trees, in the direction of the schoolhouse. "After I clean the floors, I look at the books and the pictures on the walls," he said, then cocked his head to one side. "But if you want to teach reading in English, you need books that have more words than pictures. We like to work hard."

Miss Arnold pursed her lips, holding back a smile. Tiny wrinkles branched out around her mouth. "I will consider your practical suggestion, Fausto. Your work ethic will serve you well in school, and you would be a big help to me in the classroom. I strongly suggest you come to my class." She sat on her haunches before him, her blue skirt billowing out and sweeping the ground. "A poet wrote about the difficult journey we Philippine teachers have had to undertake. The end of the poem says: 'Remember, while you try to do your parts, / That, if one single spark of light you leave / Behind, your work will not have been in vain.'" She broke out grinning. "Fausto Empleo, you already exhibit a spark of light, but you can be *more* with schooling. How rewarding that would be for you, your parents, and me—to be *more!*"

She promised to visit his house to request permission for him to go to school. After she left, he caught sight of his mother walking homeward, his baby brother joined at her hip, his sisters skipping behind her, his lelang trailing and eyeing him. Nearby, the town *presidente's* daughters greeted their American teacher with curtsies. The two girls, dressed in striped skirts and filmy *blusas* as pale as their faces, were waiting for their *calesa*, which had pulled into the courtyard. A dark-skinned man hoisted the girls to their covered seats. He sat in front and snapped his whip against the horse's oily black flank. Fausto's sisters called after him, and he ran to catch up, wincing in his shoes. He looked back as the two glazed yellow wheels spun in circles and the red-painted calesa lurched forward, dipping in and out of the ruts beyond the arched entryway. It soon passed him and his family, though he broke out into a lively gait, imagining he could outrun the horse.

———————

Miss Arnold came the following Sunday, just as Fausto and his family were returning from church. When his mother saw her, she hurried across the yard, jouncing his baby brother in her arms, ignoring the teacher. Even his lelang retreated indoors without a word. Alarmed, Fausto kicked off his shoes and outran his mother to the backyard. His father, shirtless, pant legs rolled up to his knees, had just entered the pigs' pen, scraping a knife against a sharpening stone. The only pig in the pen was the one his sisters had named "Ti Presidente" because it pushed the other pigs away from the trough during feeding time. It already weighed fifty kilos, big enough to feed the family for weeks. Fausto ran harder, hoping to reach his father before the pig's throat was slit.

"Pa!" Fausto hopped up on the fence, his arms dangling over the top rail.

His father's eyes flickered when he saw Miss Arnold crossing the yard. He threw down the knife and stone, and came to the open gate. Fausto's cheeks reddened at the sight of his father's exposed chest. His mother hesitated on the other side of the fence as Miss Arnold came shoulder to shoulder with her. Miss Arnold glanced at the tethered pig, whose back hooves scratched at the clay soil. His father retrieved the knife and cut the cord that bound the pig's feet. It kicked up on all fours, darted to the far end of the pen, and tunneled into a stack of hay. The upended straw quaked.

"Good afternoon, Mr. Empleo," Miss Arnold said in Ilocano, in a voice that Fausto decided was always bright and pleasant, no matter the situation.

When she bowed, his father's upper lip curled. Fausto dug his fingernails into the railing. He wished he'd advised Miss Arnold to wear a hat with a wider brim like that of a woven bamboo *salakot*. His father was likely thinking that her hat, which didn't shade the sun from her face, was for vanity's sake.

"I'm here to appeal to you," she went on, despite the chickens pecking at her feet. "I would like your son to join my classroom so he can receive an education."

"He does not need an education."

"Good heavens!" Miss Arnold laughed. Even her sea-blue eyes were laughing. "Everybody needs an education, especially when you are born into this world at a disadvantage. It's the only way to move up in this world! So many children here are benefiting from going to school. They have grown up to become teachers and *presidentes* in other towns. It's for the good of the community." She swept her gaze from Fausto to his mother as if trying to rally them to her cause.

"You cannot know what is good for us." His father straightened his spine, though he was still shorter than she.

Fausto buried his head in the crook of his arm. His toes began to slip from the rail. Hanging there, he felt as if his life were the thing being suspended.

"Emiliano," his mother said. "Miss Arnold is a guest in our country, in our town."

Fausto's baby brother, Cipriano, cooed in her arms.

"Do guests tell their hosts what to do?" His father's voice crackled.

His mother stepped back, pressing her cheek against Cipriano's ear.

"Mr. Empleo," Miss Arnold said, holding her head high, "I came to the Philippine Islands in 1901 with a mission to educate your youngsters. I've only been in San Esteban for two months, but I've lived in your country for eighteen years. I don't consider myself a guest anymore. More importantly, I've taken the interests of the people of San Esteban —indeed, of the Philippine Islands—to heart. Many of the teachers who first came here when I did have already gone home, trusting the future of the school system to the natives, but I confess I'm not ready to go just yet. Besides the lovely way I've been treated here and the lovely time I've had, something else has been keeping me put, although I didn't know what it was—until now." She glanced at Fausto.

His father gave her a withering look. "My son will answer for himself."

Miss Arnold clapped her hands. "Excellent! After all, it is *his* future."

The three of them turned to Fausto, who had shrunk behind the fence.

"What do you say, Fausto?" his father prodded, his words sharp, like a *talibon* knife poking at his gut.

"I would like to try," Fausto said slowly, trying to summon up the courage, the words, his desire. "Pa, I would like to go to school and get an education."

But his father shook his head. "I cannot lose his work in the fields."

"If Fausto cannot attend school during the day, we can create a special schedule for him," Miss Arnold said, her smile persisting. "When is he free?"

"Free?" His father looked skyward and wiped his brow with his forearm. "We have a longer work day than the sun."

"Sunday is our day of rest," Miss Arnold said, "but for Fausto's sake I can open up the schoolhouse a few hours in the afternoon and give him some lessons. Will that be acceptable to you, Mr. Empleo?"

"Fausto can go to your schoolhouse for two hours every Sunday afternoon," he said, "but if he is too tired to work on Monday, he must stop learning."

"I understand, Mr. Empleo." She thrust her hand out to him. When he hesitated, she added, "I grew up in a farm in Missouri. My father recently retired, although a farmer never really retires. He swore he'd rather die threshing grain than rocking in a chair. I can see you and my father have that much in common. I don't mind getting my hands dirty. It means you're a hard worker. My father would say that and he's right."

He was slow to take her hand. When they pulled away, Miss Arnold said, "We have a garden behind the school. If you care to know, I believe in the dignity of labor."

She waved good-bye, winking at Fausto as if they had secretly plotted together. When she was gone, when he no longer heard the marching footfalls of her boots, Fausto expected his father to strike his head. Instead, his father flicked off clay stuck to his heel.

"Do not be angry," his mother said.

His father chuckled. "Do you remember when that other American teacher forced Johnny to send Macario to school?" he said. "My brother told that teacher she could have him as long as his work in the fields did not suffer. She knew nothing about farming here. Maybe Fausto will last a few weeks." He cocked his head. "Maybe less."

Fausto jumped off the fence, making the rails quiver. He wanted his father to realize that he'd been listening the whole time, but his father didn't care. He spied his lelang in the kitchen window, but when their eyes met she stepped behind the curtain.

"Emiliano!" his mother said. "Do not be so cruel to Fausto."

"I am protecting my family. That is what fathers do." He tossed the cord at Fausto's feet. "Fausto, get Ti Presidente."

The pig grunted at the empty trough. Fausto would have chased it out of the yard and down the road, chased it into a field thick with *bagbagotot* bushes. Instead, he tackled the pig and tied its legs so tight the cord cut into its pink skin. Squealing, the pig flailed, flinging mud on his Sunday trousers, digging its cloven hoof into his bare toes. Fausto kicked the animal's hairy behind and dragged it toward his father, who stood with the knife in his fist.

———

Though his father worked him hard, Fausto never missed school. When Miss Arnold presented him with a map of the world for his geography lesson, he was stunned to see how small the Islands were compared to other countries, how vast the oceans were, how big the world was. He listened to stories about George Washington and Abraham Lincoln. By the end of his first year, before he turned eight, he could read and write a little in English, and he could add and subtract. He was looking forward to mastering English and learning the industrial skills she was teaching the older boys. But when he came home after mass one Sunday, Miss Arnold was at the door, talking to his mother, who was home sick. He wondered why his teacher was not at church. She rested her hand on his shoulder, and then withdrew it, her touch so fleeting he thought he had dreamed it up.

"I've come to say good-bye, Fausto," she said.

"Miss Arnold is needed at home," his mother said. "Her father is very ill."

Miss Arnold patted a handkerchief across her moist upper lip. "Your father was right about one thing: In the end, our families need us and we need them."

Fausto wanted to strike the door. He didn't want his father to be right. He didn't want Miss Arnold to admit it. But he held his arms down, digging his fists into his thighs.

"Are you coming back?"

"I'll miss the planting season. It's almost here, isn't it?" she said, as if she didn't hear him. "It's my favorite time—accordions and guitars, singing, dancing in the mud. Such a lovely tradition, such a lovely people." She fastened her gaze on Fausto. "I'm going home for good, but I hope to see you again. Perhaps you can come visit me outside of Kansas City when you're all grown up."

Fausto's father emerged from the shadows and stood in the doorway. "There is no reason for him to leave San Esteban," he said.

Miss Arnold locked eyes with Fausto. "I grew up on a farm, and look where I've been in my life! You can become anything you want."

His mother coughed into the sleeve of her *blusa*. "We can never imagine sending Fausto to the States, Miss Arnold. It is too dear a price for us," she murmured.

"I'm so sorry!" Miss Arnold's cheeks reddened. "Please excuse me for my indiscretion. I should leave now and continue with my packing. I've accumulated so many things in my eighteen years here!"

"Have you not seen your father in eighteen years?" His father's voice was sharp.

Miss Arnold stood still for a moment. "No," she whispered, blinking hard.

His father bowed his head. "Miss Arnold, we are sorry for your loss."

"Pa, her father is not lost yet," Fausto said. It was bad luck to talk about someone as if he or she had already passed away.

"It *is* a loss," Miss Arnold said. She stuffed her handkerchief beneath her sleeve and tugged on the stiff cuff of her suit jacket. "Thank you all for your kindness."

Fausto stood in her way. "What will become of our lessons?"

"Fausto!" His mother pinched his arm, but he couldn't feel a thing.

"Let Miss Arnold go," his father said.

"Josefa Zamora will be taking my place," Miss Arnold said. "She told me she will try to open up the schoolhouse on Sunday afternoons for you."

Fausto didn't know what else to say. Time would not stop. He stepped aside.

"I have fond memories of my stay here," Miss Arnold said to Fausto's mother and father. She knelt down in front of him and gathered him in her arms.

The lavender scent in her hair made him think of the bars of soap at the schoolhouse that her students used to wash their hands after lunchtime.

She touched his cheek. "I shall miss you the most, my little spark of light. So full of promise. Remember, you can do more. You have it in you."

She stood up, sucking the air around him, and hurried away. Fausto ran after her, but he stopped at the gate. He watched her arms swing by her sides. Her feet, in their brown, button-up boots, marched as they always did across the dirt road. Then she was gone, swallowed by the bagbagotot bushes, the bend in the road.

"No more," his father said in Ilocano. He clamped his hand on Fausto's shoulder. "School made you worthless in the fields. I was going to stop it, but she did it for me."

Fausto locked his knees, dug his feet in the earth. He wanted to bolt after Miss Arnold. She was still somewhere down that road. He imagined himself next to her, ignoring the blisters on his feet from his shoes, wanting to keep pace with her boots. "If I finish seventh grade, I can teach school too," he insisted. "Just like Josefa Zamora."

His father snorted, and said, "Teaching is for teachers." His father spun him around and turned his hands over. "See?" With his leathery finger he rubbed the calluses in Fausto's skin. "You are meant to work the land."

He let go and strode inside, his mother following, her head down. His lelang, quiet as a house lizard, emerged from behind the kitchen door and touched his sleeve.

Fausto turned to her. "Lelang Purificación, are you with Pa?"

Her face was full of hard lines and sorrow. "Your father has his reasons, Fausto. You are too young to understand. There is so much you must learn."

"I *was* learning!" he said. "You are all against me. Now I am alone."

"Alone?" She stared at him as if he had spoken in a foreign tongue. "You will never be alone, Fausto. You will always be with us."

He shook his head and ran out of the yard, covering several hundred meters before realizing he'd gone in the opposite direction of Miss Arnold. Each breath scalded his lungs. His legs were giving out; his toes were wet with popped blisters. He fell to the side of the road, crashing into a thatch of cogon grass. Its sharp-pointed leaves pricked his face. He rolled over and pawed at his ears, his lelang's words burrowing like a tick.

———

Fausto's scalp prickled in the Central Valley heat. He stood by the window, hoping for a breeze. The sky was as faded as a pair of old jeans, the wispy clouds billowed like worn cotton shirts hung out to dry. Palm trees in the distance rose above the flat earth. When he first arrived in the Valley, he asked an old-timer how these trees ended up lining the streets of towns in the area. The Philippines had so many palm trees, and the land was lush from the rainy seasons, not dry most of the year like it was in the Valley. The old-timer told him the local farmers sold their produce in Los Angeles. If the farmers profited from a good crop, they bought and hauled back palm trees, and planted them along the private roads leading up to their houses and nearby streets. It was a sign, visible for miles, of their prosperity. Fausto laughed. If only that had been the situation in San Esteban!

Arturo spoke up. "Hombrecito, so Miss Arnold inspired you to go to America?"

Fausto moved away from the window, each step a test for his legs. "She opened up the world for me. But after she left, nothing was going to change. Pa made sure of that. When I was twelve, my cousins—Macario, Cary, Serapio, and Domingo—left for America. Macario met some rich Filipino boys who studied at American colleges. He got it in his head that he could be like them—a *pensionado*—having the American government pay for their education in the US." Fausto shrugged. It sounded silly to him now.

He walked slowly around in circles, the room too small to hold his restlessness. "Cary, Serapio, and Domingo left with their families' blessing, but Uncle Johnny was against Macario leaving. So Macario ran off with them. Uncle Johnny accused him of stealing from the profits of their harvest of maguey. Benny and I refused to believe Macario could steal and lie to his own family. Then Uncle Johnny blamed everyone else for Macario's escape."

———————

Uncle Johnny ranted in front of San Esteban's town hall as he wandered from one acacia tree to the next in the plaza: "The Americans said they would liberate us, but they are just like the Spaniards! Our children come home from their schools wanting to be like the rich Americans! They steal our children's minds and then their bodies!" Fausto's father and his uncles carried off Uncle Johnny, who bellowed all the way home, blaming God for Macario's disobedience, his disappearance, for the fact that he would never see his son again.

Macario sent Fausto and Benny letters, accompanied by a studio portrait. After his little brother fell sleep, Fausto pulled out the photograph from beneath his woven mat and studied every detail under the kerosene lamp. During the day, when he stared at his reflection in the flooded fields, he didn't see a teenager, brown as mud, planting rice. He saw his four cousins in all their finery. In the portrait, flat-painted clouds puffed up behind them. The flowery rug beneath his cousins' leather shoes looked too expensive to be walked on. Cary and Macario stood in back. Serapio and Domingo sat straight-backed in stuffed chairs, their legs crossed at the knees. Cary clutched a pair of gloves with covered buttons. They all wore three-piece wool suits. The high, starched collars and bulbous knot of their wide ties seemed to hold up their chins, their proud smiles. Cary and Macario wore their fedoras with a corner tipped to one side, shadowing an eye. Serapio and Domingo's fedoras sat on their laps like prizes.

Macario wrote of the plentiful jobs and high wages. He bragged about the temptations—American women who flirted with them, Chinese gamblers who dared them to try their luck at winning fistfuls of American dollars—that constantly battled for their money and attention. The postmarks on the envelopes hailed from different towns and states across America, but in the last couple of years Los Angeles, California, had become their home. "Hope Street is calling you," Macario wrote. "When will you answer, Fausto?"

When Fausto and Benny transplanted rice shoots or washed maguey in the sea, they daydreamed of fine clothes, the affections of American girls, the vast campuses of American colleges. Fausto never heard from Miss Arnold again, but he kept hearing her voice in the rice fields, in the wind that tousled the ocean waves, at night when he couldn't sleep—*You can become anything you want*. Wasn't Macario proof? It was good enough for Fausto and Benny. They saved their money, and in five years they could afford the price of boat tickets.

One evening after dinner had been cleared from the table, he followed his father to the backyard. "Pa," he said, "Benny and I are going to America."

His father turned around, even in height with Fausto. He had celebrated his forty-first birthday earlier in the year, though he looked older. His arms and legs were hard with muscle, but his skin was as tough as the cured hide of a carabao. He held out his palms, slashed with rope burns from guiding the water buffalo across the muddy fields. "Do you think I will let you go when Macario and your cousins have never come back?" he said. "Your poor Uncle Johnny has no son to help him with his farm work."

"Pa, Macario is Uncle Johnny's only son, but our family is large enough to help with the fields and the animals."

Shock spread across his father's face. "Is it a matter of giving up one son so easily because I have another? Sons are not bargained with like bales of maguey!"

"That was not my intent," Fausto said. "It is fate. Like Lelong's life, your life."

"Your lelong and I chose to build our lives here." He held out his arms to encircle his land, his son. "You can choose too, only you choose to go away!"

"Pa, I want to change my luck," Fausto said.

His father looked past him, though the dazed expression never left his face. "Miss Arnold," he said finally. "After she left, I dreamed her ghost returned. She cracked your skull and everything she taught you spilled out and swept you into the sea." He rocked on his bare heels as if seized by waves. "The dream came to me again and again. I worried you would leave one day. But time passed. I thought you were happy. I fooled myself, picking which girl in San Esteban you would marry. I was going to give you the largest rice field on your next birthday." He raised his hand, which loomed like a wall that Fausto couldn't scale. "I cannot stop you. We are done here."

"Benny and I leave next month," Fausto said. "We have paperwork to complete in Manila. A doctor has to examine us."

As he spoke of his plans, which he and Benny had plotted so carefully, so secretively, they became as real as the tamped soil beneath his feet. But his father walked away before he could finish. Fausto wasn't angry. He watched his father retreat to the house and climb the stairs to his bedroom, the wooden steps creaking, exploding, echoing with each footfall—the sound, Fausto imagined, of his father's heart breaking.

The night before he and Benny left, Fausto carried out his chores. He used to hate checking the pigs, asleep in their pens, but he gazed with tenderness at the masses of pink fat glistening beneath his lamplight. He took in the smell of hay mixed with mud, the gassy stench of wet excrement. When he heard footsteps behind him, he knew it was his father, but he didn't turn around until his father thrust a piece of paper into his chest. Fausto's lantern had run out of kerosene, so his father lit a torch and held it above them. The carabao stirred in the corner of the yard, its eyes glittering beneath drowsy lids, its nose shining wetly. Light flickered over rows of mongo beans on the vine. Shadows of green bamboo shoots cut across the earth. All he could hear was his father's shallow breath.

The letter, written by Cary to his mother, announced that he had tuberculosis. He expected to die because the doctors told him he would if he didn't take care. He couldn't work to help pay for rent. Jobs were scarce or hard. It was a different kind of hard than working in the rice fields. They had no money for school. The Americans said cruel words to them wherever they went. Cary was trying to save enough money to return home.

Fausto turned his face away from the heat. "Why are you showing this to me?"

"Do you want to end up like Cary? Spending precious money and then coming home sick so your mother has to take care of you?" The torch shook in his hand. Bits of charred wood flew and skipped across the ground. "Your Auntie Lilia gave me this letter."

Fausto looked at the date. Four months had gone by since the letter was written. He tried to remember when he had received the last portrait of his cousins. He would have noticed if his handsome cousin was ill. Instead, he recalled how splendid Cary looked, his curly hair thick and healthy, his smile relaxed and sure of himself. Macario bragged that Cary had the looks to rival Gary Cooper. He could become a big movie star. It was the reason they moved to Hollywood.

Fausto swallowed hard, grimacing as if he had bitten into *parya*, the melon's warty skin bitter to the taste. "If this letter is true, Auntie Lilia would not shame Cary or herself in front of everybody. He would not want her to show this letter to anyone else."

Purple blotches the color of *tarong* deepened across his father's cheeks like a bruise. "Stupid boy! You think I am tricking you?" He slapped the piece of paper with the back of his hand. "Lilia is trying to save you at the expense of her own shame!"

His father's shouting roused the carabao, which shifted its weight and bellowed. A few pigs grunted, then fell silent. The goats crowded to the front of their pen, rustling hay beneath their hooves. Fausto stared at the crossed-out words written with such force that the onion paper was torn in places. How could he accuse his father of forging a letter that involved his cousin and auntie? The families were so close, the town so small.

"You are trying to weaken me with this letter," Fausto said.

"I am trying to strengthen you!"

"I am leaving—whether it is true or not." Fausto dropped the letter. He ran into the house, heart pounding, but stopped to spy from the kitchen window.

His father pierced the letter with the torch. Sparks flew across the yard. Smoke curled up. The letter crackled, turning into ashes. Black bits twirled away into the darkness. The rest crumbled at his father's leathery feet. He turned his back to the house, with his head held high.

Fausto retreated to the second floor. A candle glowed in his lelang's bedroom, though she was usually asleep by this time. He hesitated before pulling the crocheted curtain aside. She was sitting up, as if waiting for him. He sat on her bed and inhaled the musty, bitter scent of betel nut mixed with lime on her lips and red-stained teeth.

"Lelang Purificación," he began, "Pa will not give me his blessing."

"You should be honored by the burden of his love," she said. She sighed and stared out her window, the *capiz*-shell panels slid open all the way to let the stars in.

"What about you, Lelang? Will you try to change my mind?"

She pursed her lips as if she had swallowed betel-nut juice. "I tell you something not to change your mind but so you are not ignorant."

Fausto laughed. "Lelang, I am going to America to *gain* knowledge."

She kneaded her fingers. Veins, like thick twine wrapped around her fist, warped the shape of her hands. "You know June 12th, 1898?"

"Independence Day," Fausto answered. "The Americans helped us defeat Spain. Miss Arnold taught me about the Americans' involvement."

She pulled her shawl over her shoulders, though the air was warm. "There was another war after the Spaniards were removed, but you will not find it in American history books. Your father was too young to know what was happening in the lower provinces and on the other islands—*we do not talk of the bad times*—but I told him years later, when he could understand. He never forgot, but now you will make him think of it all the time."

"Remember what?" Fausto's voice was as taut as the woven mat stretched across his lelang's bed.

"The war with the Americans," she said softly. "I received word that my parents and sisters and brothers were being sent to a detention camp set up by American troops in Batangas, my hometown. We thought the news was false, but your Lelong Cirilo decided to bring them here to stay with us. When he left, your father was only ten years old. More than a year and a half passed before your lelong came back alone. He had lost so much weight. He would not say what became of my family. The day he came back was the day my family ceased to exist. It was also the day your lelong ceased to exist."

Cirilo, who had welcomed the ousting of the Spanish government before his prolonged absence, kept his sons out of the American schools that were cropping up across the islands. He swore under his breath at the American soldiers who passed through town. Two American Negroes arrived one day and settled in San Esteban. Cirilo welcomed them into his home for meals and went to their homes as a guest. When he returned one evening, he told Purificación that they had deserted the American army. "They will never go back to the States. They said they are freer in our country than in their own," he insisted, though she didn't believe him. He told her the white American soldiers had called him "nigger" and "savage," words that they also hurled at the Negroes. "My friends call me brother, and there is great truth to that," he said.

Fausto couldn't recall visits to their house by Negro soldiers, though he remembered seeing two Negro men at his lelong's funeral. Cirilo always had snowy white hair as long as Fausto could remember and looked much older than his sixty-five years when he passed. Each year had separated him further from Batangas, but keeping a secret from his family for so many years had aged him and kept the memories fresh.

When Cirilo lay dying, he took his wife's hand and said, "Forgive me, Purificación, for burdening you with silence and now the truth about your family." He spoke as if he'd just arrived amid the makeshift detention camps in Batangas. He was called an *insurrecto*, an insurgent, by American soldiers who captured him outside the hastily drawn boundaries. As a prisoner, he heard stories of soldiers destroying crops and confiscating possessions, and he was forced to witness the torching of houses and rice-filled granaries beyond the barbed fences. Black clouds blotted out the sun. Green fields turned to gray as ash rained down. Ash clung to the prisoners' hair and eyelashes, their arms and legs. Cirilo tasted smoke in the rotten mangos they were forced to eat. Exhausted and starving, he fell asleep to the squeal of village pigs that were slaughtered nightly and left in their pens to rot. The American commander accused the villagers of being guerrilla supporters, which made it necessary to "depopulate" the islands.

Unrest plagued the camps. Men, driven by the hope of either being released or spared death, turned on each other, identifying alleged rebels, regardless of whether the accused were guilty or innocent. Those singled out were held down on the ground, arms pinned behind their heads or tied behind their backs, mouths pried open, beneath the running faucet of a large water tank. "Water cure," Cirilo called it. The American soldiers in cowboy hats shoved their rifle butts or their boots into the prisoners' bloated stomachs for several minutes while a native interpreter repeated the Tagalog word *"kumpisal"* to the prisoner over and over again. They added the word "confess" in English for the Americans' sake. But many of the prisoners drowned.

The camps were overcrowded, allowing malaria, beriberi, and dengue fever to rage. American doctors treated the soldiers who fell ill, but they ignored the sick prisoners. Everyone in Purificación's family died of disease. Cirilo didn't know if anger or grief had kept him alive. He escaped with two prisoners one night, after smashing a patrolman's skull with his own bayonet. On his journey back to Ilocos Sur, he heard similar stories of detention camps and ruined villages. Some said the Americans were angry because the natives were ungrateful for their help in liberating them from Spain. Instead of welcoming them as heroes, the Americans complained, the natives were betraying them, using *bolos* to hack to pieces American soldiers who ventured beyond the towns they had pacified. The spears, darts, and stones the guerrillas used were as good as sticks compared to the American bayonets. They were being flushed out by the American soldiers like "quails in a shoot," one soldier bragged.

Cirilo met a man who had fled his hometown of Balangiga on the island of Samar. The American Navy fired on his village from their gunboats before they landed to invade. American soldiers, coming from the interior, joined the sailors in rounding up the townspeople and crowded them so tightly into pens that they slept standing up, leaning against one another, even in the rain. Another man who had escaped ruin in his hometown recited an order—like a drinking song—that had been handed down from an American general to all soldiers in the field: "Everything over ten" would not be spared. Cirilo didn't know what it meant until the man from Balangiga told him anyone over the age of ten would be slaughtered. They were things, not people, to the Americans. *Everything over ten.*

"This is your America," Fausto's lelang told him, and slumped against her bed's scarred wooden headboard.

"Things have changed." Fausto's voice faltered. "When I was in school—"

"Poor boy!" She sat up, spittle flecking her lips. "Those kind American women in those American schools were not teachers. They were soldiers, telling you what to do. How could I warn you then? Miss Arnold opened up the world for you. Education is good. But they came here for a darker purpose."

"Lelang, Miss Arnold is not evil."

"You are not listening!" She shook her head, her gray hair fanning across her shoulders like a *mantilla*. "Like the Negroes who have been there for hundreds of years, you will never be accepted by the Americans. Why go there with this knowledge?"

The flame hissed as the melted wax pooled around the short wick. Her dark eyes were wet in the candlelight. "You think your father is ignorant. You believe American education made you smarter, but their schools erased our past, just as the Spaniards did."

"Lelang, I am not ignorant." Fausto got up from her bed, feeling weightless, unanchored. He held on to one of the thick, carved bedposts.

"I told this story only once before, to your father after your lelong passed away." Her voice dropped so low he could barely hear her. "Until that time, Emiliano never knew why his own father was so untouchable."

"I am sorry for your loss." Fausto's words and his whole body were stiff. He pulled down the mosquito net from the four posters of her bed until his grandmother was encased in white gauze. She seemed so far away from him as she blew out the candle.

"We must make use of the bad times," she called out.

He unhooked the curtain from her bedroom entryway and let it fall in front of him. "It will make me stronger, Lelang," he said. He waited to hear her voice again. In the moonlight, wisps of smoke rose and disappeared.

———————

Fausto breathed deeply, trying to recall the scent of betel juice and lime. "My father went to his rice fields without saying good-bye the day I left," he said.

Arturo shook his head. "Damn, hombrecito. It's never easy to leave your family. I'm sorry your dad made it harder."

Fausto wanted to say more, but his throat was sucked dry. He sat mute as Arturo washed the dirty dishes in the bathroom sink. He nodded when Arturo fished his car keys from his pant pocket and announced that he would return in an hour. Arturo was going to bring back a folding cot so Fausto could talk into the night.

As the evening light began to fade, Fausto thought maybe he'd tell Arturo what happened the morning he came down for his final meal at home. He wouldn't eat the freshly baked *pan* or the fried *bangus*, milkfish, his mother had made for him. He told her he'd seen his father leave before the sun rose. It meant he didn't care. His mother shook her head. Did he not remember the birth of each of his three sisters and brother? Of course, he did, but Fausto didn't want to admit how jealous he was at the sight of his father dancing and lifting each bundled baby to the sky. His father had always been hardest on Fausto, starting him in the rice fields at an earlier age than his siblings, giving him more chores. But his mother insisted that the joy his father displayed at the birth of his siblings was just a spark from the joy that had burst forth from him when Fausto was born.

"Your oldest brother died when he was a month old, and your brother after him died at childbirth." His mother brushed away tears near the mole below the corner of her left eye. "Your father thought we were cursed. The midwife could not help us, so we went to the *albularyo*, who held his hands on my stomach and said a prayer. We were scared, but we tried again. And then—after a difficult labor—you were born." Her voice grew stronger. "Your father called you his miracle. He told me he would stop working to watch you in the fields. You were growing up too fast for him, but he was thankful you were healthy."

Fausto pushed his slice of *pan* across the table. Why didn't his father tell him these things? He couldn't recall a time when his father was motionless in the fields.

"Do you remember the year we lost the rice crop to the typhoon—the year after we harvested only half the fields?" his mother pressed. "Do you remember the mestizo who owned the *nadumaduma* store near the plaza?"

Everybody lost their crops that year. Lim Juco, the Chinese mestizo agent, extended credit to Fausto's uncles and the rest of the families to survive until next year's harvest. He couldn't forget the agent's pale folds of fat on his belly, arms, and legs—or how he lived well off the townspeople. Fausto didn't like accompanying his father to the back of the tin-walled *nadumaduma* store where Lim Juco weighed the crops and bullied the farmers to accept his low rates. He didn't like the way his father answered to this man as if he were his master, though sometimes his father spoke up. During business dealings, the agent's lazy eye seemed to follow Fausto's every move. Jabbing his thick finger at Fausto, Lim Juco never failed to tell his father how lucky he was.

Fausto's mother broke her serving of *pan* in two and gave a piece to him. "The year we lost our crop, that mestizo told Emiliano he would give us credit for free," she said, chewing her piece of bread thoroughly as if it were all she had to eat. "He told Emiliano you were obedient and strong. He wanted you to work in his house."

Fausto knew of the arrangement. It was the first time he'd heard his father raise his voice with the agent. His father stormed out, gripping Fausto so hard his arm bore bruises when they reached home. Late-night arguments erupted between his parents, and then one evening his father returned from seeing the albularyo and gave Fausto something to drink. Sitting before his mother that morning, he realized whatever he drank that night made him vomit the next day. Then he became feverish for days and feeble for weeks. As he lay in bed, he thought of the fields that needed to be cleared. His arms were too heavy for him to lift and yet were skinny as twigs.

Now he understood his father's behavior—sitting by his bed every evening until he recovered. In the glare of the kerosene lamp, his father turned over Fausto's arms and legs, examining him as a farmer inspects a sickly animal to determine its fate. Late nights, Fausto heard his father's muffled sobs in the corner where he kept vigil.

It was risky, his mother said, this powder Emiliano had given to Fausto to save him. But the albularyo promised Emiliano the boy would recover without any lasting harm. Lim Juco withdrew his offer when he heard Fausto had lost nearly a quarter of his weight, and he blamed the boy's illness on Emiliano's insubordination, arguing over rates that he generously offered for worthless crops. It served him right, Jim Luco told the other farmers. The next year, when Emiliano paid off his debt with a bumper crop—Fausto was sure his father welcomed this as a sign that he had done the right thing—he worked with a different agent, one who offered even lower rates than Lim Juco.

Fausto rocked back and forth in his bed, the creaking of the mattress coils keeping him rooted in the present. He had known about this story, but only now did he grasp what had happened. He checked the stopped clock out of habit, wishing for Arturo's return. He would tell the nurse that he had broken his father's heart, which hastened his father's death. Even as he felt the old wound in recounting his departure from home, even as he covered it up with fresh anger, Fausto could never fault his father for not saying good-bye. Fausto was softening, with wisdom, with looking inward. No, it was old age, plain and simple, he decided, crossing his arms. Perhaps it was an early sign of a heart attack or stroke. Or maybe, he countered, the memories were loosening this closed-up muscle of his. He looked out the window into the square of blackness, past the vineyards and empty fields, the gaping unknown. Deep in the fist of his heart he knew why Rogelio was traveling a great distance to see him. Sons do that, he said aloud. They find their way back to their fathers.

CHAPTER 3

Twin journeys

In the early morning, Fausto replayed Arturo's news in his head: "Hombrecito, Rogelio called me. He's coming to see you. Tomorrow." He relished the look of disbelief on the nurse's face, though he kept pinching himself. Last night, Fausto made him repeat every word until Arturo lay down on his cot, pulled the sheet over his head, and willed himself to sleep. Rogelio had come alone and was staying with Macario in Terra Bella—only twenty-five miles away. Arturo said that Rogelio had gotten in touch with him and told him, "I know we can't change the past, but I'd like to think it's never too late to go back and claim it all. It's what makes us brave enough to move forward."

What did he mean, Fausto wanted to know.

"Promise me, when I die, you will send me back to San Esteban."

"Ai!" Fausto jerked his head. "Cary? Caridad!"

The cot creaked. Fausto cried out his name again. The light came on.

"What's wrong, hombrecito?" Arturo came to his bed, droopy-eyed.

"I heard Cary's voice," Fausto whispered.

"Your cousin? Which one was he?" Arturo's voice dropped too.

"He died in 1933."

"You dreamed of him then. It's cuz you're thinking about your family."

"I heard Cary's voice same as you talking to me here." Fausto's words hung mid-air.

Arturo checked the time, first with the stopped clock and then his wrist watch. He got up and filled the coffee pot with water from the bathroom sink. "Listen," he began, and flipped the switch for the coffeemaker, "I don't want you bringing up stuff that's gonna be hard on you. I promised Rogelio I'd make sure you were ready to see him and not get too excited. You know what I'm saying?"

Arturo poured a cup for Fausto and then drained his own. "I'm wide awake now. Let's go easy," he said. "Tell me about getting here. You came by boat in 1929, right?"

Of course, Fausto chided him. But before they could get on the ship in Manila, he and Benny had to pass many tests. The doctors poked their testicles and penises with cold metal rods, and scribbled notes in silence. For a thick wad of pesos, they received papers that declared them "bacterially negative." They also paid a handsome fee for another paper that proclaimed them citizens of the Philippine Islands who could travel freely to America.

The SS *President Jackson*. Fausto hadn't spoken the ship's name in decades. Son-of-a-gun, he laughed, how the ship's propeller rumbled the entire trip! It sat below the third-class passenger section, but to Fausto it was lodged in his head like a great mechanical heartbeat gone mad. His bunk bed vibrated. In the dining saloon, cold bean-paste soup spilled out of bowls. Knives and forks rattled menacingly against steel tables.

He didn't know other Filipinos could travel outside of third class until he saw a group of them on deck one evening. The men, their hair slicked back, shiny with pomade, wore suits and bow ties. The women were adorned in high-heeled shoes and hats that sprouted feathers and hugged their heads. Fausto asked one of the men where they were staying when they walked by. He hadn't seen them, or any well-dressed Filipinos for that matter, in third class. The men and women exchanged glances.

"We speak Tagalog, not Ilocano," one of them said in English. "We are students—pensionados—not laborers. Can you not see by the way we are dressed, boy?" The women laughed behind their gloved fingers.

Benny grabbed Fausto's arm so the two of them could leave, but Fausto stood his ground. The pensionados were trying to get into one of the social rooms, but the steward, who was Ilocano and as dark as cured tobacco leaves, shook his head. The man who had spoken to Fausto poked his finger at the steward, speaking in English loudly enough for Fausto to hear. They were staying in second class and had the right to enter the smoking room. It was the third time they had been denied access. The pensionado removed his spectacles, as if to show off his fair skin or the lack of pinch marks on the bridge of his nose, which was narrow and delicate, not fleshy like Fausto's. The steward folded his arms, replying in Ilocano that only first-class guests could use the smoking room. Besides, he added, no matter how well they dressed or behaved, the white passengers would not welcome them.

"Speak Tagalog!" the pensionado barked to the steward, and turned on his heel. The group retreated, and the pensionado brushed shoulders with Fausto. As they disappeared below deck, Fausto thought to go after the man, but Benny pulled him toward the nearest stairwell and pointed at the deck above where the first-class passengers had gathered. As the

SS *President Jackson* chugged away from the port of Hong Kong, the first-class passengers gawked at the Chinese families whose sampans tossed about in the white water that churned beneath the propellers. Using their oars, mothers and fathers and elderly men and women clashed with other sampans for position. The children called out in their native dialect and waved at the passengers, who leaned over the rail, laughing. One man torpedoed fruit into the water. A red apple struck a girl's jaw. She ate it whole and licked the blood that trickled down the corner of her mouth.

Other passengers threw coins that disappeared in the froth, prompting men and boys to dive in. A fistful of coins came raining down, and Fausto and Benny gasped as a tiny boy kicked off the edge of the boat with froglike legs. The rope knotted around his waist and attached to the sampan uncoiled in the air with a snap and was pulled taut. After a few moments, an older sibling yanked at the rope and the boy's head popped up from the sea. Water flowed from his clothes and hair as he was pulled in. His arms and legs hung limp as seaweed over the side of the sampan. Then he held up his hand. Silvery disks flashed between his fingers, and his brothers and sisters piled on top of him, hugging him and patting his head. The passengers clapped. The men whistled. Soon they all dispersed. Fausto lost sight of the boy. In time, the SS *President Jackson* outran the sampans, though the mothers and fathers continued to row, refusing to return to shore, even as the sun dipped below the horizon.

Fausto took comfort in his cabinmates—four others besides Benny. Three had cousins or uncles waiting for them in America. Vermil Bienvenido spoke good English. He had worked in hotels in Manila and was counting on making more money in the American hotels. Ambo Ayson's uncle had a restaurant job waiting for him in New York City. Arsenio Magsaysay hailed from Santa Maria, ten kilometers north of San Esteban. As he rolled cigarettes made from his family-grown tobacco and handed them out to his cabinmates, he told them he expected his work in the fields would serve him well on American farms. Vermil and Arsenio were going to return home rich. Ambo wanted to remain in the States but visit his hometown, bringing gifts for his five sisters, his parents, and grandparents. Everyone's heart was still in the Philippines, except for Jun Villanueva.

Jun didn't talk much, but one evening when Arsenio spoke longingly of his family's land, Jun cut him off, blurting out that there was no future in his hometown, San Fernando. When Jun declared he would never return because he hated his country, his cabinmates wanted to fight him—even Fausto. It was as if he had spit on their mothers! Fausto convinced the others to go up deck to cool their heads so he could talk to Jun. With just the two of them in the cabin, Jun complained that the rice they served on the ship was too gritty. His mother milled rice with a mortar and pestle, which made it taste more fragrant. Fausto told him the rice would be better once they got off the ship, but Jun said it would always taste bitter in his mouth. His family had lost their fields to harsh weather and cheating agents who made it impossible to make a living off of the harvests. The new landlords overcharged, but his parents conceded just so they could stay on his lelong's land.

"I told him he did not hate his country," Fausto said to Arturo. "The people in power were dishonest. I told him he would realize that—maybe not now, but later—when he is in America and he grows homesick. I admitted I was already homesick."

Fausto massaged his eyelids, bringing up an image of the teenaged boy who sat rigid in the bunk opposite him. Jun's face and body were angular and hard. His eyes, mere slits, told everybody he trusted no one. The part in his hair was severe, a white streak. But when Fausto told him his homesickness was their secret, the hardness melted away. Jun yanked the bunk's wool blanket over his head and began wailing.

"There is no shame in being scared or angry." Fausto pulled the blanket down.

"If they had not taken our land, I would not be here!"

"Awan ti pag danagan. Shhh, it's okay," Fausto said softly. "You will get it back. You put your anger to hard work in America, eh? Then you return. But you are tired, you need to rest."

"They do not want me here." Jun sat up, amid the empty bunks.

Fausto promised to talk to them; they would understand his family's hardships. Jun lay down, crossing his arms, but when Fausto patted his hand, Jun grabbed it and held tight. Neither of them moved. As Fausto watched Jun sleep, he thought of what they had left behind. He thought of the boy in the sampan. Fausto's life in San Esteban was not so bad after all. Homesickness gnawed a hole in his stomach, but he wove his fingers with Jun's until they were entwined.

Fausto didn't know what happened to Jun when they landed in Seattle and parted ways. When he was working near Stockton years later, an asparagus crewmember told him about a pinoy named Jun Villanueva, whose story of his family's hardship in the Philippines sounded nearly identical. At the time, the US government had passed a law giving pinoys free passage to return to the Philippines. Not many took it. Fausto later found out that if a pinoy accepted the offer, he could never return to America. This Villanueva got in trouble up and down California, fighting with whites and pinoys alike. When he landed in jail in Salinas, he took the free passage, bragging to anyone who would listen that he was glad to be leaving. But Fausto's crewmember said he heard the sheriff forced him to sign the paperwork.

"You think it was Jun from your ship?" Arturo was on his second cup of coffee.

"I hoped it was not him," Fausto said. "I did not want to think he had no place to call home. When we landed, he said he wanted to keep in touch. I gave him my cousins' address in Los Angeles, but I never heard from him again." Fausto stared into his cold cup, at his watery-black reflection. "Last time I saw him he was walking off the pier. But he looked like any of us leaving the ship. He was *all of us* leaving the ship."

Waves of Filipinos pushed Fausto down the gangplank, nearly separating him from Benny. They ended up at a street corner by the pier, along with their countrymen. Some met up with relatives or friends who were already living in America. Fausto had written to Macario, but neither he nor Benny heard back before they left. Many of them headed downtown for the bus station to begin the final leg of their journey to far-flung places—Stockton, Los Angeles, Chicago, New York City.

A procession of taxicabs roared down the street and stopped in front of the pier, their engines still rumbling. A Filipino wearing a tight-fitting suit sprang out of one cab and shouted in Ilocano that the cabs would take them to a hotel. The bus station was now closed. For ten dollars a night, they could stay off the crime-filled streets of Seattle. Fausto and Benny were swept away like the rest of the newly arrived, despite Fausto's protests. The drivers deposited them on King Street, where wooden signboards announced the names of hotels, gambling dens, and taxi-dance halls that crowded the street. The cab sped off after the driver forced Benny to tip him a dollar by threatening to leave with their luggage.

They didn't know where to go. Some Filipinos entered the Alps Hotel on the same block, while others headed to the LMV Hotel down the street. But most of them ducked into the dens and dance halls as a light rain fell. An older Chinese woman stepped out of the shadows and led Fausto and Benny into her hotel lobby, lit by dim humming lights. Before Fausto could speak, two Filipinos barged in, their shiny skin leaching whiskey. Their fedoras were smashed on their heads, limp ties dangled from their necks, and their damp shirttails were caught by trouser zippers pulled up halfway.

"Sonovabeech," one of the men said to Benny, leering in his face with bloodshot eyes. "I loss ten bucks in that damn Chinese gambling den."

His companion, a short, clean-shaven Filipino laughed in Fausto's ear. "Better to spend money at taxi-dance halls. At lees you get something for your money!"

"Sheet!" the gambler spat out at his friend. "Every night you come back empty-handed. What's wrong—the white women don't like your small dick?"

The gambler's friend swung his fist. Fausto tried to grab his arm, but the drunkard knocked over a lamp, smashing it into big pieces. The woman screeched. Weaving in and out of English and Chinese, she told them they would pay for the damages. She rang a bell, and four Chinese men appeared and emptied all the money from the drunkards' pockets and pitched them headfirst into the street. The two Filipinos scrambled to their feet, their knees wet and black, their shoes catching in the crevices of the road's uneven brick and mortar. They ran off in different directions, lost among the sea of countrymen on King Street.

"You got money to pay for room?" the woman said to Fausto.

As if on cue, a heavy-set Filipino man emerged from behind a door and said, "You need jobs, boys?" When Benny told him they were only staying one night, the man flicked out his hand like a snake's tongue. "Thirty dollars a night," he told them.

Fausto dug into his pocket and felt for his roll of dollar bills. "The Filipino who came with the taxicabs said ten dollars a night."

"If you stay more than one night. That the special—a bargain, a steal." The woman, her fingers twitching, stared at his hand in his pocket.

Fausto turned to the Filipino. "*Apay saanka aya nga kailyan?*"

"*Saan!* No! I'm not your countryman anymore. Not here," the man said, twisting one of the thick gold rings around his fingers. "Did you not hear what happened? The rich lost a lot of money when the stock market crashed; it will get even worse here for people like you and me." The man sized Fausto up. "You'll learn plenny quick!"

The woman elbowed her way in between them. "How many night?"

"We will sleep in the alley," Fausto declared.

"It's against the law, boys." The man kicked a broken piece of glass from the lamp across the stained carpet. "It's harder to get out of jail than this place."

Benny leaned against Fausto's shoulder. Seasickness had weakened him, and he needed to sleep. Benny signed a piece of paper, agreeing that they would pay for anything they broke or stole from the hotel, before the woman would give them the key. The man shook their hands, his rings digging into their flesh. The woman whisked the paper behind the counter, hugging it close to her chest.

"See you early in the morning, boys!" The man disappeared behind a door.

As they trudged upstairs, Fausto saw that the hotel patrons were all Filipinos. Doors opened just enough for brown faces to peek out. When Fausto unlocked their door, a man with a shock of black hair emerged from his room and introduced himself as Prudencio. He asked Fausto and Benny which group they were in. The first group would be sent to pick apples in Yakima Valley in the morning, the second group the day afterward to Montana for sugar beets, the third group midweek to Imperial Valley for lettuce, and the fourth group later in the week to pick the early citrus crops in central California. The Filipino contractor—the man with the rings—told Prudencio they were lucky to arrive amid such bounty during the worst of times. Prudencio asked Fausto if they had money to cover their hotel bill in case they had to stay longer.

"We go to Los Angeles tomorrow." Benny lay down on the bed, the only furniture in the room. He kicked off his shoes, exposing the wrinkled, pink soles of his feet.

"If you sign that paper, you work for the contractor!" Prudencio insisted.

Benny let out a moan and covered his face with a pillow, but Fausto shook his head. He told the Filipinos who had gathered in the hallway that they were going to Los Angeles—Hope Street—where their cousins lived. Prudencio warned that the Chinese woman counted bodies late at night to make sure nobody fled because the hotel got a small fee for each person handed over to the contractors. The other pinoys retreated to their rooms as if afraid of being caught. Prudencio asked Fausto for their address, just in case he was lucky enough to escape his fate. He had come to America on his own, with no relations here. He would seek out Fausto and Benny if he didn't land on his feet, he told them. Fausto shook his hand, admiring Prudencio's confidence, the smile and wink he gave them before he wished them a safe trip and closed his door. Later that night, after the Chinese woman finished the room count on their floor, Fausto and Benny stole away.

They boarded the first bus headed for California just as it started raining. Fausto recognized some of his countrymen from the ship standing in long lines for other buses. They turned up their collars and shielded their eyes from the rain, but they were smiling and patting one another on the back. Perhaps they, too, had escaped.

"Where is Hope Street?" Benny asked.

"Where is Hope Street?"

Fausto marveled at how his ears tricked him. Arturo's voice sounded just like his cousin's. Benny had asked him that question as the bus rolled out of the station.

"I'll bet a freeway runs through it now." Arturo took Fausto's cup and dumped out the cold coffee in the bathroom sink. "Maybe Rogelio can take you on a pilgrimage to find it."

"I don't want to go!" Fausto cried out.

Arturo stood in the bathroom doorway, hands on his head as if surrendering. "Hombrecito, we'll stop for now. Okay?"

Fausto folded his arms across his chest to stop the tightness growing inside him.

Promise me, when I die, you'll send me back to San Esteban.

Arturo walked slowly to the middle of the room, his eyes fixed on Fausto.

Did Arturo hear Cary's voice too? Or did he see something in Fausto's face? Fausto's nose began to run. Without his handkerchief, he snuffled. He worked his mouth open. *"I want to talk."* He spoke the words as if he were under water. Arturo nodded and came to his side and took his hand. Fausto's eyes flickered. He mouthed the words: *I will be here when you are ready. I will still be here for you.*

CHAPTER 4

Hope Street

Los Angeles, 1929–1933

When the taxi cab driver dropped Fausto and Benny off at the corner of Hope and Main streets, the City of Angels—that's what he told them Los Angeles means—they thought they had traveled a great distance only to return to King Street in Seattle. Bold signs vied for the attention and wallets of their countrymen, who streamed in and out of gambling dens, poolrooms, and taxi-dance halls in the steady rain. Filipino grocery stores and barbershops tucked in between were empty, though still open. The faces of Filipinos who bumped into them seemed familiar but showed no signs of recognition.

Evening fell by the time they found the right apartment building, though they combed the nearby streets but could not find the shiny black Dodge sedan from Macario's photos. A knock on the door prompted scuffling on the other side, making Fausto recheck the apartment number on the envelope scrap beneath a sputtering hallway light. But then the door flew open, and Fausto stared into the blanched face, the bulging eyes of his cousin, who made the sign of the cross with a shaky hand.

"Serapio! Five years pass and you forget what we look like?" Fausto scolded him.

"I thought you were a ghost bringing bad news to our door!" Serapio laughed.

"We wrote we were coming." Benny dragged in their two suitcases.

Fausto stripped off his wet jacket. "So this is our welcome to America?"

Serapio threw his arms around them. Fausto buried his face in his cousin's shoulder and felt a sharp collarbone against his cheek.

"You two are soaked through like dogs left out in the rain!" Serapio said.

"Kumusta ka!" Domingo handed out towels. He hugged Fausto, rocking him back and forth. "I thought I was dreaming when I saw you. It is good to have more of us here," he said when they released. He smiled at them until Benny wagged his jaw.

"I thought you were going to get your teeth fixed." Benny laughed. "Maybe the Hollywood girls like all those teeth."

Domingo grinned with a closed mouth. Though they sent pictures in their letters every now and then, seeing them face to face startled Fausto. The youthful fat in Domingo and Serapio's cheeks had vanished. Once smooth, their chins were pocked with stubble. Both cousins had grown a few inches, but they were still skinny.

"*Kumusta!*" a voice called out.

In the corner of the room, Cary sat wedged between a white woman with blonde hair and the sofa's armrest. His thick, wavy black hair had thinned and was uncombed. Fausto was reminded of his father's words, the flames that turned his Auntie Lilia's letter into ashes. He turned away, but all around him was peeling wallpaper. Three mattresses rolled up and tied with string rested against a wall. Two open doors revealed a bathroom and a bedroom. Chicken *adobo* simmered on the stove, and the aroma of fried fish, vinegar, and garlic beckoned. Yet Fausto, who hadn't eaten since morning, had no appetite.

The woman elbowed Cary. "Where are my manners?" he chided himself, as he struggled to sit up. He gave her a quick squeeze, making her breasts swell between his chest and grip, and announced, "Cousins, this is my girl, April."

She sucked on her cigarette while holding a bottle in her other hand. Cary lifted his rail-thin arm, and added, "April, this is Fausto Empleo and that is Benny Edralin." The effort winded him. He rested his head on the back of the sofa.

A siren wailed outside and stopped somewhere along Hope Street. "You little beech," a man shouted, from below the window. The man's voice, thick with alcohol, had a Filipino accent. Serapio closed the window, but they could still hear the man's angry words.

Benny sat down in a nearby chair. "How are you, Cary?" he asked. He had dried off, but he kept rubbing the back of his neck.

"He's fine," April said, her words hard and defiant.

Cary doubled over, coughing. He drew a handkerchief over his mouth and held his chest with his other hand. April gave him a bottle, which he tipped on its end into his mouth and emptied in two gulps.

"This cough comes with bad weather," Cary said, and licked his pale lips. "But do not worry about me. Let us toast your arrival. Welcome to America!"

Domingo handed out cups filled with amber-colored liquid. Alcohol was illegal, but one of his bosses, an Italian grocer, smuggled in liquor from Tijuana, and Domingo delivered them to customers in grocery boxes covered with fruits and vegetables. "I am going to stop soon," Domingo promised. "Too risky."

"He thinks he needs a second job because I am not working." Cary stuffed the wadded-up handkerchief into his trouser pocket. "I will go back to work soon."

"We can start working soon," Benny offered.

Fausto pulled out an envelope thick with bills. Auntie Lilia had given it to his father, who in turn had hidden it in Fausto's cloth pouch with a note from Auntie Lilia: "For Cary's safe return home." He threw it on the coffee table.

"You need money? Here is your money, Cary! It is from your mother!" he said.

April grabbed the envelope and squealed with delight. She nibbled on Cary's ear. "We can take you to the best hospital with this. You can get better now."

"I was sending *her* money," Cary whispered. "Why?"

"Do you not remember the letter you sent her?" Fausto wanted to kick the table.

"I was homesick then. I will write and tell her not to worry anymore." He smiled, though his teeth looked dull, his gums dark and swollen. "I will repay her." Cary waved the envelope at Domingo. "You and Serapio can quit your second jobs," he called out.

But Domingo didn't move. When Macario strode in, Domingo hung his head.

Macario yanked off a black bow tie and unbuttoned his white shirt, stained with grease. "You boys finally arrived, eh?" He slapped Benny on the back.

Laughing, Cary threw the envelope at Macario. Pesos in hues of green, red, and brown flew out and landed on the floor. "Macario, Ma sent me money. Now we can get our real apartment back—next to the movie stars in Hollywood!"

Macario stepped over the bills. "Let me welcome you, Cousin!" He grabbed Fausto in a bear hug, playfully pounding him on the back and whispering in his ear, "He is going crazy lying in bed every day. But do not worry about Cary. Everything is fine."

"What has happened to you all?" Fausto demanded, pulling away.

"Let us get something to eat and drink," Macario said, and slung his arms around Fausto and Benny. "I know a speakeasy that has cigarette girls with big breasts and snake legs—you know what I mean?" He winked. "I will tell you everything."

"The truth!" Fausto looked him in his bloodshot eyes.

Macario laughed, his mouth and pores releasing a vapor of resiny whiskey. "If that is what you like, Cousin, if that is what you like!"

Macario couldn't lie about everything. Fausto could see that for himself. They never had a Dodge sedan. They couldn't go outside Manilatown or the Mexican district to eat or find entertainment that didn't involve women, drinking, or gambling. Signs posted on the doors of establishments everywhere else in town warned, "Positively no Filipinos allowed." He saw a middle-aged woman who looked like Miss Arnold emerge from a fancy restaurant with white tablecloths and china, accompanied by a man who wore a black tuxedo. As he watched them slip into a limousine, he thought to himself how Miss Arnold had created a different America for him—the real America only wanted him to wait on them at restaurants and hotels with bowed heads and gloved hands.

———————

Four months after Fausto arrived on Hope Street, Cary and Macario insisted that they send a picture back home. Cary outfitted Benny in his three-piece suit, which was too loose on him now, but also too large on Benny. Macario dressed Fausto in his old suit, and Cary posed them beside a stranger's black Dodge. Macario dictated what they should say, bragging about how well they all were doing. Fausto didn't want to lie, but when he sat down to write with the photograph next to him he wrote of the many opportunities before them—if they worked hard enough. Fausto regretted mailing the letter, even as he admired the photograph of him and Benny—they looked just like the pensionados on the SS *President Jackson.*

———————

By summer's end, Fausto had gone through two jobs. Soon after their arrival, Serapio had secured busboy positions for Fausto and Benny at the same restaurant where he worked, but a few weeks into the job, the heavyset white manager had insulted him after his shift: "Listen, brown monkey, you and your monkey friends can't eat leftovers after your shift anymore!" He grabbed Fausto's plate from him. "Brown monkeys don't eat fancy food!" Fausto was speechless; he had never been called a monkey, though he witnessed several of his countrymen being called many things. Fausto would have landed a punch had Serapio not intervened, telling the manager that his cousin understood, and pulled him into the steamy kitchen. Crates of hot glasses clanked angrily in the arms of a Filipino dishwasher. The damp air smelled of ammonia as another Filipino swung a mop back and forth across the floor. A third Filipino spilled soup from a tray of bowls in one corner, and the Filipino with the mop turned it on its end, waving the dripping head and threatening a fight because he was afraid the manager would fire him for not doing his job. Benny abandoned the garbage bag that he was dragging to the Dumpster.

"Remember your place, Fausto," Serapio warned him. "We are not citizens."

"We are human beings first!" Fausto wiped his face dry.

Serapio rapped his raw knuckles against Fausto's head. "If you fight him, you will lose your job and the police will beat you up and let you rot in jail. *Síge!* Go on!"

"Swallow your anger," Benny pleaded. "We have to eat and pay rent."

Fausto untied his apron. "Why are we here? Why do we not all go back home?"

"We still believe our lives will improve here," Serapio said.

Fausto looked around the kitchen. The two Filipinos had taken their argument into the alley. One of the Filipino cooks scraped bits of burnt meat from the grill, while another cook doused hot oil on the black surface and then scrubbed it to a silvery gleam.

"When you turn the other way every time a man calls you 'brown monkey,' how will your life improve?" Fausto threw down his apron.

Serapio snatched up the apron and folded it with care. "It makes me stronger inside," he said. "Our lives will get better. We have to try harder. For Cary."

Fausto felt as if he were talking to an old albularyo who believed he could draw poison from a patient's snake bite by writing a prayer on a cloth and applying it on the wound. But Fausto agreed to swallow his anger for Cary's sake and put his apron back on.

Cary was coughing more and his fevers returned. April took him to the county hospital, but his condition didn't improve. The lesions on his lungs—black clouds on his X-ray pictures—were growing. The doctors recommended surgery, but Cary didn't want to be cut open or die on an operating table far from home. Macario insisted that the doctors were scaring him needlessly. April watched over him when she wasn't working at the taxi-dance hall, but they stayed up late when he needed rest, and she gave in to his cravings for cigarettes and liquor, which the doctors forbade. April told Cary that the county hospital wouldn't make him pay for the surgery, but he got it in his head that the doctors would remove some other organ in exchange for repairing his damaged lungs. Macario agreed. Nothing is free in America.

————————

As Cary's condition worsened, Macario spent less time at the apartment. After his shift, he took to the pool hall, the gambling den, or the taxi-dance hall in Manilatown and blew his daily wage of a $1.50 and even his $5 tips. When he returned, he stumbled in the dark and collapsed on the mattress next to Benny. Already sleepless, Fausto could hardly breathe with the flowery perfume and the sweet odor of marijuana filling the apartment. He wanted to confront Macario and demand that they repay their Auntie Lilia and tell everyone back home the truth, but Serapio, Domingo, and Benny held him back.

"Do not challenge him," Serapio advised. "Do not spit on your own face."

"You will cause all of us more trouble than it is worth," Domingo said.

Fausto surrendered at Hope Street, but he could no longer look the other way at the restaurant. One evening, the manager scolded him in front of patrons for being clumsy busing tables. Without a word, Fausto handed him his apron and walked out through the kitchen door. The flies in the alley descended upon him. For a moment, he panicked. How would he help pay rent and send money home? His heart pumped. Yet power surged within him like jolts of lightning. This is what freedom feels like! But it was short lived. Heavy footsteps clomped behind him. The manager's large body seemed stuck in the doorway before he popped out on the other side.

"Get out of my alley you goddamn, dirty monkey!" The manager danced around, dangling his arms, the fat quaking, and scratched the armpits of his sweat-stained shirt. Then he slammed the door shut. Fausto bolted out of the alley, leaving the stench of rotten food behind, though the flies trailed after him.

Fausto got a job cleaning rooms at a brothel on Grand Avenue. Cary used to work as a cleanup boy, which was how he met April before she became a blonde and a dancer. Cary told him the money was good—business was always brisk—especially if the madam and her women liked him. Fausto was tipped often because he listened to the women complain about the inadequacies of their customers or tell him how they fell into prostitution. They liked him because he didn't leer at them like the Filipino farm workers who came from the fields outside of Los Angeles to squander their wages. But he hated cleaning the "rooms," which were sectioned off with clotheslines and sheets to accommodate the times when business picked up, mostly when the workers got paid. He held his nose when he collected the sheets stained with semen, sweat, red lipstick, and blood. He sang the Ilocano folk song "Pamulinawen" in his head when the women screamed or he had to throw out men who got too rough.

Serapio argued that he was making good money, but Fausto shook his head as he scrubbed his hands under scalding water after he came home from his shift. "It seems like easy money, but it is not *good* money," Fausto said. "We should find other work. I could look up one of the pinoys we met in Seattle. Prudencio picks asparagus up north in Stockton."

Serapio handed him a towel. "I hear it's hard work, not easy money."

"Serapio, whatever we pinoys do for work, it is never easy money." Fausto kept rubbing his hands into the towel as if he couldn't get them clean enough.

"You're not like most of the Filipinos we see," a prostitute told Fausto one evening. Her breasts spilled out of her robe as she tucked quarters into his shirt pocket.

"Well, respectable Filipinos would not come here," Fausto said, averting his eyes from the teeth marks on her neck and breasts that her last customer had left.

The moment he said it, he regretted his words. She slapped his face and puckered her lips as if to spit on him, but Fausto pushed her to the floor. The other prostitutes rushed out of their rooms.

"You're no better than the monkeys we fuck!" Tears streamed down the woman's face. "Get out of here, you bastard, you monkey!"

Fausto threw the coins from his pocket at the woman's feet and ran out of the building. He hadn't collected his week's wage, but he didn't want their dirty money. He didn't want to hear the word "monkey" again. But every time he saw a white person, no matter where he was, he flinched, expecting the word to be hurled in his face—"monkey, monkey, monkey"—like a child's cruel nursery rhyme.

In the fall, Fausto answered an ad for two positions at a small hotel called the Savoy Hotel off of Wilshire Boulevard. He didn't want to wear the stiff uniform that the bellboys wore, with its triple rows of shiny buttons that made him look like he belonged to an organ grinder. He preferred the cleaning-boy position, which didn't require contact with patrons. Two statues in flowing togas greeted guests at the front of the Savoy Hotel, with the interior decorated with Italian pottery and lace. Its thin, silver-haired owner, Mr. Calabria, was strict when it came to promptness and particular about how Fausto was to clean vacated rooms, but he never raised his voice or called his Filipino staff names. He spent most of his time reading the newspaper at the front desk, calling attention to the grim news of the day to his staff or patrons whenever they entered the lobby.

One day, Mr. Calabria related a story about Jack "Legs" Diamond getting shot in a New York hotel. Another day, he announced that a tornado in Oklahoma had killed nineteen people and injured more than a hundred. All the while, President Hoover was trying to "prevent hunger and cold." When Fausto collected his weekly pay, Mr. Calabria told him in his heavy accent that they were lucky to have jobs. He pointed at a headline about the murder of 8,000 people by rebels in Shanghai.

"We can only depend on God and ourselves. With hard work and faith, the rest will take care of itself," he said.

Fausto nodded, though he was no longer sure of that belief.

Mrs. Calabria suffered from a heart condition. After the New Year, when she returned from the hospital, a young Filipina accompanied her to the hotel. Concepción Dacanay, a student nurse who had taken exceptional care of Mrs. Calabria, needed money to help pay for nursing school, so Mrs. Calabria offered her a part-time job as a housekeeper. When Connie was introduced to Fausto, he told her that her full name was beautiful, but she insisted on being called "Connie" because it was easier to pronounce.

Connie was born and raised in Floridablanca, in the Pampanga province, sixty kilometers northwest of Manila. Her first language was Kapampangan, but she also spoke Tagalog and Ilocano. She described to Fausto the sugarcane and rice fields, fishponds, swamp, and mangrove of her home province. One day, he told himself, he would visit Floridablanca and buy gold jewelry and wood-carved furniture, which she had told him were crafted by the Kapampangans. When she spoke of the dishes her province was known for, he licked his lips. Maybe someday after their shift she would make him a grand meal of *aligi*, crab fat; *sisig*, sizzling pig cheeks; and *balo-balo*, fermented rice mixed with shrimp.

He didn't look Connie in the eye, afraid she would see the dumb expression on his face, the way he stumbled over his words in English. But when she walked down the hall carrying mops and brooms, he stole glances, admiring the curve of her ankles and of her thick calves shaped by stark-white tights. When she smiled, which was often, her face grew as round and bright as the moon. Fausto wondered how long her straight hair would be if she removed the hairpins that always held it captive in a bun. He imagined that it grazed her straight but sturdy hips. He marveled that she could change sheets with her patients still in bed. But he admired her most for the way she dismissed the names Filipinos were being called.

"Stupid, ignorant people," she whispered under her breath, when a hotel patron asked for someone else to change his sheets. "They are threatened by us, Fausto," she said later, holding out a mop and bucket of water. "They lash out because we are not like them. Do not let them bother you. Let their name-calling strengthen you inside."

Fausto nodded, like the converted before an evangelist. The hard line of her lips softened as her gaze lingered on him. He took the mop and bucket, and followed her, floating down the carpeted hallway.

It was easy for Fausto to daydream about Connie when he was back at Hope Street. Cary still refused to have surgery, even after the doctors said that the tiny holes in his lungs would soon grow fatally larger. Macario blamed April for Cary's illness. He tried to throw her out for good, but Cary stopped him. Benny and Serapio took on additional shifts at the restaurant, earning extra money and avoiding Hope Street. At times, the apartment was as oppressive as the restaurant Fausto had left, but he was thankful for his job at the Savoy Hotel. Mr. Calabria was right; he was lucky.

Fausto looked forward to Monday and Friday afternoons and weekends, when Connie came to work after her shift at the hospital. One afternoon, when Mr. Calabria had taken his wife to the doctor's, Fausto saw her sneak into the office and put a record on the phonograph. She caught him watching her, and though she was startled at first, she smiled and motioned him into the office.

"Mr. Calabria will not like," he protested, but he followed her inside.

She pressed her finger, which smelled faintly of rubbing alcohol, to his lips to hush him. "Mrs. Calabria told me I would like this song, 'Stardust,' by Hoagy Carmichael. Listen." She placed the needle on the spinning record. She swayed her head back and forth as if moved by a breeze. She played it again and again, joining in when she caught on to the words. When the singer whistled, she puffed out her cheeks, but every time she met Fausto's eyes, she put her hand to her mouth and looked down at the carpet. She sang along, bright and cheerful, though the singer's voice was mournful, the lyrics full of longing.

Connie would have played the song again, but Fausto reminded her that the Calabrias were likely on their way back from the doctor's office by now.

"Do not ruin things, Fausto." She pouted, her full lips blooming like a rose of deep-pink petals. She rummaged through the stack of records beside the phonograph and pulled out another disk. "Ah, Maurice Chevalier! Do you know the song 'Louise'?"

He shook his head as she put the record on. This time she danced around the office, avoiding the desk and filing cabinets. She waltzed over to where he stood and held out her hand. He hesitated at first and then grasped it, savoring the touch of her warm skin. She flung herself away from him, still holding onto him, and then twirled inward until his arm was wrapped around her upper body. He didn't move. He dared to return her gaze when she sang about "the thrill of being so near to you." They stood, eyes locked, even when the record ended and the needle jerked across its black, glossy surface, making scratching sounds.

Connie sighed. "My father played the guitar as part of our town's *rondalya*. It was the best string band in the region." She looked at Fausto, her smile fading. "Do you not like to listen to music?" She pulled away from him and replaced the records in a neat pile.

"I do not have time for hobbies," he said. "Where and when would I listen to music?"

"Here!" she said. "We can listen every time they go to the doctor. You should make time, Fausto. You look too serious. I should invite you to the theater to see a movie with me so you can grow laugh lines here." She ran her finger around the corners of his mouth. "And remove your worry lines here." She brushed her fingertips across his forehead.

Did she feel how hot his face had become? He stepped back. "I cannot afford to go to the movies. My cousin Cary says it is cheaper to hang around Hollywood and watch the movie stars come out of their big cars and go into fancy restaurants to eat."

"Oh, I do not care about movie stars. I like the people they pretend to be. I like the stories, the different worlds." Her gaze drifted to the wall where colorful plates from Mr. Calabria's hometown of Palermo hung. "When I am tired from studying or work, I go to the movies. When one of my patients died, I saw Charlie Chaplin's *City Lights*. I was able to laugh again." She closed her eyes and nodded, as if recalling a scene from the movie, then adjusted her apron, remembering where she was. "Come with me. I know a place where pork chops are thirty-five cents. After dinner, we can walk to the theater. It's only five cents."

"I take care of my sickly cousin. I send money to my family. I cannot—"

She pressed her lips together, petals folding, closing as if dusk had descended. "You are a good cousin and son, Fausto." She offered him a smile. "When I come back from the movie theater, I will tell you what the story is about."

After their shift on Mondays, she gave him her version of the movies she'd seen. *Platinum Blonde* pitted hardworking folks against corrupted wealthy people. She felt sorry for the monster in *Frankenstein* because the ignorant villagers misunderstood him. Listening to her was better than going to the movies, Fausto told her; here, he could stare at her as she told the story, instead of sit in a dark theater. She laughed as if he had said something silly, but she was blushing. She always seemed cheerful, though there were times when he spied her near the broom closet lost in thought.

One morning, he ran into her by the broom closet. "What are you thinking about?" he whispered boldly in her ear in the shadows.

"*Salabat* and *basi*."

Fausto was puzzled. Why was she thinking about beverages?

"I used to make my father salabat and basi, using sugar from our fields and herbs from our garden," she explained. "My father loved to drink salabat, and I liked making it because the scent of fresh ginger root stayed on my fingers for days." She stared at her white shoes. "I have not made salabat for a long time, even when I was home. My father lost his craving for anything sweet, anything with sugar in it."

"That can happen," he said. "I used to love *bagoong*, and now the fish smell upsets my stomach. I do not know why, but it does."

"Yes." She wiped her eyes with the corner of her apron and turned away. "We do not know why things like that happen."

———————

One spring day, a few months later, Connie came looking for Fausto as he was changing sheets. Her hair flowed down her shoulders, the ends curling at her waist, as luxurious as the mink stoles some of the female patrons wore. She asked him to see a movie with her.

"Why? I always listen to you." He pulled the dirty sheets off the bed with one strong, graceful tug, which he learned from her, and rolled them into a ball.

"I would like to see a comedy," she announced, as tears gathered in her eyes.

"What is wrong?" He dropped the sheets to the floor and rushed to her side.

She withdrew an envelope from her apron pocket. "My father passed away."

Fausto sat her on the bed.

Two years ago her father lost ownership of the land where his family had lived and grown sugarcane for generations. To remain on the property, he leased the land and shared half of his harvest. The landlord charged for the use of tools and animals, and the agents cheated him when weighing the sugarcane. Even the Catholic priests, who her father had asked to intervene on his behalf, turned him away, favoring the landlord's bribes. And then this year's drought diminished his crops, and he could not pay rent, fees, or taxes. Her family was evicted from their home and forced to live in the landlord's hacienda, where her father and brothers earned ten *centavos* a day. Within a month of being forced off their land, her brothers pulled her father's body out of Pampanga Bay.

"He was not a strong swimmer, yet he swam toward the horizon," she said in a flat voice. "My mother said he had lost his land, so there was nowhere else to go but the sea. My mother is scared, but she said she must be strong for our family. She and my sisters will find factory work in Manila, and my brothers will stay in the hacienda."

"I am sorry," Fausto whispered, taking her hand.

"They sent me here after we lost the land so I could help them. But I have been living foolishly here. I do not send enough money. I should not have gone to the movies or the restaurants. But it is so difficult here in the States. I am so homesick. I should go back, should I not?" She gently shook her hand and their fingers unraveled. She wiped her tears with the crumpled envelope, smearing her cheek with traces of black ink.

Fausto stroked her head, the crown of her glossy soft hair. She closed her eyes, her head tilting back. He combed out the tangles in her mane, his fingers touching her shoulder, the curve of her back. The ends of her hair fanned out across the bare mattress.

"You are almost finished with your studies," he said. "If you go back without your degree, what good would that do? Do not waste what you have already done. I know it is hard, but you should finish your schooling and then go back. That is the best way."

"And you? When are you going back?"

He thought of the letters his sisters had written on behalf of their mother, asking for more money. It was a way to show his father that he had made the right decision, his mother said. The money was also needed to help them through a meager harvest, pay for hired help in the fields so his sisters could attend school to become teachers, and send Cipriano to Manila to learn a trade. Could he not send more money? Fausto was happy to help his brother and sisters escape the fields. The news of their ambitions eased his guilt. He doubled his monthly contribution, but it was getting harder to help pay for food and rent and sponsor his siblings' education. Never mind his own dreams of school.

"I am still saving money for school. My American teacher back home told me a long time ago how important school is. When I finish college and work some more, then I will go back home," he said, though his declaration felt like an outright lie. He hadn't thought about school since the moment he stepped into the apartment on Hope Street.

"You are right. We will both stay and be strong for one another. Maybe I will take my time to finish nursing school so I can work more hours here. We will both work hard and send more money." She smoothed out the envelope. More ink rubbed off on her fingers, making the addresses illegible. "When you send money to your family, I am sure you write nice letters to them. Will you help me write a letter to my family? Will you help me explain why I must stay here longer?"

He nodded and closed his eyes, imagining rubbing the ink off her cheek. They remained seated on the edge of the bed, joined at the hip, until Mr. Calabria called them by name. When Fausto opened his eyes, Connie had dried her eyes. She leaned over and kissed him on the cheek. Her lips lingered on his skin. Then she kissed him on the lips, as fleeting as a memory. She stood up and walked out of the room, stepping with care over the crumpled sheets on the floor.

In the fall of 1932, April took Cary to a sanatorium. She didn't tell anyone where they were; she was afraid Macario would hunt them down. Cary needed sun and rest, she insisted to Fausto. In exchange for her promise to keep Cary sober, Fausto agreed to hold Macario hostage at the Filipino barbershop the day she spirited his cousin away. It was the best thing to do, Fausto told Macario when they returned and Cary was gone. He endured Macario's accusations of betrayal, Cary's absence, and the fear that he had made the wrong decision in letting Cary go where none of his cousins could be there for him. The silence at night hurt Fausto's ears. Sometimes he woke up, believing he had heard Cary cough. But the sound came from the walls creaking or a stranger coughing on the street below.

Macario began drinking more at the apartment than at the speak-easies. He got angry more than he got drunk. When Fausto asked Macario if he wanted to talk, his cousin hurled curses and a bottle at Fausto's feet. It made no sense telling him it was for Cary's good. Fausto merely pushed aside the wet, broken glass with his shoe.

Macario grabbed a full bottle of bootleg whiskey from the coffee table. "He belongs here with us. That whore will dump him and take all his money. I would never abandon him. But she tricked him *and* you!"

"He will not be gone long."

Macario hugged the bottle to his chest. "He has been gone a long time already. He is gone from us forever." He offered Fausto his bloodshot eyes. "Did you not know that?"

After Cary left, Fausto marked off the days on the calendar. Mr.

Calabria read newspaper articles aloud: eleven million people in the country were unemployed, 1,200 striking miners were jailed in Illinois, unemployed workers sparked riots in the streets of London. He declared that the world was marching to Armageddon. Fausto wasn't interested in what was happening elsewhere. Illinois might as well be as far away as London. He ignored Mr. Calabria's gloomy news; he had enough problems at Hope Street, and now he was having problems at the Savoy Hotel. He invited Connie to visit him, but she said his neighborhood was dirty. She rented a basement room from an older white woman she had met at church. The woman charged even less when Connie cleaned her house, and she sometimes invited her to stay for a cup of coffee and a slice of pie. Connie urged Fausto to find a similar arrangement, but he couldn't leave his cousins with one less wage to help pay rent.

"You are using your cousins as an excuse!" she said.

"I need to be there when Cary returns. We are his only family here."

Connie smoothed the cover of the hotel bed they had made and stomped into the adjoining bathroom. She snapped on a pair of rubber gloves and began scrubbing the toilet bowl until soapy water splashed out. "Cary, Cary!" she spat out. "How do you think he got sick? It is the kind of life he lives, his careless, dirty ways."

She anchored her gloved hands on her hips. Water dripped onto her white apron. "Do you want to end up like Cary or Macario? In the gambling dens and pool halls where they smoke opium and marijuana? They sleep with dirty women with diseases. They are bad influences on you. Can you not see that?"

Her words wounded him, but he said, "Let's not quarrel." He tried to put his arm around her, but she pushed the wet scrub brush into his hands.

"This is our future! For me, it is worth fighting for!"

"*Our* future?"

She stood rigid, her feet apart. "After we marry, we will have to move away from Los Angeles. Your cousins will be bad influences on our children."

He had dreamed of marrying Connie and raising a family, but they had never discussed it until now. This wasn't how he wanted to talk about it.

"Do you want to marry me?"

The brush wavered in his hands. "It has been my dream——"

"Do you love me?" She wrenched the brush from him and let it drop.

"You know I do." He meant it in his heart, but not like this, not here, with puddles on the tiles. *"Ta ayat mo ti biag ko,"* he whispered.

"Say it in English, Fausto!"

He raised his eyes to meet hers. "Your love is my life, Connie."

Relief swept across her face. She pulled the gloves off and threw them into the pedestal sink. "Then it is settled. I will find a family from church who will rent you a room. When I graduate in June, we will get married and then move far away from here."

As she gathered wet towels from the floor, she softened her voice. "It will not be so bad. Benny, Serapio, and Domingo can visit us. You will see—it is all for the best."

Arms full of towels, she blew loose hair away from her perspiring face. She stood on her toes and offered her cheek to him. He bent down to kiss her, but he could not feel the warmth of her skin or smell the floral scent of her perfume.

Connie pushed Fausto to leave Hope Street, but he always gave her different excuses, which prompted angry exchanges and her tearful departures from the Savoy Hotel after her shift. Fausto didn't want to leave. Cary had written that he would return in the spring; he'd had enough of the sanatorium and wanted to come back.

After the New Year, Connie joined a social club called the Filipino Federation of America. When she came to work, she talked of nothing else. She told Fausto that its president and founder, Dr. Hilario Moncado, was a scholar who had graduated from the University of Southern California and had written several books. She hoped Fausto was serious about going to college so he could enter a respected profession. She wanted him to see the mansion that the Federation bought. It was something to aspire to, owning such a grand place. Dr. Moncado enforced a strict code of behavior, but what Connie appreciated the most was that the members took care of one another, as if they were back home.

Since joining the club, she neglected the movies and phonograph records. Instead, she directed the club's cultural programs and made food for its banquets, cooking the Kapampangan delicacies she had never made for him. She spearheaded clothes drives in the Filipino neighborhoods for needy families in the Philippines and joined the committee that planned the José Rizal Day cultural activities, honoring the slain Filipino national hero. She raised money for benefit dances and convinced a few Filipinos on the hotel staff to join.

Though Connie urged Fausto to join so he could escort her to club events, he declined. Moncado was from Cebu—a small island south of Luzon with a language as foreign to Fausto as Italian or German. Fausto was at home with the Ilocanos from Luzon who hung out at the lunch counters and barbershops. She kept telling him about the club's weekly activities, hounding him as they cleaned rooms. He only gave her silence when she pressed him for an answer, which drove her to seek the fellowship of her converted co-workers. During breaks, they discussed the latest activity, while Fausto sat idle in the corner, missing her movie reviews and humming the songs she used to play on the phonograph.

Fausto came to work late one morning, shrugging when Mr. Calabria scolded him. He sat in a vacated room until its incoming patrons checked in. When the third set of patrons complained that their hotel rooms were not ready when they arrived, Mr. Calabria fired him.

"You know the rules," he said to Fausto, as he folded the morning newspaper. "Filipinos are getting hurt in riots all over California. Thirteen million people are out of work in this country. Why do you create your own trouble? Mrs. Calabria and I really liked you, but Mrs. Calabria said if we keep you, we spoil you. We must set a good example to the rest of the staff." He held out an envelope with Fausto's last pay, and Fausto took it without saying a word.

Connie huddled outside the office like a shadow. "What happened?" she whispered, her fingers creeping to her lips, when he closed the door behind him.

"I got fired."

"What?" She herded him to a corner of the lobby. "What did you do?"

"I did nothing," he said. "When I should have been cleaning, I did nothing."

"Why?" She lowered her voice as a patron walked by. "Why?"

"Cary is coming back next week," he said.

He headed for the entrance of the hotel. He didn't know what to expect, whether she would pick up the dustpan by her feet and throw it at the revolving-glass door or run after him, shouting that she would join him at Hope Street when Cary returned. Through the door—which they had both cleaned many times together, sometimes making funny faces or blowing kisses through the glass—he saw her standing in the lobby where he had left her, as still as the robed statues in front of the Savoy Hotel.

The day Cary was expected back, summer pushed spring out of the way. The view from the bedroom window was a brick building across the street, but Fausto knew that beyond Hope Street the blossoms on the trees had given way to shiny green leaves. Eight months had passed since Cary's departure. Fausto hoped his cousin had gotten rest, that giving up alcohol and cigarettes had stopped irritating the lesions on Cary's lungs. He didn't know anything about medicine—though he tried to understand what the county doctors had told him about Cary's condition—but maybe it was possible for the lesions to shrink and disappear for good. Yet when Cary walked through the door, Fausto's expectations vanished as quickly as his smile. Cary had lost more hair. His eyes were sunken in deep, black holes. His joints poked out. Some of his teeth were missing and dried blood flecked off his lips.

"What happened to you?" Macario demanded, rushing forward.

All the cousins helped Cary to the sofa. April lingered by the door, trying to hide a purple jaw and fat lip with her swollen fingers. Cary winced when he touched his chest. He had cracked some ribs in a fight that broke out a few nights ago when someone insulted April. He had to defend her, Cary went on, but Macario would hear no more. He grabbed April by the roots of her hair and knocked her down. She screamed and kicked, her heels gouging the wood floor. As she tried to twist free, the buttons down the front of her blouse popped off. The black cups of her brassiere poked out. Her ribs were tattooed with bruises. As Macario dragged her down the stairs, her body thumped against the walls. Their shouting echoed in the hallway and then rose up from the street to Fausto's ears.

"You little beech!"

"You're a goddamn brown monkey!" she shot back. "I can stop being a whore whenever I want to, but you'll always be a monkey!" Her voice broke; it lost its edge.

A car screeched. Benny and Fausto rushed to the window. Macario was alone on the sidewalk, though a crowd of pinoys had begun to grow. He kicked the taxi door shut, and it sped down the street. Cary sat on the sofa, his tongue running along his lip. Fausto glanced at the *longanisa* he had prepared for Cary's homecoming; his appetite for the pan-fried pork patties was gone.

"That whore!" Macario burst in, red-faced, as if he'd been strangled. "I told her I would break her neck if she ever came back."

"She brought him to the sanatorium when none of us could do it," Fausto said. "She took care of him."

"She took care of him all right! See how well he looks!" Macario demanded.

"I have been rough on her too," Cary said. "I am worse than a dog. No, I am worse than a goddamn monkey." He tried to laugh, but he doubled over, hugging his chest as he coughed. A fine spray of blood covered the coffee table.

Fausto rushed to wipe Cary's mouth and all trace of blood from the table with a towel.

"I thought this place was supposed to cure you!" Macario paced the room. "We let a whore take you away from us and bring you back like this!"

"Enough!" Benny took the towel from Fausto. "Can you not see Cary is in pain?"

"Who sees my pain?" Macario wanted to know, standing before the view of weathered bricks.

"I do," Cary whispered.

"You see nothing or you would not have gone!" Macario kept his back to them.

Fausto ignored Macario. He cupped Cary's burning cheeks with his palms. "You are with us now. We will take care of you."

———

Serapio found a restaurant that needed a busboy on call. Fausto filled in for workers who were sick, so the hours were irregular. He worried about not having steady pay, but he was able to watch over Cary, whose face, once bronzed and smooth, had turned ashy gray. Cary's lips and his hands and feet were cracked like mud flats in a drought.

One morning, Fausto brought in a bowl of soup and a cup of tea on a tray he had taken from the restaurant, though Cary was sleeping, his face buried in the pillow. Fausto set the tray on the chair and tiptoed out the room, but Cary called him back.

"Stay with me." Cary sat up from bed one elbow at a time, trying not to shake. "Eat with me."

"I already ate," Fausto said.

Cary tipped the bowl to his mouth. Soup dribbled from Cary's lips, and Fausto, always watchful, blotted the sheet with a napkin.

"Goddamn it!" Cary tried to sound lighthearted. "I peed again." When he moved his legs beneath the sheet, the smell of urine, strong and acidic, was fanned across the room.

Fausto held his breath. "I will wash the sheets. Macario will not know."

"He can smell it in the mattress."

"Never mind Macario! Finish your soup so I can strip the bed," Fausto snapped. He crumpled up the damp napkin, ashamed for being irritated about washing the sheets so often. How many times did Connie change hospital bed sheets every day?

He watched Cary spoon the rice into his mouth and chew slowly as if he had no teeth, before asking, "What happened the last eight months?"

Cary laid his spoon down. "We ran out of money for the sanatorium. I had to leave when my room was assigned to another patient. We stayed with April's friends in San Diego the rest of the time. They were hard drinkers and gamblers—how could I resist?" He shrugged, though his eyes looked defeated. "No matter. It is too late."

"What is too late?"

Cary lifted his chin. "I am dying."

Fausto never doubted that his cousin would recover. Now the truth was all around him, as unavoidable as dawn's arrival. "Macario is right; it *is* your fault," Fausto said in a flat voice, without a trace of anger. "Why are you doing this to yourself, to us?"

"Because I can." Cary's eyes were full of wonder. "Macario and I thought we could do anything in America because we were strong. But no more! I am weak. Like the rest of you."

Fausto removed the tray from Cary's lap. "I am going to take you to the county hospital so the doctors can operate on you."

"It is too late. If you force me, I will cut my wrists! I will do it this time!" Cary held his fists to his chest. "Let me die the way I want."

Fausto threw his arms out. "You cannot die here! This is not what you want!"

"Better to die here with you than in the hospital or sanatorium," Cary insisted. "I am asking you to do me one favor. That is all."

"What?" The word crackled in the air.

"Promise me, when I die, you will send me back to San Esteban."

"We can go home alive." He threw the bed sheet back as if to say, *Cousin, let us go now; Kasinsin, let us leave this stinking apartment, this rotten country now.*

Cary buried his feet beneath the bunched-up sheet. "Too late."

"No!" Fausto said. "As long as I am here, it is not too late. I will be here. I will still be here for you."

"Send my body back home. Do not let me be buried here. I do not belong here. Will you promise me?" Cary's hands crawled up Fausto's arms like a blind beggar.

"I promise you will go home alive!"

Fausto changed the sheets and tucked Cary in bed. Tired, he left the soiled sheets in the bathroom, but he wished he'd washed them because Macario came home early that night. Macario sniffed the air in the bathroom, though Fausto breathed in the alcohol seeping out of his cousin's pores long before he could smell urine. Macario pushed Fausto aside with a flick of his muscular arm and in his drunkenness nearly ripped the bedroom door from its hinges. He turned on the bedroom light.

"Are you a baby?" Macario stumbled across the room.

Serapio, Domingo, and Benny bolted into the bedroom. Cary's head lolled to one side of the pillow. His mouth was crusted white with drool. Before they could stop him, Macario yanked Cary out of bed and threw him against the wall. Cary's arms and legs flew out like wind-blown twigs. Macario began stripping the bed of its sheets.

"You are stinking up the whole apartment!" Macario bellowed.

"I will leave then." Cary reached for a pair of trousers on the floor.

Domingo and Benny lifted Cary by his arms. Macario threw the bedroom window open. He grabbed the lumpy mattress and heaved a corner of it out the window. He flung his body against the mattress, but the corner was lodged tight, covering the opening so that no moonlight shone into the room. Fausto and Serapio seized Macario by the shoulders and rammed him against the front door.

"You stink up this apartment with your whiskey and opium. *You* leave. *You* get out!" Fausto seized a chair and held it above his head.

He expected Macario to slap the chair away as if it were mere sticks and land a hard blow to his chin. But Macario backed down. The wild look in his eyes dissolved as if he had suddenly gone sober, and he ran out of the apartment and down the stairs. In the bedroom, Benny removed

Cary's trousers. Fausto freed the mattress from the window, and Serapio and Domingo put the bed back together so Cary could lie down. Fausto stuck his head out the window and searched the area below. Macario was in the alley, kicking newspapers and crumpled paper bags, slamming his fists into the bricks. He dropped to his haunches and shoved his knuckles in his mouth. A siren wailed down Hope Street, drowning out, Fausto imagined, his cousin's howl.

———————

Connie was somewhere in that sea of white uniforms. From where Fausto sat, in the last row of bleachers in the steamy auditorium, the graduating nursing students looked like a flock of doves in tidy rows. When her name was called out and she floated across the stage in her white shoes to receive her diploma, Fausto stood up and clapped. He could barely see her face. She must be smiling; he imagined her smiling. When the ceremony was over and the women filed out, he pushed his way down the stairs, hoping to catch up with her. The crowd had broken apart once it spilled onto the manicured lawn. He wandered from group to group, wondering what to say when he found her, then panicked at the thought of missing her altogether.

Connie was talking to two other graduates. She was thinner, her face not quite as round. He was no more than a stone's throw from her when they were joined by three pinoys dressed in crisp, tan McIntosh suits and fedoras. The last of them, a tall, slender, fair-skinned pinoy, kissed Connie on the lips. He withdrew a handkerchief from his pocket and patted her shiny forehead, then extended his arm, where she deposited her dark-navy cape. All six of them began walking in the opposite direction of Fausto, but something made her look over her shoulder. It was as if he had called her name without making a sound, and no one else but she could hear. Her eye caught his, and she held back, even as her companion touched her elbow. She stood up on her toes and whispered in his ear. The pinoy looked over at Fausto with anxious eyes, though Fausto didn't know why; he was handsome with an elegant nose. The pinoy's mouth tightened as he watched her leave his side. She stopped an arm's length away from Fausto, not saying a word, her eyes betraying confusion.

"Congratulations, Connie." Fausto said. "I wanted to come to your graduation."

"If I did not see you just now, were you going to leave without talking to me?" She lifted her eyebrows, once full, now plucked into graceful arches.

Fausto shrugged. "You saw me. You walked back."

"Maybe I'm waiting for something." Her voice was tight.

"I am sorry."

"Sorry for what?"

Her questions, the way she pounced on him, were maddening. He squirmed in the heat, feeling as if he were back at the Savoy Hotel. "I am sorry for hurting you." When he spoke, something inside his chest took flight, like a wild bird escaping.

Now she shrugged. "I can take care of myself. I *have* been taking care of myself."

"Connie!" one of the women called out.

The man who kissed her craned his neck. The anxious look never left his face, even as she waved to him.

Fausto looked away. The last beat of wings faded in his ears. "Your friends?"

"We're all Moncados," she said. "The girls—my classmates—and I met the boys at a dance. We're going to New York City in July. Letty's auntie lives there. Rose found work at a downtown hospital, where we hope to become nurses too. The boys have engineering degrees. It should be easy for them to find good companies to work for."

He tried not to sound surprised. "Ah, your friend is also going?"

"Nino—Saturnino—and I are engaged. We are going to get married next spring. That is our plan."

She seemed reluctant to tell him, but it didn't matter. How could he have missed the diamond on her ring finger? Its oval shape threw off sparks in the sun. He wanted to look at this pinoy again, and yet he couldn't bring himself to. He already knew her Nino had come from wealth back home, from a family who could afford his schooling here.

"Congratulations. I hope you two will be very happy together," he said, withering in the heat like the trampled blades of grass all around him. "Good luck to you."

"Thank you." She blinked her eyes in the sun. "Good luck to you too."

She was about to leave him when he blurted out, "Your family!"

She stood still. "They know I'm staying here. I have been sending them lots of money for a long time now. I'll be able to send even more when I work for a hospital and Nino finds a job. Nino and I are going to take care of them—from America." Her eyes hardened. "And what about your education? Will you be going to school soon?"

Fausto swallowed. "Concepción, Cary is dying."

"I'm so sorry." Her voice turned soft, just as he remembered it so long ago.

"I promised Cary—we are trying to get enough money to send him home alive."

"You will do it," she said with resolution, though he knew how hollow his promise must have sounded to her.

He didn't know what else to say or do, so he walked off. He thought he heard her call out to him. If he ran back to her and he was wrong, he would look foolish. If he looked over his shoulder now, she would be gone already. The last image he would have of her would be her arm interlocked with her fiancé, the ring catching the sun again, instead of the sad look on her face as he turned away. He walked at a fast clip. When he reached the edge of the lawn, he mopped his brow with his handkerchief. The damp cloth slid to his pinched eyes and down to his mouth, where he licked his lips and tasted salt.

———————

It was a miracle Cary lasted until the few trees in the neighborhood lost their leaves. The evenings grew cooler. Fausto, Benny, Serapio, and Domingo spent late nights dealing cards and rolling buttons across the table as they played *sikoy-sikoy*, while Macario stayed away until dawn. Sunday midmorning, Fausto woke up surrounded by empty mattresses and silence. His cousins looked away as he pushed into the room. Cary's hair was mussed up. The back of his head seemed to float on the pillow as if it had no weight. His eyes, his lips were closed. Fausto stroked Cary's forehead, surprised that his skin had already grown cool to the touch. Nobody moved when Macario came into the bedroom, holding a bottle-shaped paper bag by its neck. Benny crowded up to Fausto, their shoulders fused, to let Macario in, but Macario threw his body into a chair in the corner of the room. The paper bag clinked to the floor. He flung his head back against the wall.

"Remember how Cary and I used to swim out to sea?" he asked. "We swam for hours, trying to see whose arms would give out, whose legs would cramp first. And the time he beat me at *palo sebo?* I could not accept that he could climb that greased pole faster than me. He claimed his strength was in his hair." Macario laughed at the ceiling. "So I cut your hair when you were sleeping, remember?" He ran his thumb across his fingers over and over, as if feeling the texture and weight of Cary's thick, wavy locks.

"I promised Cary I would send him home to recover," Fausto said. "But now we will send his body home for good."

Macario sprang from the chair. "We were going to change our lives here! We cannot go back. Cary cannot go back." He leaned over Cary as if entreating his body to side with him. "We will bury him in America."

"No!" Fausto said. "I should have taken him home when I first came here."

"You have money for your ticket too?" Macario demanded. "Or do you trust the Americans on the ship not to steal the money and throw his body into the sea?"

"I will get the money *and* bring Cary home." Fausto locked his hand on Cary's shoulder. How stiff it felt! Even if he found two jobs and Benny, Domingo, and Serapio took second jobs too, it would still take a few months to earn passages on the ship.

"How much will the morgue charge you to keep his body for several months?" Macario said, as if reading Fausto's mind. He gave off fumes of whiskey, anger. "I will give you three days to get the money, and then I will prepare for his burial." He marched to the open door, deaf to their protests. "Leave me alone with Cary!"

Nobody dared cross Macario. They filed out without a word. Through the closed door, they heard a chair scraping across the floor, and then nothing.

––––––––––

The third day after Cary died, Fausto and Benny stood across the street from Fat's Gambling Den, dusting dirt from their clothes. They had won $200 at blackjack. They should have gone back to Hope Street, but Fausto, feeling both restless and lucky, convinced Benny they could win more money. When he reached $300, however, he should have known that Mr. Fat's dealer would not only reclaim their money but make Fausto lose two weeks' worth of wages too. Macario knew which gambling dens punished players who won and kept playing. He knew how to win at blackjack too, but he refused to go with them. He had even wished them bad luck—hoping for a funeral or a lizard crossing their path on their way to the gambling houses.

"What now?" Benny asked. "Ai, rice is wasted, even the bran!"

Fausto fished a coin from his trouser pocket. He held up a dime.

"We failed Cary. How can we face him?" Benny demanded, near tears and slump-shouldered.

"Cary is dead." Fausto's words broke through his own stupor. "Cary is dead."

"You sound like Macario!" Benny cried. "You are being disrespectful!"

Fausto ran his callused finger across the ridges of the dime. Tomorrow Macario would call the mortuary to take Cary's body away. They would have to leave the apartment, but Fausto knew they would not leave together. Serapio and Domingo would follow Macario, just as they have done all their lives. Maybe he and Benny would look for Arsenio Magsaysay, who was going to top beets in Montana or pick snow peas in Idaho, though Fausto had no idea when the harvests began. Or they could meet Prudencio in Stockton to pick asparagus. He massaged the bridge of his nose. He was getting ahead of himself. There were more pressing matters. Even if they couldn't send his body back—Fausto could not let go of that promise just yet—they needed money for a coffin and a cemetery plot. Cary deserved a Catholic funeral service, though Fausto, who hadn't stepped inside a church since his arrival in America, didn't know if Filipinos were allowed to be buried on American soil. But out of all the tasks that needed to be done, writing to Cary's family was the greatest burden.

Fausto caught sight of the Manila Taxi-Dance Hall. The sign above the entrance—"Ten Cents a Dance"—beckoned. He curled his fingers into a fist, the dime disappearing. This was his fate, wasn't it? Slow dancing with a tall blonde. Maybe she would pity him when he told his story and collect money from the other dancers. Maybe April was in there. She would help because she loved Cary. It was fate. He believed in fate.

Rain started falling. It was a sign to go inside the Manila Taxi-Dance Hall for shelter. He shielded his eyes as he headed for the entrance. Benny called out to him in a frantic voice. Where was he going? Benny ran after him and tugged on his jacket, but Fausto flicked his arm away. A pinoy guard pawed at his arms and legs, searching for weapons, even after Fausto told him he had nothing to fight with. The guard kicked open the door, and Fausto stumbled in. Thick smoke swirled in the room. He rubbed his eyes raw and circled the dance floor, but he couldn't find April. Hell, he couldn't find a damn blonde. My luck, he thought, shaking his head. He could ask, but he didn't know her last name. Benny pushed up against his shoulder, clambering over him like a stray cur.

"Go find your own partner!" Fausto shouted.

Benny stepped back as if he'd been slapped. Fausto didn't care. He felt nothing in his heart, and maybe that was good. He moved on, not looking back.

"Ten cents a dance!" a pinoy hawker cried out from the edge of the dance floor.

Pinoys strutted along the sidelines in their tailor-made suits. They peeled off ten-dollar bills from fat rolls, exchanging their weekly wages for a handful of tickets. Fausto deposited the dime in the hawker's palm. The hawker sneered, but Fausto would not leave until he got his one red ticket. He searched for a partner, while the other pinoys, thick-headed and thick-tongued with alcohol and marijuana, yelled at the women on the floor. He finally saw a blonde nearby. As she danced, she tore up a ticket every minute, cheating her partner out of time and his money. Before the song ended, she pulled away, all of the pinoy's tickets littered at her feet. The pinoy scratched his head and slunk away, inciting jeers from the spectators. Fausto cut in ahead of another pinoy.

"I only have one ticket," he said, as the pinoy band began to play.

"If I like you, I'll dance with you longer, for free." She breathed in his ear, her lips gummy on his skin. "This could be your lucky night."

He tucked the ticket in her bra, which peeked out of her low-cut blouse. She was probably in her early twenties, but she looked older. Red lipstick was smeared across her teeth. Face powder flaked off at the corners of her mouth. She didn't offer him her name and didn't ask him for his name, which suited him fine. Without hesitation, she pressed her body against him. He could barely breathe, pressed into her enormous breasts. He had planned to be rough with her, but her forcefulness took him by surprise. He followed her lead, as the trumpeter went up and down the scale lazily. A piano tinkled, clarinets tooted, and sandy sounds shimmered and rose up from the drummer's brush. The easy tempo made Fausto sleepy; his eyelids fluttered from the weight of exhaustion. A trombone cut in before a gravelly voiced pinoy singer sang into the microphone, jarring him awake.

"I can't give you anything but love, baby," the singer crooned, trying to sound like Louis Armstrong.

Fausto didn't want to look at the woman, at her hungry eyes. He pressed his cheek against hers as she spun him in circles. Couples were locked so tightly they looked like solitary dancers bumping up against him. His face prickled in the heat, and then he started crying. Tears seeped between their cheeks.

"Hey." She pulled away and shook his arms. "Wanna come up to my room?"

She unbuttoned her blouse to reveal her flimsy bra. He stuck one hand in his trouser pocket, his fingers groping, trying to awaken his penis, but it hung limp.

"Listen, I like you," she said in a voice that needed convincing. She withdrew the damp ticket from her bra and held up her wristwatch to his face, letting him know that his time on the dance floor had expired several minutes ago. "You owe me."

He buried his face in her shoulder and sobbed. He should be in the apartment, washing and dressing his cousin's body. He should be on his knees by Cary's bedside, praying. Instead, another song began. The woman pushed him away. She ripped the ticket in two and let it flutter to the floor where the rest of the red-paper strips lay like dirty confetti from a parade that had long since passed. She turned her attention to a pinoy who stepped in.

"Get off the floor!" the hawker yelled. "If you're not paying, you're not playing!"

Fausto wove his way through the throng of dog-tired but eager pinoys, whose suits were now wrinkled and stained. He found a door that led to an alley and smelled chicken before he saw its legs carved up by maggots in a garbage can. The door slapped shut, sucking hot air. The music seemed so distant. He looked ahead, at the slice of street between the brick buildings, and pulled up the collar of his jacket. It was raining harder now. Water spilled from the sidewalks, overflowing onto the street, bubbling blackly in the storm drains.

CHAPTER 5

Cutting 'gras

By midmorning at Agbayani Village, doors opened and men emerged from their rooms. The Mexican migrant worker who had been ill all week coughed the length of the walkway. Fausto's next-door neighbor, an Anglo with a silver crew cut, shuffled out in house slippers. Fausto braced himself as his neighbor slammed his door, making the common wall they shared shudder. The man gasped and shoved the tube wrapped around his face closer to his nose. He pulled a small oxygen tank behind him and joined the other retired farm workers for breakfast in the dining hall. Fausto shut his door.

"Are you hungry?" Arturo set his cup down. The coffee pot was empty.

Fausto's stomach roared in his ears as Arturo prepared breakfast in his room. Fausto didn't like to eat in the hall. The retirees were younger, and every harvest brought a new crop of migrant farm workers who couldn't afford to live in town. There was no reason for him to get to know them. His eyes watered as Arturo presented the tray on his lap. He sipped from the bowl, hoping Arturo would assume his tears were from the steamy chicken and rice soup. He was lucky to have Arturo here with him all these years. It made sense that Rogelio would come back into his life by way of Arturo.

Arturo brewed another pot of coffee and ate the rest of the soup. "So," he began, moving his bowl to the desk, "did you send Cary's body back to San Esteban?"

More than sixty years later, Fausto was still ashamed. One of the tenants notified the landlord, who stormed into the apartment four days after Cary had died and found the body still laid out on the bed. Fausto couldn't recall any odor. Every time he prayed at Cary's bedside he was aware of how this shrunken body had once been filled with his laughter, his touch, his good looks. The photographs of Cary captured his smile and the sheen of his health, but it was those cold fingers that last held his hand, those distant eyes that gazed at him one last time. Cary was buried in a cemetery outside of Los Angeles, without a Catholic Church service and only a plain marker on his grave. Fausto couldn't forgive Macario's absence at the burial, not even decades later when Macario had replaced the marker with a marble tombstone.

His Auntie Lilia caught pneumonia and passed away just before Cary died, sparing Fausto the burden of carrying his auntie's heartbreak, her sorrow at his failure to bring her son back home alive. The five cousins fled the City of Angels. Serapio and Domingo went north to San Francisco and then followed Macario to New York City. The three of them later returned to Los Angeles. Fausto and Benny landed in the agricultural town of Stockton, where they met up with Prudencio and his friend Ayong. Fausto kept in touch with Serapio and Domingo, but he never went to New York City—he was too angry with Macario. He was also afraid of running into Connie, no matter that the city was big. He assumed she had made a nice life for herself and her Nino in America and forgot her family in Floridablanca, even as he knew it was wrong of him to judge her.

Arturo knew Fausto never saw his parents again, but he didn't know everything. Fausto's brother, Cipriano, wrote him a letter when Fausto was living in the Delta camps in Stockton. Fausto remembered the date—April 1, 1938—because Joe Louis had knocked out Harry Thomas in five rounds in Chicago. His boss let him and his crew listen to the world championship match on the radio. The boys in the bunkhouse were cheering for the Brown Bomber and were still talking about the match when they came back from the fields. One of the old-timers picked up Fausto's letter from the Luzon Café, where the owner, Manong Claro, took in the workers' mail when they returned for the harvest. Fausto's sisters had written earlier that their mother went back to working in the fields after he left. But Cipriano wrote to tell him that she had died in childbirth, at age forty-seven. Nobody told him she was pregnant. Cipriano wrote that the baby's head was too big, but he never revealed if the baby, who also died, was a boy or a girl.

Cipriano sent the letter after their burials, and he asked for money because the funeral for their mother and the baby had been grand. Fausto sent a month's worth of his earnings, but it wasn't enough to cover all the expenses—the coffins built of narra wood, the *sampaguita* wreaths that were showered upon the coffins and burial site, the donations to St. Stephen Church, the big party that lasted for days. Fausto was taken aback by the timing of the letter; he had expected a telegram to let him know of her death as soon as it had happened. Benny was sure they thought he couldn't afford to go home, but Fausto didn't believe him. He had lain awake in his bunk, remembering his mother's face—her large, raised mole like an onyx bead adorning the end of her thick brow; the prominent fold of her lids, which made her eyes deep set and dreamy looking; her earlobes, translucent as onion paper in the morning light. As he stared at the blackness, he told God that Cipriano's actions were just. It was his punishment for having left his family when they needed him the most.

His father died in 1941. This time, his sister Marguerite's letter to him was pages long. Pa, she wrote, had suffered a heart attack in one of his rice fields during a storm. The good-for-nothing hired workers left early that day. It was nightfall when Marguerite gathered their uncles to look for him. They found him the next morning, the back of his head and his shoulder blades just above the muddy water. His face was swollen, his hands and feet shriveled up. His carabao was still tied to a nearby tree. If Fausto had never left, he would have been beside their father and brought him home, Marguerite insisted in her ragged handwriting, her words cramped across the page. If he had stayed in the Philippines, Fausto thought to himself, he might have had his own family to take care of, his own fields to tend. It didn't matter; she told Fausto that the money for his boat ticket would be better spent on their father's burial. So he borrowed money from Benny, Prudencio, and Ayong to give his father a splendid funeral.

He overcame the rift between his siblings and him by the time he settled in Terra Bella in 1950. He received letters from their children—his nieces and nephews—begging him, "Uncle Fausto, please remember us." They wrote at Christmas and on their birthdays, though relatives from Terra Bella who visited San Esteban assured his siblings that he was not rich. Cipriano argued that Fausto had no wife or children to support. Fausto imagined that his brother assumed he was hoarding his money. So he tried to send as much as he could. It troubled him to think that his nieces and nephews, whom he had never met, only cared about the money he sent monthly, but he understood life back home was still hard. When he retired in 1980, the letters stopped and he never heard from any of his nieces and nephews or their children again.

Fausto swallowed hard, as if dry grains of rice were stuck to his throat. Arturo brought him outdoors for a break, guiding him along the walkway. Fausto bent down to examine the rose bushes, which had grown in a wild fan shape and needed to be pruned. He rubbed a red petal between his fingers. Its blackened edges were curling up like lettuce leaves. Its stem was gummy with "honeydew" sap, a sure sign that aphids were attacking the roses again.

Seeing the flowers reminded Fausto of when Rogelio was a boy tending the family flower garden. One summer day while babysitting, Fausto noticed black mold all over the leaves of the geraniums that Benny's wife, Luz, had planted in the front yard. When he told Rogelio they needed to spray the plants before the aphids destroyed them, Rogelio led him to the back shed where Benny kept the gardening tools. Fausto had trouble reading the labels on the jugs and relied on Rogelio to find the insecticide. Fausto filled the spray can and attached it to the hose, and let Rogelio douse the geraniums with the milky water. Within days the plants died, and Luz punished Rogelio for not watering them by spanking him and giving his favorite toy truck to the Salvation Army.

When Fausto found Rogelio, whose face was streaked with tears, planting new geraniums in the flower bed, he brought the boy to the shed. The jug Rogelio had taken was nearly empty of its contents. Fausto rapped his own head. It was *his* fault for killing Luz's plants. If he had checked the label, he wouldn't have used the chemical that was toxic to her flowers. But Rogelio insisted that it was still his fault because he had picked the jug. Rogelio was more afraid of Luz declaring Fausto unfit to care for her children. He'd already been punished; he couldn't bear to lose Fausto too. Fausto didn't want to lose Rogelio either. So they both kept quiet, and Fausto replanted the rest of the geraniums.

As they stepped into the sunshine, Fausto wondered if Rogelio would remember that story. From the dining-hall window, they heard clinking glasses being loaded into the dishwasher. Fausto was glad he had left the restaurant business. He didn't like waiting on white people who wouldn't tip him unless he wore gloves. In the fields he was free, working all day with his countrymen.

"You know we got paid according to how much we picked in the fields," he said to Arturo. "Your father and I liked being rewarded for being quick."

"Dad was quick for a big man," Arturo said. He turned Fausto around to retrace their steps to his room.

"Your father beat me a few times when we raced to see who could pack the most crates by the end of the day." Fausto laughed. "Oh, he used to brag! He said he could beat me in the strawberry fields. But I told him the asparagus fields were harder."

"Dad was glad he never picked asparagus." Arturo led Fausto back into his room.

"We called it cutting 'gras!" Fausto curled his fingers, trying to remember the knife's position in his hand as he cut 'gras in the Delta region near Stockton. He was part of an all-Filipino crew, the fastest team ever from the *campos*—the labor camps—in the late 1930s. Many workers quit for good after spring ended, after only one harvest, because the work required a lot of bending. "Those who quit did not have the backs for this kind of work," he said.

Fausto sifted through papers in his desk until he came upon a manila envelope full of loose photographs. He handed Arturo a black-and-white picture of his crew. A lanky horse with a wooden cart—they called it a "sled"—full of asparagus stood in a field of dark soil. A group of men squinted at the sun, clutching asparagus spears and hoes. To keep the peat dirt out, they layered sweaters and suit vests over long-sleeved shirts and coveralls. They knotted scarves at their necks and wore goggles and wide-brimmed hats in the fields. Some even wore two pairs of pants. In the photograph, a few smiled. Others stared grim faced. All of them looked tired.

The workers made good money being quick with their hands. When the other crews were still cutting 'gras in the late morning, Fausto and his crew were heading back to camp. They were so fast they often had to wait for the cook to finish making lunch.

"This is you, right?" Arturo pointed at the image of Fausto, his arm draped around Benny, his straight, black hair flattened by the straw hat he held in his hand.

Fausto tapped the upper corner of the photograph where Prudencio and Ayong were huddled together. Despite years of being apart, he and Benny had kept in touch with Prudencio, who never made it to Los Angeles because he met Ayong while picking lettuce in the Imperial Valley. The two of them followed the harvests up and down California. They had been cutting 'gras for years before Benny and Fausto joined them in the Delta.

"We did not know what the hell we were doing!" Fausto laughed, holding his soft belly. "Everyone was mad because we were cutting 'gras wrong. We were losing more than we were harvesting! I told Benny maybe we should pick something else. Prudencio and Ayong made fun of us too, but they helped us in the fields and in the camps."

He showed Arturo his palms, his calluses, each layer of yellowed skin like a tree ring. Deep down, one of those layers had formed when he was cutting 'gras. The first day they joined the camps in 1934, the foreman made Prudencio and Ayong miss the cockfights on their day off to measure Fausto and Benny so they could get their knives custom made.

"Can we not use somebody else's knife?" Benny pointed at the long row of asparagus knives, of varying lengths, leaning against the bunkhouse wall.

Ayong let them examine his knife, whose handle was carved with crude swirls. The wood was a silvery gray, exposed to sun and rain for years. Ayong ran his finger down the length of the short metal shaft to its sharp blade, which was flat and notched like the fletching at the end of an arrow. "Try to cut with this. Ah, *sige!* Go on!"

The handle was too small in Fausto's hand. Its indentations didn't fit right in his grip. He stabbed at the soft soil with the blade, hunching his back, almost falling forward. Benny was shorter than Fausto, but he too had to bend low.

Only Ayong could trot across the yard, grazing the earth with his blade with ease. He pointed to his arm. "Ai, that is why we size you! If you use somebody else's knife—*bumbye*—you will hurt your hand and your back! And then you will be useless in the Delta and everywhere else too!" Ayong laughed.

He led them to a cottonwood tree outside the camp. Its trunk was massive, its crooked branches spread out several feet. They chose a branch, thicker than their fists, from which to carve their handles. Then Prudencio drove them to Gianelli Machine Shop on Highway 4 just outside of Stockton, where the shafts were measured using the length of their arms. Prudencio spit out strings of tobacco chew and said he would show them how to carve their handles—if they proved to be worthy members on their crew.

Fausto and Benny were used to working late hours in restaurants and sleeping in. On their first day of cutting 'gras, they straggled out of the bunkhouse at three in the morning, barely able to see their feet. Ayong told them some crews left camp as early as two in the morning to get to the Delta fields in nearby Terminous. Prudencio slapped hats strapped with flashlights on their heads and told them to take afternoon naps.

Fausto trained his light at the ground. How could they cut 'gras with such weak light? But he didn't say anything more as he and Benny followed the crew on foot to the fields hundreds of yards away. Fausto was amazed at how quickly the tips sprouted through the rich peat dirt. Like daily miracles, spears shot up every morning for weeks, growing as much as several inches a day in the warm weather.

While the rest of the Filipino crew trotted across the fields, Prudencio and Ayong—who lost at least a morning's worth of wages—stayed behind to show Fausto and Benny how to angle the blade at 45 degrees to the soil to avoid flat cutting and damaging the spears. Though they cut all the spears they could see that morning, they threw out 'gras not fit for market—the ones whose spears were curved by the wind or turned gray by the rain or whose heads had flowered too early. They combed the fields twice, in search of perfect, tight-headed spears. By afternoon the fields were empty of workers and any trace of 'gras, leaving the peat dirt ready to receive the next morning's crop. Fausto's crew didn't harvest white 'gras, which meant they had to be cut before they emerged from the soil and turned green by the sun. He was glad; it was too hard to spot the tips of white 'gras, which were shipped to fancy restaurants on the East Coast.

When they returned to the camps that first afternoon, they found veteran pinoys sharpening knives, tending their garden plots, or grooming their chickens. Benny collapsed on his bunk bed, but Fausto hurried to the bathhouse with clean clothes and towel in tow. Peat dust settled everywhere. The fine dust and sweat irritated his skin, making him itch beyond the hours spent on the Delta. It seeped into the pores of his scalp. It was packed into the corners of his eyes. Often, neither thick lathering of soap nor scrubbing with a pumice stone until his skin was raw freed him of dust. The cook came back from the fields midmorning to light the fireplace under the metal tub so the water would be hot when the men returned for the noontime meal. Fausto resisted the urge to use too many cans of hot water for rinsing, mindful of those who still needed to take baths. He watched the black soapy water stream down his body and disappear through the slats of the wooden floor, longing to jump into the tub itself and soak for hours. He ground his teeth at night to keep from scratching and breaking skin. The itching was worse than the early spring wind and cold, which cut through the strips of cardboard lining the inside of the crew's bunkhouse, a rusted freight car.

He was amazed that his bleeding gums were not the only thing left in his mouth by season's end.

That first day, Prudencio and Ayong had a good laugh as Fausto and Benny lay on their bunks, massaging each other's backs and necks. Prudencio congratulated them but announced that they had to make up for costing him and Ayong a day's wage. For compensation, Prudencio ordered Fausto to check the outhouse and clear the small wooden structure of sheltering black widows. Whenever Prudencio had to go, Fausto lit a rolled-up newspaper with a match and waved it over the holes to scare off the spiders, which scurried across his work boots, making him dance and shiver.

Prudencio and Ayong took them to Stockton's Little Manila, the Filipino District, to celebrate their first week. Prudencio couldn't convince them to gamble or take in a dance at the taxi-dance halls, so they settled on having meals at the Luzon Café and the Lafayette Lunch Counter. Prudencio introduced them to Manong Ambo, the owner of the lunch counter, who entertained them with stories and cooked Filipino meals in his white T-shirt and apron, his boat-shaped, paper cook's hat sitting atop his round head. When they received their first pay, they got haircuts at a barbershop on El Dorado Street and had a suit made for them at a tailor shop on Lafayette Street.

Fausto liked the District, which swarmed with attractive *pinays* who worked in or frequented the Filipino grocery stores, restaurants, fish markets, laundry establishments, and cafés. He and Benny befriended a few pinays in Little Manila, but none of the women showed romantic interest. Benny tried to get Fausto to attend St. Mary's Church and the Filipino Full Gospel Center, but Fausto thought it was disrespectful to go to church just to meet respectable pinays. Then Benny suggested they join the Filipino Federation of America. Joining the fraternal organization was a show of solidarity for the pinoys in the community, especially after Manong Ambo told them that locals had chased after "those brown boys" with baseball bats and brass knuckles. Still, Fausto reminded Benny that a group of white men had bombed the federation's building in Stockton in 1930, and instead of investigating, the police blamed other Filipinos for blowing out the front porch and injuring one member. Though five years had passed since the bombing, hard feelings still simmered outside the District. Fausto, unlike the others in the federation, didn't want to be so visible. He and Benny didn't dare venture beyond Washington and Sutter streets, the boundaries of Little Manila.

In two weeks' time, Fausto and Benny were cutting 'gras at a steady pace. They rushed the stalks from the field to the packing shed before they could dry out, so that they'd earn more money per pound. With the extra pay, they bought fedoras and spectator shoes, and Benny even bought Tabu cologne, though the strong scent made his eyes water. Their Filipino crew could cut as many as ten acres per day per man. Other crews could only muster five acres. Their crew's piles—*burros*, Ayong called them—were the highest in the fields. Prudencio and Ayong were pleased with how quickly Fausto and Benny were able to contribute to their crew's production. Ayong told Fausto the Italian farmers wanted Filipino workers because they were short, "close to the ground," making 'gras cutting "easy."

Easy. Fausto snorted, remembering the backbreaking work he and his countrymen endured in the asparagus fields decades ago.

Arturo handed back the picture. Fausto squinted. The faces in the photograph were faded, ready to disappear from the glossy paper.

During Fausto's first season, Manong Val, one of the older pinoy farm workers, warned him he had better go to school and study hard because the fields were tough. Fausto didn't tell him that Hope Street had crushed his dream of attending school. Instead, he declared that he planned to return to Los Angeles with money saved from working in the fields and get an education. Manong Val nodded, tapping with his bent finger at the scar that ran from his temple to his jaw. Fausto heard that one of the campo horses got spooked and kicked Manong Val in the head, but Manong Val told him he had worked in the plantations in Hawaii when the Hawaiian Sugar Planters' Association recruited him in 1907.

"It is hard in the pineapple fields! I join the Filipino Federation of Labor union," Manong Val said. "In 1920, we strike for higher wages. The strike las' for 165 days! But nothing happen! Another strike in 1924 spread to twenty-three of the forty-five plantations. Oh, it was big! But it only las' eight months. Then later the police raid our union headquarters at the Hanapepe camp on the island of Kauai." Manong Val pointed to his scar. "I get hit in the head. I almos' die. They kill sixteen Filipino workers. If not for my injury—I did not wake up for almos' five days—I go to prison for years. They arrest sixty of my compatriots."

Manong Val was blacklisted because of his union activities, so he came to the mainland. He found work in California and stuck with the unions, but trouble erupted in Pixley. The cotton growers jumped workers who went on strike in the fields. Two people were killed and many were wounded, but none of the farmers went to jail.

Fausto couldn't stop staring at the deep purple line along Manong Val's jaw. "Maybe if you quit the union, you would not have to suffer so much."

Manong Val's eyes were milky. "I am too old to do nothing else! If you are stuck in the fields, you better have the union fighting for you! Who else will fight for you, eh?"

"If not for the union, you would not have this scar," Fausto said.

"If I din have the union, I only make pennies in the fields."

"But at what cost, Manong Val?"

Manong Val laughed, exposing tobacco-flecked spittle connecting his two rows of blackened teeth. "I thought you were smart! You been in the States for how long? And you doan know the cost of things here? If you leave, you have no use for the unions. Too late for me to change my luck, but not for you!" He picked up his knife and walked away.

Fausto pitied the old man, whose back was curved and hands curled like a sickle. Manong Val spent his free time pulling weeds in the campo garden or grooming his chickens for cockfights. It was not a life Fausto could imagine living for the rest of his days, though he didn't know what else to do. He wouldn't have to get involved with the unions because he vowed the first harvest would be his last. Yet he came back with Benny for another season in the Delta and suffered again through Manong Val's lectures. By the third year, Manong Val was no longer surprised to see him, though he shook his bark-like finger at Fausto as if Manong Val were the one pitying Fausto. He led Fausto to an empty garden plot next to his, overturned a shovelful of dirt, and said, "I will help you grow *tarong, kamatis,* and *parya.*"

Manong Val passed away in his sleep during Fausto's fifth year in the Delta. When the 'gras season ended, he and Benny followed Prudencio and Ayong picking lettuce in the Imperial Valley, melons in Lompoc, and strawberries on their knees along the San Diego coast. Sometimes they changed their minds about what to harvest, but they always returned in the spring to cut 'gras. They returned to the big Filipino community in Stockton and in the campos. The Delta was the closest thing to home for Fausto. It was the first time he felt that way.

"I'm glad Dad never moved us north of Delano, or else I would have cut 'gras right next to him," Arturo said. "The vineyards were enough for me."

Fausto gazed at the photograph, committing the youthful faces to memory as he shut his desk drawer. "Conditions were not so good in the fields and in the camps, but every morning I would look at the spears of 'gras in the black dirt and thank God for this chance to live and work in His creation when so many in this country had nothing."

"And then you cursed the devil for the work itself!" Arturo teased.

Fausto scowled. "You cannot appreciate because you did not see what I saw. *Síge;* go on! Close your eyes!" he demanded. "Peat dirt looks like coffee grounds. Can you imagine miles and miles of coffee grounds?"

Arturo closed his eyes. Fausto closed his eyes too, willing a scene he had witnessed for so many seasons in the springtime—a swayback horse pulling a wooden sled filled with asparagus, trotting down the rows, its hooves kicking up clouds of dust. The workers galloped ahead of the horse, bending down, cutting the 'gras with their right hand and snatching the fallen spear with their left, and holding as many as twenty blades of 'gras within their fingers as they raced across the fields toward the rising sun.

CHAPTER 6

Lost and found

Son-of-a-gun! Fausto banged the stopped clock on his dresser top. Forty-eight hours later and he was still seething. Despite his protests, Arturo held firm on his decision to delay Rogelio's visit by two days because he declared that Fausto needed more time to prepare. Fausto slammed his drawer shut. He'd been waiting for decades! But Arturo fended off all arguments the night before, giving his attention to ironing Fausto's shirt and spraying too much starch on the collar, which now chafed Fausto's neck. To make matters worse, in his anger, Fausto cut himself shaving. How could he face Rogelio in this state, he asked his reflection in the bathroom mirror as he pressed a wad of toilet paper against his chin. His cheeks were ablaze. His heart was skipping stones.

Fausto tidied up his room, hoping to calm down and not think about the day ahead. But as he hung shirts and trousers in his closet, he imagined folding them into an empty suitcase that Rogelio would bring and open up like a present on his bed. It struck him then—why Rogelio agreed to wait. He wanted Fausto to be healthy enough to leave with him on a plane. The revelation made him abandon his room and wait at the entryway of the Village. As he eased onto the wooden bench, mindful that sitting too long would hurt his hips, Fausto told himself it was enough to endure physical pain—to feel this alive—for what lay ahead of him.

Arturo insisted on picking up Rogelio, as if to bring him to a secret location. Fausto massaged his hip. Maybe Arturo knew. Maybe that's why he didn't want Rogelio driving himself to the Village; he was afraid Rogelio would whisk Fausto away once the truth was revealed. It wasn't going to be easy to leave Arturo, but in Fausto's heart he knew his remaining time belonged to Rogelio.

Long before he saw Arturo's Camaro, Fausto heard the familiar drone of the white Chevy on the main road getting closer. He managed to hide behind the corner of the brick building, wiping his palms on his trousers, unable to decide whether to wait in his room or greet the two men at the entrance. By then, Arturo's car pulled into the driveway, gravel popping beneath the tires. Before Arturo got out, the passenger door swung open and a young man wearing sunglasses stepped into the heat.

Rogelio wore short sleeves and shorts, exposing thick legs and muscular arms. He was dark skinned, not as dark as Fausto got in the summer, but not fair skinned like his wife Marina. Fausto examined Rogelio's left leg to see if it was shorter than the right, if he leaned on his right leg, or if there were any scars from the surgeries he had undergone as a boy. Fausto couldn't tell. He hung back as they headed toward his room, trailing them when they were several yards ahead of him. His feet seemed to glide across the walkway like a spirit. As he approached his open door, he heard Arturo ask how long Rogelio was planning to stay. Fausto would not have recognized Rogelio's soft voice.

"You mean here today, or my stay in Terra Bella?" Rogelio paused. "I don't know the answer to either. We have a lot of catching up to do. I was hoping to spend the night here—if everything works out."

"Overnight?" Arturo questioned. "Well, we'll see how Fausto is doing."

Fausto counted to ten. As he stepped into his room, he felt suddenly lightheaded, as if the room had been sucked of air. He grabbed the doorknob, twisting it in his grip. The young man standing before him came into view. *Rogelio.* The name floated from his lips.

Rogelio kissed him on both cheeks. "I'm here," he said awkwardly. "Finally."

Fausto pressed his fingers in the hollow of his cheek as if that would seal the memory of Rogelio's touch. Rogelio took Fausto's hands in his. He was struggling—Fausto could see that—trying to say something and hold back at the same time.

"How are you feeling? Are you cold?"

Fausto shook his head, but Rogelio's hands felt like a radiator melting the icy numbness that he didn't realize had stiffened his fingers. Rogelio's cheeks were flushed, perhaps from too much sun. Or was he embarrassed because he didn't greet Fausto by calling him "Father" or "Dad" or "Pa"? Maybe nerves made him forget, but it was still disrespectful. *He did not call you "Uncle" or "Tata." Be grateful for that.* Fausto wanted more. But it was too soon. *Don't push.* There was plenty of time. Fausto expected to see a reflection of his youth, his features stamped on Rogelio's face, but there was no likeness. He didn't resemble Marina, either. Where she was delicate—her neck, her fingers—he was squared and tough. There were no moles on his face or neck. Sometimes children didn't look like either parent, he thought. What mattered was how strong and healthy Rogelio looked.

Arturo pulled up a chair, motioning Rogelio to sit. He led Fausto to his bed and then dragged his feet to the door. "I'll be at the clinic all day—unless my car won't start in this heat. Rogelio, I'll unload your stuff and leave it in the office. Page me if you need me or when you're done. Have a good visit, you two," he said, and then he was gone.

Fausto reached out to pat Rogelio's smooth, hairless arm. Rogelio moved to the edge of the chair, his knees touching the bed.

"*Kumusta ka?*" said Rogelio. "How are you feeling?"

Fausto was giddy. "You speak Ilocano? That's good! I'm all better. Everything is good." The chill from the shock of seeing Rogelio worked its way through his body. Fausto offered him a smile. "Benny said you were coming. He promised he would return. I thought maybe he would change his mind and come with you."

A shadow crossed Rogelio's face. "I was hoping I wouldn't have to tell you right away," he began, and then he paused as if he regretted making a hasty decision, a hasty announcement. He swallowed hard, his Adam's apple trembling. "I'm sorry, bringing you bad news."

"*Ania?* What are you talking about?"

"Dad recently passed away."

Rogelio spoke so softly that Fausto yanked on his ear, as if he hadn't heard right. "I saw him! He came here less than two weeks ago."

"His spirit must have come to you."

Benny's stopped watch, the absence of his shadow, the dog's uneasiness when he saw them. Fausto hadn't forgotten what his lelang once told him, that spirits come to long-lost or faraway relatives with news of their death. But Benny hadn't told him he'd died.

"What happened? *Ania?* What?" Fausto demanded.

Rogelio's eyes, as black as obsidian, became glassy with tears. Benny had suffered two strokes this year—the first one in January. Half his face and his right arm were paralyzed. Luz took him to a speech therapist and by the end of spring, he regained his words. Benny told Rogelio that he was trying to summon his memories and share them with Rogelio, so Rogelio would have them. But then he suffered his second stroke in early August. He spoke to Rogelio one last time and then slipped into a coma.

"The nurse told me to keep talking. She said they can hear you—it's the last sense that goes. I thought she was referring to stroke patients, not patients who are dying." Rogelio passed his hand over his face, just as Benny used to do. "I didn't think he was dying, that he would die. I thought he was gathering his strength to come back to us—to come back to you. That's what he told me when he was able to talk after his first stroke. He didn't want to pick up the phone. He wanted to *see* you. He was too ill to travel, but he was trying to figure out a way to be with you."

Gone. Fausto would never see him again. "Why did nobody tell me?"

"I called Auntie Rozelle and Ninong Macario to tell them I was coming," Rogelio explained. "I asked them why no one had told you. They said they hadn't seen you in years and didn't know how you'd react. Ninong Macario was afraid to tell you."

"Afraid? I don't believe him!" Fausto turned as if to spit. "Why did Luz not call?"

"She had a hard year, taking care of Dad. She's in poor health too. I told Mom I should be the one to tell you about Dad in person." Rogelio pulled out photographs from his chest pocket. "She wanted me to give you pictures from his funeral."

The first photograph was too glossy, too colorful. Ribbons bearing Benny's name were draped across arrangements of different-colored roses. The flower-studded hearts and crosses pushed up against Rogelio, his younger brother BJ, and Luz, who stood slump-shouldered between the two. Peace lilies, white orchids, and azalea plants were crowded behind them on the floor in front of the open casket. Fausto couldn't make out Benny's features. It could have been anyone in that casket. The second photograph revealed Benny's face, his waxy and pale skin. Fausto couldn't tell if Benny had shrunk in old age. He couldn't see the crown of his cousin's head, where his gray hair had thinned out, but the right side of his face looked no different than the left side. Except for the puffiness of his cheeks, this was how Benny looked when he appeared to him. The crosshatch of wrinkles on his face was the same pattern Fausto's eyes had traced that morning, so long ago now.

Rogelio handed him the last photograph. "I found this later."

Fausto and Benny stood in front of the gray-brick house in Terra Bella, their arms around each other's shoulders, wearing Hawaiian shirts and shorts that came down past their knees. The picture was taken soon after they had bought the house. The lace curtains belonging to the previous owner still hung in the windows like tattered ghosts.

Fausto laid the photographs on his lap, as if they were too heavy for his hands.

"Will you forgive me?"

Fausto looked up, startled. "Forgive you? *Apay?* Why?"

"I should have tried to reach out to you. After we moved, Mom said you and Dad had quarreled. She didn't want me upsetting Dad with questions, so I kept quiet. There were so many changes for me—the schools, the new relatives, the weather—then the surgeries and physical therapy. So much time had gone by. BJ and I forgot about Terra Bella."

Awanen. Just like that. It broke Fausto's heart to be dismissed so easily.

Rogelio took Fausto's hands in his again. "Please forgive my Mom too. She's sorry she kept us all apart."

Now? Now that Benny had brought back the past that Luz had erased from Rogelio's memory? Now that Benny was gone? Fausto turned his face away. He couldn't shake the stinginess in him that refused to forgive her.

"Mom told me the day of the funeral we should never have left Terra Bella. It was Dad's home." Rogelio squeezed his hands. "She admitted we left because of the quarrel between her and you. She knows it was wrong to blame you for what happened to me."

"It *was* my fault!" Fausto cried out. He couldn't help looking at Rogelio's leg, for some trace of his wrongdoing. "They took you away because I hurt you. They thought I would cause more harm. Maybe that's true. How can I blame them for protecting you?" He closed his eyes. *I would do the same to protect you.*

"You didn't hurt me," Rogelio said. "It was my fault—I wasn't paying attention. It was an accident. No more, no less."

No more, no less. Fausto struggled to take a deep breath, trying to make sense of everything Rogelio had said. He rapped the side of his head, angry for thinking only of his quarrel with Luz, his refusal to believe she had come to this reckoning on her own. None of that mattered when he thought of never seeing Benny again. It was a different kind of loss than if he and Benny had been together all these years and then he passed away. Not seeing him every day, Fausto could trick himself into believing that Benny was still out there—thousands of miles away, doing what he usually did day in and day out—until he realized that he couldn't call Benny and hear his voice. He couldn't write a letter that Benny would receive and read. He couldn't make plans to visit, as fleeting and futile as those plans might be. Everything was a memory now. Fausto pressed his palms against the sides of his head.

"I know this is all too much for you."

Fausto brushed the photographs onto his bed and stood up. "I need to go to the bathroom," he mumbled. He waved off Rogelio, somehow making his way to the bathroom on legs that he could not feel. Tears were pushing up as he stood above the toilet. He would not cry, he told himself over and over. He looked down. He needed to pee, but it seemed that damming up his tears had also stopped up his urine.

"Are you okay?" Rogelio's faraway voice was on the other side of the door.

"I need to pee," Fausto insisted, though he abandoned all effort. He washed his hands in hot water to chase the chill and ease the sharp pain that pulsed in the joints of his fingers. When he opened the door, Rogelio was looking out the window, his back to him. Hands splayed, reaching out as if blind, Fausto made his way across the room. "What was the last thing Benny told you?"

"I think he knew it was our last time together." Rogelio turned around as if in a dream. "He told me to go to you. You would tell me what happened. He said you remember everything. It was a gift you would give to me, now that his memory was leaving him."

Some gift! Fausto snorted. If he didn't know any better, he would think Benny was being a coward, forcing Fausto to relive the past and tell Rogelio the truth. It would be a shock—who knows how Rogelio would handle the news, or maybe Rogelio had his suspicions about his parentage—but perhaps it was best that the truth come from his father. His real father. Benny—his ghost—said as much that morning. Fausto found his way to his bed and patted the spot next to him. Rogelio took his place like an obedient child. Despite journeying with Arturo through the first decades of his life as planned, he was ill prepared for this very moment.

Rogelio put his arm around Fausto. "I've lived most of my life in Chicago, but Terra Bella is my home, just like it was Dad's home," he said. "I'm here now." He kissed him on the forehead, chasing the chill. "I'm here."

Fausto nodded, burdened and buoyed by swelling waves. Again, tears were pushing up, and again, he held them at bay.

CHAPTER 7

San Esteban Circle

Terra Bella, California, 1950–1960

Fausto never could have imagined his cousins and him settling down in the same town after Cary had died, though he longed for their familiar faces and the ties to home, especially as the years passed in America. Little Manila and the pinoy crew lured Fausto and Benny back to Stockton after their discharge from the Army at the close of World War II. Domingo returned to Los Angeles but without Serapio, who died in combat in New Guinea, where Fausto and Benny were also stationed. Fausto tried to contact Macario, but his cousin never responded. Soon after, Fausto gave up.

When they were boys in San Esteban, Macario barked commands to the younger cousins and walked with a swagger, as if he knew what the world held for him. He wasn't afraid of anybody, not even his father. So it came as no surprise to Fausto to learn that Macario had earned a Bronze Star for helping members of his all-Filipino regiment escape before Corregidor fell to the Japanese and had enjoyed a hero's homecoming in San Esteban thrown by his widowed mother. He stayed for three months to recover from an injury, during which time he courted and then married a young woman named Nida Zapanta, fifteen years his junior, and brought her to California's Central Valley. There he bought land on the outskirts of a farming town called Terra Bella, securing thirty acres of orange and grapefruit groves, an old house that needed fixing, and a shed full of rusted farming equipment. Before the war, it all belonged to a Japanese farmer who'd been relocated to an internment camp.

In his letters to Domingo, who had settled into his job as a waiter at Musso & Frank Grill on Hollywood Boulevard, Macario declared that the Valley was the best place in California to raise a family. Domingo visited a few times but complained that the town's name, Terra Bella, was misleading—it was not "beautiful land" at all. Terra Bella was muddy in the winters, dusty in the summers. The fog chilled the bones. The heat, though dry, sapped his energy. He claimed it was so hot in Terra Bella that his earwax melted. Domingo preferred living and working in a bustling city, where he stared at movie stars, such as Humphrey Bogart, who lounged in the restaurant's mahogany-paneled booths. He hadn't found a pinay to wed yet, but he told Macario he'd have better luck in the city.

Soon Fausto's distant cousins, who immigrated to the States after the War, settled in Terra Bella. When other cousins in Los Angeles got married, some moved to Terra Bella to raise their families. Even Domingo eventually got swept into the Central Valley, with the hope that the dusty town would become another San Esteban.

Domingo wrote to Fausto and Benny, retracting all claims that Terra Bella was just for cows and goats. Some good-looking pinays had moved into town, though none were as beautiful as Macario's wife, according to Domingo. His letters made Fausto and Benny envious, especially of Macario's good fortune. But it was Macario's letter sent when the new decade began that changed everything: "The War has been over for many years now. Fausto, I am asking you to join us in Terra Bella. Here, we are San Estebans."

Benny was eager to go. As they walked back to their Delta camp and considered Macario's invitation, Fausto felt as if they had traveled more than twenty years back, when Macario beckoned them to join him in Los Angeles. But now they were American citizens, having applied when the naturalization law was amended in 1946. And now Macario owned a house and land in a place he called home. When they reached their bunkhouse, Benny sharpened his knife with a ceramic stone dipped in a bucket of water. "Almost forty years old, Fausto. Maybe we already lived half our lives. We need a real home," he said.

Fausto ran his finger across the blade of his knife before leaning it against the bunkhouse wall. He wasn't sure how well he and Macario would get along. He didn't know how to tell Benny that he had gotten used to the camp, to waking up among friends and working in the fields alongside his friends. And then how could he admit to Benny that since the war he imagined his life not changing, a thought that no longer alarmed him?

Benny waved Macario's letter as they entered the bunkhouse. "Macario says the Valley is full of orange groves and vineyards, cheap land and houses. We can buy a home together. Finally, we can own something in America!" As he removed layers of work clothes, black peat dirt rained down on the floorboards like sifted flour.

Fausto sat on his bed. Such a large purchase seemed beyond the truth of their lives. But he liked the idea of buying a house with Benny. He peeled off his clothes. He licked his lips free of grit and knotted a threadbare towel around his waist. "Can we trust Macario? He forgot us so easily after the war. Maybe he just wants to show off what he has."

"Don't be stubborn! Do it for Cary and Serapio. What do you say?"

"*Intayon!*" Fausto slapped at the flies on his arms. "Let's go then to Terra Bella."

Benny let out a whoop and burst out of the bunkhouse. Fausto's bed creaked as he scraped the inside of his ear with his fingernail and scratched at the blackened creases in his forehead. He would miss everything about the Delta, except the peat dirt.

They spent one last spring cutting 'gras and said good-bye to Prudencio and Ayong, who had bunked next to them for so many years. Ayong insisted on keeping Fausto and Benny's asparagus knives. Benny had sharpened and polished his knife one last time, but Fausto left alone the dirt caked on his blade and the peat dust that filled the curlicues carved into his handle. He was sorry to part with his friends, but he wasn't sorry to leave behind what they called the "devil's tool."

"I will put your knives against the wall." Ayong laid them side by side. "Every time I pick mine up in the morning and lay it down in the afternoon, I will think of you two abandoning us. Picking grapes is for lazy people! Not like cutting 'gras!"

"Come with us. Our cousins will welcome you," Fausto said.

Prudencio shook his head, and Ayong declared, "I do not like change!"

"Remember us," Prudencio said, wagging his finger at the two cousins. He spit out a stream of tobacco juice on the ground. "*Laglagipen dakami!*"

Fausto laughed—he couldn't forget if he wanted to! He recalled mornings when the fog was so thick he couldn't see Prudencio less than ten feet away from him in the fields. Prudencio's face emerged from the ghostly white bank, his crooked teeth stained from tobacco chew and the constant squint of his eyes as if he were looking right at the sun.

———

Fausto and Benny boarded a Greyhound bus and then an Orange Belt Stages bus that dropped them off on Terra Bella's main street, the only road in town with a sidewalk, but one of many in the area lined with palm trees. It wasn't the camp that Domingo described, but it was no different than any other farming town they had passed through. Only rows of grapevines surrounded this town, and orange groves butted up against foothills still green from late spring rains. The white-capped Sierra Nevada Mountains rose up against the crisp blue sky in the east. Outside of town, oak trees towered over fields of orange poppies.

Domingo was waiting for them in front of the post office, leaning against an old, polished Pontiac. The moment they stepped off the bus, he sprang up and threw out his arms. A pinay emerged from the car as Fausto dropped his suitcases to the sidewalk. He guessed she was Domingo's wife, perhaps newly arrived from the Philippines. His cousin's face had filled out and he had a bit of a gut—no doubt from home-cooked meals. His wife, a head shorter with curly, chin-length hair, clung to his side.

"Boys, this is Rozelle!" Domingo's face was stamped with a wide grin. "Came from San Esteban less than a month ago. Her grandfather is Teroy Corpus."

Benny nodded, swiping his fedora off his head.

Fausto shook her hand, trying to remember the Corpus family back home, then boxed Domingo's ear. "Son-of-a-gun! Why did you not tell us you got married?"

"Happened so fast, you know?" Domingo winked. "Got tired of Macario and Nida lecturing me about getting too old to be by myself."

"Adda kami ditoy para kenka." Benny donned his fedora.

"You boys? What use do I have for you?" Domingo gave a wink to Rozelle, who just stood there smiling, her lips a bright coral color.

"Boys!" Fausto scoffed. "We have not been boys since we left San Esteban."

The three of them laughed. Fausto was relieved that Benny didn't remind him the asparagus growers called the Filipino farm workers "boys."

"Rozelle is the youngest of ten children," Domingo said. "Her oldest brother is my age, but her parents didn't mind—I'm American, and I brought her to the States."

Rozelle pinched his arm.

"An-nay!" He flapped his arm as if it were smarting. "You're lucky to get to America, honey. Don't be embarrassed. You should be proud."

Rozelle turned to Fausto and Benny. "I was a teacher in Lapog," she said, smoothing out the folds of her full skirt. "I cannot teach here until

I go back to school and get my credentials. But that is our plan, right, Domingo?"

Domingo rubbed his forearm. "Until then, she will pick grapes in the summer and pack oranges in the winter. Nida is going to talk to her boss on Rozelle's behalf. It's good that Rozelle and Nida get along so well, that we have friends already here. We learned that, eh? We had each other, the six of us."

It was good to see his cousin again after so many years apart, but Fausto felt restless, as if he had arrived for a brief visit and now it was time to go. But the stretch of road was empty, the Orange Belt Stages bus long since gone.

"I promised Macario I would take you straight to his place. We bought ourselves a little house in town, but Macario lives outside of town." Domingo deposited their suitcases in the gaping trunk of the Pontiac and opened the door for them to get in.

He told them the car used to belong to Macario before he got a new one. Fausto nodded at Rozelle when she turned around now and then to check on them, but mostly he stared at the patchwork of grapefruit and orange groves stitched up and down the sloping land. He rolled down the window and took a deep breath. White blossoms lay in heaps around the orange tree trunks like melting snow. The car turned down a road full of potholes. Rows of orange trees inched up an incline, and a house in a clearing appeared. A lone pine tree shaded one side of the house from the afternoon sun. Benny whistled as Domingo explained that both groves flanking the house belonged to Macario. The land produced extra money for Macario, Domingo told them as they pulled into the dirt driveway. The house's exterior wood siding was scraped bare, ready for a coat of paint. Young oleander bushes had been planted along the base of the house, and the beginnings of a fence bordered the front yard like a row of stone teeth. Macario, in dirty coveralls, came from behind the house, pushing a wheelbarrow full of river stones across the broken soil.

He dusted off his hands, shouting, *"Kumusta! Kumusta!"*

He strode across his land straight to Fausto and hugged him. "It's behind us, Fausto," he said in Fausto's ear, his voice fierce. "I'm not *kudil ti sibuyas*, you're not *kudil ti sibuyas*. We have thicker skins now. What is done is done. We go forward."

Macario's neck was browned by the sun and shiny with sweat. Fausto looked his cousin in the eye and cupped Macario's cheeks with his callused palms. Not *kudil ti sibuyas,* anymore, not thin skinned, not easily offended. He didn't want to hold grudges if Macario felt the same way. He would go forward, but he would not forget the past. He hugged his cousin again, and over Macario's shoulder, Benny smiled at him, relief washing over Benny's face.

"I have a gift for you," Fausto said, and handed Macario two photos, one of Serapio, Fausto, and Benny in uniform, dwarfed by New Guinea grass. The second picture was of Domingo, Serapio, Benny, and him in black suits, standing beside Cary's open casket.

Fausto meant for them to be a gift, but Macario's eyes narrowed as he stared at the grainy picture. Did Macario think he was insulting him, reminding him of his absence?

Fausto offered the pictures again. "To remind you of our bond."

Macario pocketed them without saying a word. He extended his arm behind him, where his wife, Nida, was waiting on the porch. She was tall and skinny, though when she came down the steps with care, she revealed a big belly. She drew close to Macario, her wavy hair pressing into his tanned cheek, her arm interlocking with his arm.

"Congratulations." Fausto took her hand and shook it gently.

"Wen, congratulations!" Benny said, and nudged Macario. "Maybe it will be a boy to help you with your orange groves."

Macario smiled and shook his head. "My sons will go to college."

"No more school for us anymore," Domingo said. "Always the oldest kids in the classroom in San Esteban. Now we're just too old!" He laughed at himself.

Rozelle clucked her tongue. She and Nida exchanged glances.

"Fausto was the most educated of us all," Macario said. "An American teacher taught him back home. What was her name?" He snapped his fingers at Fausto.

Rozelle and Nida gave Fausto curious looks. Fausto hoped his cousin wasn't making fun of him. Fausto used to brag about Miss Arnold, but now it seemed as if she had taught him about a different time and place, taught him an education that he had no use for in America. He shrugged.

"Our children are our future." Macario spread out his arms, revealing slashes of sweat in the crook of his elbows and underarms. "All this then is for our children."

"You have done well," Benny said, awestruck. "Has he not?" He turned to Fausto.

Fausto swept his gaze from Nida's belly to Macario's land. The trees, like gigantic trimmed shrubs, rose to at least twenty feet. Oranges twice the size of a fist crowded the leafy branches. There must be at least a hundred of them on each tree and tens of thousands throughout Macario's grove. Fausto shook his head. It was late in the season, and still his crops were bountiful. The house before him was big enough for a large family, perhaps a bedroom for each child. An old tractor sat by a tin shed, with a harrow mounted to it. Divots pocked the sprawling dirt yard, though when Fausto closed his eyes, he imagined toys scattered across a plush green lawn, a swing dangling from a sturdy branch of the pine tree. He even heard the echo of children's laughter. *"Wen,"* he said loudly to overcome the laughter in his head. He opened his eyes, surprised to have found his voice tight with envy, edged with sadness.

Along with Domingo and four other cousins, Fausto and Benny picked oranges and grapefruit for Macario's modest business before the two of them found work at larger farms. Instead of stooping down to harvest 'gras, they now climbed towering ladders propped up against the trees, pointing to the heavens. Fausto had to get used to the weight of the oranges and grapefruit, and to the spread of his fingers, but his pace quickened just as it had with 'gras, strawberries, melons, and lettuce. Fausto and Benny lived with Macario and Nida until their first child—christened Macario Junior—was born. Macario claimed there was still plenty of room, and in truth, the ranch-style house was spacious. But the colicky baby's constant night crying made Fausto and Benny useless in the fields. They stayed with Domingo and Rozelle until Alex, named after Rozelle's father, was born. After Alex's baptism, Fausto and Benny moved to one of the camps owned by the farmer George Cuculich in nearby Delano during the grape harvests. They returned to Terra Bella on weekends at Domingo and Macario's insistence.

After a few years in Terra Bella, Fausto wrote to Prudencio and Ayong, convincing them to pick grapes for one summer. When Prudencio and Ayong first arrived at the campgrounds, Fausto was overcome with memories of the Delta. His friends had shed a few pounds. Gray hair lined their temples and more wrinkles branched across their face, but years and hundreds of miles had not separated them. Fausto slapped Prudencio on the back, proclaiming that this was going to be their new summer home.

"I don't know," Prudencio said, dropping his cloth bag to the ground. "Too much traveling. Took so damn long on the bus to get here with hardly any stops. I need to pee."

Fausto led him to a wooden shack not far from the bunkhouse. Prudencio pranced after him. "Ai, don't tell me there are holes in the ground! Just like back home!"

Fausto kicked open the outhouse door. Prudencio peered at the deep pit dug in the earth. *"Awan iti agbaliw,* eh?" Prudencio grimaced as he unzipped his pants.

"Why should anything change?" Fausto swatted away a swarm of flies. "You brought the flies! I'll hold the door for you so you can see— just like before."

The four of them lived in the same camp, their bunks next to one another, asparagus knives, which Ayong had brought, tucked beneath their beds. Soon they would be gathering in the Filipino camp's mess hall, eating *lechon* with greasy fingers.

After the grapes were harvested and the camps emptied, Prudencio and Ayong returned north, and Fausto and Benny moved into a wooden shed behind Macario's house. Macario claimed that renting an apartment would keep them from saving to buy a house. He refused their money, and Fausto and Benny agreed to stay only if Macario let them put in electricity and a makeshift bathroom. Fausto tried to slip money on the kitchen table, but it always ended up in his work boots in the mornings. There was no kitchen in the shed yet, which suited Macario just fine. He insisted that they eat at his house. He liked drinking whiskey with company Saturday nights.

One day a new curio cabinet was delivered, and that evening Benny admired Macario's military medals, which Nida had polished and displayed behind the sparkling glass.

"I remember when Fausto, Serapio, and I were stuck in those damn foxholes," Benny told his cousins. "Every night, how we dreamed of returning home!"

Fausto poured himself a glass of whiskey and downed it in two gulps. He didn't like talking about the war, though Macario enjoyed recounting his heroics at Corregidor.

Benny held out a cup for Fausto to fill and took a long sip. "Imagine if President Roosevelt had not signed that law, we could not have joined the US Army!" His eyes glistened like his whiskey-bathed lips. "Fausto,

Serapio, and I would not have signed up for the 1st Filipino Infantry Regiment and got sent to New Guinea."

"Oro Bay was the worst," Fausto mumbled, pouring himself another glass.

Fausto was grateful to be with his cousins and hundreds of his countrymen, but when they landed at Oro Bay, nobody, not even the pinoys, was prepared for the conditions of the swamp-filled island. They used machetes to clear the sandbars along the river of kunai grass, which dwarfed them and whose dagger-like edges carved up arms and legs. Ant bites stung like cigarette burns on the flesh. They fought diseases before they even battled the Japanese soldiers. The native guides, though friendly, scared Fausto with their tall, dense cones of coarse hair and their muscular, dark bodies.

"When this war is over, maybe I will ask Macario to put our anger behind us so we can be together again," Fausto had said to Benny and Serapio one night as they crawled into their foxholes in combat uniforms and boots, fleeing the black cloud of flies.

"Maybe? What will change your mind?" Serapio rapped Fausto's helmet with the butt of his rifle. "If you make that a promise, I'll wipe out all the Japs in New Guinea to end the war sooner, just to see you and Macario make peace."

"Kill all the mosquitoes too," Benny demanded, slapping at his neck and cheeks to drive the mosquitoes away, "and the snakes and centipedes and scorpions."

Serapio laughed, his dog tags clinking against the barrel of his rifle.

Fausto leaned against his pack, pinching his nose to avoid smelling smoky metal and rotting vegetables. Within moments, it seemed, his cousins were asleep. Fat drops of rain pelted the palm fronds and the canvas sheets tied to sticks that shielded their foxholes. The walls of Fausto's foxhole were melting. The earth sucked on his boots. Rips of thunder drowned out Benny's snoring. Lightning lit up the jagged line separating the steep, rocky mountain and gray sky, and exposed the foxholes. Helmet askew, Serapio was slumped against his crumbling ledge—a small mudslide—his mouth open, receiving the rain.

A month into their tour in New Guinea, Serapio and Fausto were struck by gunfire while on patrol. Fausto hit the ground. His cousin crashed to the mud, arms and legs entangled in vines. Serapio's bloodshot eyes bulged, pulsing like exposed hearts. It was as if he could not believe what had happened to him. Fausto dragged him to the grass-covered fields as blades of kunai grass knifed his sweat-soaked uniform to shreds. He wanted to push his cousin's eyes back into their sockets and stuff the ragged gap in his stomach with the organs that had spilled out. He froze in the heat as native scouts strapped Serapio on a stretcher suspended by poles. They sprinted down the trail with his body, supporting the thick poles with their dark shoulders. Serapio was taken to the hospital ship but died later that night.

Benny spilled whiskey into his cup and on the table. "Do you remember, Fausto, what you swore to do after Serapio died?" His voice, his hands were unsteady. "We lost Serapio to get here. We have to keep remembering that; we have to keep reminding ourselves how we got here, so we do not lose our way again!"

"We are here now, Benny, out of harm's way." Fausto stood up, weak-kneed. He thrust his hands on the table to steady himself. "We should go to the shed now."

Macario's eyes were watery. "What did you swear to do after the war?"

Fausto blinked, as the room—silent and still—grew blurry. "Come home to you all," he said finally.

During harvest, Fausto didn't mind returning to the Cuculich camp Sunday evenings after spending weekends in Terra Bella, though he and Benny complained of the camp cook. Manong Flor overcooked the *kaldereta*, making the goat meat as chewy as leather. The noodles of his *pansit* dish stuck together. He deep-fried his *lumpia* too long, and instead of producing a crisp, golden-brown wrapper, the entire spring roll was soaked through with oil. The grievances were minor. As the years went by, as much as Fausto liked Nida and being around Macario's sons, he felt as if he were an old uncle, a *tata*, who always got in the way. He preferred the company of Prudencio and Ayong, and the other pinoys at the camp.

The bunkhouses were assigned according to nationality. Most of the workers in Fausto's camp were pinoys. But the next largest group was Mexican-Americans and the *braceros*, the US government-contracted workers from Mexico. The smaller group of Puerto Ricans was housed with the Mexican-Americans and braceros. The rest of the bunkhouses were filled with a mix of blacks who left their homes in Los Angeles for the harvest, old farmers from the Midwest who escaped the Dust Bowl decades ago and remained in the area, a handful of Japanese men who once owned houses and land and had to start all over again after the war, and Arabs who hailed from Yemen, a country Fausto had never heard of. Everyone spoke their own language, and most groups kept to themselves, eating in mess halls that served their own food.

During lunch break in the fields, Fausto approached one of the Arab workers, who looked to be around his age, squatting by a wooden post by himself. The man tipped his paper plate to one side and dabbed his bread in a brown stew of rice and meat. The stew's spicy aroma made Fausto's mouth water.

Fausto cleared his throat. "Where is Yemen?"

The man looked up at him, chewing and swallowing his food. The muscles in his face loosened when Fausto smiled and squatted next to him. "Do Filipinos not say 'hello' when they greet strangers?" the man said.

Fausto stared back dumbly until the man laughed. Relieved, Fausto joined him.

"Yemen is an old country," the man said. "Do you know where the Arabian Peninsula is? We are the tip of the peninsula. We are surrounded by the Red Sea and the Gulf of Aden." He spoke with an accent, though his English was very good. His skin was as dark as Fausto's. Deep creases lined his forehead like ripples across sand dunes.

Fausto didn't know where the Arabian Peninsula was, and he wasn't familiar with the names of seas other than the South China Sea, whose shores included San Esteban. Miss Arnold had never exposed him to knowledge of Arab countries or surrounding seas in his geography lessons. "What is Yemen like?" he asked.

The man dabbed the last piece of bread in the remains of his stew and ate it. He wiped his mouth with the red-and-black-checkered scarf he had pulled from his head. "Where I come from—the coast—it is hot and humid," he answered.

An Anglo foreman dropped a galvanized-steel water jug on a stack of empty crates. A group of men gathered around him, handing him nickels in exchange for water poured into their Styrofoam cups and empty soda and even beer cans. A handful of workers formed another line, and as soon as the cooler was emptied, the foreman took their quarters and gave them soda from an ice chest. When he ran out, he overturned the chest and the melted ice formed rivers of water that cut into the dusty soil. Fausto moved his foot as one stream pooled at his toe.

Fausto licked his parched lips. "Is Yemen hot like Delano?"

The man laughed. "Yes, but we have monsoons. Many families fish for their livelihood. We are at the mercy of the monsoons."

"We have typhoons in the Philippines. That is where I came from. My name is Fausto Empleo." He thrust out his hand, and the man shook it vigorously.

"I am Ahmed Mansur, the son of Mansur Ali Ibrahim."

"How long have you been in the States?"

Ahmed moved his lips, adding up the years. "Thirty-five years, maybe more."

"Ai, thirty-five years!" Fausto slapped his hand on his haunch. Dust rose from his jeans. "You came in the 1920s. Same as me!"

"When I left, there was so much unrest in Yemen, too much hardship for my family. I was looking to improve my fortune. I took a ship and came here to the Valley to work in the fields. I planned to save enough money to return to Mukalla, my hometown." Ahmed stretched his legs and sat on an empty wooden crate bearing the label *Cuculich Farms*. "But I am still here," he said, in a voice as hollow as the crate.

"Me too. Me too."

"It is hard work in the fields, but what else is there for someone like me?"

Fausto couldn't answer, his hands on his thighs, his palms open to the sky.

A woman shrieked near the road. A dark-haired worker shoved other workers aside and darted into a row of vines. Pulling up the zipper of her work pants, the Chicana chased after him, but she didn't know where he went. She stood at the edge of the vines and shook her fist, Spanish spewing from her lips. Every now and then, men spied on the female farm workers as they peed in between cars, which served as their outhouse. Laughter erupted from another part of the road. A group of young pinoys scattered, holding their noses and waving their hands.

"Whoever did this, cover up your shit!" a Filipino foreman yelled. He grabbed a pinoy, who protested that it wasn't their fault—there was no bathroom to speak of—but the foreman threw a short-handled spade at him and barked, "That's not my problem!"

Fausto shook his head, but Ahmed wasn't paying attention anymore.

"Do you miss the Philippines? Do you miss your home?" Ahmed asked.

Fausto rubbed his neck where trickles of sweat made his skin itch. "Maybe I missed what it used to be or what it used to mean to me. But I have been here longer in the States than in the Philippines. My family is like a stranger to me. Imagine that!"

"I am afraid to imagine such things," Ahmed said.

"What do you miss of your home?" Fausto wanted to know.

"Everything," Ahmed said. The rocky coast, he told Fausto, is like a school of ancient turtles sunning themselves by turquoise waters. The city, crowded with stone buildings and chalk-white mosques, crawls up the base of wind-blasted hills. The whitewashed minarets soar and pierce the sharp, blue sky. Ahmed imagined the wrinkles that have deepened around his mother's eyes, which aren't covered by her black *chador*. He is haunted by the memory of his father—alone in a boat bobbing off the coast, with hands as ragged as the nets he casts out into the deep waters.

Ahmed scrambled to his feet. He was wiry and shorter than Fausto. "I am behind on my boxes."

Fausto rose up next to him. "Come by our bunkhouse after dinner, eh? We can play cards and have some drink. I can take you around to meet the other pinoys."

"We do not drink," Ahmed said.

"Maybe we can share food. Your lunch smelled good. We have a very bad pinoy cook, but I make good Filipino food. Would you like?"

"Yes, thank you." Ahmed grabbed the nearby wooden crate and turned to Fausto, his face gone serious. "Our foreman said we do not work as hard as the Filipinos and the Mexicans. He said the Filipinos do not think we belong in these fields."

Fausto scowled. When one of their foremen accused his crew of not producing enough boxes at day's end, he told them the Mexicans called the Filipinos lazy. Once, Prudencio threatened to march over to the Mexicans' bunkhouse and challenge all of them to a fight, but the foreman said anyone who caused trouble would be kicked out of camp. The best way to respond was to work harder. "The way to win is in the fields with your clippers, boys, not with your fists in the camps. You get paid more for your hard work, and Mr. Cuculich gets more grapes into the grocery stores," the foreman told them. He nodded with approval when his crews brought in extra boxes in the late afternoon.

"What your foreman said is not true!" Fausto told Ahmed.

"Yes, this was my thought as well." Ahmed rested the crate on his shoulder.

Fausto wondered if Ahmed would have accepted his invitation if he had believed his foreman. He knew the pinoys took pride in their output in the fields. He was no exception. But he also knew that all the crews worked just as hard; it meant extra money for all of them, especially when the harvests were abundant. There was no need to create trouble and distrust. They were all poor. They were all still strangers in America—decades later.

As Ahmed disappeared into the field, the leaves slapping and swallowing him up, Fausto wondered if his new friend's religion forbade him to play cards or other sports that involved gambling. Fausto wasn't going to take any chances; he would not invite Ahmed to attend the *sabong*. He was one of the few pinoys who didn't enjoy it. After evening baths, many of them went to the far side of camp to bet on cockfights, or they piled into cars and headed to nearby Earlimart, where one clever pinoy had bought chickens to feed and train. The farm workers gossiped about how he had made hundreds of dollars on a single fight, despite being raided, jailed, and fined by the local sheriff. Manong Flor claimed that the grape growers secretly approved of the gambling. Many pinoys spent their pay on the cockfights, and after the raids, everyone, whether they bet or just watched, was fined from fifty to one hundred dollars each. Both situations kept the pinoys poor. The raids happened every so often. The pinoys scattered at the sight of the sheriff's vehicles, but they had nowhere else to go except back to their bunkhouses.

Once after bathtime, a foreman hustled all the Filipino workers into one building for an unannounced visit by Mr. Cuculich. "I won't tolerate lawbreakers," he roared, walking down the aisle of the bunkhouse. The heels of his hand-tooled cowboy boots stomped into the floorboards with splintery force. "My grandfather came here from Croatia in the 1920s and worked his way up with no one's help but God's. That's the Slavic tradition. He played by the rules because he was a God-fearing man. It's time you all learned to do the same!"

The pinoys, clad only in towels from the waist down, cowered behind their bunks. Even the flies that made their way into the bunkhouse flew away at the sound of Mr. Cuculich's booming voice. Fausto hoped that his countrymen heeded his boss's words. He didn't want the townspeople from Delano to think all they did was gamble, drink, and chase women.

He wanted to shake the image that had followed him up and down California through the years, from the time he first arrived in America.

"Do you boys understand?" Mr. Cuculich watched their heads bob. "I keep a close eye on all of you." He marched up to Fausto. "I know Fausto is a hard worker, and hard workers always tell the truth." He paused. "Did my message get through?"

Fausto didn't look at his countrymen. Goose pimples raced up his arms, though the air was thick with heat. "Yes, sir," he said, straightening up, as if he were back at Camp Beale with the 1st Filipino Infantry Regiment. Mr. Cuculich slapped him on his bare back and left the bunkhouse, his boots nearly pounding the nails out of the floorboards.

Fausto knew there were problems in the camps and fields, but he felt part of the community in the vineyards. He liked living with his friends and riding the camp bus to the fields. He got rounds of Ilocano folk songs going, in spite of the tin ear of many of his countrymen. When they reached the vineyard, his cousins who lived in Terra Bella were already there. He chatted with Lito Guzman, Macario, and Domingo, and he shared a quick cup of coffee with Fidel Europa before they seized empty crates and headed into the fields.

Benny had no patience for Prudencio's jokes, but Fausto didn't mind. Once, Prudencio warned him of garter snakes that hid in the leaves on hot summer afternoons. Fausto turned his back, dismissing him. With everybody watching, Prudencio yanked a long vine in between Fausto's legs until it snapped against his crotch. "Snake!" Prudencio hollered, and Benny and Fidel swore Fausto leapt as high as the tops of the vines before falling in a heap. "Son-of-a-gun!" he yelled, scrambling to his feet. He shook his fist at Prudencio, who danced back and forth like a boxer, waiting for Fausto to rush after him. But Fausto laughed as hard as everyone else as he mopped his face with a handkerchief.

"Get back to work!" Nick Lazaro strode toward them. The pinoy foreman oversaw Fausto's crew and was one of the labor contractors who supplied Mr. Cuculich with workers.

"A garter snake attacked Fausto." Prudencio wiggled the long vine.

Nick pushed past Prudencio and got into Fausto's face. Nick's moustache twitched in the heat. "Maybe I should find braceros who will work for less!"

"The work will get done, Nick. Don't worry." Fausto took a step back.

Benny came up behind Fausto. "We are the hardest working crew you got!"

Nick spat bits of tobacco chew in a brown pool on the ground. "Not today! You work for me. I work for Mr. Cuculich. He doesn't pay me when you horse around."

A Mexican worker emerged from the vineyard across the dirt road and took a drink from his Thermos. Nick barked at him to get back to work and headed for his parked car. Another Mexican worker came out, and the two of them spoke in Spanish. The man with the Thermos stared down at the pinoys, and then they retreated to the fields.

"What is he saying about me?" Prudencio wanted to know.

Manong Pete, one of the oldest workers in the pinoy crew, translated. "He said if Nick caught them joking around, Nick would deduct their box bonuses from their pay. He said Nick lets us get away with everything because he is one of us."

"What is wrong with that?" Prudencio cracked the vine in the air like a whip. "Who is Nick going to be loyal to if not the pinoys?"

Fausto massaged his friend's shoulder. "Forget it."

"How about I only speak Ilocano around them!" Prudencio went on. He stabbed his finger at the spot where the two Mexicans had been standing. *"Kuneng isuna!"*

Fidel swatted Prudencio in the back of his head with his straw hat. "Don't call them stupid! Do you want to create more trouble?"

"The foremen are the ones causing trouble," Fausto said.

"It's time Mr. Cuculich followed the other growers and called the immigration people to send them back to Mexico before the next payday," Prudencio said.

"Go get a crate! Nick might come back and say bad things to you in Visayan!" Benny grabbed an empty crate from a nearby pile.

"Next time, I'm gonna . . ." Prudencio trailed off.

"Next time nothing." Fausto gave Prudencio a hard shove toward their side of the vineyard. "Leave them alone. They did nothing to you."

"I was talking about Nick!" Prudencio said, sullen faced. "He was one of us last year. When he got promoted, he got too big for us. He acts like he owns the whole goddamn farm!"

Benny thrust an empty crate into Prudencio's gut. "Maybe in a few years you will be one of Mr. Cuculich's foremen, and then you will boss us around."

"Not me!" Prudencio shook his head. "I don't want to see Cuculich every day and kiss his ass all the time. I'll stick to the vineyards. I'll stay here with all of you."

"He is not that bad," Benny admitted. "We have worked for worse bosses."

It was true. Mr. Cuculich never called the immigration authorities on his illegal workers; rightly or wrongly, he cared about his crops first. He came to the fields and the camps often, striking up conversation. From what he was told by pinoys at other camps, Fausto couldn't imagine the meaner bosses like Frank Radic, Joseph Kostelic, or John Depolo visiting with their workers, let alone being pleasant in any encounter.

"If you do not mind being called 'boy,' nothing will bother you," Prudencio said. He grabbed a cluster of grapes from a nearby vine and used his clippers to snip off the undesirable fruit: the spoiled and runty, the immature grapes the growers called "water berries." He let them fall and ground them with his heel. When he lifted his foot, the flattened skins, like purple bruises, stuck to the soles of his work boots.

———

Fausto was troubled that his good friend was so full of anger. Prudencio reminded him of Macario sometimes, when his cousin was younger and hot headed. These days, Macario didn't complain. He was too busy rushing in and out of the fields, exchanging full crates for empty ones. They were paid by the hour, but what mattered to Macario was the bonus, in cents, that they earned per box. When he spoke up in the fields, he talked about how much money he had already saved for his sons' education, how much more he needed to fix up the house for Nida, and what it would cost to buy a second car. When Fausto and Benny visited on weekends, Macario showed them dog-eared magazine advertisements. His weathered finger traced the round hoods and trunks of gleaming cars. "She's a beauty, eh?" Macario said hungrily. He dreamed of a red Ford Customline sedan, though Nida wanted a station wagon now that she was carrying their third child. Fausto whistled at the price tag: $3,000! He knew promotion to a foreman was worth more in income than status to Macario, and wondered if Macario was competing for the next available position. Nida was working hard in the fields too, and she volunteered for extra hours at the packing shed when the orange season was in full production. She took a few weeks off after each birth before going back in the fields or the packing house, leaving her babies in the care of an older auntie whose hand was maimed by machinery that waxed oranges. When Fausto and Prudencio argued yet again about conditions in the fields, or when Prudencio complained about the Mexican workers, Macario pulled his bandana away from his mouth and told them they were wasting their time complaining over something they couldn't change. Find something to work for, he told them, before moving down the row.

Prudencio pointed his clippers at Fausto. "If we don't complain, how will our work improve in the fields? This is our livelihood. We have the right to make it better!"

"Our livelihood is also all these workers' livelihood." Fausto crouched to reach the low-hanging grapes. "If everybody wants to make conditions in the fields better, it should bring us together, not break us down. There is enough trouble among the different groups. That's why it's not good to keep separate bunkhouses."

Prudencio snorted. "If they only speak their language, it makes sense to keep them together. Nick said it was better to keep the groups separate. He said if we were thrown together in the camps, there would be misunderstandings and fights."

"The misunderstandings are from their lies!" In his excitement, Fausto broke the cap stems from a cluster of grapes. He cursed himself for his carelessness. "As long as we are kept separate and each group is being told one thing against the other by their foreman, there will be more misunderstandings. Ai, it does not have to be that way!"

The duct tape that kept dust from entering through the top of Prudencio's work boot pulled away from his jeans. He unwound the silver strip with an impatient tug and wrapped it tight around his calf. "Did you not hear what that Mexican worker said about Nick? Manong Pete did not make up what that Mexican said. Nick has no reason to lie." He hoisted another full crate upon his shoulder. "The more you talk nonsense, the less money you'll earn in the fields. It will cost you!" he said, and lumbered down the dirt path.

Fausto held up a cluster of grapes. Ripe fruit hung down from his fingers like strands of dark South Sea pearls. That these jewels lasted only weeks made them more precious than any gem mined from the earth or harvested from the ocean. He laid the cluster in the crate by his feet. When he stood up, pain radiated from his hand, up his arm to his shoulder. He peeled off his cotton glove to massage his fingers, knead the length of his arm in a slow crawl. How could he forget? The long, hard work in the fields, the ache in his body, the low hourly rate reminded him daily of how dear these grapes were.

When Fausto invited Ahmed to dinner, he convinced Manong Flor to take an evening off so he could cook. After his first meal at the Filipino mess hall, Ahmed returned the favor and Fausto joined him at his bunkhouse mess hall. Rice and spicy chicken stew flavored with cardamom was a grand meal compared to Manong Flor's dishes, which increasingly had either too little or too much of an ingredient as the pinoy cook's eyesight grew weaker. Fausto enjoyed *shay*, a mint-flavored sweet tea, and *bint al sahn*, sweet bread dipped in honey and butter. By then, some Yemeni farm workers had spread out dominoes on the cleared tables. A group of Okies left the mess hall for a smoke. A handful of blacks huddled in a corner talking in low voices. During dessert, Ahmed and his friends argued over the latest clash between the British government and the southern port city of Aden. North Yemen's ruler was courting Cairo for protection, and Ahmed and his friends disagreed over the need for a pact that was forming among North Yemen, Egypt, and Syria.

"Collaborating with other countries weakens us," Ahmed's bunkmate Moamar explained to Fausto. "We fought hard for our independence, but we are a small country. If we join this alliance, Egypt and Syria will take advantage of us."

A clean-shaven young man with close-cropped hair named Fahmi spoke up. "It is a dangerous world. No matter how well we fought, we are not safe standing alone. We are proud, but pride is dangerous. We have to band together with *all* our people—make concessions if we have to—or else bow down to the Western world. Which is worse?"

Moamar waved him off. "I am Yemeni. Syria and Egypt are *not* my people."

"To Westerners, we are all the same," Fahmi said.

Moamar picked crumbs from his moustache and dusted his tunic with a sweep of his hand. "I am not defined by outsiders!"

Ahmed turned to Fausto. "The Arab world is full of many different groups and clans that have fought in the past and even to this day," he said. When the British broke up the Arab countries by creating their own boundaries, with no regard to who was living where, they created a new meaning for what it is to be Arab. "Fahmi says we must come together—

no matter what our past relationship was like—to confront a common, greater enemy. We must set aside our differences if our independence, our very existence, is at stake." He leaned close, exposing the red rims of his tired eyes. "Do you agree?"

Fausto slid forward on the bench, no longer a shadow at the table. He glanced around at the men who wore checkered head scarves or lounged in cotton breeches and long, airy white tunics. "Yes," he said.

"We cannot help talking about what is happening back home," Ahmed said, and poured himself another cup of tea from a Thermos, which released the heavy scent of mint into the mess hall. "What is the use in arguing? How does it affect our lives here?"

Fahmi reached out and touched the frayed cuff of Fausto's shirt. "Do the Filipinos talk about the struggles in the Philippines?"

Fausto took a sip of tea. He felt as if the hot liquid had burned through his cheeks. "The US granted the Philippines full independence after the war. We don't follow what happens over there so much anymore."

"Why?" a Yemeni with a graying temple named Walid asked.

"Because—" Fausto halted. Lacquered dominoes clashed and clicked in a corner of the building and in his head. "Because this is our home now. For some of us, it is what we want. For others, we have come to accept this."

Silence settled over them like the layer of trapped warm air in the mess hall.

Moamar ground his teeth. "I only have a few leaves of *khat* left, but I feel a great need to chew them all tonight." He got up and swung his leg over the wooden bench, the seams of his cotton breeches straining.

Fahmi stood up next to Moamar, and said in a dull voice, "We will return." He pulled out a smashed pack of Marlboros and headed out the door.

Fausto didn't know if Fahmi meant return to their table or to Yemen.

For days he could not shake their silence, their sad eyes, the feeling that they might never go back to Yemen, that the fields and camps would be their world for the rest of their lives. Fausto greeted Ahmed's friends out in the fields, knowing that there was no misunderstanding between him and them, that whatever their own foremen told them was untrue. But whenever Fausto saw Fahmi, the boy's smile was fleeting. Fahmi's eyes were faded, like the dust-sheathed Ribier grapes they picked all summer long.

One afternoon when the workers were waiting for the tractor to deliver the packing cart for their crates, a stout Mexican named Arturo Esperanza said hello to Fausto, who was standing behind him in line. Taken by his friendliness, Fausto asked Arturo if he could translate some words for him so he could understand the language. Arturo shook his hand and said he was honored to teach Fausto words and phrases. "Maybe Spanish easy for you," Arturo told him, as they watched the tractor rumble down the road towing the packing cart. The metal parts of the cart jangled as if battered by winds that didn't exist and threatened to fall apart. "You got Spanish in your country's history. A lot of same words," he added.

"But Spain and Mexico are different," Fausto said above the metallic rattle.

A smile bloomed on Arturo's leathery face, exposing big gaps between his teeth. "Oh sure. But sometimes you think what is the same, and that makes easier, *sí?*"

"Yes, *sí.*" Fausto returned the smile.

"Harvest almost over." Arturo pointed to fermenting berries on a nearby vine. Some had already dropped to the ground like fat raindrops. Arturo squinted in the slant of late September sunlight. "They need workers to prune and plant. You apply?"

"Benny and I stay with our cousins in Terra Bella and pick their citrus fruit."

"Try to apply," Arturo urged. "You can stay in the camp. I prune and plant rest of year. Keeps me in one place, so I can buy a house and bring my wife here and start a family."

"I don't have a family." Fausto stared at their work boots.

"*Todavía no,* not yet. For now, pruning make you more valuable. It special work. You save lots of money. You be ready when family come later." Arturo tapped his forehead with his gloved finger. "That my plan. That my hope. Always keep thinking ahead. Always. *Siempre.*"

The driver hopped down from the tractor and unhooked the steel cart. The packers who had been waiting by the road gathered around the cart to hoist the metal flaps up with poles and secure the cart's roof.

"*Siempre,*" Fausto repeated. He lugged Arturo's crate onto the rack, and Arturo lifted his straw hat from his matted-down, salt-and-pepper hair and nodded his thanks.

After the last harvest, the farm workers streamed out of the camp, and many of the bunkhouses were locked up. Fausto lobbied Nick to put him and Benny on the pruning and planting crews, which allowed them to stay in the open bunkhouse during the dormant season. Macario insisted that they stay with him in the winter and spring, but Fausto didn't want to impose, now that his family, as well as Domingo's, was growing.

Fausto and Benny learned quickly under Arturo. They pruned vines in the winter and planted new ones in early spring. They fertilized the soil and pulled weeds by hand. They looked for diseases like black rot and powdery mildew and insects like leafhoppers and climbing cutworms, which could destroy entire crops. When they discovered leaves with white spots or ragged holes, a different crew came in to spray the vines with an oily liquid smelling of citrus mixed with perfume. Every now and then the pruning crew got caught in the yellow cloud, which numbed the tips of their tongues, stung their eyes and throats, and made their scalps itch long after they had taken their baths.

The dense fog made the vineyards and camp ghostly. Sometimes the sun couldn't burn off the fog until afternoon. Fausto didn't believe Macario when his cousin first told him that fog was good for the citrus crops in the Valley because it protected them from the damaging frost brought on by clear, cold nights. How could that be? The whiteness in the air numbed his gloved fingers as he gripped his pruning shears. At night in his bunk, layered in long johns, two pairs of socks, and mountains of blankets that rubbed against his skin like steel wool, he still felt the fog's chill seep through the cracks in the wallboards and knead its way into his skin, icing down every muscle and bone in his body.

———

When January mornings dawned free of fog, a brilliant pink rinsed the sky, the color of red Emperor grapes crushed in water. On such a morning, beneath a rose-tinged sky, Nick scolded a group of workers for their sloppy pruning. As he singled out Fausto as a model worker who was both quick and exact, Mr. Cuculich came roaring down the dirt road that cut through his vineyards in his big-wheeled Chevy pickup truck and hopped out to where the group had gathered. His eight-year-old son—one of five boys—leapt down, scaling the distance from the cab to the ground below with gangly legs. He peered at the workers from behind his father's hip. Fausto smiled at him. The boy returned the smile before disappearing behind his father's down jacket.

When Nick told Mr. Cuculich about Fausto's pruning and training skills, the farmer asked him to demonstrate on an Emperor grapevine. Fausto's fingers, so sure with the pruning shears at any other time, trembled under the grower's watch. He cut back the two branch canes of the vine to where they narrowed to a thickness of half an inch. He pruned to a bottom bud at the ends of the two canes and pruned the ends of the full cordons, leaving a foot-long gap between the vines. Proper spacing kept the shoots and clusters of individual vines from melding together.

Mr. Cuculich leaned over, brushing Fausto with the pillowy arm of his down jacket, and measured the distance with his stocky hand. He grunted his approval and moved aside so Fausto could wrap the branch cane once around the wire, which ran perpendicular to the wooden post about two-thirds up, and swiftly tie it at various points with string.

"In the spring, we'll prune back the shoots and sucker the crowns," Fausto said.

When he was done tightening the knots, making sure the canes were straight and secure, Mr. Cuculich nodded with admiration. A few pinoys whispered to one another, but Arturo smiled with pride as if he'd done the work himself. The Cuculich boy inched his way around his father's legs so that he stood next to Fausto. Brimming with confidence, Fausto reached over and tousled the boy's mop of brown hair.

"Next year you'll remove all the canes growing out of the trunk's crotch, but don't forget to remove the fruit and flowers so you don't weaken the vine. Remember, Fausto, it's all about balance!" Mr. Cuculich's breath fogged up in the cold air. "Hell, everything is about balance." He hooked his thumbs in the loops of his jeans, his feet spread wide apart as if he were fording a stream. He surveyed his land, tilting his head back as if he couldn't get enough of the acres and acres of his land in one view. "We had a good year, didn't we? A record year is what Nick keeps telling me. What do you think, Fausto? Are we going to have another good year come next harvest?"

Though foggy, the winter had been mild. "So far, so good, Mr. Cuculich."

Mr. Cuculich grinned. "You're a good worker. You keep taking good care of these canes, and we'll get twenty-five, thirty years of production out of them. Hell, we'll be retired by then. Well, at least you'll be retired. Farmers like me never retire. It's in our blood." He stepped back, saying in a loud voice so that everyone would hear, "I'll bet you know better than me when the grapes have just enough sugar to pick, don't you?"

"I don't believe so. I'm not that good," Fausto said.

"Don't be afraid to brag," Nick called out. "I would say most of my Filipino crewmembers could tell, Mr. Cuculich. They're the best workers you have."

"Let's hope ol' Nick is exaggerating. I wouldn't want others knowing my work better than me." Mr. Cuculich winked, the leathery skin around his eye crinkling up.

"You are the boss," Fausto blurted out, and then immediately regretted his words.

Mr. Cuculich laughed, exposing silver caps and fillings in his teeth. He opened the door of his truck, and his son scrambled up the sideboard and disappeared into the cab. As they sped off, the farm workers murmured to one another again. Fausto was glad Prudencio wasn't among them. If Prudencio's ready anger was a result of growing old, maybe Fausto's obedience sprang from the same source. He sighed, his breath white in the air, and walked between the rows of dormant vines, sidestepping canes that stuck out wildly. A faint disk hung in the middle of the sky. So much time had been lost! His stomach growled, but Fausto quickened his steps over the rocky path and gripped his pruning shears, ready to cut the weaker canes from the vines.

Four years after their arrival in the Central Valley, Fausto and Benny put a down payment on a gray-brick house in Terra Bella with their savings. It took a while for Benny to convince Fausto. Wasn't it one of the reasons they had left Stockton in the first place? Benny argued. Fausto had gotten used to living with Prudencio and Ayong in the camp, though Benny had tired of camp life long ago.

"We'll need a car." Fausto stamped his foot on a trail of ants that swarmed the cracks in the concrete walkway leading up to the front door. "We cannot ask Domingo or Macario to drive us back and forth from Terra Bella to Delano all the time."

"Nick Lazaro is going to get the new Chevrolet Bel Air, so I said we'll buy his old car," Benny said. "Our first car—a '51 Bel Air Hardtop— eh? Finally."

Fausto shrugged. Being an owner of anything didn't excite him as much as it did Benny, which surprised him after working on somebody else's land for so many years. It all sounded so expensive. How could Nick or Macario afford such luxuries, no matter how hard they worked in the fields?

"Prudencio and Ayong can stay with us on the weekends," Fausto said, standing at the edge of the lawn, which was more dirt than grass.

The house was old but located in the neighborhood where most of their cousins had settled. The block lacked a sidewalk. Only the main street that housed the library, fire department, post office, and a convenience store had a sidewalk. Macario said they should have bargained the owner down—pricy ranch-style homes were being built in the area. But the elderly white woman held her price at $8,000, and Benny was afraid to lose it to somebody else. The house had no roof-top air conditioner or heating unit. The refrigerator and stove were twenty years old. The pipes burst in the first winter freeze. The roof had been leaking for years. Water stains on the ceiling, painted over before they bought the house, bloomed like weeds after rainstorms. Still, after the first week, Fausto realized how nice it was to be near their cousins and eat meals they cooked themselves. He enjoyed the quiet evenings and taking a hot bath whenever he wanted, not just at the end of the workday.

"We'll fix everything up," Benny promised Fausto when he turned on the bathroom faucet one morning and brown water choked out.

Fausto imagined them working on the house on weekends, saving them from losing money on rummy games at parties. He pointed to the flat expanse of land behind the house. Manong Lito's chickens had stepped through the holes in the chainlink fence that separated their properties and pecked at the late frost-tipped ground. Fausto's father had bragged about making every centimeter of land he owned productive. "I would like to plant a garden. Maybe grow some *tarong, kamatis,* and *parya,*" he said.

"Just like the ones in San Esteban and the camps." Benny kneeled and grabbed a handful of soil—as rocky as the Delta peat dirt was rich.

Fausto insisted that Prudencio and Ayong stay with them during harvests. They did, but only after insisting on sharing the cost of groceries and helping fix up the house. When Fausto protested, Prudencio said he couldn't stand sleeping in another bunk.

"Iti agyan ditoy nga balay kasla agyan iti palacio," he said, settling into the sofa.

Fausto swatted his friend's work boots from the coffee table. "Then keep your feet off the furniture! This is a palace, eh?" he said. They all laughed, as the aroma of *longanisa* lured them into the kitchen.

Macario came up with the idea to establish the San Esteban Circle, though for the last four years Fausto had been proposing the founding of a social club, just like the ones back home. Macario declared himself president and appointed Nida as treasurer and Fausto as secretary. Fausto's main duty was to contact pinoys in the States who had roots in San Esteban—from Honolulu, Sacramento, Los Angeles, Chicago—to ask them to join the club and invite them to an annual celebration over Labor Day weekend. He was reluctant to include news of an annual celebration in his letter, afraid the city relatives would laugh at them. Why would they want to travel hundreds or thousands of miles to a dusty farming town?

He was wrong. The first year of the dance, the summer of 1955, relatives from all over wrote or telephoned, saying they would come. Fausto and Benny spent late nights cleaning the house. They aired out woven mats, expecting to sleep on the living room floor to accommodate guests. Benny made trips to the grocery store, packing their refrigerator, which was usually near-empty, with food. Fausto boxed vegetables that he and Benny had grown in their garden to send home with their relatives. They ironed their *barong* shirts and dress trousers, and had a pinoy barber in Earlimart cut their hair. Domingo and Rozelle delivered two butchered pigs, their bodies still warm, which Fausto and Benny were to roast in their backyard for Saturday's luncheon.

Friday night of Labor Day weekend, a caravan of cars clogged the main street of Terra Bella. Every driveway and shoulder of the road in the Filipino neighborhoods transformed into parking lots as weary travelers arrived. Fausto and Benny stayed up until the early hours, reacquainting themselves or introducing themselves to distant relatives and exchanging news about San Esteban. Fausto recognized most of the names—Europa, Empleo, Edralin, Vergara, Eala, Ayson, Orpilla, Abad, Ebat, Esperanza—though some were strangers. In the faces of distant relatives both young and old, he saw the resemblance to—or an exact copy of—older relatives recalled from his youth. The long night and leisurely breakfast conversations made Fausto and Benny late delivering the pigs and steel buckets filled with raw goat meat to the town's Veterans Memorial Building. The brick building was erected after World War II with a main hall that boasted floor-to-ceiling windows and an elevated stage, a commercial-size kitchen, and a banquet room whose walls were lined with photographs of American servicemen. Gamblers set up tables and chairs in the corner of the hall to play rummy and mahjong. Nida, an apron flared out over her bulging stomach, waved a wooden spoon at them when they barged into the steaming kitchen. They seesawed like a pair of drunkards as they carried the pigs—with blackened ears and snout—on a bowed wooden pallet.

"The *lechon* goes on the banquet table! Give the goat meat to Rozelle and the girls!" Nida ordered, weaving her way across the kitchen. "We are already late!"

Benny winked at one of the volunteers who had introduced herself as Anita Eala from Chicago. She smiled at him and brushed back her black locks with her left hand, keeping it idle by her smooth cheek as if to expose her ringless finger. Benny asked her if she wanted him to crush the garlic, but before she could answer, Nida bumped up against him without apology. She was on the verge of crying, as if the success of the long weekend, the debut of Terra Bella, the hoped-for praises for a grand event, and the promises of a return trip next year relied on this luncheon, the first event of the San Esteban Circle's festivities. Benny reached for an iron skillet to help Anita fry the meat, but Nida pushed him to the big steel sink, grabbing Fausto's arm in her sweep. She slapped aprons over the men's shoulders, commanding them to wash the pile of pots and pans. Fausto scowled at Anita, who was left with the bucket of meat. Flirting with a man at least fifteen years her senior! Benny was embarrassing himself too. They slipped the apron bibs over their heads, and Benny soaped and scrubbed while Fausto rinsed—just like at home.

After lunch, visitors roamed the neighborhood in the broiling heat. Fausto and Benny endured days like this, but out of hospitality they ran the window-unit air conditioner all weekend long, careless of the electricity bill that was sure to triple. As their guests stayed in shelter and others ducked in, Fausto and Benny served *halo-halo*, with Fausto shaving big blocks of ice and Benny drowning layers of shredded coconut meat and cantaloupe, kidney beans, sweet corn, and shaved ice with sweetened condensed milk. Their guests devoured the dessert, taking turns standing in front of the air conditioner. A second cousin from Honolulu, wearing a *muumuu* as colorful as her dessert, raised her glass of halo-halo as if to toast Fausto and asked why he wasn't married. All eyes were fixed on him. Fausto mumbled that he was too busy, working in the fields and on the house all the time. The large woman stepped in front of the air conditioner, her muumuu flapping like a flag. "And you, Manong Benny?" she demanded.

Benny stirred his halo-halo. "When you are set in your ways, you have to find someone who does not mind that. Someone who does not bend or break me!"

Everybody laughed except Fausto. Maybe the two of them will find mates at the dance, the woman wondered aloud. Laughter erupted again. As Fausto hurried into the kitchen to shave more ice, he caught some of the men grinning, winking to one other.

The dance was the major event of the weekend. Nida sang the national anthems of both countries and the San Esteban Hymn, the town song. As master of ceremonies, Macario announced the dances. He cradled the microphone to his lips, his voice booming: "Special dance for members of the San Esteban Circle." He swept his arms up like a presidente, inviting everyone to the center of the floor. The all-Filipino band from Los Angeles took up the entire stage, dressed in crisp-white dinner jackets, black bow ties, and baggy trousers. They played waltzes, the cha-cha, and traditional Filipino songs. The special dances cost money. The proceeds went to the club's fund, some of which helped out members who had met misfortune. Nida's brother, whom she had sponsored to come to the States, lost his wife to a long illness in the spring. The club helped pay for the funeral. As Nida collected money from the long line of dancers, Fausto thought of Cary—how he wished they'd had the club when Cary was alive. Fausto shook his head as the couples spun by. It was useless to think such things.

Fausto and Benny were asked to dance with the widows. Fausto chose to watch from the hall entrance, where the men preferred talking to dancing. Coming in from the fields only hours before, his co-workers were now wearing their Sunday suits or their barong shirts, which boasted intricate embroidery across the filmy fabric woven from banana fibers. The local men danced with their wives, their faces tight as if trying to remember where to place their feet on the slippery floor.

When the guests departed Monday afternoon, Benny shut off the air conditioner. Their driveway and shoulder of the road were suddenly bereft of cars. Damp towels lay heaped on the bathroom floor. Bed sheets were balled up at the foot of their beds. Glasses sat on the coffee table, half-full with warm, flat soda. Benny complained of the mess, but to Fausto it was a sign of good hosts.

As Fausto rolled up the mats that they slept on in the living room, he thought about Cary again. "If only we had a San Esteban Circle when Cary was alive," he said.

"Stop thinking of the past." Benny grabbed the mats and shoved them in the closet. *"Agyamanka iti nagunod tayo nga sanikua!"*

"I *am* grateful for what we have." Fausto retrieved a leftover dance program from the floor. "Now that we are older, I'm grateful we have each other."

Benny stared at him, his mouth twisting at the corner. He rubbed his eyes, kneading the folds of soft skin. Fausto turned out the light and they went to their bedrooms. As Benny's door closed, Fausto realized his cousin hadn't said goodnight. In the dark, Fausto crawled into his twin bed, which seemed cloudlike and big after a weekend of sleeping on woven mats in the living room. He *was* happy with their two-bedroom home, though it always seemed to be in need of repair. The cabbage-shaped water stains had spread farther down the living room walls from the ceiling, even with tarp tacked over the roof. Sections of linoleum in the kitchen came up with a kick of his work boot. If he increased his box production next harvest, they could buy a new refrigerator from Sears to replace the one that kept defrosting itself. But there was no rush. He rolled over, facing the common wall separating their rooms, hearing Benny's clap-like snoring. It wasn't what he envisioned for them in the States when they were teenagers in San Esteban, reading Macario's letters in the glow of the gas lamp. But here they were, decades later, two older bachelors in their own house in America. Two manongs and their home. He was grateful for that.

CHAPTER 8

The words to say it

As the window and doors of his square room came into focus, Fausto felt the uneven springs in his mattress, then the warmth of skin through cloth where his right thigh touched Rogelio's left thigh. Out of habit, he glanced at his stopped clock, though he knew from the angle of light from his window that it was still morning. It seemed as if half a lifetime had passed because he had talked so much.

When Rogelio asked what he and Benny had grown behind the gray-brick house in Terra Bella, summers of long ago flashed before Fausto. He and Benny had picked deep-purple tarong just before they matured, before the flesh turned bitter. Rows of kamatis plants produced enough tomatoes all summer long for Benny to dip in salty *bagoong* for his afternoon snack. Fausto swore Benny would never wash away the smell of fish paste from his fingers. They grew melons—cantaloupes, honeydew, watermelon, and casabas. Fausto would have gone on, but Rogelio kept squeezing his shoulders and hushing him. His fingers were wet with tears; damp patches stained his trousers. Stunned, Fausto realized he hadn't spoken a word when Rogelio asked him the question; his lips had moved silently as if he were praying the rosary.

"Dad told me lots of stories," Rogelio began. "He told me things I never knew."

After his first stroke, Benny couldn't stop weeping when they brought him home. Rogelio swabbed tears from his father's face, never leaving his side for two weeks, never looking away from the half of Benny's face that was as stiff as a mask. When Benny started talking again in the spring, Luz told Rogelio that he was recalling events out of the blue. He stared straight ahead of him, crying, *Cary, we should have brought you home!* Another time he looked to the side, half-smiling, whispering, *Serapio, you were so brave!* Benny was speaking mostly in Ilocano now. Before his second stroke he asked for Rogelio, who came right away. Benny talked for hours into the night, with Rogelio sleeping next to him in a rollaway bed. He was lucid. The whites of his eyes were bright, not filmy and jaundiced like the day before. But he was in great pain and full of sorrow. He needed to reach Fausto.

"I need to tell you something," Rogelio said to Fausto slowly, yet with urgency in his voice. "I don't know how to begin." His mouth hung empty, like a stream in a winter drought.

Fausto hugged his stomach. After so many years, the moment had arrived, and yet he shook with fear. Could he not handle the truth, after all? He thought of Benny lying in bed, paralyzed in so many ways. He wasn't there when his cousin needed him the most. It was too late when Benny's spirit came, but even then Fausto was stingy and selfish, wanting to claim what was his. It was wrong then, and it was wrong now.

Fausto's hand trembled, but he reached out and patted Rogelio's leg. He dared to rest his hand there, feeling warmth and hard muscle, feeling uncertain at first and then settling down. "You just came this morning," he said, full of wonder at how calmly he spoke. "You can't find the words; you're too tired from your long trip, eh?"

"I have the words," Rogelio insisted. He gave Fausto a smile that vanished just as quickly as he had flashed it. "But you're right—maybe not now, not this moment. Dad said you have a lot to tell me too. It's still your turn, isn't it? You have plenty to tell me. We have plenty of time, don't we?"

Plenty of time. Fausto nodded, then shook his head. He wanted to be in their garden again—when it belonged to just the two of them, before anything else or anyone could intrude and all those events unfolded and made their world joyful, sad, and triumphant all at once. *Remember when we built the trellis one summer, and the next summer—like magic —it was thick with string beans?* In the evenings, Fausto and Benny sat on overturned buckets beneath the trellis, shelling beans that made plinking sounds as they fell into a steel colander. It was still warm outside, but cooler in the shade. And while they talked idly, they could look out and admire the bountiful crops, which were the envy of their relatives and townmates. It was the best place to be in the garden. Those evenings seemed endless.

Fausto wanted today to be endless, with Rogelio dabbing his face with a soft cloth that smelled of musky cologne. He was weeping again. His hands and feet had gone cold, but he knew he could keep going and not be afraid. He was no longer alone. He had the words to say it. And there was plenty of time.

CHAPTER 9

Matchmaking

Terra Bella, California, 1960–1964

Light rain came down as Fausto left the post office. He was going to get soaked through by the time he returned home several blocks away because he didn't have his umbrella, but it didn't matter. The dark clouds matched his mood. There had been only bills and one letter addressed to Benny—from Luzviminda Ebat, granddaughter of the late Manong Vincent in San Esteban. Fausto pinched the bridge of his nose. He knew what the letter meant. The weekend before, at the baptism party for her fourth son, Nida had teased Fausto, saying it would soon be his "turn." She didn't say anything more, and he assumed she meant he would win the round after she had peeked at his cards. Now, as he stared at Luz Ebat's neat handwriting, he understood. In the last few months, Benny had insisted on getting the mail when it was Fausto's turn. He had written more letters in that time, composing them late at night. Once, Fausto woke up to get a glass of water. Benny was at the kitchen table, reading glasses on, a smile on his face, sheets of onion paper in his hands. As soon as Fausto walked in, Benny stuffed the letter in its envelope and went to his bedroom.

Fausto made pansit, set the table, and waited for Benny with the letter in his trouser pocket. Over dinner, Benny reported he'd heard from their cousin Fidel Europa that Mr. Cuculich was going to cut the rate for pruners by ten cents. Fausto reminded him that last year's harvest was not so good, but Benny waved him off—Fidel couldn't afford to lose money and might pick oranges in the winter instead. Many of the pruners felt that way, according to Fidel.

It was Fausto's turn to dismiss his cousin. He slapped the letter on the table between them. "Is Luzviminda Ebat looking for a sponsor to come to the States?"

Benny set his fork down. It was raining harder now. Fat drops squiggled down the window. "We are talking about getting married," he said. "Nida and Rozelle introduced us. I did not tell you because I did not want to upset you."

"*Apay?* Why? So you want to get married. Why should that bother me?"

"I never hear you talk about marriage. But I want a good wife."

Fausto shot him a look. "How do you know she will be a good wife?"

"We have been writing for months now. We had more time to know each other than Macario and Nida, Domingo and Rozelle. Look how many years they have been married, how many kids they have." Benny stared at his hands. "I want a wife and children. Ai, I'm almost fifty."

Fausto shut his eyes tight as if he could escape growing older, escape Benny's wishes. Benny would be a good father. He could see it when Macario's boys swarmed him when they visited. They hung from his arms and shoulders, wanting him to be "it" in a game of hide-and-seek in the orange grove. Benny was still quick enough to grasp the belt loop of one squirming, giggling boy and lift him off the tilled soil. Fausto shook his head, wanting the hard sweep of rain to drown out the children's laughter, the clang of wedding bells.

"What about the house?" Fausto stood up. The freezer, bought from Sears for Christmas, was still stocked with vegetables from their first harvest. He had stamped out the silverfish that had infested their closets, saving their starched barong shirts from ruin.

"We can talk about that later, when we have more time to think about it and make plans for the both of us. I'm not going to bring Luz here until next month."

"So soon? I cannot pay for the house by myself."

"I was thinking you could return to San Esteban with me and look for a wife. Where there are flowers, you know, there are butterflies." Benny winked, looking youthful for a moment.

"I cannot go back now. You know that."

"If you come with me, your sisters and brother will welcome you," Benny insisted. "Just like what happened with you and Macario."

"They would rather have the money for my ticket than see me. That's what I'm good for to them—struggling here in the US, but giving them tens of dollars for hundreds of pesos so they can live well." Fausto cleared his dishes. "When you bring Luz here, I'll go back to the camp."

"We want the house for you and your bride. That is why I want you to join me."

Fausto dismissed the frustration in Benny's voice. "I got the San Esteban Circle, Prudencio and Ayong, the camp, and the farm. That's all I need," Fausto announced, and walked out of the house. He stood at the edge of the garden—plowed under for the winter, now waterlogged.

Benny's bedroom window lit up behind him. Fausto blinked back the rain that bathed his face. He imagined Benny already packing his suitcase.

———————

Before he left, Benny patched the cracks in the exterior walls. When he was gone, Fausto found torn-out magazine advertisements for a new no-wax kitchen floor and scraps of paper with names of roof contractors on Benny's nightstand. Fausto couldn't sleep at night. They never had money to complete so many repairs all at once. By refusing to go to San Esteban, Fausto was sure the new plan was for him to leave and Benny to fix up the new bride's house. The day before Benny's arrival home, Fausto returned to Mr. Cuculich's camp. He retrieved his belongings, including the Bel Air, which he didn't feel guilty for taking.

"Not even here yet and Benny's bride already kick you out?" Prudencio asked. His feet, in soiled socks, were slung over the side of his bunk.

Fausto threw his suitcase on the bed below Prudencio's.

"I got something to cheer you up," Ayong said, and pulled out a wool army blanket from under his bed. He unrolled the four asparagus knives.

"Why do you still have those? They are useless." Fausto dumped his clothes out. They tumbled in a heap of tangled legs and long sleeves as if they'd been fighting in the confines of his suitcase.

"Souvenirs!" Ayong gave him a toothy grin. "It reminds me how many years later we are still together. *Impag pagarup mo nga daytoy ket pumayso?*"

"No." Fausto hung his head. He couldn't have imagined such a thing. "We are not all together."

"Never mind. Better to have *you* back." Prudencio sorted through the clothes and began folding jeans. "Now that you are here all the time, you can come to the union meetings with us and meet Larry Itliong, the local organizer. It will keep your mind off small matters. There are more important things going on with unionizing."

Fausto kicked his suitcase under his bunk. "I'm not interested in the Agricultural Workers Organizing Committee."

"You'll get interested plenty fast," Prudencio countered. "Things have got worse here. The bathrooms Mr. Cuculich promised are not getting built. We are talking about conditions in the camp and higher wages, especially for the pruners, in our meetings."

"We always talk about higher wages!" Ayong grabbed a handful of socks and matched them to their pairs.

"Larry says we are fighting for better jobs in the fields—not just higher wages, not just this season but next year and the year after that." Prudencio stopped folding shirts. "But we pinoys have to fight together and stick together. That way, nobody can get rid of us."

"Like peat dirt in our skin," Ayong chimed in. He examined his fingertips, as if expecting to find black dust after so many years removed from the Delta.

"*Nasayaat no agyanka ditoy kadakami,*" Prudencio said.

"Why should I not be okay with you guys, eh?" Fausto said. "Luz can take care of Benny. He's not very strong inside. The camp will take care of me."

"We all will take care of you!" Prudencio said.

The floorboards creaked beneath Fausto's feet. He was grateful to have Prudencio and Ayong welcome him back, grateful that Nick put both of them on the pruning crews. He'd invite Ahmed to dinner. Still, he never thought he would return, not after signing papers that made him and Benny homeowners, not after spending the first night drinking Dos Equis, when the two of them sang "Pamulinawen" at the top of their lungs, the lyrics calling on the stone-hearted woman who refused to give her love to them.

Fausto was restless the day Benny and Luz were supposed to have arrived, so he was secretly pleased when he found Benny waiting for him outside the mess hall.

"*Apay?* Why did you leave? I told you we wanted you to stay in the house." Benny followed Fausto into the bunkhouse. He spied Fausto's suitcase under the bed and laid it open on the mattress.

Fausto shut the lid of his suitcase. "I cannot stay there anymore. You know that."

"We still have more paperwork. Luz is not coming for two more months." Benny watched Fausto shove the suitcase under his bed. Clumps of dust shot out and settled on their shoes like white bloom on grapes. "At least stay in the house until she arrives."

Fausto agreed to stay with Benny on the weekends because he wanted to see his cousin struggle to adjust, but he was disappointed the moment he walked into the house. Fausto's bedroom was painted a bright yellow. He coughed as he breathed in the air freshener's heavy floral scent. Benny had pried up the last patches of linoleum and ordered new tiles.

The following weekend, Benny and another man on the rooftop threw old tar-and-gravel shingles into a bin. The next weekend, they finished nailing the new shingles.

"How can you afford all this?" Fausto wanted to know.

Benny dropped the hammer in the loophole of his workpants. "I took out a loan."

Fausto stepped back, his shoes crunching the loose gravel littered on the walkway. When they had signed the papers, they agreed to not take on any more debt. Their home-improvement projects were always modest and done only with the sweat of their brow.

Benny chuckled. *"Saanka nga madanagan.* Don't worry. I signed for the loan. It's not a second mortgage. You'll not be held responsible. Luz and I will be."

"But if you cannot pay, the bank will take the house," Fausto said.

"We are going to work hard to pay it off." Benny plucked off his work gloves, revealing a thin gold band on his ring finger. He gazed at the front door, gleaming white with a shiny brass doorknob. "It's a new house now—good enough for Luz."

Benny had built shutters and flower boxes for the front windows, and he planted seeds along the border of the house. Fausto squinted at the moist ground. Green shoots were shouldering their way up through the soil, bringing with them the promise of flowers.

When Luz finally arrived, Fausto stayed with Domingo and Rozelle on the weekends and still played rummy with his relatives on Sunday afternoons. During one game, Elsie Gunabe lowered her cards from her face, and declared, "Manong Fausto, I hear you have not been to the house since Luz arrived. It is so different now!"

Luz decorated each room with vases of plastic flowers and paintings bought at thrift stores, according to Elsie. She sewed and hung curtains in every window, and replaced the worn rug in the living room with a big piece of remnant carpeting. All the furniture would be replaced once she saved enough money packing oranges, but first they had to buy a car.

"Furniture and now a car? I thought they were trying to pay off improvements to the house." Fausto pretended to study the cards he'd been dealt.

Elsie exchanged glances with the women around the table. "Manong, are you keeping track of how much Benny and Luz are spending?"

Across the table, Truelino Orpilla slapped a queen of hearts atop a stack of cards. "Fausto should be concerned for Benny's sake. Women spend too much money. They say they got it on sale—a bargain—but it is hard-earned money out of our wallets just the same." He singled out the married men at the table with a knowing look. "We have to watch out for one another, or else we'll be just as poor here as in San Esteban!"

Fausto spread out his cards, but instead of seeing black diamonds and red hearts, he imagined a woman in a housecoat—sweeping, dusting, dragging a bucket of soapy water smelling of disinfectant from room to room, erasing all trace of him.

Fausto avoided the house. He tried to avoid Benny in the fields, but his cousin sought him out, inviting him to the welcome reception that Nida and Rozelle were throwing for Luz the following weekend, but never bringing up the fact that Fausto had kept his distance. How could Fausto say no? If he didn't show up, everybody's tongue would be wagging.

When Benny introduced Luz to him at the reception, Fausto recognized in her a slight resemblance to the late Manong Vincent. She wore her hair, as wiry as her lelong's, swept away from her broad face. She had Manong Vincent's long-lobed ears and gray-green eyes. But she was still a stranger.

"Thank you for moving back to the camp." Luz extended her hand, waiting for Fausto to exchange his bottle of Dos Equis from one hand to his other. "I scolded Benny for being so thoughtless." She threw Benny a look that Fausto guessed was meant to both tease and scold him. "I told Benny you understood we need time alone before children come."

Fausto raised his eyebrows. "Children?"

"We are starting a family." She wrested her arm from Benny's pinching fingers.

"You are expecting?" He shifted his gaze to Benny, who shoved his hands in his trouser pockets. The few times Benny forced him to eat lunch together he didn't talk about Luz. Fausto thought that maybe marriage wasn't agreeing with Benny after all, but all hope vanished with her announcement.

"Not now, but I am sure any time soon." Luz pulled Benny close to her.

"That's why everybody gets married." Fausto drained the last of his beer.

Benny grasped Luz's elbow. "You should greet the relatives from out of town." He steered her toward a group of women. He beamed at her, though it was clear to Fausto that he seemed unfamiliar, uncomfortable, in his new role. Luz called for him when they were separated for more than a few minutes. He hurried to her side, giving her a puzzled look when he realized she didn't need him for any reason. Luz joined Nida and Rozelle but kept her eye on Benny as he offered a bottle of Dos Equis to Fausto.

"It was never my plan to have you move to the camp." He whispered, even though Luz was out of earshot. "I was hoping you would marry too. So now we change our plans. We will get you in another house in town. We will help pay."

They stood in silence, cold bottles sweating in their hands. Fausto couldn't imagine where all this money was coming from, but he didn't want to argue, even if Benny and his bride were making decisions for him.

Benny took a swig of beer. "Did I tell you we had so much food left after our wedding reception in San Esteban? What luck!"

Fausto held up his bottle. Food left over after a wedding banquet meant Benny and Luz would become prosperous. "That's good. *Maragsakannak para kenka.*"

"Really? You are happy for us?" Benny's eyes shined. He was giddy, drunk.

Fausto nodded his head, thick from too much drink too.

The party wore on into the evening, with players crowding the rummy and mahjong tables in the living room and bedrooms. Fausto left after a hasty meal, though he sat in the Bel Air in the dark to catch his breath. Benny stepped outside and scanned the sea of parked cars. Then Luz came up from behind and tugged him back into the gray-brick house.

———

Fausto began to eat Sunday dinners with Benny and Luz before heading back to Delano. One weekend a newer car sat in their driveway, beneath a makeshift carport Benny had made with a discarded garage door and sheets of corrugated tin. He and Benny used to take turns hosing gnats and bird droppings off the Bel Air. They draped it with tarp to keep the frost from crusting on the windows, and they covered the top of the dashboard and the cloth seats with towels. Fausto was still just as careful. The Bel Air, with its rounded top and hood, was a few years old when they bought it; now it looked ancient next to the new cars that sported longer, boxier bodies.

Over dinner of chicken adobo, Benny bragged about their new car's spaciousness and power. "I bet it goes zero to sixty in half a minute. Is that not right, honey?"

Luz watched Fausto eat the chicken meat right off the bone. She sighed. "It is a good enough car, but it is not new, like I had hoped."

Benny waved her off, saying the previous owners had taken good care of it. Besides, it was only two years old, practically new.

Fausto laid the bare bone on his plate and licked his fingers, with Luz still watching him. At the start of dinner, she had insisted that Benny use his utensils. Fausto's fork lay untouched by his plate. For the third time, she reached over with a wet rag to rub off the sticky ring Benny's cup of 7-Up had left on the plastic tablecloth. Benny shook his head and took another piece of adobo.

"We are giving you the Bel Air," Benny told Fausto, and laid the pink slip of ownership on the table. "This is just the beginning of how we will repay you."

Fausto wiped his hands on his jeans. "This is plenty."

"It's just to start. Go on. Take it. Keep it in a safe place."

Fausto felt Luz's disapproval as she cleared the table. He imagined she must have been thinking that they would have purchased a new car if they had sold the Bel Air.

When Benny walked Fausto to his car, the pink slip safe in his shirt pocket, Fausto asked, *"Makarurod maipanggep diay lugan?"*

"She's not angry about the car." Benny glanced over his shoulder. Luz had already gone back in, having said her good-bye at the door. "Don't worry about Luz."

So he hadn't imagined her disapproval or the way she watched him eat, as if she were adding up the cost of everything on his plate! He thanked Benny again and settled into the driver's seat, feeling comfortable for the first time all evening.

———

When Arturo Esperanza invited him over for Sunday dinners, Fausto shortened his weekends in Terra Bella, coming into town Saturday afternoons after work and leaving for Delano midday Sunday. He spent time with Arturo Junior before dinner, helping him build houses with wooden Popsicle sticks. Whenever Fausto had loose change, he bought plastic cars for the stick houses because the boy didn't have many toys. As they played, he could smell the *menudo* and *mole* tamales Arturo's wife, Georgina, usually prepared. She didn't know any English, having newly arrived with her son months before, so Fausto thanked her in Spanish with the few words Arturo had taught him—*gracias, muy buena comida.* She smiled and offered him second and third helpings. He tried to follow Arturo's conversations with Georgina. He had heard Spanish spoken for several decades but still couldn't grasp much of the language.

Arturo invited farm workers who lived nearby to dinner as well. Sometimes heated arguments erupted. The grape growers, including Mr. Cuculich, were balking at the higher wages the farm workers wanted. At the dinner table, they compared how much of their wages the contractors were keeping for themselves. The sanitation in the fields was growing worse—only so many holes could be dug as toilets before the shoulders of the asphalt roads and dirt paths in between the fields became cesspools. Raúl, a thin man in his early twenties, insisted that the rumors about contractors demanding bribes and sex from women who were looking for work were true.

"A man named César Chávez is recruiting members for his organization—the National Farm Workers Association." Raúl reached for a roasted ear of corn. "Papi and I heard him talk. I like what he said. We're going to host the next meeting on Thursday."

"Another union?" Fernando, an older Mexican man, rolled his watery eyes. "The AFL-CIO's union—the Agricultural Workers Organizing Committee—is just a bunch of Anglos telling us what's good for us. *Han trabajado siempre en los campos?*"

"No, they have never worked in the fields," Raúl answered. "Their leaders aren't even in the area. They don't know what's going on in Delano. The trouble with AWOC is it's too friendly with the contractors and growers. But Chávez is one of us. He knows what it's like in the fields. His organization is different."

"I have heard of Chávez," Fernando said. "He has been here for a couple of years now and only has 200 paid members. Even AWOC has more Mexicans than him."

Arturo put two links of *chorizo* on his son's plate and passed the platter to Fausto. "AWOC have lots of Mexicans and Filipinos. It have Filipino organizer, yes?" he said.

Fausto nodded, though he didn't like this kind of talk at the dinner table. Georgina and Arturo's parents were restless in their seats. Arturo Junior hadn't eaten his chorizo.

"What that Filipino organizer's name?" Arturo pressed.

"Larry Itliong," Fausto said. "But I never met him."

"You don't belong to AWOC?" Raúl said. "Not any union?"

"No." Fausto pulled off bits of silk from his ear of corn.

"Why not?" Raúl set his corn down. "You don't think we need protection in the fields? Do you think our wages and our working conditions are good enough?"

"No, no!" Fausto said. "There are many problems in the fields and camps, but sometimes it's too dangerous to be in a union. In the asparagus fields, I saw what kind of trouble happens when unions strike." He looked each one of them in the eye. Workers got beat up. After the strikes ended and wages rose, the foremen who supported the unions got fired and blacklisted. Then the following season, the growers lowered wages again. "Every year there is always a fight, but the price of a strike is too dear when what is won does not last," he said.

"That's the trouble with unions," Raúl said, and wiped his mouth with his sleeve. "They think all they have to do is strike during harvests when the growers need workers and return to the fields when the growers raise wages. A union should do more than strike for higher wages; it should protect members from growers who bully them for their union activities. That is what Chávez's group wants to do. He wants to solve all the problems farm workers face. He says the NFWA won't strike until we have built up a strong membership. Only then can we be effective."

Arturo leaned over to Fausto. "Listen to him. This *hombre joven,* he smart."

Fausto nodded as Raúl drank his beer. When Arturo first introduced Fausto to Raúl at the Cuculich farm, he told Fausto that Raúl's father had come from Mexico around the same time Fausto arrived in the States. Raúl was born in Watsonville and picked strawberries with his parents and his brothers when he was a little boy. They moved to Delano two years ago and now Raúl and his family picked grapes.

Fernando tossed grapes in his mouth, talking and eating at the same time. "I saw the same things but in the lettuce fields in the Imperial Valley. We'll see what happens with Chávez. I hope you're right. *Para una vez,* I hope we can live like decent people in this land of plenty. *Merecemos nuestra dignidad en este país, no apenas en nuestro propio país.*"

"We will have dignity here. It will take time and a lot of sacrifice," Raúl said.

Fernando pressed his gut into the table as if to continue the talk, but Fausto cleared his throat and turned to Georgina, whose knife and fork had sat across the edge of her plate during the talk of unions. "The menudo was *muy bueno*. Thank you," Fausto said.

"*Sí, gracias por la cena, señora* Esperanza," Raúl said. "*Tal chorizo dulce.*"

Georgina smiled at Fausto, then at Raúl. Arturo Junior ate his chorizo in two bites. Then he attacked his chili rice. Fernando ground his knuckles into the top of Arturo Junior's head. Rice and red beans spilled off of the boy's fork. "Let's eat your *madre's* good food, but you could stand to eat less of it. *Usted no lo piensa es demasiado gordo?*"

"Fernando!" Arturo scolded as Georgina opened her mouth but didn't speak.

"*Qué?*" Fernando spread out his doughy hands. "I'm doing your son a favor. It's not good to be so big. I should know. Life is already hard—*la vida es ya dura*—don't we all know from working in the fields for Anglos?" He searched around the table to find a sympathetic face but found none. "I've been in the States long enough to know: he doesn't need one more burden in this country besides his birthright."

Arturo Junior's cheek bore two red splotches. His shoulders hunched up until Fausto melted the hardness away with his gentle rubbing. He offered Arturo Junior the last ear of corn, and the boy sank his teeth into it as if it were Fernando's leg.

The farm workers went home after dinner, but Fausto insisted on helping Arturo and Georgina clean up. Though Georgina protested, she gave in and left the kitchen to help her son get ready for bed. Arturo and Fausto cleared the table. Now and then, the boy's sobs pierced the walls.

"He not like school," Arturo said, craning his neck to listen.

"The farmers' kids are being mean to Arturo Junior?" Fausto guessed.

Wrinkles deepened across Arturo's forehead as if a disk harrow had plowed into the dark earth of his skin. "I take years to learn so little English. Children learn faster, but I want Junior to learn more faster. It hard to be old like me and know I never can speak good, never can write in English, but it harder to watch him struggle."

Fausto stacked mismatched cups in the sink. "Do the teachers not scold the kids?"

Arturo ran the faucet and told Fausto how he'd gotten off work early to meet with his son's teacher about the bullying. She had stared at Arturo's work clothes and said she'd talk to the kids, but the next day Junior came home with dirty clothes; he had been dumped in the garbage bin after school.

A cloud of steam rose from the sink. Arturo swiped at his moist cheek. "I tell him I talk with the teacher again, but he say 'no more' to me. Makes me think he ashamed of me," he said.

"No!" Fausto insisted. "I bet those kids thought Arturo Junior told on them. The teacher scolded them, so they made things worse for him."

"I never stop worry since he born early, born too small." Arturo held his hands inches apart. "Now he too big! Now he have big problems for such a boy." He tilted his head at Fausto. "Your English good. Maybe you teach him. Junior like you."

"An old man like me?" Fausto said, though Arturo Junior's face always lit up as he ran down the dirt driveway of their house when Fausto pulled up in his Bel Air.

"You not tease him," Arturo said. "You play with him, have patience with him."

Georgina emerged from the bedroom and exchanged words with Arturo. Then she drove the men out of the kitchen with a wooden spoon, speaking in rapid-fire Spanish.

Arturo led Fausto into the cramped living room. "She say kitchen is no man's place because we break the dishes. She get mad when I say, 'How we break plastic?'"

Fausto laughed, then turned serious. "What did she say when she came out?"

Arturo sank into the sofa and sighed. "Junior sleeping now. Only time he not worry."

Fausto joined Arturo on the sofa. "I'll help you, eh? I'll teach Junior English."

With red-rimmed eyes, Arturo met Fausto's gaze. *"Gracias,"* he said. *"Muchas gracias."*

Fausto's weekends in Terra Bella shrank even more. He collected magazines from the pinays in town and used them in the same way his American schoolteacher had done. He pointed out pictures to Arturo Junior and named them in English. "Car," he said, stabbing his finger at a sleek new car in an advertisement. *"Carro,"* Arturo Junior said, staring intently at the picture, then said with more deliberation, "car." Fausto slid his finger across the page to a tree in the background and tapped the glossy leaves. "Tree," he said. *"Árbol,"* Arturo Junior said first, and then, "tree." Fausto smiled at him. "Good, *bien,"* he said. *"Bien,* good," Arturo Junior said, returning the smile. As Fausto tousled the boy's hair, he thought this was how Miss Arnold must have felt when he had correctly named all forty-eight states in the Union during a geography test.

After one Sunday afternoon lesson, he asked Arturo Junior if knowing more words in English made school better for him. The boy pushed aside the magazine and drew his legs to his chest. Fausto balled up his hands. "Those kids still say mean things to you?"

"I not let it bother me. One of Papi's friends teach me how to box." He sprang up and raised his chubby arms, his fists orbiting in tight circles in front of his face, eyes narrowed to slits. His thick calf knocked up against the coffee table. Bits of particleboard crumbled to the rug. "Next time they call me something, I hit them between the eyes."

Fausto leapt up. "No, no! That is not how to act!"

Arturo Junior twisted his lips. "Nothing else work."

"You try this," Fausto offered. "Call me something they call you. Go ahead."

Arturo Junior hesitated, then blurted out, his voice hard, "Stupid wetback! Go walk home! You can't swim back. Can't drown, stupid fat wetback!"

Fausto wanted to march to the schoolyard and find out who had said those terrible things. He would box their ears, drag them home, and scold their parents—even challenge the fathers to a fistfight. He had fought back the urge to throw a punch after being called a brown monkey. But this was different, hurting a child like that.

"When they say those things to you, you walk away!" he finally said.

"That not work." Arturo Junior's voice was small. "They follow me and say more bad things. Then I cry and they laugh."

"When they see their words hurt you, it makes them feel powerful," Fausto said. "You have to be strong inside, feel good about yourself inside." He gently thumped the boy's chest. "Then whatever they say will not hurt you. It takes time to learn how to be strong inside. For now, you think of something in your head, far away from the playground."

"Like what?"

"Think of a song your mother sings to you or think of your home in

Mexico—anything that takes you away from the playground and makes you feel better inside."

Arturo Junior plopped down on the sofa and picked at the fibers sticking out of the worn upholstery. "I had a dog back home. Papi make me leave him there."

Fausto gathered the boy, his body warm and squishy, in his arms. "What kind of dog was he? A big one? A small one? What color was he? What was his name?" He pulled out his handkerchief and swabbed the boy's tears, as if removing a splinter from his tender skin.

Arturo Junior had found a straw-colored mongrel in a box on the roadside and took the puppy home, much to his mother's dismay. But she let him keep it because he played with it all evening, sometimes forgetting to cry over his father's absence during harvests. He fed his food to the dog, assuring his mother he had plenty to eat—couldn't she tell by how big he was? He named the dog Afortunado, meaning "lucky," because he had saved the little runt. Afortunado followed him everywhere. On cold nights, he snuck the dog in and let it fall asleep within his fleshy arms. If only he could tell his mother it was good to be big, to be able to offer his body like a thick blanket!

Once, a drunkard tried to steal Arturo Junior's money after the boy came out of a store. But the dog drove his teeth into the man's calf. Arturo Junior ran away, and Afortunado soon followed, prancing around with a piece of the drunkard's pants caught in his teeth as if it were a trophy. "But he not really *afortunado*," Arturo Junior said.

"You remember Afortunado. He was lucky for *you*," Fausto said fiercely. "That was his reason for you finding him—to protect you. When those kids call you names, you say nothing and walk away. You think about Afortunado, and then you see in your head that little dog chasing them away with his sharp teeth." He pointed at the drab ceiling. "Afortunado is watching out for you," he added, believing every word he was saying.

Arturo Junior looked up, his nose glittery with snot. "Maybe this not work."

"Try, you try!" Fausto prompted him. "Promise me, eh?"

"Papi says if I make a promise, I must keep it," Arturo Junior said.

He took Fausto by the hand and led him outside. As they stood on the lawn, the boy stared at the sky. Fausto couldn't tell if Arturo Junior believed that Afortunado was in heaven or whether the boy would have the courage to walk away from taunting schoolchildren. Fausto hoped he would try. Arturo Junior had made a promise, but Fausto knew sometimes promises were hard to keep.

He knelt down. "After Afortunado chases the mean kids away, he will lick your face. He will be so happy to be by your side again," he said, and wrapped his arms around the boy.

Arturo Junior looked Fausto in the eye. "Maybe it work," he said, and bit his lip.

Benny was the only one home when Fausto came to pick up Luz's magazines one Sunday afternoon. "You are becoming a stranger around here," Benny said, trailing after him as he went to the washroom where the magazines were stored. "How come you don't come around much? What's the matter with you? *Ania iti napasamak?*"

"I been busy." Fausto scooped a stack of magazines into a grocery bag.

"I been meaning to talk to you." Benny crouched down so they were eye level. "I don't want you hearing from somebody else, especially Nida, Rozelle, Macario, or Domingo."

Fausto dumped another stack of magazines into a bag. "Hear what?"

"Luz petitioned her niece from Vigan to come here. We want you to meet her. We thought you and Marina would be a good match." Benny offered a smile.

"Good match? *Apay?* Is she old and lonely?" Fausto carried the bags in each arm and walked out the washroom back door to the Bel Air.

Benny chased after him. "She is thirty-two, the eldest of Luz's oldest sister. She helped her five brothers and sisters through school so she never had time for marriage."

"I'm fifty-two, maybe older than her father. What will she do with an old man?" Fausto put the bags down. As he lifted the hood of the car trunk, he felt a twinge in his lower back.

"She can take care of you. She can give you children, if you like."

"I'm too old!" Fausto massaged his back.

"You are strong and healthy!" Benny deposited the first bag in the trunk. He reached for the second one, but Fausto wrested it from him.

"What is wrong with her?" he asked, and threw the bag in the trunk.

Benny's wispy eyebrows bunched up. "What do you mean? Does she limp? Does she have a crippled hand? Is her face full of moles with hair sticking out?" He laughed, holding his stomach. *"Awan iti pagkunaam kenkuana*—nothing! Wait, I have a picture of her." He hurried back into the house and returned with a photograph of Luz's niece. "This is Marina Ayson."

In the black-and-white picture, Marina Ayson stood beside her seated parents, who were round and healthy looking. She was skinny, as if she were the runt of a litter, not the firstborn. She couldn't have supported her family with manual labor. Her legs were so thin, her knees like knots. Her fingers looked delicate; they would surely bruise easily when grabbing oranges that tumbled down steel chutes and packing them in crates. Her fingers would go numb from clipping grapes ten hours a day. Maybe after a few years they would be as useless in the fields as berry shatter on the ground. The woman's hair was pulled into a bun, the part in the middle a severe white line, but she looked younger than her age. He expected her to look older—like Luz, Nida, or Rozelle after a season in the fields and packing house. He expected her thick eyebrows to be furrowed, not relaxed—with a bitter look on her face for being forced to make such a harsh sacrifice, but she was smiling. She wasn't ugly or pretty, just plain.

"She will not want me for a husband." Fausto handed the photograph back.

Benny pored over Marina's image, as if looking for flaws that Fausto had caught. "But she has your picture already. Luz and I sent it to her. She is coming to meet you."

He gave Benny a hard look. "Did you send an old picture of me from the army?"

"No!" Benny laughed. "I sent the one of the two of us our first summer here, in front of our house, in our Hawaiian shirts and shorts, for Macario's birthday party."

Fausto ran his fingers through his graying hair. He refused to dye his hair like Orlino Vergara did and didn't suffer Lito Guzman's fate—a bald spot that kept growing. What did Marina see in him? Luz probably told her he was living in the camp and had no savings. Maybe the plan was to divorce him after a year—she would have her papers to stay here and be free to marry a younger man who could give her a future. Was Luz behind this, and Benny simply blind? But Marina looked too proud in the picture to have agreed to such a scheme.

"What is she like?"

Benny scratched at his graying temple. "I don't know. Luz says she is quiet but determined. Luz had to convince her sister it was wrong not to let Marina live her own life. She is old to be a newlywed back home, but not so much here."

"Ah, that is what we have in common!" Fausto forced a laugh.

"We don't pity you or Marina. *Kayatmi laeng iti tumulong.*"

"I don't want your help in these matters!"

"You will not meet her at all? Ai, I'm just asking you one favor. Just meet her."

Too old at thirty-two for a husband back home. How could anyone promise her life would be better in the States? Fausto couldn't say whether his life was better now than when he had first arrived, when he was full of the worlds Miss Arnold and Macario had created for him in his head. He thought of the pointed arch of her brow, her pressed lips—how mysterious it all was! He slammed the trunk shut, aware of the veins on his hands.

Marina Ayson arrived midsummer 1964. Fausto didn't see her until Luz threw a welcoming party in her honor a week after she had come. Everyone knew Fausto was the handpicked suitor, though he never said a thing to anyone in the fields or at gatherings. He endured the ribbing of Macario, Orlino, Lito, and even Fidel.

"The next party is the wedding, eh?" Lito joked as Fausto came up the walkway to the gray-brick house. The yard was crowded with men inhaling cigarettes and downing beers. Domingo took Fausto aside, guiding him to the farthest tree in the yard.

"Don't listen to them. When they are not playing rummy, they have nothing better to do," Domingo said, blotting his temple with the back of his hand. The air was thick with heat, even in the shade.

"Ania iti sawsawen yo?" Fausto said, annoyed.

"You know what I'm talking about." Domingo poked Fausto's soft midsection. "You are lucky! Benny is thinking of your best interests!"

"How lucky for me." Fausto massaged his stomach.

"We are all thinking of your best interests." Domingo leaned into the tree, his face gone serious. "I heard you joined Larry Itliong's union, AWOC. Is that true?"

"Saan. No. I have too many things on my mind."

"Unions are troublesome. Better to leave them alone," Domingo advised. "You should move back here. There is too much union agitation in the camps." His face relaxed. "So, you got things on your mind? Thinking about settling down?"

"Let's go inside. Let's not roast in this heat!" Fausto said, gritting his teeth.

He spotted Marina in the crowded living room. She was wearing a cornflower-blue dress with a hemline of puppies spilling out of woven baskets, a dress Fausto recognized as once belonging to Nida. Marina looked even skinnier in person. Her collarbone stuck out above the square neckline. The self-belt was cinched as far as it would go, but it was still loose on her waist, and the skirt flared out, making her legs look like twigs. She wore her hair in a bun, revealing a neck as fragile as a baby bird's. From the kitchen entryway, Benny raised his eyebrows when he saw Fausto. Flanked by Elsie Gunabe and Pilar Europa, Marina didn't notice Fausto. They swept her into the kitchen, brushing Benny aside as if he were a curtain. A moment later, female laughter erupted from the kitchen. Fausto sighed at Benny. He couldn't leave without meeting her, unless he wanted to spark a new round of gossip at the rummy tables. But Marina was never by herself, and when he introduced himself to her he didn't want anyone spying on him, especially Luz. Marina seemed overwhelmed by the attention, but at the same time, she kept looking over her shoulder. When she finally locked eyes with him in the living room, she lowered her head and pulled at her bun at the nape of her neck as if trying to loosen it and hide behind her hair. Benny finally rescued Marina from Luz's care and brought her to Fausto, who had fled to the deserted front yard.

"Marina, this is Fausto Empleo," Benny said, as if exhausted.

She held out her hand, her fingers as weightless as feathers when he held them. He offered to get her a cup of Coca-Cola, but Benny trotted off, insisting he'd bring it to her.

"What did Luz tell you about me?" Fausto blurted out.

"Auntie Luz said you and Uncle Benny are close first-cousins, and the two of you came over in the 1920s. She said you work in the vineyards in Delano all year."

"Did she tell you I live in the labor camp? Did she tell you how old I am?"

She blushed and nodded. "Did Uncle Benny tell you how old *I* am? Did he tell you what my circumstances are?"

His cheeks grew hot. He didn't mean to be rude, but he wanted to know. Had Benny told her everything about him? He dared to take in her dark eyes before Benny coughed to announce himself. He gave Marina a paper cup full of Coca-Cola and excused himself to carve the rest of the pig he had roasted in the backyard.

"What are your circumstances?" he asked softly, though they were alone. Maybe people could see the two of them from the front windows. Maybe they were giggling or hushing one another, straining to hear through the screens. It seemed too convenient that at a big party they were the only ones in the front yard. But Fausto didn't care anymore.

She took a sip from her cup. "My mother wanted me to take care of her and my father after taking care of my sisters and brothers. She did not want me to get married and move away from Vigan as my sisters did—as she once did. She said I was the reliable one. My sisters needed to be taken care of, but I was strong on my own. For the longest time, I believed her, but Auntie Luz intervened. She said even if it was true, it was not fair. She promised me a better life here. She told my mother a better life for me here meant a better life for her in Vigan."

"Sometimes it's not so good to be the reliable one in the family," he said.

She nodded. He stared at the cup resting against her bright pink lips. He wished he had a drink, something to hold onto. Out of the corner of his eye, he spotted Luz watching them through the screen door. He asked Marina why Luz had intervened.

Marina swished the ice in her cup. "Auntie Luz knew how hard my life would be. She got away from her situation when Manang Nida and Manang Rozelle matched her to Uncle Benny. She wanted to help me."

Benny pulled Luz back from the door. Fausto gazed at the empty spot where she had stood. He had never seen this side of Luz. "Did she say why she wanted us to meet?"

"Uncle Benny suggested you. Auntie Luz was thinking of someone younger, but I told her I did not mind." She took another sip, a longer one.

Impatient, he came closer to her. "You did not mind what?"

"I told her I did not mind how old you are as long as you are as good and kind as she is to me. What good is a younger man if he is cruel?"

He couldn't tell if she regretted being so truthful. "What about love?"

She drank the rest of the Coca-Cola, the delicate lump in her throat gliding up and down as she swallowed. "I have never been. My mother would not let me. What do I have to compare it to? If you marry someone who is kind, why should love not come later? Is it wrong to think that?" Her voice was plaintive in the summer heat.

"There is no right or wrong."

She tilted her head to one side, her shaped eyebrows raised, full of expectation. "And you? Are you looking for someone special? Is that why you have not married yet?"

"Benny did not tell me how outspoken you are. Maybe you scared away all your suitors." He forced a laugh, but it died in his parched throat.

"Am I scaring you away?" She wasn't upset, though she stared at him with unwavering eyes.

Sparrows twittered and dove into the tree. The leaves shivered with their presence. He swallowed hard, wishing the two of them were somewhere else, though the din of the party seemed far away. He looked down and noticed old grease stains on his shirt, scuff marks on his shoes, his frayed trouser cuffs. He wasn't thinking about what kind of an impression such an outfit would make when he got dressed that morning. How shabby he must look to her. How blind or desperate she must be. But she was waiting for his answer.

"No," he whispered, though he kept his eyes locked on the blades of grass at his feet. "I'm not scared. I'm standing right here."

She overturned her cup. Cubes of ice slipped to the lawn without making a sound. "I am still thirsty. Do you want something too?"

"Sure," he said. "I'll drink what you are drinking. Coca-Cola is fine."

"I will be back," she said, lingering at the edge of the tree's shade.

"I'll be right here," he insisted, and that seemed to satisfy her.

She strode across the lawn. Fausto rocked his feet on an exposed tree root. Was it lust or tenderness that stirred in him? Marina disappeared into the house, swallowed by well-wishers, her full skirt a swish of cornflower blue. He only knew one thing: to stand beneath the canopy of leaves, as entrenched as the tree, and wait for her return.

After dinner one evening, Prudencio took Fausto outside the mess hall, where Ayong was talking to a short pinoy. Fausto knew the man with the black, horn-rimmed glasses and crew cut was Larry Itliong. He had often seen Larry talking to the pinoys in the camp. Prudencio had been threatening to introduce Fausto to him for weeks.

"Larry, this is Fausto Empleo," Prudencio said when they reached Ayong's side.

Smoke swirled in the air as Larry transferred his cigar from one hand to the other. He grasped Fausto's hand in a vise and pumped it vigorously, as if he didn't have three fingers missing. "You're from Ilocos Sur?" He spoke out the side of his mouth, as if the cigar were still dangling from the corner of his mouth. "I'm from San Nicolas, Pangasinan, in Ilocos Norte. Cigar?" In vain, he frisked the pockets of his shirt and his corduroy pants, rolled at the cuff.

"You want to know why I have not joined AWOC," Fausto guessed.

Larry sized him up. "We need to be united for the good of the union."

Fausto shot a look at Prudencio. "Maybe unions are not the answer to our problems in the field. I have been here long enough to see what happens *after* a strike is settled."

Larry chomped on his cigar. His cheeks, dark and leathery, swelled with the effort. "Unions are not just about strikes. Unions negotiate, protect, and advocate," he said, as smoke billowed through his lips. "The Constitution says everybody has equal rights and justice, but only for the white man—not for us. Hell! We have to fight for it!"

"AWOC is talking about striking, but strikes don't always work out," Fausto said.

"There is a time and place for everything," Larry said, squinting at him even as the haze cleared from his face. "I have been here for thirty-five years and I have seen progress from the canneries in Alaska to the fields in Salinas and Coachella Valley. We have to continue to do more. We have to make great sacrifices if we want to create lasting changes, and right now it means going on strike. If we do nothing, if we don't speak up for ourselves now, the growers will set our wages, and our conditions in the fields and the camps—conditions fit for dogs, not humans—will never improve. We will continue to be nothing in this country."

"How is your union better than César Chávez's organization?" Fausto asked.

Larry spit out bits of tobacco from his lips. "We have the strength and the funds of the AFL-CIO behind us. Chávez has 200 paying members. Those membership fees aren't enough to do anything."

"Larry's been organizing for a long time," Prudencio said. "He's a pinoy. He'll take care of us."

"I stand for *every* farm worker in these vineyards. We work hard for Filipinos, Mexicans, blacks, whites, Arabs." Larry straightened up, though he was still shorter than Fausto. "You and I know Filipinos have always been exploited by everyone here—even after the Filipinos fought for this country in World War II. I became a labor leader because I saw crimes committed against our countrymen. I won't let it continue with my children or your children." His words were spirited, but Fausto held back. "How long have you been working in the fields?" Larry asked.

"I cut 'gras in the Delta in the Thirties until the war. I came here in 1950."

"What do you have to show for all those years in the fields, all those years in the camps?" Larry stabbed his thumb in the direction of the bunkhouse. Fausto was shocked into silence, but Larry went on like a bulldozer: "Don't you believe you deserve to have good wages and working conditions, decent benefits, job security? Enough money to buy a home and a car, support your family, and send your children to college?" Frowning, he raked his hand across his crew-cut hair. "If you better the life of farm workers after you, would that effort make your life worthy? Will all your struggles then not be in vain?"

An image of Marina flitted by and then vanished in a breath. So many years gone. It was too late for him, but he would fight for a better life for his children. He could say that now with certainty. He shot out his hand. "I am with you."

Larry shook his hand and smiled, his broad nostrils stretching across his cheeks, the thin slashes of his moustache parting in the middle. Fausto tried to imagine how Larry had lost his fingers as he strode off the campgrounds, his two-fingered hand holding his cigar, its thread of smoke trailing, then disappearing in the gathering dusk.

———

Throughout the summer, Fausto continued to give Arturo Junior English lessons after Sunday dinners at the Esperanza house. The boy had picked up many words, much to his father's delight, though helping him with his grammar was beyond Fausto's ability. He told Arturo Junior that in the fall his teacher should be able to help him put together complete sentences in English. It would be easier now that his vocabulary had grown. At the mention of school, however, the boy stiffened, but all Fausto had to say was "Afortunado," and Arturo Junior gave him a brave smile. When the lesson was done, Arturo Junior asked if he could come over Saturday afternoons too, after he finished picking grapes, but now that Marina had arrived, Fausto had to decline. If not for the Sunday dinners and English lessons, he would be spending his weekends at Luz and Benny's house. Marina was staying in his old room, which was supposed to be a nursery but now served as a temporary guest room. One side of the closet held baby clothes, receiving blankets, and crib sheets; Marina's hand-me-down dresses hung on the other side.

Fausto didn't feel comfortable staying overnight at Benny's house, so he slept on the sofas at Macario's and Domingo's homes and went to Benny and Luz's for Saturday dinners. He escorted Marina to weddings, funerals, baptisms, birthdays, and occasional welcome parties for relatives who had been successfully petitioned for—but the two of them were never alone. He had gotten so used to this arrangement that he wasn't sure when he would feel comfortable being in a room with just her.

Once, Benny left them alone in the kitchen, so that he could return empty crates to Truelino Orpilla, who had dropped them off packed with grapes. While he was gone, Marina bustled about in the kitchen as if it were her own, arranging bunches of grapes by color in colanders and lining them by the sink.

"You are going to wash the grapes all at once?" he asked, joining her at the sink.

"Yes," Marina said, her sleeves rolled up, the faucet running. "That way Auntie Luz will not have to wash them when she and Uncle Benny are ready to eat."

Fausto turned off the faucet. "If you don't eat washed grapes right away, the fruit will go soft and spoil faster. Only wash what you are going to eat now."

She paused, holding a colander brimming with golden-yellow berries, and then pointed to a bunch of deep-red grapes. "Which one do you want to eat?"

His arm grazed her cotton blouse as he plucked an oblong-shaped berry. "Do you want a grape with seeds or no seeds?" he said. She looked at him blankly. "They have names. This is a Thompson Seedless." He held it up to the window. Sunlight made the pale-amber skin almost translucent. "Thompson Seedless grapes are green, but when they are left on the vine longer, they turn honey colored. They are sweeter and juicier than the green ones. Most people don't know that. They want their Thompson Seedless green. But the honey-colored ones are better."

He turned the berry in his fingers. It looked like a yellow sapphire in the afternoon light. He offered it to her lips.

She wrinkled her nose. "We should wash it first. It is dirty."

He laughed. "This white dust—they call it 'bloom'—is how Nature protects the berries from getting moldy and losing moisture in the fields. It does not change the taste."

She examined it with uncertainty, then took the berry from him and slipped it into her mouth. "It is good!" she said. "And what are those?"

He turned to the darker grapes. "Emperors have seeds. They are tart." He placed a berry in her open hand. The moment she bit into it, her mouth rippled.

"So we will eat the sweeter grapes for now," Fausto said, and smiled.

He held up a small cluster, pulling the berries off with his teeth. He chewed slowly to squeeze out as much juice as he could. Soon the only thing left in his hand was the grape stem, its ends furred like tiny yellow stars. As she ran water over the colander, she turned her lips inward, as if suppressing a smile.

"What?" Fausto dipped his head to catch her eye. She shook her head, but it only made her smile bloom. "*Ania?*" he repeated, this time in a whisper. Was it possible to become drunk eating ripe grapes? That would explain his giddiness. Perhaps in the morning he would be embarrassed by his behavior. He would remember his place, the truth of their situation. But not today, not at this moment. He came closer, but she pulled away. The screen door creaked open. Benny stamped his feet on the welcome mat. Fausto and Marina stole glances at one another before moving to opposite ends of the kitchen.

———————

Marina mentioned to Benny and Fausto that it would be nice to see a movie, but Fausto ignored her request. It bothered him that ushers at the Delano Theatre seated the Filipinos along the aisles, where they had to angle their heads to face the screen. Not much had changed in the movie theatres since he had first arrived in the States. There was no reason to be reminded of their place in the community. As Benny walked Fausto to his car after dinner one evening, he suggested that Fausto take Marina to the Filipino movie theatre in nearby Earlimart, but Fausto said he was too old for movies. Benny leaned into the open car window, his eyes disappearing from laughing so hard. "You don't need to read the subtitles, and you don't need glasses—yet."

Fausto wished he hadn't spoken up. He didn't feel old in the fields; he could fill the same number of crates per day as a man twenty years younger. He could carry as many lugs of grapes from deep in the vineyard to the roadside packing station as anyone else. But he felt old when he left the camp and when he spent time with Marina. She slowed her pace when they walked around the neighborhood. He felt silly courting Marina. Since she had come, younger pinoys who were petitioned for arrived in Terra Bella, but she didn't notice them. She was too intent observing his actions and paying attention to his words, as if looking for deeper meaning, which made him uneasy. And then just when he found the courage to approach her, she turned him away, confusing and wounding him. He hadn't solved the mysteries of women when he was with Connie. He hadn't thought of her in years, and yet her name still brought up his hurt—as fresh as when they had parted on the lawn that June afternoon. Their time together was too brief to come away with anything learned. He also knew that this understanding of women was no longer within his reach now that he was older.

Benny gave up lobbying for the movies. At dinner in early August, he told Marina about the San Esteban Circle's activities during Labor Day weekend.

Marina's eyes gleamed. "Auntie Luz told me about the dance. How exciting!"

"I'll escort you, if you like," Fausto mumbled.

"I would like that very much," Marina rushed to say. "Do you like to dance?"

Benny laughed, pounding the table, rattling the forks and knives. He pointed at Fausto, and said, "He's got two left feet. Just like me. But a good dance partner fixes that."

Luz reached over to stroke Benny's hand. Fausto looked away, embarrassed. He had never noticed any public displays of affection between them. Seeing them touch one another made him feel lonely. It made him wonder if Marina was a good dancer.

"And you?" he asked, wishing that the plastic-draped table wasn't between them.

She pressed her lips to her napkin. "I am not very good. I did not dance much back home. But Auntie Luz can teach me. I learn quickly. I can be a good partner." Her voice blossomed. She turned to Luz, who nodded, her fingers still resting on Benny's wrist.

A week before the dance, Fausto came by the house. Marina answered the door, wearing a cotton housecoat that covered her knees and rubber flip-flops on her small feet. She held a pair of scissors, a pincushion was strapped to her wrist, and a tape measure hung down from around her neck. Cut-out shapes lay on the sofa. A cutting board with grid marks and tissue paper tacked to white fabric took up most of the living room floor.

She knew why he had come, gesturing at a bag full of magazines by the door. "Auntie Luz and Uncle Benny are picking up tables for the dance," she said. "I am making a gown for the dance. I do not want to wear somebody else's dress."

"You sew?" He felt bad not knowing this about her. She had asked him once what his hobbies were, and all he could think of was gardening, watching boxing on television, and playing rummy—things that didn't mean as much to him as sewing seemed to mean to her.

Marina pointed to a wooden cabinet with a black sewing machine on top and a black-iron treadle suspended a few inches off the floor. "I could not bring my sewing machine, so Auntie Luz bought this second hand. Something is wrong with the tension. The thread keeps breaking. If I keep my foot light on the pedal, it still works."

"You sewed a lot back home?" He stepped over a plastic box of steel thimbles and bobbins wound with different colored threads.

"I was hoping to be a seamstress once my youngest sister finished school, but we had no money." Marina deposited a stick of white chalk in her sewing box. "I worked in a clothing factory sewing the same things over and over. I like making my own patterns, but the factory helped me become a better seamstress. You must make use of unpleasant conditions. When you do something for many years, you had better be good."

Fausto laughed. "I must be good in the vineyards, then."

She picked up her scissors. "You are. You know so much about grapes. Uncle Benny also told me you were one of the best on the crew for cutting asparagus."

"Benny did not have rough hands for farm work in the beginning. I always did. Maybe that's why I'm so good." Fausto's father would have agreed that he was destined to work in the fields. He was better at farm labor than anything else he might have tried that required an education. He sat on the sofa, careful not to touch the patterns she had cut out.

She kneeled before the board and began cutting out more shapes. "Uncle Benny always tells me how good you are to everybody—like Severo Laigo."

Severo Laigo was one of the older pinoys who had been working for Mr. Cuculich for almost twenty years. He had injured his hand last harvest and couldn't hold his clippers properly. But he had to work; he was sickly and needed his medicine. Severo could only fill a couple of crates per hour, so Fausto worked twice as hard and gave him half of his boxes the rest of the summer until Severo's hand healed. "I did not need all that money, living in the camp," Fausto told her, palming his cheek to feel how hot it was. "Prudencio and Ayong helped too. And then the other pinoys contributed their box bonus here and there."

"But you acted first. You gave all the time, not just here and there," she said fiercely, stopping her handiwork. "You hid his injury so he could keep his job." Marina put her head down and resumed cutting. "Uncle Benny told me about your cousin Caridad."

"What about Cary?" His voice hardened.

Her head turned, following the direction of the tip of the scissors. She cut around the black points, the little nips in the fragile brown tissue. "Uncle Benny said you wanted to grant him his last wish to have his body returned to San Esteban."

"But I did not do it."

She looked up, the scissors hanging in her hand. "Yes, I know. It was difficult for you, but you tried very hard. You tried and it broke your heart not to succeed."

"And what do you think of that?" He leaned down on one knee, next to her.

Marina didn't look away. "It shows how generous you are."

Fausto stared at her face. Flecks of emerald, like tiny fireworks shooting off, glittered in her eyes. He had never noticed the mole, as small as a pinhead, near the outer corner of her left eyebrow. Her skin was the color of earth. The way she twisted her lip, he knew she was expecting him to say something. It was another hot day. The air conditioner was off. Wet patches seeped from his underarms. A shimmer of sweat matted down whispers of hair on her upper lip. He resisted the urge to roll his finger across the fine beads.

"Are you afraid you will have to go back home if you don't get married soon?"

It was a cruel thing to say, but she didn't seem upset. "I am afraid I have nothing to give to anybody. That is what you mean, is it not? That I have nothing to give to you?"

The living room walls were caving in on him, squeezing out his breath. He was afraid to tell her what he had wanted to say the first day he had met her, but that fear thrust the words up like a diver, with aching lungs, bursting to the ocean's surface. "I'm too old for you, Marina," he blurted out.

She laid the scissors on the cutting board. "It is not a problem for me."

"It is a problem for *me.*"

She rose. "Then go away." She grabbed his shirt by the shoulders and tried to push him toward the front door, but he scrambled out of her reach. "Go away! Take your *problem* with you! I do not need your *problem!*"

He stumbled back, straightening his shirt. "I have been by myself for so many years. I don't know how to live with a woman."

"I do not know how to live with a man, but I would try. If you gave me a chance, I would try very hard." Marina was crying now, pressing the cut-up fabric against the corners of her eyes. She threw the wet piece of fabric to the floor.

"Ai, what are you doing?" Fausto picked up the tangle of frayed-edged material and torn paper, even as the pins jabbed at his skin.

"No need to make this dress." She plucked the pincushion from her wrist.

"Why? I'm still taking you to the dance."

"*Awan bali na!* No use!" She shook her head. "I am no use."

"I have a week before the dance to fix my problem. Or did you not want to go to the dance with me after all?" He grabbed her wrist and held on, even as she whimpered. Maybe she could feel the calluses on his palms and the thick, hard ridges of his fingertips. He let go. Things had happened so quickly. "I did not hurt you!"

"No," she said, as she massaged her wrist.

"I'll take you to the luncheon the day of the dance. The dance begins at seven, but I'll pick you up at eight." He pointed at the pile of fabric. "We'll come in when everybody is already there. We'll show off your dress, and everybody will whisper, 'Ah, Manong Fausto, what a lucky man he is.'" Tears began to stream down her cheeks again. "Ai, why are you crying?" he exclaimed, exasperated.

"I am *not* crying." She pressed her fingers below her eyes to stem the flow and smiled through her tears. "I am lucky," she said. She grabbed the grocery bag and handed it to Fausto. "This is for Arturo Junior?"

He nodded and took the bag of magazines, the brown paper crackling between them. Her cheeks, rosy with heat, were bathed in tears.

"He is lucky too," Marina said.

She opened the door for him and he numbly stepped out into the warm air. As he drove away, he imagined that she had dried her face and returned to the cutting board, smoothing out the fabric and putting the pieces of her dress back together again.

Fausto was an hour late picking Marina up for the luncheon. He told her she had every right to curse him for wanting to fill a few more boxes, imagining that he was still as swift as he used to be, thinking about his per-box bonus and her the whole time in the fields. She insisted she wasn't angry or hungry, even as he heard her stomach growling.

"How can I be upset? You were working hard." She slipped her arm under his as they entered the Veterans Memorial Building.

Only a few people were left eating in the ballroom. Players and onlookers had gathered at the rummy and mahjong tables. All the ballroom windows were tilted open, but it was still warm indoors. Fausto felt as if the sun were trailing him from the fields, the way his cheeks flushed when everyone turned away from their games to look at the two of them. He steered her to the banquet room where food was still laid out across a long line of tables. Nida and Rozelle stood at each end, waving paper plates to shoo the flies.

Nida rushed over to hand them clean plates. "So good to see you, Marina! We were wondering why you weren't here yet." She wasn't pregnant this time, though her youngest, a toddler, another boy, was sleeping in a bassinet by the table with desserts.

"You'll be coming to the dance tonight? Together?" Rozelle scooped rice from an enormous pot and slapped a ball on each of their plates.

"Rozelle, we can get our own food," Fausto said in an irritated voice. "The flies are all over the *lechon*. Go shoo them away."

"Like you are shooing us away!" Rozelle giggled.

Nida leaned into Marina. "Manong Fausto has lost his sense of humor. Maybe you can help him find it." She and Rozelle retreated to the opposite end of the table.

He was about to say something, but Marina hushed him. When they filled their plates and got their drinks, Fausto tried to lead Marina to a table closer to the entrance. Macario, Benny, Domingo, and some of his cousins were huddled at a table near the stage. But Macario saw them and waved, and Marina headed their way. Fausto reluctantly followed— he knew what all the men were talking about.

"Fausto! What do you think of Larry Itliong's union?" Macario took Marina's plate and set it down. He eyed Fausto, and said, "I hear AWOC will strike next harvest."

"White men run that union," Domingo spoke up. "AWOC hired that Mexican unionizer, Dolores Huerta, to appeal to her people, and she hired Larry to get the Filipinos to join. *Mabalin nga para baon laeng dayta nga lalaki.*"

Fausto swallowed his mongo beans whole. "Larry is not a lackey," he responded. "He is a warrior. If anything needs to get done, Larry is the person everyone trusts and turns to."

"I heard he lost his fingers riding the railroads when he first came to the States," Melchor Vergara said. "You want to entrust your livelihood to someone who is careless?"

"I heard he lost his fingers during a strike." Lito Guzman held out his hands. His knuckles were scarred from replacing the chainlink fence that separated his backyard from Benny's backyard. "Is losing your fingers worth higher wages that don't last?"

Marina rested her plastic fork on her plate and pursed her lips as if she had lost her appetite. Fausto wanted to spirit her away, but instead, he fisted the table, and said, "Why don't you ask Larry instead of spreading rumors? If you want to know the truth, he lost them in the canneries in Alaska. Some of you know how hard that work is. Larry got nothing for losing his fingers! That's why he's been fighting for so long. That's why he joined the unions. AWOC is fighting for more than just wages. AWOC is fighting for our basic rights in the field." He took a swig of Hawaiian Punch and ground his teeth on ice cubes to cool his temper. "Nick is telling everyone that the Filipino community thinks Larry is no good. He and the growers are afraid because Larry and AWOC can change our situation in the fields. Nick's loyalty is with the growers." Fausto grappled with a leathery piece of *lechon* before he tore it in two with his teeth and began chomping on it miserably.

"Larry said the camps were terrible." Macario faced Fausto. "Is it so bad there? I thought Mr. Cuculich was going to rebuild the camps. You know he's not a tyrant."

Marina kept her head down. Fausto wouldn't allow her to visit him at the camp. There was talk of draining the pond near the bathhouse because of mosquitoes, but every summer the mosquitoes multiplied and forced Fausto and the pinoys to hang mosquito nets over their beds, just like in San Esteban. The showers were outside. The outhouses stank, especially in the summer. Mr. Cuculich told Fausto he might consider indoor plumbing when the farms produced bumper crops for a few years in a row, though machinery repairs and upgrades were his main operating concerns. He realized that Mr. Cuculich's constant talk of new bunkhouses and bathrooms was meant to keep those who lived in his camps hopelessly hopeful, distracted from the truth. The grower pointed out that the paycheck deduction of $2.25 a day covered camps, buses, cooks, and mess halls. It consumed nearly 15 percent of their pay, though Mr. Cuculich was quick to argue that the workers could reduce that amount with their per-box bonuses, if they worked hard enough. He said, "Don't look a gift horse in the mouth." Fausto didn't know what it meant, only that he knew not to bring up problems in the camp again. He would leave that for Larry and AWOC.

"The conditions are not ideal." Fausto was mindful of Marina's eyes on him.

Benny gave Fausto a withering look. "Ai, they are bad!"

Macario crushed his paper cup. "I don't like what I hear of the camps. But I don't trust Larry." He threw his napkin on his plate. "Our biggest responsibility is to make sure our children get a good education and profession to take care of us when we're old."

Marina nodded her head.

"Larry approached me after work." Benny turned to Fausto. "He told me he talked to you already. He said you have joined AWOC. Why did you not tell us?"

The men crowded the table, with surprised looks on their faces.

"Too many things going on right now," Fausto said.

"I told Larry I would wait and see what it means to be in this union," Benny said.

"Too much is at stake for me to cause trouble now. When you have children, you think different." Macario addressed Marina, who stared at the leftover food on her plate.

Fausto almost let his guard down. *When you have children, would you not fight even harder to make the future better?* he wanted to ask. It didn't matter if their children never set foot in the fields. Ideal wages and improved working conditions for all the pinoy fathers meant a better future for their sons and daughters. And for the manongs without children? It was a greater sacrifice to fight for everybody else's children. But he kept his mouth shut. When he rose, Marina stood up too. *"Siesta.* Time to get some rest," he said, but he soon regretted his choice of words when some of his cousins snickered behind their paper cups.

"No visiting with out-of-town relatives?" Lito Guzman winked.

"Or maybe just getting old!" Truelino Orpilla sighed, shaking his head full of thick, salt-and-pepper hair.

With Marina standing by his side, Fausto bristled at Truelino's comment more than Lito's. He turned to Macario. "We will see you this evening at the dance, eh?"

"I'll announce a special dance for you and Marina," Macario promised, smiling.

When they got in the car, Marina asked Fausto if the union was a good thing. "Yes," he said, as they drove off. "I did nothing to change conditions in the Delta. We gave the growers all the power. In the fields, we pay five cents for a cup of water, fifty cents for soda. We sneak in our breaks. The union will make us strong to stand up to the growers."

"You never told me about your union activities," she said, her voice accusatory.

"Why should I bore you with such talk about unions and bad work conditions?" He tried to joke, but she scowled at him.

"You know I am going to be picking grapes next summer. I would hope you would tell me everything, especially if it is bad!"

"If the union is successful, then you have nothing to worry about next summer." He imagined putting his hand on her knee to reassure her.

"What will happen if some of your cousins join the union and others oppose it?"

"We disagree and then we don't bother each other with it." He wondered if Benny or Luz told her about the ill feelings that had lasted for years over Cary's death.

When they returned to the house, lingering at the front door, she asked if he wanted to see her dress. "It is almost done," she said in a small voice.

The heat was getting to him. The muscles in his shoulder stiffened up. "I'm going to take siesta at Domingo's place. I'll see you at eight," he answered. When she looked disappointed, he added, "I need to be well rested to dance with you."

She smiled. "I am looking forward to dancing with you."

He couldn't imagine dancing with her in front of everybody. When she lifted her chin, as if expecting a kiss, he said good-bye and left her standing at the front door.

When Fausto woke up, groggy from the heat, Domingo, Macario, and Benny were arguing in Domingo's living room. He threw a pillow over his head. He knew Benny felt the same way he did. Benny had lived in the camps. Macario and Domingo had never set foot in the camps. Fausto didn't want to get up. Union talk exhausted him.

Domingo peeked into the room, already dressed in dark trousers and a white undershirt, which showed through his sheer, embroidered barong shirt. "So," he said, smoothing out creases in the fabric in front of the dresser mirror. "It has been a long courtship. Will you marry Marina soon?"

Fausto fisted the sleep from his eyes. "She has to accept first."

"Hah? You don't need to ask! She has already accepted."

Domingo left the room, laughing. Fausto edged off the bed. He knew Domingo was right. She was waiting for him; he had felt it the moment he had met her. He was being pulled toward her like a magnet, which he accepted and fought, flailing under the weight of everyone's expectations. The mirror loomed before him. In the lamplight, his gray hairs, flecked among the black, glowed like filaments. He could finally marry, have children, own a house, and be happy. Yet, he couldn't shed the image he had of himself—the elder bachelor uncle, one of the last manongs in Terra Bella.

It was light outside at eight o'clock. Gnats and moths spun around in circles beneath the porch light of the gray-brick house. Before he could knock, Marina threw the door open and stepped back, twirling around for him. The white dress she wore was simple, with thick straps and a modest neckline. The top was fitted, but at the waist the fabric flared out. A row of cloth roses, the color of Emperor grapes and the size of his palm, hung from her left shoulder, crossed in front, and attached to her right hip like a banner.

"*Napintas,* very beautiful."

She nodded, plucking at the floppy petals as if to make them bloom more fully.

He came up behind her, smelling flowery perfume on her neck. Her bare shoulder revealed a spray of tiny moles. "Let's go," he said in a hoarse voice that surprised him.

At the Veterans Memorial Building, a long line of people waiting to get in snaked out the door. Loud greetings and tearful reunions erupted in the lobby. The windows of the ballroom were open, and bright light splashed out onto the hedges and front lawn. The band was playing, its music flowing out into the lobby. Elsie Gunabe and Rozelle were exchanging programs for money at the reception table. "You look nice, Marina. Did you make your dress?" Elsie said. Marina nodded, but then a confused look crossed her face. She looked down and examined one of the flowers. Elsie turned to Fausto. "Manong, I cannot remember the last time I saw you dressed up like that! Are you wearing cologne?" She sniffed the air.

Fausto slapped dollar bills on the table as his response.

Marina went ahead of Fausto and stopped at the entrance of the ballroom. The lobby pulsed with laughter. She peeked in as dancers pulled away from one another and clapped when the music ended. She clapped too. The crown of Marina's head looked like the waxy bloom of a black orchid. Fausto leaned forward, as if smelling a flower. Her perfume grew stronger in the warm air. He stepped back, his penis hardening. She reached behind her and groped for his hand. When he touched her wrist, her fingers wrapped around it like ivy to a tree.

The packed ballroom was as humid as a hothouse. Some couples never left the dance floor. A group of teenaged girls huddled next to Fausto and Marina. One of them stared at Marina and whispered to the girl next to her. Soon all five girls were giggling. They scurried into the ballroom and lined up against a wall, still giggling. Fausto glared at them for being disrespectful, making fun of an old man with a younger woman.

Macario, waving a microphone above his head, made his way to the front of the stage. "Special dance for San Esteban Circle members!" His voice boomed from the speakers. He pointed at the Filipino band posing on stage with their instruments. The moment the band started up again, the chairs emptied as people flocked to the dance floor. Fausto touched

Marina's elbow, tracing the taut skin across her bone. She jerked around. He raised his eyebrows as if to ask if she would like to dance. But she backed out into the lobby, against the tide of people pushing forward. He followed her all the way to the bathrooms at the other end of the hallway.

"I look ugly!" she announced, and tugged at the rose that drooped at her waistline.

The bathroom door swung open and out stepped four young women with painted faces and bouffant hairstyles. Their strappy heels clacked against the linoleum floor. One wore a shimmery dress above her knees, revealing her thighs. The other three wore long dresses embellished with spangles in bright colors. They linked arms, their laughter echoing down the hallway. Marina gazed at them with longing.

"*Napintas ka.*" He lifted her skirt, exposing her fabric slip-on shoes.

"I'm not beautiful!" Marina stepped away. "My shoes are like house slippers. I look like I came from a farm." She yanked hard on one of the flowers. It came off in her hand, the petals unraveling until the flower was just a wad of fabric with hanging loose threads.

He laughed, despite her nearness to tears. "Terra Bella *is* a farm!"

"Maybe those girls bought their fancy clothes and shoes in a department store in Bakersfield and had their hair done at a salon." She lifted her stockinged foot out of her shoe as if abandoning it.

"Nobody is rich here. Ai, who cares what they look like?" he said, irritated.

"*I* care!" She shoved her foot back into her shoe. "I care how I look."

"You should not," he said roughly. The hallway was warm and stale. It stifled his penis, which hung limp with their quarreling.

"Everybody dance!" Macario's voice boomed all the way from the ballroom.

"Can you take me home?" she asked.

"We just got here!" He scuffed his dress shoe, leaving a black streak on the floor.

She plugged the tiny hole in her dress with her finger. "I do not want to be seen."

What a shame! She had been so excited when he picked her up. If Elsie's words had hurt her feelings, he would demand an apology. Then he would scold those girls who—he realized now—had made fun of her dress. But it was useless.

He softened his voice. "Everybody will wonder where we went."

"Let them wonder!" She kicked open the back door and stumbled into the parking lot, a sea of cars. In the shadows, she began to cry. "I am sorry. I am trying to belong."

"When I first came to the States, I did not belong. Every new place, I did not belong," he told her. "But now I have my cousins and relatives in Terra Bella. You already have Luz here. And others. Me, if you like."

She dabbed at her eyes with the unraveled cloth rose, but she seemed distracted, unconvinced. She walked deeper into the parking lot, stopping beneath a lamppost. Thunderous clapping erupted inside the building. Macario announced that the band would take a break, and a song from a record player scratched and hissed over the speakers.

"Marina," he whispered, as a cloud of gnats and moths swirled in the flood of light. "When do you want to get married?"

"Soon," she said, both hands clutching the cloth rose.

"After the harvest, when it's not so busy." He was surprised by this plan he had thrown together in a heartbeat and was sharing with her with such calmness, such clarity.

She balled up the fabric between her palms. "I would like to have children."

The parking lot blacktop loomed before him. Benny and Luz had been trying for a few years now. Maybe Benny was too old. Maybe age would be *his* problem too.

"I will work in the packing house this winter, and then pick grapes," she said in a dizzying rush. "When we get married, Uncle Benny said he will give us the house as a wedding present. Auntie Luz wants a bigger house to make room for children."

He searched her face, dazzling under the lamplight, the night sky.

"Uncle Benny wants us to have the house. But we both have to work very hard." Her eyes were focused beyond the darkness around them. Perhaps it was their future, unknowable and yet within reach. "I will have to work right away; we will need money to set up our house, but I would like to start a business as a seamstress." She opened her hands. The swatch of fabric unfurled, no longer a rose. "That was my plan in Vigan. Manang Rozelle was a teacher back home. She tells me she is going to leave the fields and packing house soon to become a teacher here. Can I have such a life too?"

He held her hands. How delicate they were! How many years would pass before she could become a seamstress? Rozelle still had not gotten her teaching credentials. She was too exhausted to even think of studying after long days in the packing house and fields. Domingo could not afford to have her quit so she could go back to school, not even if in the end the temporary hardship meant a more prosperous, easier life! They had to think about their children's needs, Domingo had told Fausto, which was greater than Rozelle's dream for now. But Fausto did not expect Rozelle to admit defeat. It was what got her up early mornings. His dream of being part of Miss Arnold's America had kept him here, had pushed him out of bed before dawn. It had melded the asparagus knife and clippers to his hands for years—despite the buried doubt.

"Yes," he told Marina. "I promise your dream will come true."

Loud voices bellowed at the other end of the parking lot, though as he caressed her cheek they seemed to fade away.

"When I first met you, I knew you would be good to me," she said. "You pretended not to care because you were afraid. But fear cannot hide kindness."

Her reasoning confused him. "I'm just me. Fausto. No more, no less."

"Will you take me home and stay with me until the dance ends and everybody goes home?" She pressed against his chest and groped at his crotch.

His penis throbbed. He could barely speak. "Are you sure?"

"*Okin inam!* Bullshit!" A voice pierced the night, rending them apart. A group of men gathered under the lamppost just outside the back exit. Fausto recognized Macario's angry tone, the word "AWOC." Benny was talking now.

"Bullshit!" Macario interrupted him, his voice thick with too much whiskey.

Marina's hand tightened around Fausto's wrist as she pulled him toward her. "Why are they arguing?"

"Never mind." He tried to sound soothing. "When Macario drinks, he argues. Benny will reason with him." He wrapped his arm around her shoulder so she wouldn't look back. "Let me take you home now. Let me stay with you. Tonight is special, eh?" he said in her ear because Benny's voice had matched the anger in Macario's voice.

"Yes," she whispered, though she tilted her head in the other direction.

Fausto squeezed her shoulder. He was glad the Bel Air was parked away from where his cousins were arguing. He kissed her on the forehead—the first time ever. They were walking in the shadows now, but he imagined he could see the emerald fireworks in her eyes throwing sparks. Soon, he would touch all the tiny moles he imagined were sprinkled across her body, hidden in places that were his alone to find. He would sweep his finger from one mole to the next, as if connecting stars of a constellation.

He threw his head back. A million stars blazed above them. The night air pulsed with the sound of male crickets—maybe hundreds of them rubbing their wings in the open field by the building. The record player had stopped, but the band hadn't returned. For a few moments, all he heard was the chirping of crickets. In this parking lot, his life had just changed, and it would continue to change, for the better. He allowed himself to smile. Yes, he would let Marina see him smile as they passed under the last lamppost in the lot, a cloud of gnats and moths hovering above them like earthbound stardust. He touched her chin. As she gazed into his eyes, he heard Macario's voice, like an insistent, intruding drumbeat, crying out, "Ai, *okin inam!* Bullshit! *Okin inam!*"

CHAPTER 10

Back to Marina

What was Marina like? Fausto turned Rogelio's question over as if it were a berry he was examining to determine its ripeness. Fausto imagined that when, or perhaps if, Benny had told Rogelio the truth, Rogelio must have posed the same question to Benny and Luz—after the shock of it all, of course. What was Marina like? Did Benny have enough time to fill in all the years, the details? Did Luz release any stories from her tight lips? Fausto hoped that they were kind in their judgment of him, so many years later.

Rogelio hesitated. "Mom couldn't remember when you two got married."

Fausto snorted. How could Luz forget? "January 23, 1965—the happiest day of my life," he declared. The words seemed hollow in his small room, but the hungry look on Rogelio's face brought them back to life.

———————

In the days leading up to the wedding, fog roamed the valley like trapped ghosts. Marina worried that everyone would stay home because nothing could be seen ten feet out. When a heavy rainstorm swept in the night before, she said it was a good sign for their future. But Fausto saw things differently. He told Marina that they didn't need to buy more food and drink, convinced that not everyone would show up because the rain had turned the streets into a shallow river. But everyone came, crowding into the house, leaving puddles on the linoleum. Their bodies close together, they kept the air warm and humid, rendering the heater, which had broken down while they were at the church, unnecessary. Guests slowly left, however, once the food was all gone, though the rummy players sat hunched over the card tables into the night, fingering the edges of their empty, oil-soaked paper plates. By morning, hours after everyone had left, the house was chilly, reminding them of a repair that had to wait until the next paycheck. Fausto and Marina hunkered in bed, fused together under a mountain of blankets. Marina spread his fingers across her flat stomach.

"What do you think?" she whispered. "Did we make a boy or a girl?"

Fausto didn't answer. Instead, he tickled her, making her squeal and arch her back. How long could he keep her laughing? In truth, he was nervous about such talk. Benny told him at their party that he and Luz had begun talking about adoption. Nobody knew just yet because Luz wanted to try another year before giving in.

"I picked names for a girl," Marina said. When he laughed, she sat up, exposing her shoulders and small breasts. "Make fun of me. I don't care!" Shivering, she pulled the blankets to her chin.

"What names have you already picked out for our little girl, then?"

"Ilocano names, so they never forget who they are. Ballailaw, Bituen, and Ulep."

Fausto thought of Arturo Junior. "Her classmates will make fun of her name."

"But I like what they mean: rainbow, star, cloud," Marina said softly. She looked to the window, beaded with condensation, turning the steely sky into a watercolor.

"What about Pamulinawen? It means our girl will be solid as a rock. And then everyone can call her Pam or Lina."

"My favorite is Lulukisen," she said. "Orange—warm like the sun. They will call her Lulu at school." He didn't mind the name—though he was partial to Pamulinawen—but he warned that once she started work in the packing house, she would come home and their daughter's name would remind her of the fruit that tumbled down the chute and smashed into her hands ten hours a day. "I'll not pack oranges the rest of my life!" she declared. "I'll sew fancy outfits, with Lina in a bassinet and Lulu in a playpen next to the sewing machine."

Fausto grinned at the largeness of her dreams, the image of her huddled over a sewing machine. Lulu's pudgy fingers poked through the playpen netting, trying to reach the red tracing wheel that looked like a rattle on the floor. She pulled herself up, grunting for attention. Marina slipped a pacifier between Lulu's lips. "Shhh," she said, and pointed to a white-wicker bassinet on the floor on the other side of the sewing machine. Lina, bundled up in a pink gown trimmed with lace that Marina had sewn, gurgled, lulled to sleep by the whir of the machine. But those scenes required so many things: his ability to make her pregnant, money saved to buy a new sewing machine and start her business, customers. The challenges made his vision fade, his penis shrivel.

Marina threw back the blankets and hopped out of bed. She laughed all the way down the hallway to the bathroom and turned on the shower. He imagined hot water cascading down her body, erasing her goose flesh. She was waiting for him in the steamy room. But he sat in the middle of the bed, numb in the chilly air.

They didn't make a baby their wedding night. Marina was disappointed, but she told Fausto much had to be done before she could welcome a baby into their lives. Benny and Luz had moved into their new house months before the wedding but still faced paperwork to transfer ownership. Fausto was glad Marina felt that way, glad she was taking extra shifts at the packing house. It meant getting closer to realizing the part of their dreams they could control. She said she didn't mind the work, though she asked him to rub Tiger Balm into the joints of her hands at night. Her fingers were stained by the bright-blue dye used to stamp "Sunkist" on the citrus fruit. Constant scrubbing only made the ink fade to chambray.

———————

When the gray-brick house was officially theirs, Luz left a plastic bouquet that resembled Marina's wedding flowers as a small housewarming present. Marina created a repair list for Fausto. The septic tank needed to be replaced with a sewer line. She wanted to tear down the flimsy carport Benny had built to make room for a two-car garage. Fausto refinanced the mortgage to pull out money, and they spent evenings at the kitchen table drawing up plans to push out the laundry and washroom and convert it into another bedroom. Of course, she told him, their grown children will insist that their parents live on the property and build a small house in back, though Fausto maintained that the vegetable garden must remain untouched.

When Benny and Luz lived in the house, Benny let the garden go— he was too busy making extra money in the fields—and then Luz paid someone to plow it under, trellis and all. Fausto was determined to bring back the garden. He and Marina began planting a few months after they were married, when the rains softened the frost-encrusted soil. He remembered which vegetables and fruits were planted in which part of the garden grid. When she told him she preferred honeydew over cantaloupe, no other melons made it back into the melon patch. They slogged in the mud in rubber boots. As she stooped over the earth, covering up seeds with her muddy fingers, he thought of his father's rice fields and a dull ache formed in his chest.

Do you want to go to San Esteban and Vigan?" he asked her, when they rinsed mud from their hands in the washroom.

She swiped a towel across his cheek. "*Apay?* Why go back?"

"To meet our families."

"Our families are here now, and once we have our *own* family, there is no need for me to be reminded of what I left behind," she said. Her face clouded over for a moment. "This is my home now. You have been here for more than thirty-five years, more years here than in San Esteban. Is America not your home now too?"

"Home is where you and all my cousins are," he answered.

She wrapped the towel around his neck and drew him close. "Then we are home."

Marina began planning for the next San Esteban Dance. She was married and a member of the Circle now. Nobody was going to make fun of her. In early spring, Fausto drove Marina to Porterville to look at dress patterns and sewing machines at Montgomery Ward. When he threatened not to go to the dance, embarrassed by his two left feet, she borrowed records from Luz so they could practice, sometimes in the dark. One evening, he undid the top buttons of her housecoat. She pinched his behind, ordering him to keep practicing so they could show off how well they danced together.

"*Awan aniaman na dayta?*" He unbuttoned her housecoat to her navel.

"It matters that everyone sees how far I have come."

"You care too much what others think." He pulled her down to the sofa.

"You are afraid to dance in front of everyone." Her voice grew husky as he pried her thighs apart with his knee. Her legs gave way like earth in a landslide.

In the morning, he found her curled up on the sofa, the curtains open. The moon hung like a pearl, the sky an oyster's mantle in soft, mottled shades of pink and blue.

"This is a good sign, is it not?" she whispered, her face glowing, bathed in tears.

The August heat seemed to smother the air, making it hard for Fausto to breathe, making him believe he was still in the vineyards with the dust swirling all around him. But he was back in the Village. Fausto paced his room, his muscles tightening. He stopped in the middle as if there were no other place to go. "Marina and I never went to another San Esteban Dance," he said to Rogelio, who was refilling their glasses with ice water. "When the grape season started in the spring of 1965, everything changed." He sat down again, but found no release, even after draining the glass Rogelio had offered him. "By summertime, our concerns had changed."

Every season, the harvest began in Coachella Valley, the southern end of California, and worked its way up the Central Valley, with grape picking in Delano peaking in late summer and early fall. But in 1965, a firestorm erupted in Coachella and spread to the Valley as spring turned to summer. The US Department of Labor's braceros program, which allowed guest workers from Mexico to work in agriculture, had expired. The growers fought to restore it, arguing that they were shorthanded for the harvest. The federal government gave in—just for the season. When the Filipino grape pickers took to the fields in Coachella Valley that spring, they discovered that the growers were paying the braceros $1.40 cents per hour, while their base pay was $1.10 to $1.20 per hour. By law, domestic workers could not be paid less than the braceros. Most of the Filipino workers, including Fausto and Benny, were AWOC members. The workers in Coachella immediately went on strike. Ten days later, with the grapes ripe on the vine, the growers gave in and paid all workers the same rate.

Weeks later, the same scenario played out in the Central Valley. The Delano growers set the domestic workers' rate lower than the braceros' rate, angering local and migrant workers alike. The pinoys called several meetings in the late summer evenings. Soon, Fausto was missing meals, as well as the dance lessons that he had come to enjoy after dinner. Marina was so angry with him that she didn't want to hear what they had discussed in the meetings. When he came home late, she was already in bed. But he knew she couldn't ignore him forever.

"Going out again?" she said at dinnertime, when he looked at his watch and got up, leaving his plate of pansit half-eaten on the kitchen table. She trailed after him to the front door.

"This is important," he said, and dared to offer his cheek to her.

She kissed him without enthusiasm. "What could be more important than spending time with your wife, time spent making babies?"

He held open the screen door, with one foot on the welcome mat, the other still in the living room. "There is talk of a strike to try to settle the matter, to get our wages up."

"Well then, strike!" She pushed her way through so that they both stood outside.

"It's not so easy," he said, though he was pleased with her response.

"Why not?" she persisted.

Fausto explained that the pinoy farm workers had asked Larry Itliong to get involved, so he sent registered letters to the growers to meet with them, but none showed up. Talk of a strike circulated, but nobody was willing to walk out when Larry took a vote. He got mad and told everybody to go home, which stunned the pinoys but made them think hard about what they wanted to do. The next day they went back to Larry, united and determined. He tried to organize another meeting with the growers at the Filipino Hall, but again they ignored him.

"Now we are going to vote whether to strike or not," Fausto told Marina. "It will not be easy. The growers in Delano are tougher than the growers in Coachella."

"So strike for twelve days instead of ten," she said, her voice impatient. "After the strike, you are back home in the evenings again."

"So you would be for this strike if it happens?" he prodded her.

"We cannot afford to lose twelve days of wages between the two of us," she said.

His heart sank as her gaze traveled to Luz's old sewing machine, whose treadle had been sticking for some time now. He hadn't taken it to a repair shop because of other, more immediate, expenses. He had bought a second car, a used but newer model Ford Falcon. Though she was sharing rides to the packing house with the pinays in the neighborhood, he wanted to buy her something grand and showy. He worried about setting them back moneywise, but she cried when he handed her the keys and declared that sky-blue was her new favorite color. Then last month, Marina bought a Philco television set on store credit without his permission. The twelve-inch set was on sale for ninety-nine dollars at Sears. He scolded her for making a big purchase without asking him and made her promise to return it, but he changed his mind when he plugged in the set and sharp images of two boxers in a ring appeared on the screen and crisp sounds of cheering crowds boomed from the speakers.

Marina twisted her lips, lost in thought. "If the workers in Coachella got more money after ten days, then we can make up for it. It will take time, but we can sacrifice ten days of pay for now," she said, though the uncertainty in her voice betrayed her words.

She walked him to the car, linking arms with him. His whole body twitched with restlessness. When he started the car, she leaned in and kissed him hard on the lips, as if to remind him what was waiting for him at home. But Fausto was already gone before he pulled out of the driveway. He recalled Larry Itliong's words to him and his fellow pinoys the first time they approached him to strike: "If you go out, you're going to go hungry, lose your car, lose your house, maybe lose your wife." The married pinoys got scared. When Larry took the first vote, they shoved their hands under their thighs and averted their eyes like spooked dogs with tails between their legs. The second vote would come before Labor Day. Fausto wiped sweat from his palms onto his trousers. He gripped the steering wheel, feeling as if he were being hurtled forward on the dusky stretch of road to Delano, with no way back.

———————

"Let's go outside, eh?" Fausto said to Rogelio. "I will show you what I have called home for so many years."

Rogelio slipped on his sunglasses. As Fausto shut the door, a strange sensation overcame him. It wasn't the tingly urge to pee, which he ignored because no matter how many times he went to the bathroom nothing came out. He was going to leave Agbayani Village with Rogelio very soon—he felt it in his bones. While Rogelio would see the grounds for the first time, Fausto would be saying good-bye. In the afternoon, after they had seen the entire village, Rogelio would take him to the gray-brick house. Fausto didn't care who was living in it now. There was something there that would make the house, the land meaningful to Rogelio.

Rogelio offered his arm to Fausto. "Marina wanted to be a good wife to you. I'm happy to hear it through you. You deserve that kind of love."

Fausto could only see the reflection of his astonished face in Rogelio's mirrored sunglasses. He hung his head. The sun beat down on his neck. "I didn't deserve her," he said. "She should not have trusted me."

"She trusted you because she loved you," Rogelio declared. "You gave her a new life here. You loved her too. I hear it in your voice. Nothing is lost. *Nothing!*" He took a deep breath. "Marina was a loyal, loving wife.

She was a good mother. You have to know that. I know you know that."

Fausto leaned into Rogelio, wishing he could sit down. His legs felt as if they were giving out on him, as if a temblor deep in the earth were rocking him. Everything about him quickened—his breath, his heartbeat, his blinking back tears that threatened to surface. He wanted to know, and yet he wasn't ready to ask where she was, how she was, what she had done with her life all these years. Maybe his next journey—their journey—would be to the Philippines, back to Marina.

They stopped at the edge of the blank field. Fausto turned to Rogelio. "You have something to tell me, eh?" he dared to ask.

Rogelio stood still for a few moments. Then he smiled, even with his sunglasses looming like an unscalable wall. "Stories are never told from the beginning," he said, looking out at the vast land before him, the vineyards, the open field, the union buildings, the village. He took Fausto's hand. "You have a part of the story and I have another part. At some point they come together. But not yet—it's still your turn. *Take me back with you.*"

CHAPTER 11

Empty fields, empty house

Delano, California, September 1965–May 1966

"Friends, come out of the fields! Join us in our struggle! We must all be together to succeed!" Fausto shouted from across the road. When the workers didn't respond, he cupped his hands to his chapped lips and repeated in Ilocano, *"Gagayem, rumuar kayo amin! Masapul nga agtitit nulong tayo! Tapno magun-od tayo ti karang-ayan!"*

Benny grabbed Fausto's arm and squeezed it. Fausto imagined that his own face mirrored the mix of surprise and giddiness on his cousin's face as they watched their fellow pinoys slowly stream out of the fields. It was mid-afternoon. At full strength, the sun was scorching the earth. At exactly noon, the farm workers supporting the strike had dropped their clippers and walked out of the vineyards. But there were tens of thousands more still in the fields. When their countrymen crossed the road, Fausto and Benny threw their arms around them, congratulating them for their bravery, but the look in their eyes told them they were not yet convinced they were doing the right thing. None lived in the Cuculich camp or had attended any union meetings. Fausto recognized a handful as regulars at the pool halls and barbershops in Delano; they were local workers, some with families—not the migrant pinoys who had struck down south.

"You heard about the strike in Coachella, eh?" Fausto asked the group of men. "Our countrymen struck for ten days in the spring and the growers gave in. Some of these pinoys have come to Delano expecting the same wages. But the growers here are only paying a $1.10. Is that fair to any of us?"

All eyes were on Fausto as they shook their heads.

"We must fight back!" Benny answered. "We must strike for what is fair."

"But what if the growers doan give in?" asked an elderly pinoy with milky eyes. "I seen what happen in the lettuce fields when nobody backs down."

"The pinoys who struck down south don't live here like we do, and they have no families like we do," another one said. "Delano is our home. We don't want our town mad at us and our families."

"I have a wife and four kids," a man in the back called out. With his gray hair, he looked to be the same age as Fausto and Benny. "We cannot feed on uncertainty."

"Can you guarantee us the strike will end soon?" a stubbly-faced pinoy demanded.

"We make sacrifices now to secure our future, manongs." Fausto hoped that by using the term of respect, "manong," to mean "brother," they would be more comfortable around him. "All we are asking for is decent wages and a union contract. If we can get all our brothers out of the fields—maybe 1,000 today, 2,000 tomorrow—then we have power. The strike cannot survive more than ten days. The growers cannot afford to lose their whole crop." As the men looked at the vines thick with leaves and the ripe berries pulling down the branches, Fausto said, "Two years ago, these growers paid more than any other place in California. This year they are paying less. Do you have such short memories? They are paying less because they can, manongs. Ai, think with your heads!"

"We want the growers to sign contracts to guarantee us fair wages," Benny said, when the men stared at Fausto in silence. "We are asking for a $1.40 an hour and twenty-five cents a box. This is what you all deserve, manongs. Please listen to us."

"Then what do we do now?"

"Where do we go?"

"My boss, Mr. Radic, will kick me out of camp," the milky-eyed pinoy said.

"Manong, how many years do you have left in the fields?" Fausto asked in a gentle voice. When the old man shrugged his shoulders, he went on, "I heard Radic kicks out old pinoys when they can no longer work. He tells them his bunkhouses are not retirement homes or hospitals. He's not keeping you in his bunkhouse out of charity! He has been overcharging you for years, making money off of you! Will it matter if he's angry with you?" He couldn't help but laugh. "Manong, Radic has deducted ten cents every hour you worked in his fields for how many decades now? You own that camp!"

The old man began to weep in his hands, the dirt on his fingers turning muddy. Fausto pulled out his handkerchief to wipe the old man's eyes.

"I don't live in Radic's camp," the man with the family spoke up, "and I got years of work ahead of me, but I cannot afford to have Radic mad at me. I cannot afford to have *any* grower mad at me!"

Fausto told them thirty farms were being picketed. "Go find work with the growers who are not on the list," he said. "When the strike ends, then you can go back to Radic."

So far, he and Benny had avoided scouting and picketing the Cuculich farm. As owner of one of the largest farms, Mr. Cuculich employed hundreds of workers. If all of them left, Larry Itliong told Fausto, the strike would end sooner. Fausto argued that Mr. Cuculich was not like John Depolo, who had a reputation for having the highest number of workers suffer from heat exhaustion and heat stroke. But to Larry, all the growers were the same. Larry advised Fausto and the rest of the pinoy AWOC members to picket the farms of other growers to avoid being punished by their long-time bosses once the strike ended.

The idle workers shifted their feet, hands deep in the pockets of their jeans, waiting for Fausto to speak. "With your help, the strike will end soon," he assured them.

"Go! Go now!" Benny said, and waved his arms to shoo them away.

They herded them toward the small lot of cars by the shoulder of the road and stood there until everyone piled into their cars and the caravan drove away.

"Can it be this easy?" Benny said to Fausto, as the last of the red taillights disappeared around the corner of the road.

"Ai, nothing worth fighting for is easy. This will be a long journey," Fausto said.

Down the road small bands of picketing AWOC members—all pinoys, including Prudencio, Ayong, and Fidel—hung around Frank Radic's property, but Fausto wanted to return to the Filipino Hall, AWOC's headquarters. Within an hour of the strike commencing, Fausto heard that the hall was filled with veterans—elderly pinoys who had weathered strikes in the lettuce and asparagus fields since the 1920s—and farm workers, many with families, who had never engaged in strikes or other union activity. The newcomers were eager to help, but they needed to be educated. Even Fausto didn't know what to do beyond picketing farms and getting his countrymen and strikebreakers out of the fields.

"Maybe later we'll picket the packing sheds and the cold-storage plants along Glenwood Street," Benny said.

As they walked to the Bel Air, a pickup truck veered onto the shoulder of the road and shuddered to a halt inches from Fausto, who stood on shaky legs. He recognized the man with sideburns who hopped out of the cab as Frank Radic's only son, Clifford. Benny stepped back as the man raised a shotgun above his head, but Fausto didn't move.

"Get off my land!" Clifford said, waving the shotgun.

Fausto pointed to the vineyards across the street. "We are not on your land."

"Don't act like you know more than me!" Clifford said.

"All we are asking for is a decent wage," Benny managed to say.

"You ought to be working like every red-blooded American in this country!" Clifford swallowed hard, his Adam's apple bobbing up and down his skinny neck. "My great grandpa was a sharecropper, but he built this business from the ground up by himself. Now you're trying to cheat our family without working hard yourself!"

"The government gives growers water for free, and these farms live off the sweat of the braceros, Chicanos, Filipinos, blacks, Puerto Ricans, and Arabs." Fausto spoke in a loud voice to drown out his thrashing heartbeat. "This is how these farms grew."

Clifford worked his mouth open as if he hadn't expected an old Filipino farm worker to know anything beyond picking grapes and pruning vines. "You don't know what you're talking about!" He straightened his arm, muzzle pointing skyward, and pulled the trigger.

Fausto shook his head to stop his ears from ringing. Benny grabbed his arm and their eyes met, but Fausto brushed off Benny's hand and the fear in his cousin's face. As picketers rushed toward them, Clifford jumped into the driver's seat. He revved up the engine and spun the pickup truck around, spitting out dirt beneath the fat tires before rocketing onto the blacktop and down the road.

"Are you okay?"

Fausto recognized Ayong's voice and his friend's knotty fingers on his shoulder. He nodded, though his numbed neck felt as if the Radic boy had aimed for his throat.

"This is not good," Benny whispered.

"I'm going to cut off that sonavabeech's balls off with a *buneng!*" Prudencio sliced the cold air with his straw hat, as other pinoys gathered around Fausto.

Fausto raised his hands. "They're angry because they're scared. If enough workers leave, they will lose the whole harvest. They will not risk such a loss."

"But even if they raise our wages, they will still be angry and harm us somehow," Benny said in a quiet voice. "I'm afraid."

Fausto gave Benny a withering look. "Ai, if you are afraid, then don't show it."

"Listen to Fausto," Fidel said, leaning in.

"Listen to us all!" Prudencio clapped Benny on the back. "They can break us if we are weak and scared. So be strong, manong. Let us all be strong."

The pinoys, grim faced and silent, raised their fists above their heads as they retreated to their cars. Prudencio and Ayong were going back to the Cuculich camp to check up on their bunkmates who had refused to leave camp for work. As Fausto and Benny left, they passed rows and rows of berries hung low on the vines. Like Mr. Cuculich, Frank Radic would not let his grapes be picked until they were sweet. Let them drop to the earth, Fausto entreated. Let them drop until the growers give in. Let the flies be more plentiful in the fields than the rotting grapes and the vanishing workers.

The day the workers left the fields, the growers, including Mr. Cuculich, locked out the striking tenants from their camps before dinner, just as they were returning from the picket lines. Those who stayed to stage sit-ins found the water and gas shut off and the kitchen closed. Armed guards nailed shut the doors of the bunkhouses so the men could not retrieve their belongings. The evicted tenants fled to the Filipino Hall and told stories of guards dumping the contents of their suitcases by the road. Severo Laigo, one of Fausto and Benny's old bunkhouse mates, said that Mr. Cuculich had stomped and yelled: "If you want to abuse my hospitality and the privileges I gave to you, then get the hell off my property! The goddamned welcome sign is no longer up. I'll let my grapes rot first before I bargain with the devil!" Severo left before Mr. Cuculich finished. Along the roadside, he saw bands of his countrymen hunched next to campfires cooking their dinners. He kept his head down as the police stopped their patrol cars and kicked over pots, spilling chicken adobo and rice and links of *longanisa* onto the ground.

When news of the evictions reached Fausto and Benny, they drove to the Cuculich farm in search of Prudencio and Ayong. Pieces of clothing were strewn across the shoulders of the roads. A torn shirt and pair of pants, missing one leg, dangled from the grapevines like parts of a scarecrow that had been ripped apart and scattered by a fierce dust storm. Beside a row of young vines, a big plastic doll had been uprooted from its stake. Ayong had given the discarded doll new life as a scarecrow to keep the birds from eating the tender grape leaves. Now it lay on its back, string trailing from stiff arms and legs that stuck out at all angles, its butcher-paper dress ripped, its curls sprinkled with dirt. Farther down the road, cooking pots littered the ground, some crushed like paper plates by car tires. Flies swarmed the feral dogs that ate the spoiled food, while crows cawed from their perch on telephone lines.

Fausto drove by the entrance of the Cuculich camp while it was still dusky. There were no burly, hired guards waving pistols. He wanted to stop, but Benny locked his hand on the steering wheel and told him to return to the Hall. Prudencio and Ayong wouldn't be on the grounds. There was no reason to invite trouble. As Fausto turned a corner, he saw something hunched in the middle of the road. He flipped on his headlights and the shadowy mound rose up before them.

"Manong Flor!" Fausto cried out, as a small man threw his arms across his face. Fausto pulled over, and he and Benny rushed to the camp cook.

"Manong Flor, where are your glasses?" Fausto touched the crosshatch of cuts on the camp cook's nose and cheeks.

"I loss them." He tossed his head from side to side, squinting at the blacktop. "Twenny-nine years I been living in Mr. Cuculich's camp. Now I got no place to go!"

Fausto pulled Manong Flor up and hugged him tight. He smelled fried fish in the cook's thinning hair. When he touched the old man's cheek, his skin was as greasy as the meals he prepared. Even his clothes were tacky with grease. They drove back to town, with Manong Flor laughing then sobbing, huddled in the corner of the backseat.

"Listen, Manong Flor," Fausto said, as they pulled into the Filipino Hall's parking lot. "I heard AWOC needs a good cook to feed all the strikers. I'll talk to Larry Itliong, AWOC's organizer. We'll put in a good word for you."

Manong Flor peered out the car window, at the pinoys who were smoking and pacing across the front entrance. "You tell Larry I make the best pansit in the whole town." Fausto and Benny helped Manong Flor out of the car. The cook grinned at them. "You like my cooking? Sometimes I think you two doan like."

"You're the best, Manong," Fausto declared. "Your cooking is better than my wife's." He paused. "My wife," he repeated, liking the way it sounded out loud.

Manong Flor threw a light punch into Fausto's gut. "Aiee, doan tell your pretty wife that! You bring her to the hall. I teach her how to cook." He limped ahead of them.

When they entered the main hall, they found Prudencio and Ayong sitting at a table, drinking coffee. Fausto slapped them on their backs, happy to see them. Ayong stifled a yawn and proclaimed that he was so tired he could fall asleep sitting up in his chair. Prudencio said they would sleep in the hall, though the place was crowded with pinoys stuffing rice and adobo into their mouths. Fausto kicked their work boots out from under the table and ordered Ayong to go home with Benny and Prudencio to come home with him.

Prudencio spit tobacco into his coffee cup. "We don't want to cause trouble."

Fausto yanked on Prudencio's collar. "Marina would not want you to stay here."

"Luz would feel the same," Benny said, though his voice was unconvincing.

Prudencio and Ayong laced up their work boots. As soon as the strike ended, Prudencio kept saying, they would move back to the camp. Until then, he and Ayong offered free labor to make up for their trouble, but Fausto and Benny waved them off. Fausto went to look for Manong Flor to see if he needed a place to stay, but the old cook had made friends with another elderly pinoy who was cleaning up in the kitchen. Manong Magno was from Pinipin, near Manong Flor's hometown of San Jose. Both men, shrunken to the same height, gray haired, and with limbs as dark and brittle as charred sticks, removed their aprons. Fausto couldn't imagine Manong Magno lugging crates, though he knew many pinoys in their late sixties who still picked grapes.

"He lives in town. I doan even ask, and he tell me to stay with him and his nephews," Manong Flor said. He grasped Fausto's arm and shook it. "If you doan find me, I would still be in the fields. Now I got a job in the kitchen and a place to stay."

"You should thank Manong Magno for his generosity," Fausto said.

Manong Magno snorted. "Generosity? It is our duty to help our brothers." He hung their damp aprons on a rack to dry. "We will come early to make breakfast for the boys."

The two manongs left the kitchen, stooped shoulders bumping into one another.

It was late when Fausto and Prudencio tiptoed into the gray-brick house. Fausto put a blanket and pillow on the sofa for Prudencio. There was no space in the second bedroom, which Marina had turned into her sewing room. Patterns, yards of fabric, and a half-cut blouse took up the middle of the room, though the broken sewing machine was collecting dust. Marina didn't stir when Fausto climbed into bed. He lay on his back, unable to sleep.

When Fausto woke up, Marina's side of the bed was empty. She had made coffee for Prudencio, who was wearing one of Fausto's shirts. She was holding a carton of eggs, asking him how he liked his cooked. Fausto flew into the kitchen and twirled Marina around, until she scolded him that the eggs would get broken the way he was carrying on with his silly behavior.

"*Diyos iti agngina,*" he whispered into her ear.

"Why are you thanking me?" She pecked him on the check, then turned to wink at Prudencio. "You are home."

A week later, Ayong showed up at Fausto's door. Benny told Luz that Ayong would be at their house for a week and then he would move in with Fausto—an arrangement that was news to Fausto. Benny explained to Ayong that the strike was giving Luz headaches and she couldn't cook for another person.

"I will be gone the moment the growers give in," Ayong declared, as Fausto threw his arm around him and brought him inside. When Ayong saw Marina at the kitchen entrance, he added, "Marina, you let me know when you have grown tired of us, okay?"

Marina nodded, forcing a smile. "Manong Ayong, as long as I can feed you, you and Manong Prudencio are welcome in our house."

Fausto knew the refrigerator and cupboards would soon be empty. He was going to talk with her before bedtime, but she was distant that evening and he soon lost the courage to approach her. After a day of picketing, he and Prudencio and Ayong brought home rice and ground beef donated by churches, civic groups, other unions, and businesses like the bakery from Los Angeles that provided day-old bread. When

Marina said she didn't like taking charity, Fausto told her she didn't have to eat the food. By the end of the second week, they hardly talked. The first few days of the strike, she asked questions when he returned from the Filipino Hall: Would they agree to both the hourly wage and the per-box bonus? Would they sign the union contracts? She had even gone to the picket line for the first time to bring Fausto his lunch. When she heard gunshots, she feared for Fausto's well-being. But ever since Ayong came to live with them, she went deaf and mute, turning away when Fausto tried to tell her the latest news.

In the evenings, he tended the garden, coaxing the plants to produce more *tarong, kamatis,* and *parya.* He thought about planting broccoli, cauliflower, and winter squash instead of letting the garden go dormant after the fall. As he scrubbed vegetables in the washroom sink, Marina retrieved laundry from the clothesline. Though Prudencio and Ayong protested, she insisted on washing their clothes, tossing stiff undershirts and boxers from the line in the basket without a glance. She carried the basket, overflowing with white clothes that glowed in the dusk, into the house.

"Let me help you," Fausto said, but she brushed past him.

She refused Ayong and Prudencio's help. "You are the ones working hard on the picket lines," she said in a cheerful voice, though Fausto knew her words rang false.

She excused herself from their game of rummy and retreated to her bedroom. Fausto joined them for a few rounds of rummy before retiring for the night. He made his way to his side of the bed in the dark and tried not to rustle the sheets.

"I'm scared," Marina called out in a plaintive voice.

"*Ania?* What are you scared of?" His voice was gruffer than he meant it to be.

"Two weeks have passed and nothing has happened."

"How would you know? You never ask when I come home." He kept his back to her. The last few nights, when he knew she was still awake, she had hugged the edge of the bed. Now there was a paper-thinness between them, but he had no desire to touch her.

"More workers are coming out of the fields—not just pinoys," he said. "The Teamsters Union vowed not to cross our picket line, so nobody is loading the grapes or driving the trucks. Even if strikebreakers are picking grapes, they are rotting in lugs!" Fausto's voice grew lively as if he were in the Filipino Hall. "César Chávez and his National Farm Workers Association voted to join our cause. The more people we have, the better our chance to break the growers' backs."

Fausto ran into Chávez after the labor leader addressed the strikers in the Filipino Hall, where people spilled into the parking lot. Fausto squeezed his way in and got caught as the farm workers surged out, spreading the news that the National Farm Workers Association would support AWOC's strike. Fausto turned and bumped into Chávez hard. He didn't realize how short Chávez was—the same height as he—nor how dark his skin and hair were up close. He wore a plaid shirt. His hair was parted on the far left side in a straight line and combed across like a thick tongue. When Chávez met his gaze, Fausto understood that his face had been burnished by the same sun, in the same dusty fields.

"I'm César Chávez," he said, extending his hand. "How are you doing, brother?"

Chávez's hand was small, his fingers short, his voice soft and musical.

"I'm good," Fausto said, surprised.

"We support you, brother." Chávez smiled, exposing the gap between his two front teeth, and he patted Fausto's back. "If we suffer, we all suffer together."

In the darkness, Fausto turned to Marina. "We all suffer together," he echoed.

"*Apay ngay?*" She sighed into her pillow. "Why must we suffer?"

"I have been a member of AWOC since before we got married. You know that. You supported me then. Why are you changing your mind now?"

He turned on the lamp on the nightstand. They blinked at each other in the light. She shrank to the edge of the bed, her shadow on the wall hunched over.

"*Apay ngay?*" Because everything is falling apart." She drew her legs up.

He resisted the urge to touch her toes, sticking out from beneath the hem of her nightgown. "Have you forgotten that our wages were cut this season? Or your shame when the foreman watched you pee? Have you forgotten the long hours without breaks?"

"*Saan,* but—" Her mouth sagged. In the yellow glow, she looked years older. Maybe he looked even older to her. "I cannot wait until the citrus season begins. I need to find work." She searched the room, its darkened corners. "Maybe we can work for another grower. That is what you tell all those workers you lead out of the fields."

"You go work for another grower," he said. "I already have a job. So many pinoys have left town to find other work. AWOC needs people on the picket lines."

"The ones who left are smart. We need food. The car payment is due next week. The mortgage is due at the end of the month. We still owe Sears fifty dollars."

He hadn't forgotten about the bills. When he turned off the television set and watched the glowing blue dot in the middle of the screen grow dim until it disappeared, he wished he hadn't been lured by its crisp images. With their savings account drained, he had no idea how they would pay their bills.

"*Bumbye*, we will eat bananas—two pounds for a quarter—and potatoes—fifty-nine cents for a ten-pound bag—because that is all we can afford," she said.

"Ai, we will not starve! It will not get that bad, Marina!"

"But Fausto, everybody—the townspeople, the newspapers, the growers—is against the strike. The union is alone. Even the San Esteban Circle has not endorsed it."

"They have not condemned it!" He sank his head back onto his pillow.

"Same thing!" She shifted her position, pressing close. "Nida tells me their house is going to be picketed because Macario is a foreman. Why should he be punished because he has chosen to keep working to take care of his family? He has done nothing to deserve the union's anger. And yet, AWOC is calling him a strikebreaker!"

The union had ordered picketing in front of strikebreakers' homes. Large signs proclaiming, "A scab lives here!" were staked on their lawns. Some defied Chávez's call for nonviolence and threw rocks at their windows. A few picketers even threatened to burn down their houses. Now there was talk of targeting foremen and contractors because, as long-time bosses, they held considerable influence over many of the pinoys. Before the season began, Mr. Cuculich promoted Macario. It meant a bigger paycheck and greater standing. But now it meant trouble. Fausto and Benny were afraid Macario would lash out at anyone who came near his house. They were afraid for Nida, who was expecting again, and their five boys. They tried to persuade the strikers that it was only the growers who deserved their anger. Fausto told Larry that they could sway Macario to support the strike and draw pinoys who were loyal to him to AWOC's side.

"Larry and I are going to talk to Macario in the morning," Fausto told Marina.

She retreated to her side of the bed again, her long, dark hair flowing away from him. "Nida said Macario will not change his mind. You know that."

"I have faith in my fellow brothers. We must work together or lose everything."

"You *will* lose everything!" She curled up in a ball.

He would have massaged her shoulder until the hardness melted away, kissed her on the mouth until she opened up, and promised again that they would have a baby. Instead, he turned out the light. He thought he heard her weeping, but he didn't go to her. He gave her his back, as rigid as Mr. Cuculich's vow to let his grapes rot before giving in.

Macario agreed to meet with Larry. As he and Larry stood on Macario's porch, Fausto kept wiping perspiration from his forehead. Before knocking, he asked Larry not to light a cigar in the house, even though Macario smoked cigarettes. Fausto was thinking of Nida and the boys. Still, Larry's corduroy pants and jacket gave off a musty odor that burned Fausto's nose when he stood next to him. When Macario opened the door, Fausto took a deep breath and said, "Macario, this is Larry Itliong."

Macario shook Larry's hand. Without saying a word, he led them past the living room, its floor littered with plastic trucks and an army of miniature soldiers, to the dining room table, where he offered them a platter of rice cakes cut into diamond shapes.

Fausto took the piece of sticky yellow cake from Macario to keep his hands busy.

Larry bit into his piece. "You're lucky to have a good cook!"

"All this is not luck." Macario watched Larry eat. He rested his arms, sun-burnt up to his biceps, on the table. "Listen, I'm not opposed to AWOC or unions."

"Then you'll support the strike?" Larry smiled, exposing brown-stained teeth.

"I will join," Macario began slowly, "if the union pays my mortgage and car payments and utilities, if you can feed my wife and children and put clothes on my children's backs so they can go to school."

Larry scratched his bristly crew cut with his stumpy right hand. "You know the union has no money to take care of all the strikers."

"Then I cannot afford to support you." Macario leaned back in his chair.

"Will you still recruit workers?" Fausto asked faintly.

"Yes." Macario reached for a piece of cake.

"Many of the strikebreakers told us they didn't even know a strike was going on," Larry said. "When the rest of them find out, they'll leave."

"The harvest will be over by then," Macario said, chewing with his mouth open. "But it does not matter. How many of them can afford to strike? They have families. They buy gasoline to drive their cars. They go home to houses they rent or pay mortgage on. Many come from far away, with obligations to their families back home and in the Philippines. They have sacrificed enough. You're asking too much of them." He scooted his chair back off the plush area rug and onto the polished hardwood floor. "I'll not ask that much of them. I'm here if they need a job," he said, and strode across the room to the front door. The muscles on his arm tensed as he held onto the knob.

Larry puffed out his chest as he followed Macario. "The unions are trying to make these jobs good jobs. Shouldn't that be everyone's goal?"

Macario spread out his arms. "I have a good job because I work hard and I was rewarded. Can you not see that in my home?"

Larry looked over Macario's shoulder, at the expansive living room. "You have done well, but not everyone can be a foreman. Somebody has to pick the grapes. Why not treat them with dignity?" He smiled. There was no trace of defeat in his weathered face as he extended his hand. "Let's keep talking."

Macario shrugged. He shook Larry's outstretched hand, though he eyed him warily.

As he left Macario's house, Larry reached for a cigar in his chest pocket and lit it before getting into his dark-blue car. Fausto hung back, and Macario shut the door behind them.

"I should convince you and Benny to leave AWOC, eh?" Macario said. He walked back to the kitchen.

"Ai, it's getting too dangerous!" Fausto said.

The growers were unleashing Doberman pinschers on the picketers, chasing them in their trucks, stepping on toes to make them fight back, and firing buckshot at picket signs. They drove tractors with rigs that sprayed pesticides on the picket lines, making the strikers choke on white fumes. One grower and his sons even broke strikebreakers' noses for distributing leaflets to scabs.

Macario cleared the table. "Mr. Cuculich has not resorted to these tactics. I told him he had to give me security guards because it's too risky for me and my men. Mr. Cuculich has to pay forty-three dollars a day for security guards."

"Why does he not give that money to his workers who have been with him for so many years?" Fausto followed his cousin into the kitchen with the platter of rice cakes.

Macario whirled around. "Mr. Cuculich did not start this! The strikers throw rocks and marbles into the fields. We put up sheets of plastic across the rows and move my workers deeper into the fields. They scratch paint off our cars with nails and throw jack nails on the road to give us flat tires. They threaten to follow my workers home and beat them or smash up their cars and homes. The other day Nida drove, while I laid down on the floor of my own car. We take different routes home every day because Nida is afraid."

Macario laid a dirty, sharp-pronged jack nail on the kitchen table between them. Neither union tolerated violence, but Fausto had heard of such tactics. It was difficult to keep everyone in line, especially the older pinoys who'd had enough—who this time around had nothing to lose—and the young Chicanos who were full of bravado.

"You know," Macario said, leaning forward, "Larry does not have the respect of all the pinoys. He is too outspoken for his own good. I hear there are grumblings even inside AWOC."

"If people are offended by what Larry says, it's because he speaks the truth," Fausto said. "Many pinoys don't want to draw attention to themselves, even if it means they suffer."

Macario studied Fausto. "That used to be you, Cousin. Now you are married, now you have something at stake. You want to risk it all?"

"I want a better life for my family and every family who works in the fields," Fausto countered.

"So do I, Fausto! I am with you and our fellow pinoys. We are both for improvements in the fields, but this is no time to be noble." Macario shook his finger at Fausto. "And mixing Chávez's Mexican union with AWOC is not good. You wait and see. They'll overtake the Filipinos until the Filipinos have no power and run them out of the union."

"If *everybody* joins, the strike will end soon and *everybody* wins," Fausto said. "But you cannot be with us and provide scabs to the growers. I cannot stop them from picketing your house."

"So you know what's going to happen." Macario turned away.

"Ania? What will you do?" Fausto wanted to know.

Macario crossed his arms. "My job is to get the grapes picked before they spoil," he said with unflinching eyes.

It was useless for Fausto to ask Larry not to target Macario. Not only did Macario work for one of the biggest growers in the area, but he was actively recruiting. One pinoy AWOC member claimed that Macario was getting a bonus from Mr. Cuculich for every strikebreaker he brought in. Word spread that a picket line was going to form in front of Macario's house, the first picket called outside of Delano. Fausto and Benny were going to go—to make sure no violence broke out—which Fausto had promised to Macario.

When they arrived, they found Domingo's and Nick Lazaro's cars lined up behind Macario's station wagon, forming a blockade across the dirt driveway. A handful of picketers gathered in front of Macario's house across the country road. They carried huelga signs with the insignia of a black thunderbird—its head of an eagle against a red-and-white background. Raúl, whom Fausto had met at Arturo's house, assured him that the group, which grew to two dozen, would be peaceful. Raúl led the picketers up and down the road, crying out, "A strikebreaker lives here—*un esquirol vive aquí!"* or *"Huelga! Huelga!"* Most of the men were Mexican-American, though some older pinoys from Delano had come. At dusk, as lights were being turned on in the house, Nida, stomach heavy, drew the curtains of the picture window in the living room.

Mr. Cuculich's eldest son, Matthew, drove up in a black pickup and made a wide turn, scattering picketers before parking in front of Macario's stone fence. He stepped out, along with two older men, whom Fausto didn't recognize.

"Go home!" Matthew yelled. "You don't have a right to harass innocent workers."

"He's hiring scab workers!"

"He lies to them, tells them there's no strike!"

Matthew stood with his feet apart, just like his father. His head jerked back and forth, trying to pinpoint who had spoken up. "It's a free country," he said.

An elderly pinoy with gray-streaked hair came forward from the back of the crowd. "If it is so free, then we can picket his house!"

"And I can make you all leave just like that," one of Matthew's companions said. The bearded man stuck his hand inside his denim jacket. His arm twitched.

The elderly pinoy slunk back as loud murmurs arose. The three men crossed the road. Matthew made his way to Fausto, pushing away picketers and their huelga signs.

"Fausto Empleo, what are you doing here?" Matthew blinked as if stunned to see him. "You should be inside the house."

The heat rushed to Fausto's face. He could smell beer on Matthew's breath. Matthew's buddies elbowed the picketers in the ribs, and while the picketers protested, they kept their hands wrapped around their signs. "I'm here to make sure this is a peaceful demonstration," he answered.

Matthew stared at him with eyes as steely gray as his father's. "You're going to break my dad's heart," he murmured. He spit on the ground, spraying tobacco juice and chew. "I guess you have to keep tabs on these strikers and their so-called nonviolent practices. It's all a lie. I'll prove it to you."

Matthew made eye contact with his buddies. They returned to the other side of the road and picked up loose rocks in front of the fence. The picketers gasped, expecting to be stoned. But the three men hurled rocks at their cars, smashing headlights, breaking windows. Fausto stood paralyzed as Matthew stabbed the front tire of a white Ford Thunderbird with a switchblade. Maybe it was the same knife he had used years earlier to carve a wooden horse for a 4-H fair contest. He won first place, and Fausto remembered his shiny face, the braces on his teeth as he smiled and showed off the carved horse and purple ribbon to the pinoys at camp.

The picketers descended upon the cars, shouting in Spanish and Ilocano. Soon sirens whined and lights flashed in the distance. A squad car from the Porterville Police Department stopped in the middle of the road. Fausto left Benny sitting on his haunches off to the side to explain what had happened to the police officer, who heaved himself out of his car. But the officer, a thick-necked, blond man, turned to Matthew. He yawned, and asked, "What happened?"

"These picketers are harassing our labor contractor and foreman." Matthew pointed to Macario's house, whose lights were now all turned off.

"Liar!" Raúl's voice rang out. "They slashed our tires and broke our headlights and windows!"

"But nobody got hurt, right?" the officer said, without looking at any of them.

"They stepped on our toes and struck our chests!" Raúl moved to the front.

"But nobody got hurt, especially that innocent family in there." The officer stabbed his finger in the direction of the house. He flapped his hairy arms. "All right, everybody leave the premises now! I got here in time to prevent a big mess."

"They destroyed our cars!" Raúl said. "They should be arrested for assault and battery, and for being drunk and disorderly."

"I said everybody leave now before I start making arrests for not dispersing!" The officer rested his hand on his revolver.

"What about them?" Raúl pointed at Matthew and his friends.

"You leave too," the officer said to the three men, who were leaning against the side of the pickup, but Fausto knew that wasn't what Raúl meant.

The picketers tramped back to their cars, muttering to one another. Raúl examined the slashed tires of his Thunderbird. When he retrieved a jack and a spare tire, the officer ran over and made him put them back in his trunk.

"That jack is a potential weapon," he informed Raúl. "Get your car in the morning."

"I don't want to leave it here." Raúl eyed Matthew across the street and laid his hand on the fin of the Thunderbird's backside.

The officer tossed a glance at the car. "Nobody will touch that old thing." He stamped his foot, fingering the billy club at his side. "Everybody get goin'! I said *now!*"

The picketers dashed for their cars as if being chased out of town. Raúl shook his head, though he too left in another car. The Cuculich truck pulled away, laughter hurtling out of the open windows. The squad car, its revolving lights turned off, soon followed, leaving only Fausto and Benny standing by the roadside.

"Good thing Matthew Cuculich came after all, eh?" Fausto said.

"Something could have happened." Benny was breathing through his mouth. "What if they got into the house? What would have happened to Nida and the boys?"

"They would not do that. But it does not matter; nothing happened."

"*Agayat?*" Benny marched to the broken glass and kicked it across the blacktop. The shards scattered, tinkling in the night.

"Macario's property was not damaged. I'm grateful for that. You should be too." Fausto examined his cousin's face in the moonlight. "Benedicto, are you weakening?"

Benny passed his hand over his face. "We have come this far, but I'm worried. Nida and Rozelle are avoiding Luz because of my union activity. Luz's cousins in Chicago said they can send us money if we need, but she does not like to ask. If the strike goes on for several months, we will get work elsewhere. You too. We cannot lose our homes."

AWOC and the NFWA were encouraging strikers to leave the area to find work. It was costly to run the kitchen. The strike fund was being drained. Yet both unions needed picketers on the lines; it was important to show numbers for the television news cameras. Volunteers came to Delano to support the cause, but there were grumblings from within both unions and on the outside that the strike was being taken over by non-farm workers.

The lights came back on in the house. The door swung open, and Macario's silhouette loomed. He crossed the front yard to the stone fence. Another figure took up the post in the doorway. Fausto thought that it was Domingo smoking a cigarette, but Domingo didn't smoke. The man tossed the cigarette butt on the porch and returned indoors. Fausto and Benny met Macario at the fence when it was clear that he wasn't going to leave his property.

"We came to make sure nothing would happen to you," Fausto said, running his hand along the stone fence, feeling the rough pores with his fingers like a blind man.

Macario didn't acknowledge him. "Benny, are you with me or with Fausto?"

"Hah?" Benny took a step back.

"Domingo is with me," Macario said. "Everybody in Terra Bella is with me— Melchor, Lito, Truelino, Pete—everybody!"

It was useless to point out that Fidel had joined AWOC. Fausto moved into his cousin's view. "You said you agreed with improving conditions in the field."

"Not like this," Macario said, still not looking at Fausto. "We are for workers having the right to choose to come to work."

Fausto kicked at the base of the fence, the river rocks he had stacked years before firmly entrenched. "That is not a choice!"

Macario's voice was even. "Benny, *bagayannak wenno saan?*"

"There is no such thing. We are all together," Benny said.

"Then you are with Fausto." Macario walked back to the house. The front door opened before he reached it, and Nida appeared. Macario pulled her in and kicked the door shut. The porch light was extinguished, then the living room lights. Fausto imagined them moving to the back of the house, just as Macario's workers had to retreat deep into the fields to escape the sight of the waving red-white-and-black flags and signs, the shouts, the army of picketers amassing at the edge of the vineyards.

——————

On the way to a rally at Ellington Park, Fausto saw Mr. Cuculich walking on the other side of Glenwood Street, toward the Elks Club. Fausto pulled the brim of his straw hat down. The incident at Macario's house weeks earlier was still fresh on his mind. He scolded himself; he should be proud of his stand. Why, then, did he try to talk the protestors out of picketing the Cuculich farm and Macario's house? The strike was going to test him—didn't Larry warn them all? He removed his hat.

"Fausto, is that you?" Mr. Cuculich boomed, as he flipped up his sunglasses. He dodged cars to get to the other side of the street. "Fausto Empleo, either you're too good to talk to me now or shouting '*huelga*' has made you deaf," he said with a smile.

Fausto shooed Benny on to the park so he wouldn't miss the rally.

Mr. Cuculich stood with his fingers latched around the belt loops of his jeans. "A rally, hmmm?" He craned his neck as a group of Chicanas carrying huelga signs crossed the street. Behind them followed a mix of young white men and women, some with styled hair and pressed trousers and skirts, and others with shaggy hair and torn clothes. "The park's going to be full of rabble rousers, professional agitators, and college kids protesting on their parents' dime," Mr. Cuculich said. "Where are those phony ministers I've been reading about in the papers? Ministers ought to be giving sermons, not agitating on the picket line."

Mr. Cuculich clamped his hand on Fausto's arm. "You know those outsiders invading our town are Communists. They call us racist. Doesn't that make you mad? We've got all kinds of races—we're a Little United Nations right here in Delano—and we get along just fine. But now these pinkos are drawing all you union lovers to them like some damned Pied Piper. Both Trotsky and Chávez in our town. Don't you know it looks bad for noncitizens to be associated with those kinds of people? It makes them look un-American."

"I'm a citizen of this country, Mr. Cuculich. I became a proud citizen after the war." Fausto shook free of the grower's grasp.

"I wasn't talking about you," Mr. Cuculich said. "I was talking about the other farm workers. They're brainwashed, and you're heading in that direction. Matthew told me what happened at Macario's place. His wife is having another baby and she doesn't need all these outside problems. And there you were on the side of the protestors. Such a shame!" He slammed his fist into the palm of his other hand. "Macario tells me he hasn't talked to you since that night and that your cousin Domingo has stopped talking to you too. Back where I come from, families stick together. I thought they did in the Philippine Islands too."

Mr. Cuculich shifted the sunglasses on his sweat-glistened head. "Macario tells me he's bitter about what happened. He's embarrassed for you. I'm embarrassed for you. I was going to make you one of my next foremen. I should have done it sooner. Maybe you wouldn't have turned out this way. You were one of my best men, my best workers."

Fausto kept his voice calm. "Mr. Cuculich, you say 'my, my, my,' but we don't belong to you. We are human beings, asking for decent wages and working conditions."

"Now, don't get me started on this idea about decency again!" Mr. Cuculich yanked his sunglasses off. "My grandparents came here with nothing but their sense of decency. Decency is something you have or you don't. Nobody can take it away from you. My grandparents never got any help here—not from protestors or clergy or snot-nosed college kids. Why, these agitators have never picked a grape in their lives. What do they know about hard work?" He narrowed his eyes at a couple of students wearing ripped UCLA T-shirts and cut-off denim jeans as they walked around him. They returned his look of disdain with a toss of their heads. "My family applied their grape-growing skills from the homeland. That's what decent people do. They contribute to the new country's economy. My family came around the same time as your kind and look how far we've come."

"But we did not have the same opportunities," Fausto said.

"I keep hearing that asinine excuse—inequality!" Mr. Cuculich spat out. "Sure you had the same opportunities. But we worked hard to get where we are today."

A small band of pinoys was walking on the other side of Glenwood Street. When they heard Mr. Cuculich's rising voice, they shot a look at Fausto. *Are you okay, brother? Do you need our help, manong?* their eyes said. Fausto raised his chin at them. They nodded and continued on their way. Half were in their fifties, like Fausto, the other half even older. Their faces were as wrinkled as raisin grapes drying in the fields by the roadside.

"Do you think we did not work any harder?" Fausto demanded.

"Well, no," Mr. Cuculich stammered, as if he wasn't expecting Fausto to fight back, "but we took advantage of opportunities." He hitched up his jeans by the belt loops as if by habit, though his gut hung loose. "Listen: if you work your way up honestly and become successful, look at your feet. You'll have someone from another country coming over here, yipping at your heels, claiming that what's rightfully yours is now theirs. You'll know what it feels like then."

A balding man wearing a pin-striped suit stepped out of a white Cadillac he had just parked. The man approached them, sticking out his hand to the grower. "George Cuculich, you look well," he gushed, pumping the grower's hand, his back to Fausto. "Did my secretary call you about that special low-interest rate we're offering to you and the other growers?"

Mr. Cuculich winked. "Mr. Preston, I heard that rumor through the grapevine, no pun intended. But it's nice to hear it from the president of the biggest bank in town."

"I assure you it's no rumor." Mr. Preston clutched a briefcase close to his side.

"I'll keep your offer in mind, but I'll tell you right now: The only ones suffering hardship from this so-called strike are the crows who are hoping for rotten grapes in the fields," Mr. Cuculich said. "Our business won't be affected."

"I know." Mr. Preston stole a glance at Fausto. "But I wanted to offer my support. The people of Delano need to show community spirit, especially with all of this unwarranted attention." A television van whizzed by in the direction of the park. A pinched expression crossed the banker's face. "I have business to attend to—much more important than a Communist-infested rally—so if you'll excuse me." He shook Mr. Cuculich's hand again and walked away with quick strides.

Mr. Cuculich stared at Mr. Preston's back. "That man used to snub me and my family and most of the growers in the area for years. The businessmen and townspeople didn't like us Slavs. Maybe they were jealous of our success, or maybe they didn't like how we stick together— that's the Slavic tradition. But now the townspeople, the newspaper, even the law-enforcement agencies are on our side." He spread out his arms, embracing the whole town.

The sidewalk was now empty. Fausto imagined Ellington Park so full of union supporters and placards that they spilled out into the streets. Distant rumbling came from the park. He longed to be there, but Mr. Cuculich showed no signs of leaving.

"I know you're not against *me*, and you know I don't have anything personal against you," Mr. Cuculich went on. "But I got a beef with Itliong and Chávez and this so-called strike. It's dangerous for Filipinos to mix with Mexicans and Chicanos. Haven't we been telling you that for years now? You know what one of Chávez's union officers told my brother the other day? He said, 'This union is for Mexicans.' Didn't want blacks, Arabs, Filipinos, not even the Puerto Ricans around. Just Mexicans. You want proof? Nick Lazaro tells me Chávez created that huelga bird with the head of the eagle from the Mexican flag and the wings to look like upside-down Aztec pyramids to appeal to *his* people. You're being used, and it hurts to see my Filipino workers—the ones who've been with me for twenty, thirty years—get tricked. That Chávez, he's just replacing me with himself."

"With all due respect, Mr. Cuculich, what you and the foremen have been saying is hurtful," Fausto said. "I don't believe it at all."

"You'll believe solid evidence." Mr. Cuculich pulled out Polaroid pictures from his chest pocket and handed them to Fausto. "I've been taking pictures and turning them over to the police, the sheriff, and the FBI. They have files on your people."

Fausto sifted through three pictures. The windows of a bus, the kind he used to ride every day before he and Benny bought the Bel Air, were blown out. Chunks of concrete and glass littered the ground. A cold-storage house stood charred. A bicycle with melted tires and no seat or handlebars leaned against a fence. Mr. Cuculich let his youngest son ride on the dirt roads that separated the rows of vines while he examined the grapes. It offended some of the workers, but it didn't bother Fausto to hear the boy's laughter in the fields. What would a ten-year-old know of their hardships? Why should they expect him to be concerned with such matters? Fausto hung his head at the sight of the mangled bicycle.

"It's one thing to go after us growers—we're man enough to take it," he said. "But when someone does something like this to a kid...."

"There has been violence on both sides."

Mr. Cuculich snatched the Polaroid pictures from Fausto's hand and stuffed them back in his chest pocket. "Does that make it right?"

"No!" Fausto said, startled at such a question. "Both unions have condemned the use of violence. Everyone is tired, and we are letting our anger get the best of us."

"Damn right," Mr. Cuculich muttered.

"Maybe it's time, then, to come to the table and make peace."

Ahmed, Moamar, and Fahmi were walking toward the park, their white tunics flowing, red-and-black checkered scarves wrapped around their heads. They quickened their steps as shouts of *"Huelga! Huelga!"* pulled them forward.

"That the language you speak now, Fausto?" Mr. Cuculich sighed. "I'm truly sorry about all this mess. Go on, don't believe me, but I am. We're not monsters, but all these outsiders who don't even know us are painting us that way. When you're attacked, you fight back." Mr. Cuculich glanced at his watch. "I'm late for a meeting, and you've got a rally to go to. Well, good luck to you, *hermano*, and good luck to me."

Fausto stood rooted, even as the grower crossed the street. "Mr. Cuculich," he called out. "Macario says you will let the grapes rot first."

Mr. Cuculich turned around, laughing. "We're smart farmers and businessmen. We'll turn the grapes into wine." He pulled his sunglasses down.

Fausto knew the growers would only pocket a quarter of their usual profits. Table grapes were never meant for wine. But it didn't matter. He turned his back on his old boss as shouts from the park grew. *"Viva huelga! Viva la raza! Viva César Chávez!"*

The strike carried on as the early November air turned cold. On the picket line across the road from John Depolo's farm, Fausto watched elderly men and women labor under the thick canopy of leaves and vines. When they emerged, bunches of grapes shook against their chests as they wheezed in the dust. With armed guards patroling the property line, all he could do was beg them to come out. Boys and girls who might have been old enough for kindergarten were dragging crates of grapes instead of wooden push-and-pull toys in the classroom. Even drunkards, with bottles tucked in their back pockets, wove in and out of the rows of vines, smelling as fermented as the berries on the ground.

At Jack Dragovich's ranch, all-female crews picked grapes as their babies lay in crates turned into bassinets. Toddlers played in the dirt. The women were picking the last of the grapes—raisins now—for jelly production. AWOC and the NFWA succeeded in keeping local workers out of the fields. But the growers recruited scabs from Bakersfield, thirty-three miles to the south, and Tulare, thirty miles to the north, and now as far away as Arizona and Texas. The growers lied to the workers about their wages and then charged as much as thirty-three dollars for bus fare. Disgusted, scabs told Fausto and the other strikers that they were promised fifteen cents a box but only got ten cents. When scabs walked off the Depolo fields, a rock fight erupted and Depolo himself beat an AWOC volunteer unconscious.

Fausto came home dejected, but he took comfort in the fact that Marina's mood had changed. He didn't know—and didn't want to know—why. She no longer complained about Prudencio and Ayong, who spent most of their days on the picket lines, took their meals at the Filipino Hall, and came back after she went to bed. Marina asked them to come home for dinners, which she made out of the donated food Fausto brought back. She massaged Fausto's hands when he told her about the desperate people the growers preyed on to work as scabs. Everything will work out, she kept saying. Her newfound faith amazed him and boosted his own flagging spirits. He looked forward to coming home, especially as the situation in the fields worsened.

When Marina asked if they could see a movie, he agreed because she had begun work at the packing house in Terra Bella. Her paychecks weren't enough to cover the mortgage, though she sent what she could to the bank. The citrus season wouldn't pick up until after the holidays, so long as harsh weather didn't damage the crops. Fausto borrowed money from Prudencio and Ayong, who were relieved to return the favor of room and board.

Fausto agreed to see *Mary Poppins* at the Delano Theatre, despite being led to the outer seats by the ushers. He wasn't interested in seeing a children's movie, but Marina was happy. When they left the theatre, she talked about how big the girl's dollhouse was in the movie and wondered out loud if Fausto could build such a structure. When she kissed him in the car, his tongue tasted buttered popcorn and waxy chocolate from the box of Milk Duds he had bought for her.

That night in bed, as Marina slept clinging to his side, Fausto held on to the memory of her smile and laughter when they walked out of the theatre, not wanting that moment to vanish. He kissed the crown of her head. She sighed, warming his bare chest with her breath. He held on to her tight to keep from crying. In the morning, with money borrowed from Severo Laigo and some pinoys from the bunkhouse, he traded in the old machine and bought a used Singer "Touch and Sew." Marina cried when he wheeled the wooden cabinet into the living room. She fingered the push-button bobbin and the silver knobs, reading aloud what each knob controlled. She tested all three stitches—straight, zigzag, and chainstitch—on fabric scraps.

She didn't ask where he had gotten the money. Fausto wasn't worried about the new purchase. "Don't pay me back," Severo had told him, flexing his right hand—his clipping hand—long since healed. "You were there for me when I could not work in the fields. It's my turn to help you," The other pinoys who pitched in said, "Pay us back when the strike is over."

Fausto yielded to Marina's advances at night. Making love made him momentarily forget near-empty cupboards and the growers' relentless determination. It seemed to do Marina more good than it did for him, though he ran his fingers across her back, connecting her moles with his touch, to induce himself to come. When he finally did—after she had already come—she pulled up to his chest, her eyelids fluttered shut, and her breathing grew soft and restful. He was afraid to move out from under her, so he lay under the weight of her, thinking of the grandparents, children, and mothers in the fields. Where were they sleeping tonight? The utility bills, the monthly bills for the Ford Falcon and the Philco television set, even the mortgage statement no longer made him panic when he retrieved them from the post office and shoved them in the kitchen drawer. There were more important things. Every cold fall morning in the fields, he saw what was more important.

———————

In mid-November, the rains came to the Valley, turning the vineyards into a sea of glossy mud stamped with dead leaves and smashed berries, which made the fields smell like an open vat of musty red wine. Fausto stood outside and let the rain wash his face. Perhaps now the strike—almost two months old—would soon end. But no matter how hard the rains came and washed away the crops, the growers did not yield. Still, with each rainy day everyone at the Filipino Hall and the NFWA headquarters, which members had christened "Huelga House," waited with optimism. Checks poured into the unions; a steady stream of clothing and food trucks arrived from San Francisco and Los Angeles. But Fausto heard that NFWA scouts and picketers could no longer put gasoline in their cars. The local gas station operator, who previously honored NFWA's credit cards, now turned them away, announcing that César Chávez was broke. Strike operations swallowed up all monetary donations the moment the checks were cashed.

By December, Fausto couldn't make the car payment for the third month in a row. He and Marina had scraped and borrowed enough money to pay the utilities and part of the mortgage, but at the expense of the Ford Falcon. Fausto had called the creditor and spoken with a sympathetic manager, but he made the mistake of promising not only to make the third payment but to start paying on the two missed payments as well. When he received a notice that required him to settle the balance in full within thirty days, he called the creditor, asking for the same manager. But the manager rebuffed him.

"It's not my place, Mr. Empleo, to judge you on what your priorities ought to be, but next time think about the consequences of your decisions," the manager said. "A representative will retrieve the car at the end of the month, after the holidays."

"Please understand my situation," Fausto said, keeping his voice low because Marina was in the next room. "Let me explain my circumstances to you again."

"I understand your situation only too well." The manager sighed. "This is off the record, Mr. Empleo, but the American Dream isn't for everybody. That's the hard fact of life I tell everyone whose file lands on my desk. Don't bite off more than you can chew; don't buy more than you earn. The sooner you learn, the better off you'll be next time."

"Next time?" It was getting harder to keep his voice down. "I still have until the end of the month."

The manager put his hand over the mouthpiece. Fausto heard muffled voices. Maybe he was going to do something after all. But when he came back on the line, his voice was frosty. "I've got calls coming in. It's our busy season. I believe we're finished with this conversation, Mr. Empleo. I hope you and your family have a happy holiday."

The receiver clicked. The silence on the line whistled in his ear. *Jingle Bells* was playing on the stereo console, the volume turned down low. Marina crept up to him.

"They are going to take the Falcon away," she whispered.

"I'll leave town and find work," Fausto declared. He slammed his fist into the kitchen wall calendar, its picture of a blond-haired family decorating a Christmas tree. The second hand was speeding around the face of the stove clock. He took a deep breath, but his lungs felt as if they were clogged with sand. His whole body felt like an hourglass. "I have until the end of the month. If they take it away, I promise I'll get it back for you," he said.

She drew a pink crocheted blanket tight around her shoulders. "We have each other. There are other things more important than a car, more important than the strike, yes?"

He cupped her face with his hands. Her patience made him lucky, luckier than Benny, who was looking for work in Lodi to appease Luz. Fausto kissed Marina's forehead, shutting his eyes tight to dam the tears.

Manna from the sky, that's what Manong Flor told Fausto. He overheard Larry Itliong talk about César Chávez securing strike funds from the United Auto Workers. "The UAW president is suppose to come here," Manong Flor said in a low voice.

Fausto couldn't imagine the head of the national auto workers union coming to Delano, a farming town. The AFL-CIO, which sponsored AWOC, didn't officially endorse the strike yet, so why would another influential union lend its support when the strikers' own sponsor had been wavering for so long?

"Shhh!" Manong Flor shoved his thick glasses up his nose. "You din hear it from me, okay? I doan spread rumors." He rested his broom against the kitchen wall. "We gonna get money and their support. But doan tell nobody, not even Benny. I'll tell you when, okay?"

Fausto wasn't about to spread such a claim. Maybe Manong Flor's hearing was getting as bad as his eyesight. Yet days later, news reached the Filipino Hall that UAW president Walter Reuther was coming as the AFL-CIO gathered for its annual meeting in San Francisco. He arrived in Delano on the heels of the AFL-CIO's formal endorsement. Fausto caught a glimpse of Reuther. He was clean shaven with a thatch of brown, combed-over hair. He looked out of place in a suit and tie, but he shook hands and struck up conversations with ease, as if he had been standing on the picket line since the beginning.

A march through town was hastily announced. Marina begged off; she wasn't feeling well and it was too cold for her to be outdoors. So Fausto, Benny, Prudencio, Ayong, and Fidel picked up their signs and joined the gathering. They exchanged waves with Arturo and Ahmed, who were soon lost among the sea of farm workers, students, volunteers, clergy, and picket signs. Fausto waved to newspaper reporters, who took his picture. Sullen-faced police officers, their breath clouding in the air, did not make good on their threat to arrest the strikers who lacked a permit to march—for fear of bad press. Chávez and Itliong flanked Reuther at the front of the line for the march through the streets of Delano and on to the Filipino Hall for a rally. There, Reuther announced that the UAW was pledging $5,000 a month to both unions until the strike ended. A collective gasp rose. Then the Hall erupted in deafening clapping, and the floor rocked as work boots stomped on wooden planks.

Amid the celebration, Manong Flor pushed his way through the crowd to Fausto and yelled into his ear, "What did I tell you, huh?" He grinned, his mouth full of brown-streaked gums and tobacco-stained teeth. "Manna from the sky. We gonna be all right." Fausto threw his arm around him, happy to inhale the ingredients of chicken adobo in the cook's white work shirt: vinegar, bay leaf, and peppercorn.

Chávez moved to the front of the room. "This strike will last until we win—this year or next year or the year after," he thundered. "This strike will not end until the workers have a union contract and can live like dignified human beings."

Cheers erupted again. Ahmed and Arturo hugged their fellow countrymen. Benny clapped and whistled. People were standing shoulder to shoulder, but Fausto felt a chill as he thought of the possibility of years of endurance. After the rally, he found Marina swaddled in her pink crocheted blanket on the sofa, drinking hot milk. When he told her that the UAW was pledging thousands of dollars a month to AWOC's strike fund, she smiled weakly.

"When the growers hear about the money and the support of the bigger unions, they will get scared," she said. "They will not let another harvest spoil." Her voice tapered off.

Fausto stared into her watery milk. He didn't repeat what Chávez had said in the Hall—what they might very well expect—that the strike could last for years.

———

The farm workers were still talking about the UAW's financial donation a week after Reuther's visit. While picketing the cold-storage buildings on Glenwood Street, Fausto and Ahmed made up a list of things the money could cover.

"You could get your car back." Ahmed said, and raised his sign above his head.

"That car is a luxury!" Fausto's breath clouded up in the light fog. "The money should go to families who need it more. We have to take care of the children first."

As they turned the corner, Severo Laigo and another pinoy waved and approached them.

"*Kumusta!*" Severo said. "You guys are doing a hell of a job!" He lifted his chin in the direction of the padlocked steel buildings, the rusty Southern Pacific boxcars sitting on the silent tracks as if shipwrecked. "I bet those grapes are spoiling in the coolers!"

He smiled wide, wrinkles deepening all over his face. His countryman, a smaller pinoy whose nostrils flared like dark mushroom caps, laughed and clutched his thick midsection. Behind them, the picketers began chanting, "*Huelga! Huelga!*"

"This is Paulo Agbayani," Severo said, as the man extended his hand to Fausto and Ahmed. "He worked for John Depolo."

"No more!" Paulo scowled. "Now that the UAW is giving us money, we will be taken care of."

"That money will not end up in our pockets," Fausto warned.

Severo shrugged. "We will still benefit. Manong Flor said he heard Chávez wants to build a retirement home for farm workers. Chávez is thinking big with that money."

"Retirement home?" Fausto didn't know whether to laugh or spit on the damp ground, though Ahmed laughed. "They should take care of those of us still working!"

Paulo pounded his small chest with his fist. "I am only in my fifties! I got lots of years of work left in me. The unions need to get our jobs back before anyone can retire!"

A pickup truck with its window rolled down turned onto the street. Mr. Cuculich leaned out. He shuddered, perhaps from the cold, perhaps from the sight of Fausto and the picketers. He gunned the pickup around the corner, showing off a large sign taped on the back window of his cab that instructed in fat, bold letters: "Fight Communism in Delano!"

Fausto grasped Paulo's arm, squeezing what little muscle was left on the pinoy's bone. "We will get our jobs back. It will take some time, but we'll do it."

"That is my only fear. It will take time." Paulo gulped air as if winded. "How much time do you have? How much time do I have?"

————————

A few days before Christmas, after Benny had dropped him off after picketing the packing sheds, Fausto found Marina still in her nightgown, curled up in a corner of their bed. A cup of tea sat on the nightstand, a cold hot-water bottle on his pillow. He asked her what was wrong, but she didn't stir. She wouldn't let him rock or hold her. When he went to the bathroom to get a thermometer, he saw clots of dark blood at the bottom of the toilet bowl. At first he thought she was having woman problems, but he noticed smaller clots of mucus floating in the pink-stained water. Resting in the center of one large blood clot was a curved mass—little more than the size of his thumb, with a nub on one end, a tail on the other, and sprouted buds in the middle.

Fausto gasped and grabbed onto the shower curtain; it snapped off of its hooks with metallic clinks. Marina's cotton underwear was hanging from the bathtub spout, dripping water. He put the toilet lid down and sat on the seat with his hands over his ears. How strange it was to try to slow down his racing heart when it felt rock heavy! For a brief moment, he grew warm with guilty satisfaction. He *wasn't* too old. But then he thought of their loss and rushed to her bedside.

"So sorry, so sorry," he murmured, though she only offered him a blank face.

She heaved herself up to sit. "I was pregnant for five weeks and four days."

He reached out and touched her stomach, imagining the deep, empty cave. "Why did you not tell me when you found out?"

Marina frowned as if scolding herself for bad judgment. "I could not believe it myself, even when the doctor told me it was true. Maybe it came out of me because I did not believe it was real." She covered her face. "I was waiting for a good time—the end of the strike—to tell you."

"I promise the strike will end soon." Fausto gently rubbed strands of dried hair that had stuck to her forehead and neck. "We'll try again."

She lowered herself, laid her head back on the pillow. "I was going to take a bath this afternoon, but my stomach hurt. I went back to bed and drank tea and used the hot-water bottle, but the pain was too much. I did not think to call the doctor. Maybe it still would have come out. When I finally got out of bed, there was blood on the sheets."

White sheets lay balled up by the door. His heart ached, thinking of her, doubled over, changing sheets.

She held up her hands. "I ran to the bathroom. I tried to catch my baby, but it slipped through my fingers." Her wet eyes gleamed for a moment. "Do you know a baby can hear its mother's voice in the womb? And its heart begins to beat when it is only twenty-one days old. It's true!" She nodded, transfixed. "I saw pictures in *Life* magazine. I was trying to find our baby's heart. I think I found its eyes."

He tried to picture what he'd seen in the bathroom. It didn't look like a baby at all. But what did he know? He had her word that it was something they had created, living and growing inside her until it was snatched away.

Marina rolled onto her side. She was thinking only of the baby, how they needed money for the baby, she'd said. She ran her hand across his thigh, but he couldn't feel a thing. Yesterday, she had called the pawnshop Luz once used. The owner showed up with his truck, and took the sewing machine, television set, and stereo console in the morning. On the dresser was an envelope with money to pay the long-due balance and late fees of the television set and to buy a crib and a stroller for the baby.

He sat back on his haunches. How could he have missed the empty spaces: next to the heater where Marina's sewing machine once stood, in the corner where the television set hid the loose tiles of linoleum, and by the front window where the stereo console played Ilocano folk music and Elvis Presley records while Marina cleaned?

"Why did you sell the sewing machine?" he demanded. "Severo gave me the money and I borrowed the rest from the pinoys at camp to buy it for you!"

"But we need things for the baby." She swallowed hard. "The *next* baby."

"I'll go find work up north." Fausto spread out his hands. Could he still cut 'gras? It would soon be asparagus season, though he wondered whether his back could handle bending down for hours. Maybe they wouldn't even take him, with so many younger, quicker pinoy strikers migrating northward.

But she shook her head and sat up on her knees, her sharp bones digging into the soft mattress. He kicked off his shoes and climbed in bed. She drew his arm around her, but he was afraid to touch her stomach again. She pulled away, grimacing in pain, and stared at the ceiling. "I did not want to flush the toilet," she whispered. "Will you find a safe place for our baby here? We will not tell anyone. No one must know."

He would need to retrieve it before Prudencio and Ayong come home. There were empty jars in the washroom. He could find a shoebox, a handkerchief. His head spun. In a corner of the vegetable garden. He remembered a story from one of the black farm workers whose mother had come from a long line of midwives. *They buried the placenta to remind the child where he was born.* But this was the opposite.

"The baby needs a proper burial," he said. "We'll go to Our Lady of Guadalupe. Maybe St. Mary's is better. *Agkararag tayo kin apo tapno lawlawagan na ti panunot tayo.*"

"Why do we need God's guidance?" Marina snapped. "He damned my life!"

Fausto drew back. "This life?" Stunned, he stared at the four walls of their bedroom.

"All the things He took away from me from the moment I was born! I will not see a priest! You take care of the baby tonight. Promise me!"

Fausto didn't trust himself to make promises anymore, but he was afraid that if he refused she might storm into the bathroom and flush the toilet in anger. He nodded.

"We will try again. You need to stay home so we can try again." She held his face in her hands in a vise-like grip.

He stroked her stomach, her damp flannel nightgown. "I can take care of you with a job. Then you'll not worry and we'll have our baby.

We need to keep the house for our family. After Christmas, I'll go away and find work."

"No," Marina insisted. "The strike will end soon. Everything will be okay. Listen!"

He pressed his face into her hair, smelling spicy Cotillion perfume and dried sweat. He strained to hear beyond their breathing. It was raining again, raining hard. He imagined great puddles of water turning into lakes across the earth. He imagined the last of the grape harvest succumbing to the rain. He told her he would get them all back: the sky-blue Ford Falcon, the stereo console, the "Touch and Sew" sewing machine, the Philco television set. And the baby. He stroked Marina's cheek again and again until he felt her go limp against his chest. *The baby*, he kept telling himself. Most of all, the baby.

After Christmas, Prudencio and Ayong went north to pick olives in Lindsay. They promised to return in the spring either to rejoin the picket line or, they hoped, to work under union contracts. They vowed to send money, though Fausto told them to take care of their needs first. Deep down, he was relieved to see them go. Before they had returned that night, he scooped the remains out of the toilet and swaddled it with a handkerchief, which grew pink and wet. He buried it in a shoebox where honeydew grew plentiful in the summer. In the morning, he realized it wasn't a good spot, but he didn't go back. He wondered if he could ever walk in the garden again.

Marina insisted that they make love every night, but as the weeks and the strike wore on and nothing happened, she grew despondent. Temperatures plummeted; frost was damaging the citrus crop, keeping the packing houses from operating at full production. Depending on her mood, Marina blamed everything on their lack of luck. Other days, she was sure it was because she had done something wrong in the past. Fausto cursed God under his breath, though at night as he watched her sleep he asked for God's forgiveness, for God to watch over her because he was losing his ability to take care of her.

When he was within walking distance of St. Mary's, he slipped into the church and sat in the back pew, staring at the stained-glass windows surrounding him. Families had donated all the little windows of saints in memory of loved ones. It was the growers' and townspeople's church—big enough to fit 400 parishioners. Mr. Cuculich's grandfather died more than fifteen years ago; Fausto was sure the family had paid for a window of a saint somewhere along the walls. He picked a window for their baby—St. Francis of Assisi, surrounded by animals and trees. For a moment it brought comfort. But he ducked out of the church, feeling bad for going there instead of Our Lady of Guadalupe, where the farm workers worshiped and prayed for an end to the strike.

Marina didn't go to the backyard anymore. He found her staring out the washroom window, perhaps trying to find which part of the garden held their secret, a secret she kept even from Luz. There was no television set to watch programs or stereo console to play records while she scrubbed the linoleum with the overturned half-shell of a coconut. There was no sewing machine to keep her hands occupied. Before the strike, she had sewn scraps together to make a quilt but stored the unfinished piece in the second bedroom closet.

Marina didn't leave the house for weeks. When Fausto came home, she was often on the sofa, rolling the edges of her pink crocheted blanket on her lap with nervous fingers. She looked at him expectantly as he sat down beside her, as if she'd waited all day for him to return. But when he touched her wrist, she hid her hands beneath the blanket and turned away, willing him to leave the room, the house even. There were few places in Terra Bella for Fausto to go besides Benny's house. Fausto occasionally visited with Fidel when his cousin came home every other weekend from picking lettuce, though Marina begged off Pilar Europa's invitation to join them. When he couldn't bring himself to spend another evening with Marina staring out the window in silence, he began to stop by Arturo's house on his way home from the Filipino Hall. He'd only been by Arturo's house a few times since the strike began, and Georgina and Arturo Junior were happy to see him. Raúl came over too, but when Raúl and Arturo argued in the kitchen about the duration of the strike, Fausto took Arturo Junior to the living room. The boy knew his father was leaving for the Imperial Valley, and when the strawberry season commenced he would head straight to Ventura County.

"Are you sad your father is leaving home for work?" Fausto dared to ask him.

Arturo Junior shook his head. "Papi needs to find work so we can eat and keep our house. This strike is important."

"You are a brave boy, do you know that?" Fausto lifted Arturo Junior's chin. "You know why the strike is important?" The boy stared back, motionless. "If we give in to the growers, all our years of hard work will be worth nothing," Fausto told him. "It would be a shame to live a life that is useless, meaningless. Do you understand?"

"*Sí, entiendo,*" Arturo Junior answered. He stood up, ran into the kitchen, and threw his chubby arms around his father's neck.

———————

As winter marched on, Fausto took refuge with the idle farm workers at the local hangouts: the Monte Carlo, the Guadalajara, Divina's Four Deuces. He didn't drink or spend money he didn't have or borrow money he couldn't pay back. He just wanted a dark, noisy place to escape to, a place where other pinoy strikers—most of them single, some of them married but without children or with spouses who had gone away to find work—exchanged stories of what had been repossessed or what they had to sell to make ends meet. They dreamed up schemes of how they would get their possessions back.

He took refuge in the picket lines and the Filipino Hall, where picketers congregated for lunch to eat the greasy or bone-dry meals that Manong Flor cooked. Larry strutted in the dining area with the puffed chest of a rooster, giving pep talks to strikers who nursed their cups of black coffee. "We are just as good as any of those white men! We have the same rights as any of them!" he thundered. "But we have to go get equality and justice because they don't want to give it to us!" By the time Larry left the Hall, the pinoys were talking about their worth, not just the raises, per-box bonuses, and health benefits that the growers would give them as the spoils of their victory.

At the Hall, Fausto shook hands with the clergy who were active in the pickets. He met college students who came for the weekend to protest. Some belonged to groups like the Free Speech Movement, the W.E.B. Du Bois Club, the Student Nonviolent Coordinating Committee Students for Farm Labor (SNCC), or the Congress of Racial Equality (CORE). Students arrived from Mississippi and Alabama, fresh from witnessing civil rights abuses against blacks. Some had spent time in prison farms as a punishment for participating in sit-ins in public places. At night, outside the Hall, they sang "We Shall Overcome."

The students used big words that were beyond Fausto's grasp. At their young age, they were smarter than Miss Arnold. At the same time, he was awed by their confidence and grateful that they marched in the fog or muddy fields when they could have been on vacation. Many of them had long hair and dressed in clothes as worn as the farm workers. He didn't know if they were showing solidarity, not wishing to offend the farm workers, because most of the students came from wealthy or middle-class families.

Wendy Whitman, a student from Stanford, drove down to picket every other weekend in her new Ford Mustang convertible. She reported to the Hall wearing a leather coat over white blouses and pleated skirts, with leather gloves and boots. She looked out of place with her bouffant hairstyle and manicured nails. Fausto kept his distance until she joined him for lunch one day in the dining area, greeting him in a cheerful voice, *"Kumusta, Manong."* Wendy knew a few words in Ilocano, and her favorite Filipino dish was lumpia. He learned that she had spent a month in Manila. He asked her what she was studying and what her family did, but she wasn't interested in talking about herself. Her round, peach-complexioned face was so serious. "The Philippines is a beautiful country with beautiful people," she said. "I felt a kinship with the Filipinos when I was there, and I want to show my respect for them here."

Ted Enebrad, a skinny young Filipino, emerged from the kitchen, patting Manong Flor on the back. Fausto had already met the student from San Francisco State who introduced himself as Teddy and immediately told Fausto, "The growers are cutting your people low, and that's uncool." He came almost every weekend, sporting faded jeans and a denim jacket and rotating no more than three different T-shirts throughout his visits. Fausto wanted to take a pair of barber's shears to Teddy's straight hair, which fell past his ears. Most of the time, he drove up alone in his weathered Volkswagen Beetle. Sometimes he crammed in as many as four other students whom he convinced to join the "cause." In the beginning, Teddy was clean shaven, but as the months wore on, he grew a wispy moustache and beard.

"Hey, Wen," Teddy said, as he plopped down beside her and Fausto on the long bench with a cup of water and a stack of tortillas. "What's happening, Manong Fausto?"

Fausto shrugged. He left Marina curled up in bed in the morning. Work at the packing house had slowed down. Lacking seniority, she was one of the last to be called when production picked up. She slept in most days, but even when she woke up, she stayed in bed, silent as night. As far as he was concerned, his problems at home were nobody's business, whereas in the field it was everybody's business. "Somebody threw rocks at the Depolo farm in the afternoon," he reported. "The sheriff came, but nobody got arrested."

Teddy pulled out a pencil from his shirt pocket and started scribbling in a spiral-bound notebook, asking Fausto for specific details.

"More field notes for your thesis?" Wendy asked, peering over his shoulder.

"My thesis is growing into a tome!" Teddy rolled a tortilla and ate it in two bites. "Who knew that the unionization of Filipino farm laborers in California would be such a hot topic? This thesis is going to blaze my trail in academia. It's going to be one of the reasons California's university systems establish full-fledged departments and degreed programs in Asian American Studies."

"No more toiling under the tyranny of the history department?" Wendy teased. "Fight in the fields, fight on the campuses. You've got your work cut out for you, Theodore Enebrad, but you'll come out on top on perseverance alone."

Teddy drummed the table with fingers that pulsed with abundant energy, matched only by student picketers who returned to the hall, still chanting *Huelga!* "I just need more hours in the day!" he said.

"Ai, you cannot be too busy to take a bath!" Fausto touched the back of Teddy's long hair. "If you're going to be a professor, you need to start dressing better. You look like one of us in the fields." He lifted his chin toward a corner of the hall, where farm workers leaned against white walls plastered with posters, wearing their work clothes, although none of them had been picking grapes or pruning vines for nearly six months.

"How you look isn't important, Manong Fausto." Teddy grinned wickedly at Wendy.

"Right on!" Wendy stood up and put on her lacquered black coat.

She was looking for company on the picket line at the Cuculich ranch. Fausto hunkered down, passing on her invitation. He wondered what Mr. Cuculich would say if he saw her, wearing expensive clothes, stepping out of her convertible; he wouldn't be able to call her a professional agitator, a college kook, or a Communist. But if he saw her on the picket line, he would call her a rabble-rouser. She enjoyed irritating the security guards and strikebreakers by rubbing the handheld microphone against her wool skirt for as long as she and the rest of the picketers could stand the scratchy sounds blasting out of the electric megaphone.

Fausto watched Teddy reread what he called his chicken scratch. "You are ambitious," he told Teddy. "You are going to be a good professor in a good college."

Teddy snapped shut his notebook and pointed it at Fausto. "It's people like you, Manong Fausto, who've fired up my ambition."

"Me?" Fausto's cheeks grew warm. "You should follow César Chávez or Larry Itliong. They are the leaders. I just go where they tell me to go."

"No way!" Teddy shook his head. "Who would Chávez or Itliong lead if not for you guys on the front lines? You're the ones making the most sacrifice. You're still here while so many of the strikers have left. Chávez is getting all the press coverage. Everyone will remember him. Everyone will be saying, 'Viva César Chávez!' years from now. But will anyone say the same things about you or any of those guys?" He pointed at the other end of the table where young and old pinoys were bent over, scooping chicken adobo and rice into their mouths. "Who will sing your praises, Manong Fausto? Who will even know it was the pinoys who had the courage to sit down because it was the right thing to do, even if Chávez said it was the wrong time to strike and had to be talked into it. As if there was a wrong time to fight for your dignity!"

Fausto opened his mouth, but nothing came out.

"I will; that's who." Teddy pocketed his pencil and notebook. "I'll be standing right next to you when this is all over, and I'll be shouting your praises to the next couple of generations of Filipinos, so everybody knows."

Fausto sighed. "When this is all over," he repeated, his voice trailing.

At a nearby rummy game, an elderly pinoy lay his head down on his cards. He scratched his chin, crusted with white stubble like frost. His face was blotted with age spots and scored with wrinkles, his skin like a map of his life. The man's eyelids drooped, his mouth sagged open. His elbow jerked and a penny fell to the floor. It rolled under the table and rested against his overturned house slipper.

Teddy held out his hand and offered Fausto a smile. "*Wen*, Manong. *Wen.*"

Fausto reached for Teddy's hand, the warmth of it, the strength of his pulse.

In February, Marina was heartened when weekly money orders came from Prudencio and Ayong. Fausto wrote back, insisting that they were sending too much, but he was glad to receive the money. They had already missed a month's mortgage payment entirely. One sunny, cold day, two pieces of mail arrived: another money order and a letter from the bank informing Fausto that he was in default and asking for prompt payment, as well as late fees. *Default*. The word sounded so final, damning. Because Marina's paychecks had dwindled, the sum of money he had sent to the bank was laughable. How could he have thought that sending the bank any amount would delay receiving such a letter? The feeble citrus season was coming to a close, with the freeze—no longer just a cold snap—ruining acres of oranges and grapefruit in its wake. As soon as the packing house idled, Marina would be out of a job. It was useless to fret over having bought the Ford Falcon. It was futile to question why he had refinanced the home mortgage.

For a week, Fausto sat at the kitchen table late at night, blowing on his fingers to warm them, staring at the typed letter on crisp, heavy paper. How long ago last spring was! He didn't like the yeasty taste of beer, but he drank it for the numbness that washed over him. If they missed a second payment, the bank would refer the case to its collections department. He threw the letter away. It was not possible to pay even the late fee. The end of the month was days away. All he could do was wait for the next letter that would tell him that someone from the collections department would be contacting him soon. Maybe he would have better luck with this person than with the man who had taken away their Ford Falcon. He would have to keep the mailbox key and collect the mail so Marina wouldn't know. The beer was losing its power over him. But instead of getting another bottle, he stumbled his way to the bathroom in the dark and threw up in the toilet.

He didn't tell Marina about the letter. She was already upset over the utilities being shut down. It was as if the vital organs of the house were expiring one by one. Long before the telephone company stopped their service, the relatives who sided with Macario no longer called to invite them to parties. Nida and Rozelle hadn't called Marina since the incident at Macario's house. It didn't matter, she insisted, as long as she had Luz. Fausto didn't ask what they talked about, though Marina told him that she didn't want anybody to know how bad their money problems were—not even Luz or Benny. He knew Luz was pushing

Benny to quit the strike and the union, though Benny remained steadfast. When Marina came home from her visits, she talked of ways to save money. She stopped the newspaper service. Benny let them put out their trash with his. The most important bill to pay as much as they could, she said, was the mortgage. He kept quiet. How could she not know the consequences of paying only a little bit each month?

The food donations to the unions came irregularly. Sometimes they had to eat the same food—potatoes or rice—for days. Marina was hoarding a whole turkey, which had been donated to the unions at Christmastime, in Fidel's freezer. She was saving it, she said, for when the strike ended. But several weeks later, Fausto came home to turkey soup on the camp stove and grilled turkey legs on the kitchen table. When they sat down to eat, Marina stripped all the meat off the bones and sucked out the marrow.

Ahmed showed up at the Filipino Hall with purple blotches beneath his eye. He and some picketers had discovered truckers loading grapes bound for Tijuana, to be sold in Mexican grocery stores. It was illegal, Ahmed warned them, and they would be arrested at the border. The lie worked; the truckers abandoned the grapes on the docks. But that's not what got him a black eye. He was assigned to gain access to the fields as a union spy, or a "submarine," as they were nicknamed, so he got hired at the Cuculich farm and persuaded many scabs to walk out of the fields. One of the foremen caught him.

"Your cousin Macario told me I had no right to lie about who I was and what I was doing," Ahmed said. "He was too angry to recognize me. So I said, 'Macario, I am a friend of your cousin Fausto Empleo.' Then he struck my face, and I passed out."

Fausto winced. "What has come between us should not involve others."

Ahmed touched Fausto's sleeve. "I should thank your cousin for bringing me fame at Huelga House." Ahmed was referring to the list on the back wall of NFWA's headquarters honoring strikers who had received the "Order of the Purple Grape," the NFWA's official distinction for those injured in the line of duty. Fausto hadn't heard of the award. Instead, he thought how Macario's words would have hurt him more than any blow from his cousin's fist.

Fausto came home late one night and sat in the Bel Air for the longest time, fingering the bandage on his nose. At the end of the day, after spending hours picketing at one of John Depolo's farms, Depolo and his security guards descended upon the picket line without warning. The picketers had been taught to keep their hands to their sides, their emotions in check. When Depolo stamped on picketers' toes, the victims suppressed their cries. Depolo jabbed picketers in the ribs. When they didn't fight back, he swung his burly arm and smacked Fausto in the nose. The sky turned black. Fausto tasted blood in his throat and felt the crack of his kneecaps as he hit the ground. When he awoke, he was at the Filipino Hall getting cleaned up. A volunteer nurse explained to him that his nose was bruised not broken, though the slightest touch was like a knife stabbing bone. Severo told him everybody wanted to pummel Depolo, but nobody went after him. Fausto was glad, though he wondered if he could restrain himself had Depolo struck Benny or Ayong, who were smaller and weaker. When he finally got out of the car, he stretched his back and arms. His whole body was still tense. How would Marina react? In the evenings, she often looked at him as if he were a ghost. But the moment he walked into the house, her face looked pained. He sat down on the sofa next to her, the pink crocheted blanket between them.

"*Ania?* What happened to you?" She lifted her hand but didn't touch his face.

"John Depolo hit me." His voice came out wheezy. "It is just a bruise."

"So you fought with one of the growers and he almost broke your nose?" She clicked her tongue against the roof of her mouth and cupped his chin, examining his cut and bruised skin.

"He struck me in the nose once. I did not fight back." When she shook her head, not understanding, Fausto added, "I was honoring the unions' vow of nonviolence."

"But he hit you. Can you not defend yourself?"

Fausto pushed off from the sofa; he didn't want to see the look of scorn on her face. The living room loomed so large without the sewing machine, the stereo console, and television set, and yet he felt trapped. He escaped to their bedroom, but Marina was right behind him, blanket in tow, when he pulled out the envelope that contained the money paid out by the pawnshop. Fausto tried to take the money once before to pay bills, but Marina begged him not to touch it. It was for the baby. Now it seemed a waste. She wasn't pregnant; maybe she'd never get pregnant. And here they were, ready to lose everything, with money stashed away.

"We need to pay the bills."

"You promised me you would not touch this money!" She tried to grab the envelope, but he held it above their heads. Her eyes were wild. "We agreed the money is for the baby."

"If you'll not let me use this money, then I'll go up north to find work."

"You promised to stay. What about the baby?" Her hands pressed down on her flat stomach and slid out to her hips again and again, as if the motion, the desire, would make her belly grow, but she was more bone than fleshy skin.

Fausto put his hands on his head, the envelope like a weight bearing down on him. He didn't know whether to hug her tight or shake her hard. She had stopped making sense when she lost the baby, and he still didn't know what to do. He slumped to the bed, holding the envelope close to his chest, though she kept trying to reach for it. He pushed her away.

She tripped on the blanket and fell back softly on the rug. "What kind of a union comes between a husband and wife?" She gave him an accusing look as she gathered herself, balling up the blanket to her stomach. "A devil of a grower tries to break your nose and you do nothing! You come home and try to steal from our baby. Then you strike me! Is this what the union has done to you?"

"I did not hit you, Marina." His shoulders caved in. His fingers loosened on the envelope. Like a crow in a vineyard, she swooped down and snatched the envelope. He didn't fight her. His nose was throbbing. "Either you let me go find work, or we use this money."

She shook her head, her jaw defiant. As he stood up, his whole body went rigid, just as it did when he was at the Filipino Hall and he wanted to storm Depolo's house and knock him senseless. He grabbed the envelope, tore it in half, and emptied its contents. Marina dropped to the floor like a beggar, gathering ragged bills. He couldn't look at her. His mouth was full of bitterness. He stepped over her blanket and found his way to the bathroom.

Fausto didn't know how long he stood leaning against the door, the bathroom lit only by the ghostly moonlight in the window. Marina was crying in their bedroom. When her sobs echoed down the hallway and her body shook on the other side of the door, he threw open the door and embraced her tight. Her face, her body was lost in his hug. He didn't want to see how much he had hurt her. When she stopped crying, he told himself, he would tell her that they would tape the torn bills together. They would put the envelope safely back in the dresser drawer. And he would stay. He would stay.

Fausto tried to get Marina to join him at the meetings. She needed fresh air to put color back in her face. She needed to keep busy. Sometimes Fausto found her jittery, as if waiting for something to happen—not just for the strike to end. Other times she stared at the worn rug, sitting up but in a tight ball, knees hugging her chest. She grew anxious when he came home without any kind of meat and took to sucking orange slices. Fausto didn't know how she could eat them. The frost had robbed the season's crop of their juice and shriveled their pulp. Yet oranges had the power to calm her.

At one meeting, the SNCC suggested boycotting products by Jack Dragovich, one of the biggest absentee growers in the area. AWOC and the NFWA were asking for volunteers to lead boycotts in out-of-state cities and even Canada. The assignment appealed to Fausto. Nothing was changing the minds of the growers—not the backing of other more powerful unions, the growing public support, the donations of food and money flowing in, and especially the prospect of losing another harvest. If the strike was going to last another year, he and Marina would be better off gone from the area but still helping the union.

He had received a letter from the bank's collections department representative, who couldn't reach him by telephone and had asked him to call her. He used the pay phone outside the Hall, and while he politely listened to her explain that he had fifteen to thirty days to pay off the delinquent payments, he told her he could not.

"I'm having a hard time hearing you—there's a lot of noise on the line," she said. "I thought you said you couldn't do a thing."

He turned his back on a caravan of picketers that had pulled into the parking lot. "That is what I said, ma'am. What happens next?"

There was a long pause before she said, "We initiate foreclosure."

He leaned into the telephone booth's glass wall streaked with fingerprints.

"To initiate foreclosure, we have to prove you're in default," she said. "If we can't work something out, our attorneys pursue court action. They'll also try to work with you, but if you can't pay off the default an action will be filed in court. You're given a reinstatement period, even if it gets beyond the Notice of Default filing with the county clerk's office. You can still do something. Do you have family members who can help?"

He kept his promise to Marina not to tell Benny. He didn't tell Prudencio or Ayong. What could they do? "How long before we have to move out?" he asked.

"Maybe two or three months, depending upon the expediency of the courts and the sale of the house to the highest bidder in an auction," she said, and gave a short laugh. "Believe me, we'd rather not have to expend this much energy on a losing transaction."

The picketers filed into the Hall, their signs hanging down by their sides. Even if the strike ended tomorrow, he wouldn't have enough money to pay or enough time to amass the large amount he owed the bank. After receiving the bank's second notice, he thought to go to Larry Itliong for help, for a loan, but he was too proud. Didn't Larry tell him what the consequences of a strike might be? Wasn't he one of the pinoys who got angry when Larry told them to go home because they weren't serious about changing their situation in the fields? They came back the next day and convinced Larry they could endure the struggle. Benny survived. Luz's cousins from Chicago were sending money, though Benny had taken it with great shame. Pride and determination to brave the strike were all Fausto had left—that and Marina's love. It came down to what he was willing to lose because some kind of loss, as Larry had reminded them all, was the price everyone had to pay for a greater good.

"Mr. Empleo, foreclosure can be a very difficult process," the woman on the other line confided. "When you default, a Notice of Sale is advertised widely and repeatedly. A sign is posted on the property. Sometimes the public auction is held right in front of the house. I'm sure you and your wife wouldn't want that."

He slammed the telephone handset into its cradle. He said he couldn't pay. Was she deaf or mean, rubbing his nose into the mess he'd made? He stepped out of the booth. The cool air refreshed him. It made his whole body tingle. *Two or three months*. He and Marina could be gone by then. He went straight into the Filipino Hall and signed them up to organize a grape boycott out of state. But when he told Marina what he had done, she looked up, shocked, and shook her head.

"Why not?" Fausto demanded, his voice brittle with frustration. He followed her as she wandered into the kitchen. "We can start our life all over again."

"I cannot leave our home. Our family is here." She opened the unplugged refrigerator—still not cleaned out of moldy food—and slammed the door shut. She wrapped herself tighter with the pink blanket that had become a second skin to her.

He stood rigid, though something was cracking inside him. He didn't know what it was—his heart, his resolve? How could he tell her they were months away from losing the house? "We don't have family here, anymore," he said.

"We have Auntie Luz and Uncle Benny, Manang Pilar and Manong Fidel, and when this strike is over and time has passed, we will have everyone else in Terra Bella."

He cupped her cheek. "We'll go away for a while. The strike will be behind us—by tomorrow, if you like. It will be good for us, just you and me, like a real honeymoon. You can even pick where you want to go. I'll ask Larry. I'll make sure you get your first choice of city." He kissed her on the damp forehead. "What do you say? *Ania?*"

Her eyes, her emerald flecks, were dissolving in tears. "We cannot," she said, just as simply as he had told the woman at the collections department that he could not pay.

He kicked the refrigerator door and stormed into the living room.

"Fausto, *sadinno iti papanam?*" she cried out.

"To the Hall, to tell them we cannot go!" he answered. He slammed the front door behind him, only to have the cold March air slap his hot cheeks.

Fausto returned home late. He stacked donated canned goods on the kitchen table and took to sleeping on the sofa. The first night on the sofa he told her he was too tired to move. She left him there without another word. It was true; he *was* tired. Notices. Defaults. Letters from the bank. Calls to the bank. Indifferent managers on the line. Every night, when he shut his eyes, sleep was a blink away. Soon she stopped leaving cooled bowls of whatever canned food he'd brought the night before. It made no sense to light up the camp stove twice and waste butane.

He stopped all talk about the strike, but he told her that Senator Robert Kennedy, as part of the panel on the US Senate Subcommittee on Migratory Labor, was coming to town to conduct hearings on farm worker abuses. She didn't care. She stayed home when Fausto, Benny, and Fidel, anxious to get a glimpse of the famous Kennedy, tried to get inside the Delano High School auditorium. The building was packed, and they were forced to hear the proceedings through speakers that had been set up outside. They were thrilled when the senator spoke up on their behalf and stunned when he paid a visit to the Filipino Hall after the hearings and declared his support for their cause. A large crowd gathered around Kennedy, but Fausto managed to squirm his way through and stuck out his hand. He could hear Kennedy's nasally voice thanking all of them for their courage and strength. Then a hand grasped his and gave it a firm shake. He stood in the same spot for a few moments, even as everybody followed Kennedy outside. He fairly flew home to share the news with Marina and show her his hand.

But she stared at his fingers as if they were foreign objects. "Did you bring home powdered milk?" she asked with anxious eyes, as if the milk were medicine, a painkiller.

She was getting particular about what foods he brought home, requesting bottles of milk or boxes of powdered milk, which were handed out to families with children first when the scarce dairy supplies arrived. "They were all taken," he said.

"Are the other women and children more important?" Tears gathered in her eyes.

"I'll get you a box tomorrow. I promise."

"I cannot wait for tomorrow or the strike to end! It is always beyond *tomorrow!*" She twisted the blanket in her hands, pulling apart the patterns of delicate needlework. "If it does not end soon, something bad will happen." He tried to touch her, but she stumbled out of his reach, disappeared down the hallway, mumbling, "Tomorrow! Ai, always tomorrow!"

One morning in late April, Fausto wandered into the café near the Filipino Hall, a busy west-end restaurant where farm workers and union supporters hung out. The Hall ran out of coffee, and Fausto needed a cup of coffee more than he needed food, though the smell of bacon and eggs clawed at his empty stomach. He took his coffee and joined

Wendy and Teddy, who pored over a stack of *Delano Records* with grim faces. Fausto didn't read the newspaper after Marina had canceled their subscription. Few pinoys read it; most of the manongs sat or squatted on the newspapers on the sidewalks and watched people and cars go by as the strike wore on.

"This reporter wrote an article today about a striker provoking a security guard to beat him up." Teddy folded the newspaper and returned it to the top of the stack. "Do you think a five-foot-tall manong would start a fight with a 300-pound, six-foot 'rent-a-fuzz' who has two Doberman pinschers on a long leash?"

Wendy put her newspaper down. "Did you read the hate mail from the locals because Senator Kennedy embarrassed that sheriff during the subcommittee hearings? You can't hide ignorance!" She rolled up her sleeves to avoid getting newsprint on her white blouse. "At least some of the national press is objective."

Fausto used to read the *Stockton Record* in the Little Manila barbershops. "We were always at fault when we were stabbed or shot at. If I was not Filipino and I read those stories, I would be afraid of Filipinos."

"Some progress!" Teddy moved his sausage links around in their pool of grease.

Fausto leaned back in his chair. Thirty years. Such a long time for something to remain the same; here he was, so much older now and not in any better position in life.

Teddy slid his plate of buttered toast and sausage links in front of Fausto. "I'm full and I hate wasting food," he said, and folded his skinny arms. "It's going to change, Manong. It's taking blacks a lot longer, but it's going to change for the pinoys too."

Fausto's stomach growled as he held the wedge of toast. He wanted to lick his finger, slick with melted butter. His mouth was already watering. "If I was your father," he told Teddy, "I could not be prouder."

"Be proud for taking a stand, Manong Fausto. Everyone on the front line has given up a lot." Teddy studied Fausto as he ate. "I read that Joseph Vukelich signed with Chávez. Have you been able to get any work there?"

"Vukelich has many vineyards, but there are more strikers than openings in the fields." Fausto laughed. "It's not so good to be strong in numbers this time, eh?"

Teddy didn't smile. "How are you doing in terms of money?"

Fausto made a sandwich with the sausage. "Marina and I are fine," he said.

"The American Friends Service Committee donated thousands of dollars to help strikers pay for rent and utilities, and social workers are volunteering to help union members get welfare benefits," Wendy offered. She put her full glass of orange juice next to Fausto's cup of coffee. "You're entitled to that, you know."

Fausto eyed the orange juice. "I did not come to this country to beg for money. My father would be ashamed of me. Miss Arnold, my American teacher in San Esteban, taught me that Americans are self-reliant. I have been an American since 1946. We get food donations. That's enough."

Wendy and Teddy exchanged looks. "Are you sure?" she asked gently. She hesitated, her hand on her purse. "My father works in the banking industry—" But she cut herself off when Teddy gave her a quick shake of his head.

"We have no kids. There are families who need help more than Marina and I do." Fausto drained the glass of orange juice. His plate was empty, but he was still hungry.

Teddy scratched at the stubble on his chin. "Manong Fausto, pride makes a lousy shelter. It doesn't keep you warm or fill your stomach. I'm just saying there are resources out there to help with hardship cases."

"I will find work up north. We have lost a few things, but we have each other." Fausto sipped his coffee. "We have not lost each other."

"I've heard some families broke up over the strike. But that's so great that your wife is as committed as you are." Wendy nodded, the bow on top of her bouffant hairdo bobbing. Her lively voice, which reminded him of Marina from long ago, made his chest ache. She went on, "Things will turn around by next harvest most definitely—if not sooner."

Fausto had lost track of the days, the week, the months. He never called the attorney assigned to his case. Instead, he wrote a short letter: "Regretfully, we cannot pay off the default. We understand the outcome. As a farm worker who has toiled many years in the fields to put food on your table, I have a greater cause to fight over saving one house." He mailed it knowing that the last sentence was as useless as standing ground when Frank Radic's tractor sprayed a white cloud of pesticide across the picket line. He knew the attorney was awaiting court approval to begin foreclosure procedures. Could it be May already?

He stood up and thanked them for the meal. Wendy held up a fist blackened with newspaper print and gave him a hug. *"Viva la huelga, Manong Fausto!"* she declared.

"Viva Manong Fausto!" Teddy gave him a hug too.

Fausto wove through the slow-moving crowd and stepped outside, his ears ringing with their words. He stared at the hard sun in the midday sky. After several moments, he saw only blackness, and then he was stricken by a sprinkling of tiny false stars.

It was still light outside on a mid-May evening when Fausto came home. He had taken his dinner at the Hall and brought a paper plate of warm pansit and lumpia covered in aluminum foil. He expected Marina to be in bed already, but maybe he could draw her to the kitchen with hot food. Getting her to talk had become impossible. When her gaze wasn't off into space or fixed, it seemed, on the cracks in the walls, she was anxious, hands always in motion. He felt guilty that he was leaving her alone so much, and he'd stopped trying to get her out of the house. But for a few months now, she had pushed him away, closing him off by curling up into a tight ball. He proposed looking for work up north again, but just like that she dropped out of her stupor and accused him of trying to abandon her.

He felt stuck. Here but not here. Trying to help her but doing nothing. Useless in the house when he should have joined Prudencio and Ayong, who left to pick prunes in the Sacramento Valley and clingstone peaches in Modesto. Severo Laigo and most of the pinoys from the Cuculich camp migrated to Stanislaus County to harvest cherries. It was easier to stay away, hang out in the Filipino Hall, but he knew he needed to spend more time with Marina now. She wasn't eating much beyond the oranges and powdered milk he diligently brought home. He was worried about her health. Late one night, in his half-sleep he thought he heard her vomit in the bathroom. But when he asked her if she wanted to see the volunteer nurse, she insisted that she was fine.

"I brought you some pansit and lumpia," Fausto called as he came in the door. "You need to eat more." He was surprised to find Marina huddled on the sofa, dressed in slacks and a long-sleeved blouse, wrapped in the same pink blanket she had used all winter. He laid the paper plate on the coffee table. "I thought maybe we can talk, for once."

She stood up and slapped an opened envelope against his chest. The letter was certified and hand delivered to the house, requiring her signature. As he took out the official letter, he tasted yeast in his mouth as if he'd drunk beer, though he hadn't had a drop in days. He recognized the law office's letterhead. The attorney was informing him that he had filed a Notice of Default with the county clerk's office. A copy of the Notice was included. The total amount of the default made him dizzy. Fausto still had a 30-day reinstatement period to pay off the amount. But the two or three months' deadline had vanished. Where had he been all that time? He looked at Marina. *It's useless, Marina, useless.*

"I called the attorney's office," she said. "How foolish I looked! Why did you not tell me this has been going on for several months now? *Apay ngay?*"

"You know we have not been paying the full amount for months now and we have not been paying at all since you stopped working at the packing house," he said.

She paced the living room, the blanket, its yarn unraveling at the edges, sweeping the floor behind her. "I knew something bad would happen, but I did not expect this," she said.

He let go of the letter. It landed on the coffee table. "You knew we were running out of money, but you would not let me look for work to support us."

"You needed to take care of me. You still do. How can you be a husband hundreds of miles away?" She bit her lip. The pressure seemed to make her whole face ashen. "I could have asked Auntie Luz for help if I had known. You could have gotten work at one of the farms instead of being on the picket lines. Now we have nothing."

"How could you *not* know? You told me not to tell Luz or Benny how bad things were!" He pulled on his hair. "Ai, it does not matter. We have each other. That is what is most important. We can still go to another city and picket."

"We have nothing, Fausto, nothing to raise a family in!"

She kicked the coffee table on its end. Lumpia and noodles were slopped on the floor like scraps for pigs. He kneeled down and scooped up the noodles onto the paper plate, which was soaked through by now. The floor hadn't been swept for days. Dust motes clung to the noodles. He righted the table but gave up on the plate of food.

"For all my hard work, putting my brothers and sisters through school, I received nothing but more expectations from my mother and father." She hiccupped as she gulped for air. "I came here for a new life.

Now you are making decisions for me, just like my parents, without my knowledge and consent, without a care about me. You lied to me. You kept things from me, just like my parents. You betrayed me."

"You are not being fair." His foot slid on the grease-stained floor.

"Fair?" Her voice cracked. "Yes, you are right. What do I know of fairness?"

"I know you are unhappy, but I did what you told me to do!" he said miserably. "A house is a thing. A house is something we can get back later. The strike will end."

"We were not rich, but we were happy before the strike. That was enough for me!" she said. "I want our baby to be born without violence, to come home to our house. And now that will not happen."

How could he tell her what he'd been thinking, that maybe what he had buried in the melon patch was the only chance God had given them? That it died was his fault. That he couldn't satisfy her was his fault. When she woke him at night, straddling him, she stroked his penis until it hardened, and then it became a quest to get him to come. The times he collapsed on top of her, panting as if he had cleared an entire field of 'gras by himself, telling her he was sorry, she kept pressing him. Again! She mounted him, and they tried once more, though he was worn out, drained of pleasure. Her eyes, nose, and mouth scrunched up as if she were trying to unscrew a stuck lid from a jar. When he failed her, she rolled off of him and clung to her pillow at the edge of the bed. The times he came, she wept and then fell into an exhausted sleep. He lay on his side of the bed, feeling empty long before he had emptied out. When she stopped seeking him in bed the last few months, he was buoyed with masked relief yet burdened with failure.

"Marina." He'd forgotten how tender his voice could be.

She stared back, unblinking. "You cannot do anything anymore."

He yanked the blanket away and threw it on the floor. He grabbed her arm, but she jerked back and stared with disgust at the dark smudge on her sleeve. Early in their courtship, he didn't want her to see him dirty. He shaved and showered before seeing her. But she told him she wanted to see him when he came from the vineyards, that hard work was honorable. She touched the grit that had become part of his face, the texture of his skin. Somehow, the dirt on his body made him more desirable. Now she rubbed her arm.

He upended the coffee table with a swift kick. The corner of the table landed in the middle of the plate of food. It was cheap—particleboard with thin laminate strips curling up at the edges—like everything else in the house.

Marina retreated to the opposite side of the room. "I'm going to stay with Auntie Luz for now," she said. "I cannot outlast the strike here. It's not good for my nerves. Auntie Luz said she would take me to Chicago." She grabbed the vase of plastic flowers on the other end table and held it against her stomach. A runaway bride.

He rushed up to her and wrapped his hands around the vase. "In the morning, I'll sign us up to lead the boycott in Chicago." For a moment, he felt uplifted, holding their wedding bouquet together. But when she let go of the flowers, he realized she meant to leave him behind.

"You told me to stay here and take care of you. And now *you* are leaving *me?*"

"I am not leaving you." The spark in her emerald-flecked eyes was gone, as if that had been turned off too. "I will go away with Auntie Luz for a few months. Until I get better. Until everything is better. Then we will know what we have and what we must do."

"How can we decide what to do if we are not together? You kept me here because you said a husband needs to be with his wife."

She flinched before he lifted the vase above his head and hurled it in the corner of the room. She stared at the jagged pieces of glass and flowers strewn on the floor. But when she turned around, her face was full of wonder. "I'm doing this for us. I love you, Fausto!"

He sat down on his haunches, his lungs squeezed of oxygen, as if a massive landslide had knocked him down. It was all he could do to stand up again. It was all he could do to try to breathe. He hadn't heard her say those words for so long. It rang false.

"What do you know of love, eh? People sacrifice for love. We lose a few possessions, and now you are leaving! Well, then, get out! Go back to Vigan because I'll not be waiting for you whenever you feel like returning! I don't want you back!"

The words shot out. He wasn't sure he meant it. But she looked as if she were expecting it. He glanced wildly about the room, looking for a suitcase. Was Luz waiting outside? He lunged at the front door and threw it open, but he was only met by the full moon and the faint sound of crickets.

"You mean it," she said, shivering.

He stared at the door, open mouthed.

"Look at you!" Her voice was full of disbelief and sadness as she inched her way to the front door, groping the wall behind her.

He turned away. Her face was like a mirror—showing him how shameful he was behaving. His hand twitched on the doorknob. He could close the door. They could sit down on the sofa and talk. He would appeal to Larry first thing in the morning for a loan. He would ask Teddy and Wendy what to do about the foreclosure. He didn't think he was imagining that Wendy was offering help from her wealthy father. For love, he could shed his pride, he could beg. He could make it all up to everyone in the end.

But her face had a faraway look to it. "Useless! So useless!" she whispered to the floor, as if confiding the truth, what was deepest in her heart.

"Go back to Vigan!" he said. *"Go!"*

He grabbed her arm, which felt thinner than he'd remembered, and with all his might he pushed her out into the front lawn. She tumbled across the grass, her arms and legs splayed, her hair twirling in the air. She rolled in the grass, clutching her stomach with one hand, her face hidden by the other. Before he could find his voice, she stood up—everything about her like jelly—and ran off into the darkness. He tried to will himself to go after her, but he was stuck in the doorway, useless, so useless.

CHAPTER 12

Union and division

Delano, May 1966–July 1970

For a moment Fausto thought Marina had slept next to him all night—the cinnamon scent of her Cotillion perfume was heady and steeped in her pillow. He thought she had risen to make breakfast because the bedroom was already brilliant with May sunshine. But the house was silent. When he got up, still wearing his clothes from the day before, his work boot knocked down two empty bottles of Dos Equis. His tongue was thick with the aftertaste of beer. Its sourness clung to his skin.

The living room smelled of pansit. The plastic flowers and broken glass were still scattered across the floor. A swarm of ants had claimed the food. Soon they were pinching his ankles. It was good to feel pain, however slight, though the pricks soon ended and a dull ache began to seep out from his chest.

"Fausto!" Benny yelled from outside. "Fausto Empleo!"

Benny jiggled the front doorknob violently. Fausto unlocked it, afraid the door was going to come crashing down. Benny tumbled into the living room and stopped in front of the overturned coffee table. One of its legs had broken off.

"Marina is gone," Fausto mumbled.

"Yes, I know." Benny whirled around. "Luz took her to Porterville Hospital."

Fausto searched the room, trying to find the keys to the Bel Air. "I need to go get her!"

"Come here." Benny sat down on the sofa and patted the cushion next to him. His eyes were rimmed with dark circles. "She's not there anymore."

Fausto sank, the feeling gone from his legs. "Where is she?"

Benny stamped at the ants near his feet. "I wasn't home when Marina came to our house. Luz said she was limping and complaining of pain in her hip and stomach. Luz left me a note saying she was here helping Marina. But she had taken Marina to the emergency room and told the doctor she had fallen."

Fausto pulled himself to the edge of the sofa. "She is okay?"

Benny said the doctor examined and released her. It was past midnight when they drove back to Benny and Luz's house. Benny had fallen asleep on the sofa waiting for Luz and didn't know that in their car in the driveway Luz was trying in vain to convince Marina to stay with them. Marina didn't want to go to Chicago anymore. She wanted to go back to the Philippines. She had no suitcase, no passport, but Marina talked Luz into sneaking back to her house. Benny gave Fausto a withering look. Luz reported that Fausto was passed out, face down on the bed, stinking of beer. Fausto didn't even stir when Marina threw clothes in an overnight bag, pulled her passport from the dresser, and slipped away into the night.

Fausto held his head in his hands. If he had stayed sober and up all night, she would have seen that his vigil meant he cared. He would have talked her into staying.

Instead, Luz gave Marina money meant for the next mortgage payment, assuring Marina that their cousins in Chicago could wire her money in a day. With misgivings, Luz drove her to the Bakersfield airport, some forty miles away, and waited until early morning when Marina boarded a twin-engine plane headed for Los Angeles. Benny had woken up while she was still gone. Sick with worry, he had put on his shoes to walk to the gray-brick house when she returned home. Luz, hollow-eyed and exhausted, sat down at the kitchen table and cried.

"Luz called her sister in Vigan to let her know," Benny said. "Marina is at Los Angeles International. By tonight, she will be on her way back to the Philippines."

"I'll drive to LA." Fausto glanced at the wall clock. It was almost two in the afternoon.

"Let her go. Ai, Fausto! You told her to go back to Vigan! *Ai sus!*" Benny slapped at his ankle and fled from the stream of ants.

Fausto looked away, ashamed that Benny and Luz knew what he had said to Marina. Benny dragged a trashcan from the kitchen and picked up the food with paper towels. Fausto cleaned the floor with a sponge and took the broom Benny handed him.

"Why did you two fight?" Benny asked finally.

Fausto swept the broken pieces of glass. He found the letter from the bank behind the sofa, collecting ants, and handed it to Benny.

"Stupid!" Benny punched the piece of paper. "Why did you not tell us when you missed the first payment? We would have helped."

"*Gasat mo?*" Fausto retreated behind the coffee table. "You had a mortgage too. I could not ask Luz's cousins, either; Marina did not know. I had no one to ask here."

Benny's whole face seemed to throb, his eyes, the veins in his temple. "We are in Terra Bella, Fausto, surrounded by family! We have come this far! Why did you not come with me to find work before it got this bad?"

"Marina wanted me to stay here with her." Even as he said it, he realized how foolish he sounded.

"You are making nonsense!" Benny kicked the trashcan. "We bought this house. We put so much work into it! It was Marina's and your house. And now—*awanen!*"

Fausto stood the coffee table on its three legs. "When the bank said it was going to take the house away, I told Marina we could lead the grape boycott in another city far away from here. We would not need a house. But she did not like that."

"Luz was not interested, either," Benny said. "It has been hard on her to be treated so poorly by Nida and Rozelle and the others, but she did not want to leave town like this." He threw the large pieces of glass in the trashcan. Benny stared out the front door, at the lawn kept green by spring rains. "Where will you go? You cannot stay with me, you understand. *Ipahamak nak met.*"

"I have caused you enough trouble. I don't want my problems to become yours."

"They are one and the same—the way it should be." Benny picked up the plastic flowers, shook the ants out, and handed them to Fausto.

"Prudencio and Ayong wrote. They are looking for an apartment in Delano," Fausto said. "I'll stay with them. I'll be okay."

Benny shook his head again as he turned to the front door.

"You will not tell anyone else what happened, eh?" Fausto asked.

"I cannot tell Luz to be quiet," Benny said. "She's very angry."

"Will she not protect Marina? Does she hate me this much?"

"Don't push me!" Benny struck the doorframe with his fist. "Luz did not want me to come here, and when I insisted, she tried to come. She thinks I'll side with you because I always do. But you and I had to talk alone." He gave the trashcan a push. "Ai, Fausto. It will not be easy. Once everyone in Terra Bella finds out—" He gave Fausto a fierce hug before walking out of the house.

Fausto wandered in and out of the rooms. He walked out into the garden, where green sprouts poked through the earth and vines of parya inched their way up their wooden stakes. He eyed the young vines in the melon patch. Should he dig up the shoebox? But where would he put it? He glanced around him, dizzy with decisions to make when moments ago he thought he had none. He caught his breath as the sound of a gavel came pounding down again and again. The cracks echoed in his head like thunder, though it was the silence afterward that brought him to his knees.

————————

A few days after Marina had fled, Fausto woke up to a different-colored ceiling. The sheets were crisp, not soft and sour smelling, the clothes he had worn the day before, clean and folded on a nearby chair. Arturo Junior lay sprawled across a mattress on the floor beside the bed, yet when Fausto shifted his position, like a guard dog the boy rose and came to his side. Fausto flinched, afraid that he stank of beer. But he smelled of the creamy soap that the boy used in his bath. He couldn't remember how he had gotten to where he was. Arturo Junior placed his hand on top of Fausto's. Everything in the room was still.

————————

Prudencio and Ayong returned in early June. Fausto found them in the Filipino Hall, finishing a plate of tamales and catching up with Manong Flor, who was now working alongside a Mexican cook in the kitchen. As they walked to the parking lot, Prudencio told Fausto that they would pick cherries in Tulare County during the week and picket on the weekends. They were staying with Severo Laigo and his friends until they signed the lease for an apartment on the west side of the railroad tracks. They were only gone for six months, but they looked older. The skin on Prudencio's cheeks was peeling. It was as if he had spent the entire six months, night and day, exposed to sun and wind.

Prudencio scraped a mound of tobacco chew from a tin with his fingernail and packed the fine grounds between his lower gum and lip. "Did you hear what the union's volunteer boycotters have been doing in the grocery stores?"

They heard these stories when they were harvesting rice in Sacramento. Upstart college students loaded food on top of bunches of grapes in grocery carts and caused scenes in front of shoppers, demanding store managers to tell them if the grapes were union grapes. If they were not, they left the carts full of squashed grapes in the aisles.

"Is it true?" Prudencio said.

Fausto frowned. "I never heard about this in the Hall or in the fields."

"We thought the growers are spreading rumors to make the boycott look bad," Ayong said. "We saw many boycotts in the grocery stores in Sacramento, and nobody behaved that way. But if it is true, it makes the unions look bad."

Prudencio moved the chew to his other cheek. "We heard the Teamsters union is coming to town. The packers, truckers, and cannery workers are supposed to be honoring our picket line! Now they are crossing the line and loading and transporting grapes?"

"They say they are interested in field workers now," Fausto reported. "The growers see the Teamsters as their friend. Joseph Kostelic invited them to organize his workers on his farms."

Ayong whistled through his missing teeth. "He has twelve thousand acres in this area and an army of field workers. What's he trying to do?"

"There is talk he has bribed the Teamsters or promised them something to help him divide AWOC and the NFWA," Fausto said.

"Everybody knows the Teamsters are crooked!" Ayong's lip curled up in disgust. "They are with the Mafia. Kostelic favors a crooked union over an honest union?"

"I tell the workers who are impatient not to join the Teamsters." A trickle of perspiration slid down Fausto's neck. The blacktop was hot under the June sun. "I tell them the AFL-CIO kicked the Teamsters out because of their corruption, but they say we are making things up about the Teamsters because Chávez is losing the fight."

"So we have a lot of work to do—with our own members." Ayong grimaced.

"There has also been talk of merging the two unions," Fausto said.

"AWOC should not merge with Chávez," Prudencio said. "We have to find a way to keep the Teamsters from stealing AWOC members."

"Prudencio!" Fausto scolded. "The two unions have been on the picket line together for almost a year now."

"I don't have a problem with the NFWA supporting AWOC." Prudencio spit chew on the blacktop. "But Chávez's organization is 100 percent Mexican-American. There's no room for pinoys. Chávez wants our membership and our money. Let him be a politician in his own organization."

"Ai, we cannot be divided on the issue of improving conditions in the fields!" Fausto said. "You know the strike has weakened AWOC. The pinoys who walked out of the fields last September left a long time ago. We need more people, or else AWOC will die by its own hand. What is the matter with you, huh? You were not talking like this before you left Delano."

Prudencio pulled on his collar. His neck was red and chapped. "I've been reading about Chávez in the newspapers. He's always speaking for the strikers. Where is Larry? He was the one who first stood up to the growers. They had to drag Chávez into this."

"This is not about Chávez or Larry," Fausto said. "I have no problem with Chávez. If Larry did, he would say so. But Larry knows we must stay together for the good of all the farm workers. We are all working for one common goal."

"I'll vote to merge." Ayong peeled off a baseball cap bleached with sweat stains. "It is worth it if it ends the strike. Too many people lost too many things."

"We can worry about votes later. We need to find a place to live!" Prudencio said.

Fausto coughed into his fist. "I was thinking maybe I could stay with you two when you get your own place."

Prudencio and Ayong exchanged glances. "Of course, you can stay with us," Ayong said. "But we will not let you pay for anything—not rent or food."

"Stay with us as long as you want," Prudencio said.

Fausto nodded. He didn't know how much Prudencio and Ayong knew. He never told Larry or the other Filipino organizers. Wendy Whitman left for France for a family summer vacation, and Teddy Enebrad regretfully announced that he would not be able to come up to Delano until the fall because he had to work to pay for summer school.

———————

When Fausto moved in with Prudencio and Ayong, he told them what happened between Marina and him.

"It cannot be helped if Marina could not understand your devotion to the union," Ayong said. "Wives need to support their husbands' beliefs, or else what is the use?"

"You talk like you know these things!" Prudencio scoffed.

"That is why I am *not* married." Ayong grinned, his weathered teeth poking up like old tombstones.

Prudencio waved off Ayong. He told Fausto that some pinoys took their foreclosure notices to Larry, but Larry couldn't do anything about it—even though they were pinoy, even though they had been loyal to the union and stood on the picket lines since that September morning. Nobody expected the strike to last this long. Union funds were running low, Larry explained. He told them to leave the area and find work anywhere, even as far away as the canneries in Alaska. The wives of some pinoys and Mexicans left to find work and swore they were not coming back. Fausto was not alone, Prudencio pointed out. But Fausto wasn't going to feel better at the expense of somebody else's troubles. He dropped his suitcase in the windowless second bedroom. Gashes in the wall revealed two layers of paint, but not even a fresh coat of paint could mask the odor of cigarette smoke. Prudencio and Ayong shared the bigger bedroom, with a view of the railroad tracks.

Prudencio handed out three bottles of Dos Equis. They raised their beers around a small table that crowded the kitchen. Outside the window empty cotton cages and rusty-orange Southern Pacific boxcars sat on one set of railroad tracks. An oncoming train rumbled not far away as the crossing signal bell rang.

————————

Fausto went back to the house to clean it out. He kept to himself, though he knew he was being watched. Blinds were being bent and drapes pulled aside in the neighboring houses. He knew it was useless, but he sat down and wrote a letter to Luz, telling her he was sorry for what he had done to Marina, that he was going to bring her back and get the house back too. The list of things to retrieve seemed to grow. On his walk back from mailing the letter at the post office, he saw Pete Gunabe watering his front lawn. He was going to cross the street, but Pete waved him over.

"*Kumusta,*" Fausto called out on the other side of the chain-link fence. Pete turned the water off and dragged the hose with him. "*Kumusta!*"

"Did you hear?" Fausto said. The words about Marina's departure rushed out as if from a guilty child wanting to confess and receive swift punishment.

"Which guy was it, Manong? Which pinoy boy did she run off with? Anyone we know?" Pete looked over at the kitchen window. His wife,

Elsie, leapt out of view. "Was it someone she picked grapes with in the fields? I heard it was a Visayan."

Fausto stepped away from the fence. "She did not run off with anybody!"

"Mabalinmo nga ibaga kaniak." Pete winked and scratched his belly.

"I don't have to tell *you* anything." Fausto doubled up his fists. "You son-of-a-bitch! She did not run off with anybody!"

Pete dropped the hose and held up both hands. "I know how angry you are, but *saan-nak nga pagpapasan panggep ta pungtot mo,* ah? You already took your anger out on her. You gave that whore what she deserves."

Fausto spit on the chain-link fence.

"I'm not going to get angry with you, Manong, because of what you have been through. I pity you," he said, smirking. Fausto walked quickly away, but Pete called after him, "What a shame, Manong, losing your house and your wife. What a shame!"

Fausto drove up to the house on a Saturday morning in mid-June. A for-sale sign—as big as the huelga sign Fausto carried in the fields—was staked in the front lawn. It announced that the house would be auctioned off the first week in September. He had been expecting this next step, but as he stood there, he couldn't have anticipated what he was feeling, or rather what he wasn't feeling. He didn't care that the neighbors were probably spying on him. He imagined they came out to watch when the sign was driven into the grass, talking to one another about how Manong Fausto had lost it all with one push. He threw up his fists at the neighboring houses. *If you insult me, if I catch you gossiping about me, I'll break your bones.* Chin jutting out, he jerked his head from one neighbor's window to another, though the drapes and blinds on either side of him were still.

In truth, he didn't really care about the auction, though he had scrubbed the house. He had washed and rehung the white voile curtains, sheer as a bridal veil, in the living room windows and tacked Marina's spring wreath on the front door despite the sparrows' theft of twigs and leaves for their nests. He brushed dirt off the welcome mat and then he sat on his haunches, moaning like a house settling on its foundation.

He threw open the bedroom closet doors and removed Marina's clothes from wire hangers that rattled on the rod like bones. As he loaded the boxes to take to the Goodwill store in Porterville, he knew he would have to sell the Bel Air, which meant he would have to depend on Prudencio for either a ride or permission to drive his friend's old Dodge Dart, which leaked quarts of oil wherever it was parked. His Bel Air was reliable, whereas the Dart would surely not make it beyond the Central Valley, but he couldn't afford the gas or insurance. In the morning, he taped a "For Sale" sign on the back passenger window of the Bel Air and parked it in front of the house. Fidel offered to buy it for seventy-five dollars above the asking price.

"I know you and Benny took good care of the car. It's worth more than what you are asking," Fidel said, as he peeled back wilted bills from his wallet. "Pilar's nephew is coming from the Philippines, and once he gets his driver's license he will need a car to find work."

Fidel fingered the key Fausto had given him. "Manong, you have to come to the dance this year." When Fausto shook his head, Fidel clapped him on the back. "There are a few of us who are active. There are many in the Circle who support the strike. They are just quiet. It's important to show our solidarity to everybody there. Maybe the quiet ones won't be so quiet. The dance is a few months away still. Think about it."

Fausto could only shrug. After Fidel left, he picked ripe vegetables from the garden. Lito Guzman came to the fence that separated their backyards. Fausto knew Lito was being kind, watering the section of garden closest to his property, as far as his garden hoses could reach. He extended his hand and told Fausto he was sorry about what happened. When Fausto removed his work gloves and shook Lito's hand, a warm rush greeted him as he returned his neighbor's smile. Lito offered to clear out the garden shed and sell the tools at the flea market in Bakersfield.

"You won't get much money, but it's something," Lito said, and pulled on a baseball cap to hide his bald spot. "If you like, I can work your garden and harvest the vegetables." He kicked back a chicken that had wandered to the fence that he was forever repairing.

Fausto surveyed the garden of tarong, kamatis, and parya. In another month, it would fill two freezers with vegetables. He nodded, rubbing his eyes hard enough to punch black spots in his vision. "But leave the honeydew—they are no good," he said.

Lito cast a doubtful look at the corner of the backyard, at the swelling globes of honeydew, before returning to his yard. Fausto strode over to the melon patch and began pulling on the vines. They didn't give easily. Why should they? He grunted and heaved until every last root was wrenched from the soil. He pulled a half dozen melons, smooth and rock hard, the rind chalky white with a wash of pale green. He sniffed their blossoms—they gave off no fragrance. One by one, Fausto took the melons and smashed them into the ground, splattering webs of pulp and seeds on his work boots.

Fausto understood little of the negotiations being conducted in San Francisco among the grower Jack Dragovich, Chávez, and Bill Kircher, the AFL-CIO's chief of organizing, who represented AWOC. In the Filipino Hall, AWOC members crowded around the dining tables, reading newspaper reports. Dragovich intended to hold elections at his farms in Delano and offer four choices: AWOC, the NFWA, the Teamsters union, and "no union." Manong Flor told him that the Teamsters would "fix" the election with bribes and intimidation. Many feared that putting NFWA and AWOC on the ballot would split the vote and ensure an easy victory for the International Brotherhood of Teamsters.

Dragovich held the elections, and, as expected, the Teamsters won. Fausto tried to keep up with the news accounts of the political maneuverings that followed, including Governor Brown intervening by asking Dragovich to hold new elections, but he was still confused. All he knew by midsummer was that Dragovich agreed to schedule another election at the end of August.

Rumors of AWOC and the NFWA merging began to spread, though leadership on both sides remained tight lipped. It wasn't until late July that union leaders announced a vote to merge. Members at both the Filipino Hall and Huelga House argued whether such a move was in each other's best interests.

Fausto and Benny had just sat down in the dining area to eat lumpia when a thin Chicano with a strip of a moustache and long sideburns walked to the front of the hall's meeting area and spoke Spanish into a microphone. A crowd gathered around him, and he stopped to answer questions before continuing to read from a piece of paper. Soon, a handful of men, mostly pinoys, left. The remaining pinoys moved to another part of the hall and resumed their conversations. A group of

Yemenis filed out. A few Anglos remained on the fringes of the crowd.

"Ai, this happens all the time—they make announcements in Spanish and don't translate for everybody else!" Benny scowled and ate the last of his cold lumpia. "We pinoys are already invisible. Chávez should know what his left hand is doing. Maybe he knows, but he looks the other way."

A young Chicano standing near their table leaned toward them. "We have concerns too!" he blurted out. "The growers always choose the Filipinos first to work their fields and then promote them to foremen. Will that change when this strike is over?"

"It is not our fault if the growers prefer the pinoys," Benny said. "We have worked for the growers for twenty, thirty, thirty-five years."

"But you strike, no? Then something must be wrong between the growers and the Filipinos." The Chicano gave Benny and Fausto a dismissive look and moved into the crowd.

Fausto pushed his plate away and stood up. "Let's go outside. I'm not hungry," he told Benny, and left the hall.

In the parking lot, Filipinos converged on Larry Itliong as he stepped out of the dusty-blue Chevy Impala that AWOC was leasing for him. Fausto made his way through until he was close enough to smell cigar smoke on Larry's rumpled shirt. Larry removed his black, horn-rimmed glasses and surveyed the men.

Prudencio planted his knuckles on the hood of the Impala and spoke to Larry. "Ben Gines and Pete Manuel are threatening to quit AWOC if the unions merge. Ben says more than half of AWOC's organizers—not just the Filipinos, but the Anglos and Mexicans—will quit in protest. What will become of us if all AWOC's organizers leave?"

Paulo Agbayani, who was standing beside Prudencio, addressed Larry too. "Ben says in your heart you are against the merger," he said. "Ben told me you are afraid the Filipinos will lose their representation. Is that true?"

"There is a greater argument for merging," Larry began, but the men stirred like restless hornets. He put up his good hand. "This is the first time in the history of the agricultural labor movement that we can build one strong farm workers union to improve the working conditions of *all* farm workers." Larry spoke in a loud voice as rumbling swept through the crowd. "If Ben and the rest of the AWOC organizers leave, the Teamsters and the growers will celebrate. César is our friend. The growers are our enemy. Don't confuse the two! If you desert the union, you are aiding the growers' cause and we will *never* win the struggle in the fields."

Fausto's heart pumped wildly. He began clapping. A few pinoys joined him, though most of the men remained mute. Off to the side, a group of Yemenis and Chicanos clapped as well. Larry gave Fausto a quick smile and plucked a cigar from his chest pocket before marching into the Filipino Hall. The crowd thinned, with many following Larry inside.

Benny emerged. "So Larry is for the two unions coming together," he said.

Prudencio leaned against his Dodge Dart. "It did not sound as if he believes in it."

"I heard no such thing!" Ayong pulled on Prudencio's ear, a leathery flap. "Do you need a hearing aid?" he demanded, as Prudencio swatted his hand away.

Benny leaned forward as if harboring a secret. "I know Larry is worried Chávez will push the Filipinos aside. Manong Flor told me Larry was already talked out of leaving AWOC once before for the sake of the strike."

Fausto reminded them that Chávez told Senator Kennedy and his committee that farm work can be a decent job for his son if there is a union. *"Our* children will be in courthouses, schools, and hospitals—not in the fields," Fausto said. "But somebody has to work in the fields. Maybe it is the Mexicans who are coming to America. That is the direction of the union. Chávez has to think about the future of his people. Is that wrong?"

"We are still here," Prudencio said, pounding his chest.

"Yes, *adda tayo pay laeng ditoy,* but that is why we must unite: for better conditions for all of us, just like Larry said," Fausto told him.

"But at what cost?" Benny spoke up.

"You lost many things in America already," Prudencio said in a quiet voice. "Has the cost been worth it to you?"

"There are always costs." Fausto wasn't angry, though Prudencio looked as if he wished he could take back his words. Fausto looked Benny in the eye. *"Saanmo nga mabilang iti abakmo."*

"Wen," Benny said, looking away, "you cannot measure the things you have lost."

The August sun was unrelenting. By midday, the picketers had drunk all the ice water from the coolers the picket captains supplied along the property line of Frank Radic's farm. Fausto's straw hat did little to protect him from the heat. He took a break from marching up and down the shoulder of the road and sat in the shade of the Dodge Dart.

Fausto recognized Paulo Agbayani in the picket line when the short, stocky pinoy peeled off an old fedora to cool his damp head. He kept shifting the placard on his shoulder, making the black thunderbird insignia quiver. As he mopped his face and neck with a handkerchief, he got further behind in line. Suddenly, Paulo dropped to his knees as if in prayer. The sign tipped in front of him and he fell face forward. Fausto stood up, still feverish from the heat, as picketers surrounded Paulo's body.

"We need a car!" a black man shouted. "He needs to go to the hospital!"

Fausto froze, even as picketers from his side of the road ran over to help move Paulo to one of the picket captains' car.

"Paulo will be fine—just too much heat," another picket captain informed everyone on the bullhorn. "Let's get back to the picket lines!"

Everyone raised their signs and chanted *"Huelga! Huelga!"* including Fausto, though they did so in a daze. When Fausto, Prudencio, and Ayong returned to the Filipino Hall after their shift at Frank Radic's farm, Manong Flor told them Paulo had suffered a heart attack and died within hours of being admitted to the hospital.

A few days after Paulo Agbayani's funeral, a meeting to vote on the merger was called. Fausto heard the news while trying to convince scabs not to unload grapes at a cold-storage plant, and he knew many of his countrymen were picketing in faraway fields or were gone harvesting other crops. When Fausto returned to the Filipino Hall, Manong Flor pulled him into the kitchen and reported that the merger had gone through. The approval was overwhelming, with volunteers allowed to vote. It bothered Fausto that he didn't get to vote, but Manong Flor reminded him that AWOC was an organizing committee—not really a true union—directed like absentee landlords by AFL-CIO leaders in Washington, DC.

"Ai, doan get mad," Manong Flor counseled, wringing his hands with a damp dishtowel. "This is what you and me wanted, eh? It's good for AWOC."

Prudencio stormed into the galley kitchen, with Ayong hurrying after him. "I did not get to vote!" Prudencio threw his placard down.

Manong Flor insisted that if everyone had voted, the results would have been the same. The United Farm Workers Organizing Committee—the new union—would make its headquarters, called Forty Acres, in a labor camp west of town. An executive board of Chicanos and Filipinos named Chávez as director and Larry as vice director.

"So Larry has been demoted to Number Two?" Prudencio shook his head.

Manong Flor raised his hands, raw from dishwashing. "Larry was a paid organizer for those guys in Washington. He got more power now with UFWOC."

"As Number Two!" Prudencio spat out. "What will happen to us?"

Fausto shouldered his way to the middle. "We are now *united* farm workers."

"But for how long?" Prudencio glared at Fausto. "At what cost?"

A week after the vote, Benny sought out Fausto at the Filipino Hall. "I have been looking for you all day," he said, panting. "We need to talk."

Fausto motioned Benny to sit on the bench across the table from him, but Benny shook his head. "Not here," he said.

"Ania ti napasamak?"

Benny gave an abrupt laugh. "Nothing is wrong. But we need to talk." His face tightened up. "Did Fidel talk to you?"

Fausto nodded. The other day Fidel had asked Fausto again to attend the dance to show solidarity with the San Esteban Circle members who belonged to UFWOC or were sympathetic to the strike and boycott. Labor Day was the following weekend.

"Did Fidel tell you Macario knows he asked you to come to the dance?" Benny asked.

"Then I'll not go."

"Saan! No!" Benny said. "Macario is not angry at you anymore. He wants you to go to the dance so he can talk to you. He told me he is ready to join a union."

Fausto leaned back. Dusty tinsel hung like cobwebs from the ceiling lights. Faded red-and-green crepe paper drooped from light to light. So much had happened since December. He grew hopeful until Benny said Macario realized that the unions could no longer be ignored; he had to think of his future. Mr. Cuculich told Macario that the growers saw the merger as a scheme to throw the Teamsters out of the fields.

"So he wants to talk me into joining the Teamsters? A crooked union?" Fausto shook his head. "Is he changing your mind too?"

"*Saan!* I would not betray UFWOC!" Benny said. "Listen, Macario wants to talk to you. He has other things on his mind." Benny passed his hand over his eyes. "Come by the house before Saturday. We'll think about what to say to Macario." He pulled his straw hat down low over his eyes and hurried out of the hall.

Fausto wasn't going to go to Luz's house. He had accused her of spreading lies about what happened, though Benny defended her, saying all she told people was that they had disagreed over the strike and Marina returned to Vigan. *Dayta aminen!* That's all! Benny argued that it wasn't her fault if someone twisted the truth. If she had kept quiet, maybe everybody would have believed the lies, but those who heard it from Luz knew the truth. What did it matter? Fausto asked himself as he stepped out into the hot August afternoon. He would go to the dance. If they faulted him for destroying his marriage, they couldn't fault him for his loyalty to the union.

––––––––

Fausto yanked on the damp collar of his barong shirt. Even though Prudencio had rolled down all the car windows, Fausto's legs and back were moist with perspiration. He felt as scorched as the dry, yellow fields on either side of Highway 65.

Ayong fidgeted in his seat. "I am from Saoang, not San Esteban." He dusted the sleeve of his cotton barong shirt. "I do not like to dress up, and I cannot dance!"

Prudencio swatted him with his free hand. "We already told you! We are going to talk to all pinoys about the grape strike—not dance!"

"There are many relatives who are not from the area," Fausto reminded Ayong. "We need them to support the grape boycott."

"We have to let them know the Teamsters are crooked and UFWOC is the only union we need in the vineyards," Prudencio said. He had come to accept the new union, despite Larry's "demotion." Now that the battle was set between UFWOC and the Teamsters, Prudencio had become a loyalist.

The Dodge Dart bounced over railroad tracks intersecting the road. They were now on the main boulevard in Terra Bella and the Veterans Memorial Building was several blocks away. All the houses along the road were dark, the driveways and shoulders of the roads empty. The Veterans Memorial Building parking lot was packed with cars. Fausto surveyed the entrance where people were squeezing in. A group of men stood on the lawn. When they saw Nick Lazaro and Fidel—their faces inches apart—talking to one another, Fausto, Prudencio, and Ayong hurried to take Fidel's side.

"This is a family gathering," Nick was saying. Though he didn't hail from San Esteban, Nick's second wife did. He pointed at the UFWOC's black-thunderbird button pinned chest high on Fidel's barong shirt, and spit on the grass. "You better take that union button off before you go in. This is the Veterans Memorial Building, not the Filipino Hall."

"I served in the US Army in World War II," Fidel declared. "I fought for equality and freedom—what this country stands for. I can wear whatever I like."

When Fidel turned his back, Nick grabbed his arm, whirled him around, and yanked off the button with lightning speed. He threw it on the lawn where he had spit. Nick wasn't big, but his wiry arms were all muscle and he used to be a boxer, known for his left hook. Fidel pressed his fingers into the hole in his shirt. Nick stood his ground, his fists raised. Bug-eyed, some of the men retreated to the building. The ones who remained tightened the circle around the two men. A few clapped their hands and whistled as if they were at a cockfight. Prudencio rolled up his sleeves, but Fausto pulled him back.

When Nick took his eye off Fidel, Fidel pounced on him. They scuffled on the sidewalk and tumbled onto the grass. Fidel landed a solid punch. Nick's head snapped back as he fell to his knees, but he scrambled to his feet, his black patent shoes scuffed and pasted with blades of grass, and lunged after Fidel. Prudencio broke free of Fausto's hold and grabbed the back of Nick's shirt. They both fell over onto the sidewalk. Fausto and Ayong helped Fidel to his feet, and Fausto mopped up the blood on Fidel's face with his handkerchief. The tail-end of the crowd at the entrance began trickling to the lawn, the women on their tip-toes to see what had happened, the men shielding their wives' eyes. The crowd parted as Macario, trailed by Benny, emerged from the building.

Macario made big sweeping motions with his arms. "Everybody go inside now!" His voice was forceful, yet cheery, a master of ceremonies directing everyone to the ballroom to dance. "I'll take care of this."

Nick smirked at Fidel, ignoring the corner of his mouth, where the end of his moustache was sticky with blood. Fausto backed away and hid behind a hedge.

"Goddammit!" Macario said. "I warned you both to leave your opinions at home. Do I need to call the security guard to escort both of you to your cars?"

Nick's smirk vanished. "He started it first, wearing this," he said, and kicked Fidel's union button at Macario. *"Di pay naluto ti paria simmagpaw ti karabasa."*

"I'm in charge here; I'll jump in whenever I like, especially if somebody's going to get hurt," Macario said. "Fighting with our fists makes us look like thugs. We already have too much bad news spoiling our community."

Benny wiped the button on his trouser and handed it back to Fidel, who pinned it on the right side of shirt. As Nick continued to argue with Macario, Fausto caught Prudencio's attention; Prudencio nudged Ayong and they crept away.

But the moment they stepped into the lobby, Fausto wished he were still outside. At the reception table, Rozelle and Elsie Gunabe were exchanging money for programs. Elsie looked up and suddenly broke out into a coughing fit. Excusing herself, she rushed down the hall to the bathroom.

"Manong Fausto, what a nice surprise to see you," Rozelle said in a smooth voice.

Fausto couldn't tell if she was being sincere. She wasn't smiling, though for Domingo's sake he gave her the benefit of a doubt. He pulled out his wallet in silence.

Rozelle glanced at Prudencio and Ayong. "Are you members of the Circle?"

Fausto slapped six one-dollar bills on the table. "They are my guests."

Rozelle counted the bills and deposited them in a steel moneybox. "I didn't know you could be so generous, Manong, especially with the strike going on for so long."

Fausto walked away from the table and into the steamy ballroom. More than a dozen Teamsters members, including his townmates Bonafe Evangelista, Lito Guzman, and Melchor Vegara, stood by plastic vats of Hawaiian Punch set on the kitchen window counter. Fausto knew Macario had convinced them to sign with the Teamsters because the Teamsters were less trouble than UFWOC, though they were also boycotting grapes in the stores. Fausto recognized the other pinoys; he had shooed them away from the Filipino Hall parking lot before the merger, where they were trying to persuade AWOC members to join the Teamsters. Five UFWOC members stood at the other side of the ballroom, exchanging glances with the Teamsters members in between the dancing couples.

Fausto leaned against the ballroom's brick wall and took a deep breath. He hadn't seen many of his relatives since the incident with Marina. He spied Luz approaching Nida and kissing her on the cheek near the kitchen. Nida didn't return the kiss. Instead, she excused herself, made a beeline to the reception table, and whispered in Rozelle's ear. Fausto watched the two burst out laughing. In the ballroom, Luz walked along the edge of the dance floor toward the entrance as if she were dancing the foxtrot. Fausto stepped into her path. She moved aside and brushed up against his shoulder, her eyes filled with tears, and dashed past the reception table to the bathroom.

Prudencio motioned Fausto to join Fidel and Benny, who were walking toward the UFWOC members. They were halfway across the ballroom when Fausto felt a tap on the shoulder. He spun around, and Domingo grasped his hand and pumped it.

"*Kumusta!* I'm glad you came." His cousin's cheerfulness sounded forced.

Fausto inhaled cigarette smoke in Domingo's pomaded hair and barong shirt. "*Kumusta*," Fausto said, and embraced his cousin.

Macario strode to the front of the stage. His voice boomed into the microphone and out the speakers: "This dance is for everybody!" The band, in their black bowties and white dinner jackets, began playing "Night and Day."

"You look good," Domingo said in a loud voice over the music.

"Have you taken up smoking?"

Domingo examined his yellowed fingernails. "I was getting too nervous, so the doctor told me to take up a hobby." He laughed, shifting his weight, his eyes darting back and forth like fish trapped in a small bowl. "It's hard working in the fields these days."

Fausto grasped his cousin's wrist. "Then don't do it."

Domingo pulled away. "I cannot make the sacrifices you made. I got a family to support." His whole body went rigid. "We should not be talking like this."

"*Apay?* Why? Who said? Macario?" Fausto demanded.

"Macario has been in danger the most," Domingo spoke into his ear. "He brings a shotgun to the fields. It scares Nida, but she wants him to protect himself."

"How does a gun offer protection?"

Domingo reached for his chest pocket, lumpy with a pack of cigarettes that crinkled beneath his thrumming fingers. "You want a drink, Hawaiian Punch?" He looked over Fausto's shoulder and a sigh escaped from his lips.

Fausto expected Macario to clamp his hand on his shoulders, but it was Benny who was cutting across the ballroom in a straight line, bumping into dancing couples without apology, eyeing Fausto the whole way. Domingo excused himself when Benny came, as if they were changing shifts, and went outside, a cigarette twitching in his hand.

"Why did you not come by?" Benny wanted to know, as the band ended a slow tune.

"Luz would never let me in her house."

The wrinkles in Benny's forehead deepened. "We needed to talk before tonight. I thought maybe you were not going to the dance. What a coward I am! *Ai sus!*" He turned his back on Fausto. Macario was watching them. Fausto caught Macario lifting his chin at Benny, as if signaling. Benny whirled around.

"Macario wants to talk to you. He will try to change your mind, so maybe you should go home." Benny's words tumbled out as he nudged him toward the lobby, but Fausto sidestepped him.

Macario had vanished. The door leading to the courtyard was propped open.

"What is this all about?" Fausto demanded.

Benny touched the cuff of Fausto's barong shirt. "I have to find more work. Luz can't be the only one working. We need the money. I cannot picket anymore."

Someone other than Macario was announcing the next dance. The band began a lively song. Fausto turned his back to the stage. "*Apay?*" he whispered.

"We have decided to adopt a baby from back home," Benny said.

"Luz is going in November. She'll be gone for a few months. She says it will be easy to find a baby there—so many poor girls having babies. They need money more than babies."

"Why now—with the strike still going on?"

"When will the strike end? I don't know what is happening now that Chávez is head of UFWOC." Benny stared at the linoleum floor, his shiny shoes. "Ai, this is not what I was going to say, Fausto! We are not getting any younger. I wasted too much time because I could not admit my failure. We have accepted too much money from her cousins. I need to support Luz's decision and be able to provide for her and the baby."

"Are you quitting the union? Is this what you wanted to tell me?"

"I did not say that!" Benny passed his trembling hand over his face. "There is more. I have something to tell you. Let's go to the parking lot where it's quiet and talk, eh?"

Benny tried to herd Fausto to the lobby again, but Fausto shook free.

"I'll go see Macario now." When Benny's eyes grew wild, Fausto accused, "Benedicto! You already know what he is going to say!"

He headed for the courtyard as Nick joined his Teamsters friends by the kitchen. His shirt, its embroidered flowers soiled, was torn at the shoulder, but he was laughing.

Fausto escaped the ballroom's hot breath. The courtyard was lit by weak overhead lights, but he saw Macario standing next to a picnic bench, where his tuxedo jacket was draped. His cuffs were unbuttoned and starched shirtsleeves rolled up to his elbows. The ends of his bow tie hung loose on his chest. He stamped out his cigarette with the heel of his polished shoe and lit another cigarette, tossing the match into the brick barbecue.

"When I saw you talking to Benny," Macario said, and dragged on his cigarette, "I thought you would leave the dance instead of come out here to see me."

"*Apay ngay?* Why would I stay away?" Fausto walked around the barbecue to compose himself, until he ran out of room and stood inches away from Macario.

"I'm sorry about what happened to Marina." The end of his cigarette glowed red as he took another drag. "But tonight I want to talk to you about the house."

Fausto raised an eyebrow. "What house?"

Macario's whole body shook with laughter. Sparks flew from his cigarette and disappeared once they hit the patio. "Have you forgotten your house already?"

"It's not my house anymore."

Macario threw the cigarette into the barbecue. *"Manag selas ka? Agimon ka? Igim-i mon ka?* I never thought I would see you quit so easily. This is not like you. You haven't lost the house yet."

"I'm not a quitter," Fausto shot back, "but I cannot pay off what is owed. It's good as gone." He pointed his chin at the brick building where couples waltzed on the dance floor, their shapes distorted through the tall plates of glass. "What does Benny like to say? *Bendisyon bagas, agraman tuyo.*"

"Everything is not lost!" Macario yanked down his shirtsleeves, wrinkled and striped with bands of sweat, and pinched the pearly buttons through their buttonholes. "I have an offer for you." He tied his bow. "I'll pay off the default amount that is owed on your house. I'll even buy a roundtrip ticket for you to go to the Philippines and bring Marina back to Terra Bella. Of course, I'll pay for Marina's one-way ticket."

The charcoal in the barbecue gave off a faint trace of charred pigskin. Fausto's nostrils felt as if they were suddenly clogged with ashes. "You must be doing well to make such an offer!" He sized up his cousin's expensive-looking tuxedo, his fancy shoes. "Is Mr. Cuculich rewarding you for being loyal to him?"

"I invest my money well," Macario said.

The song ended, and the man taking Macario's place announced that the next song was open for all San Esteban Circle members. Couples packed the dance floor as the band broke into another tune.

"Why are you doing this?" Fausto moved away from the barbecue and its smell.

"I don't want us to be divided," Macario said. "I'm honoring Cary's memory. Let's not let what happened in Los Angeles repeat itself."

"This has nothing to do with Cary!" Fausto's voice cracked.

"This strike has divided our community—maybe for good if we let it. I don't want us to be divided. I want our community to be united. I want our Filipino community to be respected in our town."

"Your community." Fausto shook his head. "What do you want me to do, eh?"

"Quit UFWOC and the strike. *Dayta aminen!"* Macario clapped his hands.

"That's all?"

"Make Benny quit too. He's only following you. He always has."

"You know Benny has stopped picketing."

"But he hasn't quit the union. I offered him a job, but he won't take. He thinks going up north to find other work is more honorable." Macario sneered. "I can offer both of you good jobs. You can have your seniority back, plus a little extra per-box bonus. Nobody needs to know that." He winked at Fausto. "Benny would quit for good if you quit too. He needs all the money he can get his hands on now. So what do you say, eh?"

Fausto wanted to spit. "You think you are being generous—making me do something that benefits you in exchange for your money?"

"I am not dismissing what happened to you, Fausto," Macario said gravely. "I know how much you lost, and it pains me, Cousin. But now you have a chance to get it all back."

"This is not the way to undo my mistakes." Fausto resisted an urge to pummel his cousin's face. If Marina were behind the nearby eucalyptus tree, would she be sad or disgusted that he would not even consider getting everything back for her sake? It wasn't that easy, he would have pleaded with her. He stole a glance at the shadowy corner of the courtyard, where the eucalyptus branches hung limp, their leaves still in the warm air.

"This is not a bribe!" Macario's voice was edged with panic. "I'm looking out for you. If you keep up with this foolishness, you'll be alone. Maybe that's what you want! You have been given so much in the States and yet you squander it. After all these years, you're the gambler, not me! Not Cary!"

Fausto started walking. He would tell Prudencio and Ayong it was time to go.

"Fausto!" Macario called out from the patio's edge. "Do you want to throw away your marriage for good? Do you hate her so much you would disown your own child?"

Fausto rotated on legs he didn't feel connected to anymore. The concrete beneath his feet became rubbery and uneven. *"Ania?"* he mouthed without uttering a sound.

Macario's eyes widened. *"Ai sus!* I thought Benny already told you!"

Fausto pushed his way into the ballroom. The last notes the band played were muffled. Applause rang in his ear. Somehow he made it to Prudencio, Ayong, and Fidel.

"Fausto, did you like my boxing match with Nick?" Fidel grinned. He pointed to his back where grass stains bled into his cream-colored barong shirt as if it were a badge of honor. "Like hell Nick used to box for a living! He fights like a girl!"

"Where are Benny and Luz?" Fausto demanded.

Fidel's smile faded. "I saw them in the lobby a few minutes ago."

"What happened out there?" Ayong lifted his chin at the ballroom windows.

Fausto didn't answer. He wove his way through the crowds, unbuttoning the top two buttons of his barong shirt. He spotted Benny and Luz at the end of the lobby. She was dabbing at her eyes with a wad of facial tissue while he hovered over her.

"How long have you known about Marina?" Fausto called out before he reached them.

Luz wasn't startled. "I only told Benny a week ago," she answered, her eyes wet.

"In seven days, everyone else found out the news, except me, her husband!"

Benny came between Luz and Fausto. "I should have told you right away. I was not thinking clearly." He pointed to the side exit. "Let's talk outside—it's cooler."

At the other end of the hallway, Elsie leaned out of her chair, defying gravity. Macario's voice boomed across the hall. *Another dance for the San Esteban Circle members!*

"Who told Elsie?" Fausto asked. "Maybe Elsie made her gossip more colorful. Maybe in her retelling, the baby belongs to Marina's lover, the Visayan farm worker, and not me!"

"It's your baby, Manong Fausto," Luz whispered.

"You tell this to me *now?*" Fausto drove his fist into the concrete wall.

Luz gasped. His hand stung, but he kept his face rigid. He would not crumple.

"You knew she was pregnant before that night, eh? But you did not tell Benny for how many months? And this is how I find out about it? Luz, *kaguranak la unay.*"

"I don't hate you, Manong. I promised Marina not to tell you."

Fausto wrapped his hand around his swelling knuckles. "She could not make any decisions!"

Luz pursed her lips as if she were trying to contain herself, but then she blurted out, "Neither could you, Manong. Not that night and not tonight."

"That's enough." Benny put his arm around Luz. "Fausto, let's talk in the parking lot. Just the two of us."

"*Awanen!* No more!" Fausto said, and walked away from them.

"Manong Fausto," Luz called out. "I pity Marina, but I pity you more."

There was no anger in her voice. Fausto would have gone out the back, if not for Benny. Instead, he walked past Elsie and Rozelle. He laughed in spite of himself. His sorry life—that was all he had left to bet against. The bright lights of the lobby dazed him. Then someone opened the glass door. The hot draft made him aware of every part of his body that was moist—his underarms, the crook of his elbows, the back of his knees, his neck, his upper lip, his swollen eyes. A hand, slack with loose skin, took his hand.

"We'll get you out of here." It was Prudencio, his voice fiery and defiant. "I should make them return your money. They know six dollars is very dear to you."

"Never mind. *Bay-amon,*" Ayong murmured. "Let us go home, Fausto."

Fausto nodded, as the band played on.

After Labor Day weekend, Fausto borrowed Prudencio's car and drove to Benny's house. "Give me some money so I can see Marina," he told Benny straight up.

Benny stared dumbly through the screen door before pushing it open and letting Fausto barrel in. "Macario's offer is for Marina and the baby's sake," he said.

"It's a bribe!" Fausto said, exasperated. "I'll not abandon the union or the strike."

Benny's pants were speckled white. A wicker basket on wheeled legs and an open can of paint sat atop a spread of newspapers. He stood in front of it as if to shield it from Fausto. "How can you sacrifice your family? I could never live with myself," he murmured.

"Benny, whatever I do, I cannot live with myself." The rigidness in Fausto's body abandoned him. "She'll not come back. The look she gave me that night was not full of hate—it was full of regret."

"I don't believe you." Benny sat on his haunches. "Then why go there?"

Fausto stole a glance at the bassinet—how sturdy it looked. "My baby," he said.

"You cannot take the baby away!" Benny cried out.

"She'll not have to live with me anymore, but I'll take care of them, give them everything they need," Fausto insisted. "I'll give the baby a good education here."

"You'll provide everything? With what?"

"The strike will end soon, and all the growers will sign contracts."

Benny wiped his hands with a rag. "How do you know she will even keep it?"

"Hah?" Fausto's mouth gaped. For many months, having a baby was the one thing she had wanted more than anything else. Of course, she would keep it!

"Raising it by herself is too hard," Benny said. "Her family would not approve."

Fausto thought about the shoebox beneath the melons. "She would not get *rid* of it."

Benny passed his hand over his face. "Ai, don't say such things! I would never imagine it," he whispered, as if saying it out loud would make the deed come true.

"Do you think she would give the baby away? A stranger would raise our child?"

"Maybe she would give the baby to someone she trusts," Benny said slowly. "Maybe that person would be someone who can afford to take care of the baby."

"She would not do such a thing! Loan me money for a plane ticket. You owe me this favor."

"I cannot." Benny stood up. "I'm sorry. I have no money of my own."

Fausto withdrew his hand and left, banging the screen door shut.

Fausto sent a telegram to Marina's family in Vigan, asking for her whereabouts. He knew Benny would have counseled him not to do such a foolish thing, but he needed to know his fate. He wanted to tell Marina he knew about the baby. Maybe they were done, but they still shared this baby. Once he got in touch with Marina, he'd offer to take care of them. She would want an American education for her child. Maybe the gesture would open her heart to him again.

But weeks passed without a reply.

In early October, he received a letter from Marina's sister, Trinidad, but didn't open it until he downed two bottles of Dos Equis. She wrote that nobody in the family, especially Marina, wanted to see or hear from him again. If he ever came to the Philippines to try to take the baby away, he would be "taken care of once and for all." "We are making arrangements for the care of the baby," she wrote. "By your actions, you have given up all your responsibilities as husband and father."

Fausto longed to tell Benny about the telegram and Trinidad's response, hoping Luz could intervene. But Benny went north to find work and Luz left for the Philippines in mid-October, weeks ahead of when Benny said she was going. Why didn't Benny tell him? It was as if he didn't exist to Benny anymore, either.

Forty Acres was open, but the Filipino Hall still hosted some UFWOC activities and served as a hangout for many pinoys. A few days before Christmas, as Fausto handed out frozen turkeys from the Filipino Hall kitchen to families, Benny appeared by his side.

"*Kumusta!* Do you need some help?" Benny asked.

Manong Flor wiggled his way in between Fausto and Benny, staring at them with his scratched-up glasses. "Go with Benny. I will finish up," he said. Although his eyesight was growing worse, Manong Flor seemed to see and know everything that was going on.

Fausto blew on his numb fingers. "Do you need a turkey?"

Benny hunched his shoulders. "It's just me for Christmas. I don't need anything."

Fausto headed into the kitchen, where a big vat of menudo was on the stovetop. He ladled big spoonsful of diced beef tripe and hominy into two bowls. He could smell the cloves of garlic Manong Flor, who had been taught how to make menudo by the Mexican cook, slipped in to make the stew more flavorful.

Fausto set the bowls at the far end of one of the dining tables. "Did you hear who bought the house from the auction?"

"A young Visayan family. The husband is a farm worker too."

The menudo burned Fausto's tongue. "Lucky family got a bargain," he said, and spit a piece of rubbery fat into a paper napkin. "Have you heard from Luz?"

A smile bloomed on Benny's face. "The baby we are adopting was born."

"That's good," Fausto said. An ocean roared in his ears.

Luz and the family survived the typhoon that had struck Manila. It meant good luck for them all. The baby—more than a month late—was a healthy boy, with lots of hair, a big head that got stuck in delivery, and a howl that struck at her heart as if she had birthed the baby herself. Luz named him Rogelio, after her late father. As soon as she returned in March, she told Benny, she wanted the baby baptized. Benny was beside himself, holding his head in his hands as if he could barely contain his happiness.

Fausto wondered if he would ever find out how Marina fared in childbirth. Her bones were so delicate, her hips so small he couldn't imagine her pushing out a large baby. Maybe there were problems. Maybe she or the baby hadn't survived. Not knowing troubled him. "Has Luz visited Marina?"

"Huh?" Benny's smile faded.

"Did she visit Marina to see how she is doing?"

"She never mentioned anything about it." Benny stared at his bowl of menudo. "After the dance, Luz told me she did not want to talk about Marina anymore."

"She had the baby already. Does Luz not care about her and our baby?"

"*Hustoon, hustoon,*" Benny said, hushing him. "We did not talk about Marina when she called, but it does not mean she does not care about her niece. Fausto, Luz went to Manila to adopt our baby!" He slumped on the bench, the excitement of the news drained from his face.

"So Luz met the woman before the baby was born?" Fausto persisted.

"I don't know how these agencies work," Benny admitted. "They verified the mother's good health. Luz did not meet the mother, but she was there at the hospital."

"Why did she leave in October if the baby was going to be born in December?" Fausto drummed his fingers on the table, counting off the months with each tap. "Did she not already have the mother picked out before she left? Was this a different mother?"

"I don't know. She took care of all the papers." Bewildered, Benny rubbed at his eye with the heel of his palm. "I just wanted a baby."

Fausto remembered his mother complaining to him when he was

naughty that she should have known he would be difficult because she had a difficult delivery with him—his head was stuck in her pelvis.

"Fausto, do you hear me?" Benny called out. He rattled the spoon in Fausto's bowl. "Maybe you cannot forgive us for our mistakes in judgment of you and Marina, but I will keep trying to make it up to you. Luz was so happy she told me to decide who will be Rogelio's *ninong.*" He grinned. "I want you to be his ninong at the baptism."

"Luz has agreed to this?"

"I asked her if I could ask you. See, Fausto? Luz does not hate you. This is our present to you. Will you give us that honor?" He reached out and held Fausto's hands.

Fausto nodded, his hands warming up, because he couldn't find his voice.

In March, white blossoms adorned the orange trees. In the vineyards, scab workers pulled weeds and coughed as wet sulfur poisoned the cold air with the first mildew treatment of the year. The duration of the strike forced another wave of families and single men to leave Delano in search of work in the only possession they had left—their cars. More volunteers from outside the area arrived to replace departing strikers on the picket lines.

Over beer at the People's Café, Fausto told Prudencio, Ayong, Severo, Arturo, and Ahmed that Benny asked him to be Rogelio's ninong. He didn't tell them the baby was likely his. They would talk him out of believing this fantasy, if only to protect him.

"It is great honor to be baby's *padrino,*" Arturo said, and raised his beer in a toast. Everybody around the table raised their bottles; Ahmed lifted his glass of water.

"But I have nothing to give to Rogelio." Fausto held out his hands, wet from his sweating bottle of beer. "I should give him a welcome present, but I have nothing."

"The best gift is to teach that kid to be a good citizen of America," Severo said.

"What welcome present would you give Rogelio?" Ayong asked.

"Father Worthington at Our Lady of Guadalupe said a ninong's responsibility is to help the boy be a good Christian," Fausto said. "He recommended a simple rosary or a Bible for children. If I gave him a rosary, it would be fancy. The beads would be crystal, and the metal and the crucifix made of sterling silver. It would come in a small sterling-silver box with an engraving on the inside of the lid: 'For Rogelio, Love, Ninong Fausto.'"

Severo whistled. "That's some gift."

Fausto drained the last few drops of his lager. "It's for a special baby. That baby——" He stopped, aware that the beer was making his tongue loose, his mind fuzzy.

"Yes," Ahmed spoke up. "He is a special baby because if not for Benny and Luz, where would that baby be?"

Everyone nodded, but Fausto looked away. Billiard balls crashed into one another across the pool tables. Someone slipped a coin into the corner jukebox and loud music blared in the crowded café, making the walls and tables tremble.

———

Fausto hoped to accompany Benny to Los Angeles, but Benny left without asking him to come. Benny's boss from Lodi gave him two days off because he was planning to stay in Los Angeles overnight. The evening that Benny left, Prudencio and Ayong dragged Fausto to the People's Café despite his protests. Ahmed, Severo, and Arturo were waiting at a corner table. Fausto tried to smile, but he imagined that his lips looked more like a snarl. Nobody seemed to notice. They were all in good spirits. A pitcher of beer had already been served. Prudencio shoved a full glass in Fausto's hand.

"So we hear Rogelio is arriving tomorrow," Severo said.

Fausto raised the glass to his lips and paused. "That is what Benny told me this morning."

"Will you visit Rogelio tomorrow?" Ahmed asked.

"If they ask me, I'll come over." Fausto took a big gulp of cold beer.

"Then you better not go empty-handed," Prudencio said.

Arturo slid a black-velvet pouch across the table in front of Fausto. Inside was a small sterling-silver box, its lid decorated with a cross of inlaid black onyx. When he sprang the lid, the silver box revealed a mound of black-onyx beads. He lifted the rosary from the box, holding it high enough so that the pebbly beads gleamed in the lights and the sterling-silver crucifix and medal flashed. Arturo held the box open for him to read the engraving.

The grins around the table grew blurry as Fausto blinked back tears. "When the strike is over, I'll pay everyone back."

"Ah, no," Arturo said. "This our gift to you, *hermano*. You no pay back gifts."

"But this is too dear a price to pay, even for five people." Fausto insisted.

"You have already paid us back in so many other ways," Severo said, resting his right hand on the scarred wooden table.

Fausto fingered the delicate etching across the silver box. Prudencio raised his glass of beer. Soon five glasses of beer and Ahmed's glass of water clinked together.

"To Ninong Fausto!" Prudencio led the toast.

Ayong suggested a game of pool. Everyone got up quickly as if they understood that Fausto wanted to be alone. Fausto made the sign of the cross. His lelang had recited the rosary thousands of times—it was as natural to her as breathing. Now he would have to remember, for Rogelio's sake. He stumbled along, reciting the Apostle's Creed. The first black-onyx bead rolled between his fingers as he began the Our Father.

"Forgive us our trespasses," he said aloud, and tilted his head back. The cobwebbed ceiling turned glassy.

———

Fausto was waiting for Benny and Luz's return. He'd sat on the wooden lawn chair in the front yard for hours, not knowing their time of arrival, not caring what their reaction might be. When the newer Bel Air pulled into the driveway in the early afternoon, Fausto stood and waved. Benny got out, but Luz remained in the front seat, holding the baby close to her chest.

"*Kumusta!*" Benny called out, a wide grin on his face. "You want to meet the baby?"

"Our baby," Luz said, halfway out of the car, still holding Rogelio close to her chest as if she were nursing him, though her blouse was buttoned up to her neck.

Fausto was afraid to hold out his arms, though his muscles ached with desire. He brushed his lips against Luz's cheek, surprised that she would let him approach her. As he stepped back, her eyes flickered with either sadness or pity—he couldn't tell. But the look on her face vanished so quickly he thought he had imagined the softening of her mouth. The baby squirmed in her arms, its skinny legs kicking out from a blue blanket. Luz shifted him in her arms and hurried into the house.

Fausto could hear Rogelio's strangled cries coming from the second bedroom, the nursery. The cries tore at Fausto's heart. He was around Macario's boys when they were infants, but he'd never heard such desperate shrieks—as if Rogelio had been abandoned. Luz emerged with Rogelio—who was stiff, with arms up in protest, mouth gaping, tongue suspended as if electrified—over her shoulder. She worked with one hand, mixing tap water with a white powder. Fausto tried to help, but she kept moving away from him, as if in a clumsy dance. Benny inched his way into the kitchen.

"Heat the water, but don't boil it," Luz said, above Rogelio's cries, and handed Benny a pan. "When the water is just warm enough, take the pan off the burner and put the bottle in the water for only a few minutes."

Benny's smile turned down. "Maybe he does not like it here."

Luz poured the formula in the bottle, capped it off with a nipple, and shook the bottle before handing it to Benny. She felt the baby's crotch, the plastic diaper crinkling beneath her fingers. Rogelio released a new round of wails. As she left the kitchen, she told Rogelio that his bottle would be ready as soon as she changed his diaper.

Benny held the pan and bottle up as if he still didn't know how to heat the water. "I'm no good at this, Fausto," he said. "All this crying makes me nervous. He cried all the way from the Grapevine to Bakersfield. Luz tried to make him suck on her finger, but he did not like. I did not know what to do. He looked like he was in such pain."

"You'll forget about all this when he is a little boy, running around," Fausto said, longingly, as Rogelio's cries grew muffled down the hallway.

Luz returned later to check on the bottle, which was too hot. She ordered Benny to cool the bottle under a running faucet. Luz retreated to the living room, patting Rogelio, whispering in his ear, though Fausto imagined the baby hearing only the inside of his own cries.

Benny shoved the bottle into Fausto's chest. "Ai, you do it!"

Fausto held the bottle under the rush of cold water, thinking of Marina asleep in the early morning. Could she hear her own baby's cries an ocean away, wrenching her from her dreams? If she were on the sidewalk amid a crowd and heard her baby crying in somebody else's arms, he hoped she would run to it blindly, milk weeping from her breasts. Marina told him that babies could hear in the womb; they recognize their mother's voice. He thought it was island superstition.

Now, in Luz and Benny's house, he believed her. He never had the chance to watch her belly grow, to press his lips against the swell of her stomach to whisper: *Hush now, I'm here.* His soft voice sounded foreign to his own ears.

Luz yanked the bottle from his hand. By now, Rogelio had fallen asleep in her arms. His lips were pliant as she prodded with the nipple, but he didn't latch on. Defeated, she lowered Rogelio on his stomach in the bassinet and tucked the blanket around him. Fausto came up behind her as she stood over the bassinet.

"Very handsome face," he whispered, though all he could see was Rogelio's blotchy red cheek. "Big baby."

Luz didn't move. "It hurts to think about the delivery. I did not go through the pain, but I felt it here." She placed her hand over her heart.

"The mother," Fausto said slowly. "Was she in much pain?"

"It was hard on her."

"And after she delivered, she gave up this baby so easily?"

"She did not want it." Luz tossed her head back. "Her husband did not want it."

"*Apay ngay?*" He watched Rogelio's fingers travel to his mouth, his cheeks suck in and out. "How could it be then that a husband and wife do not want their baby?"

"It was not for me to ask." She turned on her heel and left the room.

Fausto waited until the end of dinner before asking Luz, "Did you visit Marina?"

Benny put his glass down. Luz stopped twirling the leftover noodles around her fork. She looked tired all of a sudden, her face melting in the steam of the pansit.

"I received a letter from Trinidad," Fausto said.

She eyed him, her fork suspended in her hand. "From Trini? *Kaano?*"

"Around the time you left."

She put her fork down. "Marina did not want to be bothered."

"But you saw her then, *wen?*"

"She did not want to be bothered. Not even by me. *Awanen.* That's all." She lowered her head. "Leave her in peace."

"I'm sorry." Fausto pushed his plate away. He laid the sterling-silver box in front of them. "I wanted to give Rogelio this now—not wait until the baptism."

Luz's face tightened as she sprang the lock, as if it were hard to open. A shadow crossed her face when she read the inscription. "Oh, there has been a mistake," she said.

"What do you mean?" Fausto stood up, panicked. "They spelled 'ninong' right."

She glared at Benny, who seemed to be as bewildered as Fausto, and then turned to Fausto with unrepentant eyes. "We are asking Manong Macario to be Rogelio's ninong." She ignored Benny's dropped jaw and pushed the box across the table, her eyes hard as flint, the flat line of her lips razor sharp. "Benny should be the one to apologize; I told him not to say anything until I got home because Nida had called me before I left Manila. It's no use, Fausto. You have no means to be a ninong."

Fausto pocketed the rosary—a silvery blur in his eyes. "I better get Prudencio's car back to him," he rushed to say. He was already in the living room.

"You'll come to the baptism this Saturday? We are having it at St. Ann's Church in Porterville." Luz trailed him but stopped by the bassinet.

The slant of sun through the living-room window made the wicker so brilliant white it hurt Fausto's eyes. Rogelio began to whimper. Luz rocked the bassinet. Fausto walked out without answering, without checking on Rogelio. He didn't expect Benny to come after him, but as he got to the Dodge Dart, Benny grabbed his arm.

"It's my fault," Benny said. "I told her I wanted you to be Rogelio's ninong, and she said she would think about it. I thought if I told you, she could not take it back."

"You could have told her on the long drive back, but you did not do it," Fausto said. He couldn't see into the living-room window, but he knew Luz was still rocking the bassinet, watching the two of them argue, maybe even gloating. "Why Macario?" he demanded.

"Luz wants Nida to be her friend again," Benny murmured, his eyes downcast.

"You think I can be treated so badly?"

"*Saan!*" Benny insisted. "I'll pay you back. I know it cost you a lot of money—money you do not have." Benny pulled two crisp twenty-dollar bills from his wallet.

"There is no need to pay me back."

"But it's useless." Benny looked up, startled, and added, "You cannot give it to anybody else."

Benny tried to give the bills to him, but Fausto let the money fall to the ground. He drove off, the sterling-silver box in his fist.

———

Fausto arrived at St. Ann's Church wearing the barong shirt from his wedding. If Luz or Benny were surprised to see him, they didn't show it. During the ceremony, Fausto imagined himself not in Macario's place, standing before the altar between the priest and Nida, but in Benny's place. After the ceremony, Fausto hung off to the side of the church's entrance. A photographer positioned Benny, Luz, Macario, and Nida around the priest, who held the slumbering Rogelio, while relatives snapped pictures with their Instamatic cameras. Fausto was hoping Benny would see him and ask him to join them, but Benny was giving Rogelio and Luz sloppy kisses. He whirled around to accept Macario's pumping handshake and a pat on the back from the priest. When the other guests streamed up the steps to congratulate Luz and Benny, Fausto returned to Prudencio's car, where Prudencio and Ayong were reading the newspaper while waiting for him.

Prudencio folded his newspaper section. "Are you okay?" he asked.

"You don't have to go to the baptism party, if you don't like," Ayong insisted.

"Let's go—to Benny and Luz's house." Fausto pulled on his trouser pocket to keep the corner of the sterling-silver box from jabbing into his thigh.

Luz waved to him from across the room when he first arrived at the party, but never spoke to him, which suited him fine. At first, she wouldn't let anyone hold Rogelio. When Benny called her to the kitchen to unwrap the sheet cake she'd ordered from the bakery, she surrendered the baby to the pinays in the living room. That's when Fausto made his way to the sofa. The pinays shooed him away, giggling, claiming he had no practice holding babies, but Pilar Europa, Fidel's wife, who was not much older than Marina, lifted Rogelio from Feliza Vergara's lap. She stood, adjusting her balance with a baby in her arms and one bulging from her stomach.

"Manong Fausto, come here," Pilar entreated, holding Rogelio out to him.

Rogelio blinked at Fausto with wide eyes. He was big underneath all that starched fabric and yet he seemed light in Fausto's quaking arms. The pinays laughed as Pilar dangled a furry white sock in her hand and slipped it over Rogelio's bare foot, his nubby toes. Fausto tried to soothe him by whispering in his ear, soft as a rose petal. He was afraid he'd drop Rogelio, but he wanted to keep staring at Rogelio's face. He imagined watery flecks of emerald in the baby's eyes, but he couldn't be sure. He needed more natural light. He needed more time.

At the sound of Luz's voice, he bolted outside. Several relatives stopped talking and eating. Macario raised an eyebrow, though he didn't speak or move from the rummy table. Fausto turned his back on the house and the crowd on the lawn, and rocked the baby again. His heart pounding, he tried to remember the words to "Pamulinawen" to sing to Rogelio. But then he felt a hand on his arm, fingernails digging into his loose flesh.

"Give him to me!" Luz demanded under her breath and held out her hands.

"It's my first time to hold him," Fausto said.

She pulled Rogelio away, the long, crisp gown rustling across Fausto's arms. The tugging startled Rogelio, and he began to cry. Every part of his being seemed to tremble, from his tongue and lips to his arms and legs. Luz pressed him against her chest and began patting his spine, shushing him, as she started back to the house.

"Luz, if Marina were here, what would she think of all this?" Fausto said, not as a demand but as a simple question.

For a moment, sadness washed across her face, and then it drained just as quickly, leaving her lips withered, her eyes arid. "Marina is *not* here," Luz said. Rogelio's legs kicked out from beneath his gown, swimming in air. She disappeared into the house, slamming the screen door shut, a furry sock left lying on the welcome mat.

Fausto used to mark time by the passing of the seasons, the beginning and ending of each harvest, but the strike changed all that. When he strung together days on the picket line, he often woke up confused as to the day of the week. Weekends he might see Teddy Enebrad or Wendy Whitman, but the weekdays blurred together. When he moved in with Prudencio and Ayong, the end of the month meant rent was due, and they scrambled to find work in a constant dance of avoiding eviction.

Sometimes his old way of keeping time was restored when the pinoys who were part of the original group of strikers returned to Delano after summers in the salmon canneries in Juneau, Alaska. The elderly pinoys were barely able to clean salmon sixteen hours a day. They came back hoping for the end of the strike. But after days of hanging out at the Filipino Hall and sleeping on the apartment floors of the pinoys who had remained, they moved on to pick other crops. After each harvest they returned—their stay confined to picketing and idleness—and then they left again like restless ghosts.

Fausto also measured time by visiting Arturo Junior, who was shooting up in height, though his weight was expanding as well. Now he measured time by how fast Rogelio was growing. When he had arrived at three months, Rogelio's arms and legs were so thin Fausto was afraid he would be undersized for the rest of his life. But at six months, Rogelio's cheeks filled out. When he learned to sit up, rolls of fat on his thighs popped out like rising dough. At nine months Rogelio crawled across the living room, keeping up with Fausto's gait. At eleven months he outgrew baby food in jars, preferring fresh fruit—peaches, apricots, plums, and especially grapes. Fausto made sure the grapes Benny fed him bore the union label, which now only came from Joseph Vukelich's farm.

He didn't bring up Marina's name again to Luz. It occurred to him one night that if he angered her she might not let him see Rogelio ever again, and that was something he couldn't imagine surviving. Every time he recalled Trinidad's words he was reminded that Marina was gone for good. He had banished her, and she had banished him from her life. He deserved it. But now that Rogelio was in Terra Bella, the boy was all he had left.

For Rogelio's first birthday, Fausto scraped enough money to buy a brand-new tin top at a thrift store. He sealed a few dollar bills and coins in a card and handed it to Benny when Rogelio was plopped in the center of all his presents.

"You should not be doing this," Benny said when he opened Fausto's card.

"This is for Rogelio's college education," Fausto said, pushing the envelope back.

"But you cannot afford to." Benny fingered the wilted bills.

"The strike will end soon."

"We have been saying that for years."

"Manong Flor told me that Larry said Jack Dragovich is going to sign contracts," Fausto said. "Dragovich has so many farms. So I can afford to give Rogelio presents. There is nobody else to give gifts to."

A cry of delight erupted from the middle of the room as Luz displayed a sailor suit and plunked its matching white hat on top of Rogelio's head. The outfit was from Nida and Macario. Nida waded through the sea of crumpled paper and planted a kiss on Rogelio's cheek. Standing in the back, Macario waved at Luz and Rogelio, and he lifted his chin in Fausto's direction. With Fausto coming to Terra Bella more often, their avoidance of one another gave way to gestures of acknowledgment. Fausto returned the greeting from across the room.

"What about *your* needs?" Benny said.

"I don't need anything." Fausto smiled as Rogelio waved the bright wrapping paper above him. It was true. The strike's duration had weaned him off all material goods.

"Will you sign up for work at the Dragovich farms?" Benny said.

"As soon as the contracts are signed." Fausto turned his attention away from Rogelio. "Will you sign up for work there too, or will you keep your job in Lodi?"

Benny's face brightened. "I would like to work under a union contract. We still have to pay off Luz's trip. She is talking about going back to adopt another baby."

"Will she go back to the same mother?" Fausto held his breath.

"Ah, no!" Benny said in a tone that seemed almost chiding. "Luz told me a long time ago they agreed not to contact each other at all. Even so, why would this woman get pregnant again? She gave up Rogelio. She's not really a mother."

Fausto flinched at how casually Benny talked of Rogelio's birth mother's abandonment. Maybe Luz never revealed her identity to Benny. But it was true. *"Wen,"* he agreed.

"It will be nice to have steady work nearby," Benny said. "I don't like being so far away from home during the week, especially with Rogelio here."

Rogelio let out a whoop, exposing two front teeth spaced apart, as he held up the top. Luz placed his chubby hands on the knob and helped him pump it. The train engine and its cars became a blur of bright colors—red, green, blue, yellow. His nails scratched the image of the train, his drool bathed the tin. He would wear out the top in no time! And then Rogelio laughed. It was Marina's laugh—high and clear. It made Fausto's heart sing.

In early summer 1968, UFWOC announced that Jack Dragovich had signed union contracts. Fausto felt he could breathe again, but union members didn't know where to report. Two days passed before Fausto, Prudencio, and Ayong met Benny at the union's new hiring hall, the old Azteca Tortilleria, to be dispatched to pick wine grapes. They weren't worried about being turned away despite the long lines; Dragovich owned several large vineyards on the outskirts of Delano and scattered throughout Kern County. Prudencio said he would spend his first paycheck fixing the Dodge Dart. Ayong would sleep in peace knowing the landlord wouldn't be bothering them anymore. As they moved up the line, Benny informed them that many pinoys were walking out of the hall, complaining that union officers were only giving jobs to Chicanos and Mexicans. From the back of the line, they could hear their fellow pinoys arguing at the front table. Manong Magno tried to tell the two Chicano dispatchers how many years he had been working for Dragovich.

"We don't have anything for you today," the clean-shaven man said, and he pushed the elderly man's union card across the table. "Come back tomorrow."

But Manong Magno wouldn't leave. According to UFWOC, seniority counts, he told them, and he had more seniority with Dragovich than the Chicanos and Mexicans sent there this morning. He struck his straw hat against his knee. He hadn't been working for months, yet his dungarees released a fine cloud of dust. He demanded his old job back.

"Did you hear, old man?" the other man barked. "Come back tomorrow."

"Ai, you dirty, double-crossing Mexican!" Manong Magno shouted.

Talk in the hall died down. All eyes turned on Manong Magno. The clean-shaven man stood up and leaned across the table. He stared down the elderly cook. "Talking like a grower won't get you far here. You better hope we have short memories if you come back tomorrow." He exchanged glances with his partner. "But I doubt it."

Manong Magno stomped off on legs Fausto was sure would snap from pounding the floorboards. Fausto stepped out of line to calm him down.

"It takes time to find a good way to get everybody back to work," Fausto said.

"I doan have time!" Manong Magno said.

Fausto spied Philip Vera Cruz, one of three Filipinos appointed to the executive committee of the new union, on his way out of the hiring hall. His hands were submerged in his trouser pockets, his head down as if lost in deep thought.

"Philip!" Fausto called out, dragging Manong Magno with him. When they met up with him outside, he said, "Manong Magno has seniority, but he was turned away."

Philip shook his head. His hair, parted in the middle and swept back like two waves, cascaded down. "We cannot establish seniority ranking because the growers are withholding information or giving us wrong information," he said.

Manong Magno pulled at the curly hair sticking out of the mole on his chin. "Everybody knows I been with Dragovich for thirty years, but those big shots will not listen. Why should I pay dues when they will not give me my old job back?"

Philip adjusted the black-rimmed glasses on his nose. He spoke in a quiet voice. "I'm going to Dragovich's office right now to make sure they comply. Be patient." He glanced back at the hiring hall. "Then we will try to take care of the other problems."

Benny, Prudencio, and Ayong came outside. They watched Philip drive off in his old Karmann Ghia as a silver Cadillac sped by in the opposite direction. Manong Magno slapped his straw hat on his head and headed for the street.

"Where are you going, Manong Magno?" Benny asked.

He marched back. "Philip cannot change things for us," he said. "He speaks too soft. I should have listened to Nick when he tried to recruit me for the Teamsters. The growers like them. They will be the ones the growers sign contracts with. Wait and see!"

"That is what the growers want you to do." Fausto shook Manong Magno's arm as if to wake him up. "The growers are sabotaging the hiring procedures to make UFWOC look bad. They prefer the Teamsters because they are crooked, just like them."

"What do I care as long as I get my job back under any union contract? The Teamsters will protect me." Manong Magno stepped off the curb.

The silver Cadillac, like a circling shark, slowed down and a blond-haired Anglo man stuck out his head. After a short chat and a handshake, Manong Magno hopped in the back seat and the car roared away. Fausto scanned the street up and down. Were there more Teamsters in the area preying on frustrated UFWOC members?

"We should have asked Philip if that rumor is true about the union wanting to get rid of all labor contractors and foremen." Benny folded his arms tight across his chest.

"There should be no favoritism," Fausto began.

"When Nick and Macario were the foremen, we knew we would get the best assignments," Benny said. "But now we'll end up like Manong Magno. No job here at home, no security. What do we do then? I need a steady job now. *Ammom dayta!*"

A small pinoy farm worker with a curved back spoke up. "When I hear Dragovich sign, I go straight to the farm and ask for my job back. Mr. Dragovich son tell me I have to go to the hiring hall to get a work order. But they turn me away at the hall and tell me they don't have a work order for me. So I go back to Mr. Dragovich son and he tell me if there is no union he would hire me just like that." He snapped his brittle fingers. "After thirty-five years working for Dragovich, maybe I do not want a union now."

"The growers are pretending to cooperate, but they are causing trouble. UFWOC will make them comply, but we have to be patient, Manong." Fausto put his arm around the elderly pinoy and gave a little squeeze, trying to gain his trust, just as he'd seen Larry do to members who were faltering.

A young pinoy with biceps like balls of iron straining his work shirt held up a piece of paper. "I got a work order, but when I went to the farm, they wouldn't take me, wouldn't say why. I came back here. I was told UFWOC would go to court and make Dragovich take me, but until then what do I do? I can't be patient; I have no job, no money." He frisked the pockets of his shirt and pants. "I asked Larry how long it will take in court, but he didn't know. He was helpless like me. There's work in the fields now, but it's all going to the Mexicans." He wadded up the piece of paper and threw it on the blacktop. "*Malokloko tay laeng amin nga Pilipino.*"

"It's true!" another pinoy said. "The Filipinos are getting cheated."

The elderly pinoys marched off like a lynch mob, their fists raised as if wielding pitchforks. The younger pinoy left too, crying out, "The only dispatching going on here is with the Teamsters recruiters. They know something crooked is happening here."

Fausto clapped his hands over his head. "Ai, *umaykan, intayon!* Let's get our assignments. There will be other growers signing by and by. There will be enough work for everyone."

He led them back into line. Some pinoys who Fausto didn't know brought up the rear, but after several minutes, when the line didn't move, one of them whispered to the others. The huddle broke up, and they all left. One by one, the pinoys left the table empty-handed. Helpless, Fausto witnessed the hiring staff issuing work orders to the Mexicans and the Chicanos, and turning away the Filipinos.

Within a week, Prudencio, Ayong, and Benny were assigned to a Dragovich farm outside of Delano. Arturo got dispatched to one in Arvin, but Fausto was still without work. At the Filipino Hall, over watery coffee and fried eggs, Arturo said he would talk to someone at the hiring hall about getting Fausto on his crew. But Fausto declined.

"I want to help you," Arturo said.

Fausto touched Arturo's worn sleeve. "Then put another pinoy on your crew."

"I see what I can do." Arturo sopped up all trace of runny yolk on his plate with a slice of toast. "Georgina want you to come to the house for dinner again. She say she miss you. Junior say he miss you too."

For nearly eighteen months, Fausto had spent all his free time with Rogelio. He tried not to wear out his welcome; he was afraid Luz would limit his visits. Though she seemed strained whenever he came over, she held back. Did she know that he suspected the truth? Maybe guilt was gnawing at her. Maybe Benny had asked her to be nice—if he knew the truth in the first place. Fausto didn't want either their sympathy or, worse yet, their pity. He was greedy with his time with Rogelio, but at the expense of his friendships.

He answered Arturo, "I'll come by next Sunday to visit with Georgina and Junior. How is Junior?"

"He turning nine pretty soon. Growing up so fast. He gonna be taller over me." Arturo's face turned serious. "Sometime I look at him and think he gonna be on his own before I ready to let go. That day gonna be hard."

"It's hard, eh, to be a father?"

"*Dios mío!*" Arturo said. "Many time Junior do something make me angry, but I look in his eye, I touch his hair, I lay blanket over his big-boy body when he fall asleep." He made the sign of the cross. *"Agradezco a Dios.* I thank God for this blessing."

"I feel the same way about Rogelio," Fausto confided. He longed to say more.

"Somos afortunados." Arturo's smile returned. "Now I got to go to work."

Fausto didn't feel lucky. A rush of guilt and greed overcame him. It ought to be enough. He could have ended up with nothing. Yet, a voice inside him kept saying, *You could have ended up with much more.* And he responded to the wall before him, *"Wen."*

Fausto finally found work pruning vines in the winter at a smaller vineyard in the Dragovich empire. On Sundays, he carried boycott signs in front of local supermarkets that sold nonunion grapes. The national boycott of all table grape growers from the area was going strong. Fausto was heartened to read in the newspapers how housewives across the country were avoiding the produce section where grapes were being displayed, and even boys and girls were declaring they no longer liked to eat grapes. The Defense Department was buying millions of pounds of grapes and shipping them to the troops in Vietnam, though several thousand boxes ended up over the side of navy destroyers by officers who supported the boycott. It didn't matter that Ronald Reagan, the new governor who succeeded Edmund Brown, made a show of eating grapes and denouncing the boycott as "immoral" before television cameras and newspaper photographers. Fausto knew it was the actions of the common man that would determine the outcome of the strike.

Leading the boycott efforts in Delano was hard. The wives of local businessmen and growers argued with the picketers. Some women carried their own signs into the grocery stores—"Freedom for All, and Outsiders Go Home," "Agriculture is the very foundation of our nation," and "What about our rights?" A few even tried to ram their shopping carts into the picketers. Teddy Enebrad, who had earned his bachelor's degree and was accepted into graduate school, came up several times during the semester. He liked "escorting" the women into the local Safeway food store, explaining to them why the boycott was not anti-American. He was fond of a short, squat woman with cat-eye glasses perched on her pointy nose, who helped found the self-proclaimed Citizens for Facts organization on behalf of the growers soon after the strike had begun. He liked that she carried a sign proclaiming, "Win in

Vietnam!" whenever she went grocery shopping or ran errands.

"The boycott and strike have nothing to do with Vietnam," Fausto complained.

The picketers barely missed getting clipped by the cat-eye glasses woman as she peeled out of the Safeway parking lot in her boat-sized Lincoln Continental.

"Actually, they're quite connected, Manong Fausto." Teddy dusted himself off after hitting the blacktop to avoid the car's front fender. "I'd like to believe people would have cared about the farm workers at any other time in our history, but the truth is if it weren't for the passion and outrage fueling the Civil Rights Movement and the antiwar protests, I don't know where we'd be."

At the entrance, boycotters and housewives were engaged in a shouting match and batting down each other's signs. "I would hope we would all still be here," Fausto said.

"You and I would, that's for sure." Teddy pointed to a hole in the knee of his jeans, and laughed. His breath clouded up in the cold January air. "Another battle scar!"

Fausto plucked a loose thread from another tear near Teddy's thigh. "How can you tell which hole is new, eh?"

Teddy pulled apart the most recent tear, exposing scraped skin and pinpoints of blood. "The latest one is usually stained with fresh blood."

Fausto took out his handkerchief and applied pressure to Teddy's scrape.

Teddy whipped out an adhesive bandage. "A Boy Scout dropout is always prepared, especially in enemy territory," he said, and held up a two-fingered peace sign.

Fausto shook with laughter. "You were never a Boy Scout!" he said. He wadded up his soiled handkerchief and stuffed it in his pocket. "Look at your clothes and your hair!"

"Right on!" Teddy laughed. He turned Fausto's hand over, dusted off the gravel and tar pressed into Fausto's skin, and gave Fausto a firm squeeze.

One Sunday in February, Fausto was crossing the street to join boycotters at an eastside supermarket when he heard Mr. Cuculich calling him. He was surprised to see his former boss's gut shrunk to half its size, a dusting of gray on his sparse head of hair.

"How's my favorite striker doing?" Mr. Cuculich smiled, thrusting his hand out. "Has it really been a year since I've seen you?"

Fausto shifted the placard that read, "Help Farm Workers Help Themselves: Do Not Buy California Grapes," to shake Mr. Cuculich's hand. "Time flies on the picket line. I'm doing well." He couldn't resist adding, "Just like the boycotts."

"I suppose you've heard about some of the tactics your people have been carrying out in the supermarkets," Mr. Cuculich said. "Shooting up grapes on the shelves with diesel fuel, making scenes, and smashing grapes in the stores. Is that the kind of union activity you support, Fausto? Because if it is, then I've got you all wrong."

"We cannot monitor everyone's behavior," Fausto said. He immediately thought of the incident at the produce section of the local Safeway supermarket a few weeks ago. He had caught four long-haired, college-aged boys in ripped-up jeans and football jerseys injecting what smelled like gasoline into the berries. They dropped syringes and bottles, and fled the store when Fausto flew into a rage, demanding to know what the hell they were doing. Fausto swept up the needles and bottles and tossed them in the parking-lot Dumpster. He would turn them in if he saw them again, but he didn't report the incident to the store manager or the police; it would look bad on the part of the union. He was going to tell the union leaders about it later, but he didn't say anything yet.

"If somebody is doing bad things, they are not for us," Fausto insisted. "This is not how our supporters are supposed to behave."

Mr. Cuculich jabbed his finger at a black student with wiry hair carrying a stack of placards in the parking lot. "Come on, those Commies don't know how to act decently! I've seen you spending too much time with that long-haired hippie. Chávez has loaded up his union with Trotsky radicals. Are you being duped too? Brainwashed?"

"No, I'm not brainwashed." Fausto planted the end of the placard's wooden handle on the sidewalk, its words facing out.

The grower's eyes flickered over the letters. "It's too easy to say you reject the ones causing the violence. Those agitators never take responsibility for their own actions. Like the devil incarnates who blow up our irrigation pumps and beat up innocent workers for being supposed 'spies.'" Mr. Cuculich paced the sidewalk as if to calm himself down. He stopped and took a deep breath. "I hear there's grumbling in the rank and file. Sounds like *disunion* instead of a union." He laughed at his cleverness. "Most of the original strikers aren't even around, and those who stuck it out are mad that Chávez is acting like a messiah, not a union leader. But you know: God is on our side, on the side of those who work hard and worship even harder. And that's us." Mr. Cuculich thumbed his chest.

"God does not take sides," Fausto said. "The will of God is for justice to prevail."

Mr. Cuculich's face grew red. "That's what I'm talking about—justice everywhere. The sabotage is spilling out of the vineyards and into our country's grocery stores. The police need to put an end to these tactics." He pulled on his silver belt buckle, the loose waist of his blue jeans. "The grocers are just selling the same goods like they've always done. Now they're being dragged into this mess. Can you blame them when they tell us they don't care what the outcome is—they just want us to settle our problems so they can go back to selling their goods?"

"Then why not sit down with Chávez and UFWOC and settle these problems?"

"I'll take care of my problems and you take care of yours." Mr. Cuculich looked him up and down. "Nick tells me you lost your car, your house, and your wife. Now is all that worth a few cents an hour more?" The tight line of his mouth loosened. He gave Fausto a wistful look. "We could have set you up nicely. Dammit, I would have done that for you, Fausto, so you could save yourself. But you're like the guy who bites the hand that feeds you. Let me tell you, pride brings people down. Pride is worthless."

Fausto's cheeks were enflamed at the thought of the grower and foreman talking about his personal life. "Dignity is worth everything," he said.

Mr. Cuculich offered his face to the gray sky. "Dammit, Fausto, everybody has dignity. Why are you listening to a union that says you don't have dignity and here's how to suffer and get it? You don't need UFWOC for that. How long are you going to picket and boycott, waiting to get some of that so-called dignity they say you don't have? Forever?"

"It has always been simple, Mr. Cuculich, since the first day we walked out of the fields," Fausto said, surprised at his steady voice. "When all the growers sign the union contracts, then we will have dignity, then we will have respect." He lifted his chin and went on his way, never looking back, clutching the placard, its words facing inward.

———————

In the four-and-a-half years since the strike began, Fausto witnessed dozens or more friends and acquaintances whose cars had been repossessed. He could count on two hands those whose homes were foreclosed by the banks. One evening in the Filipino Hall, Prudencio singled out the men who had lost their families. There weren't many of them, but Fausto was still overcome by their grief. The men's wives packed up their children and belongings and drove out of the Central Valley, moving as far away as another state or even Mexico. Some workers came home from the picket line to find closets and garages empty.

What was gone was gone. But Fausto had hope. Arturo Junior won a fourth-grade science contest at his school. Though the award sparked jealousy among his enemies, his new passion gave him a thicker skin. He wanted a microscope to look at things like butterfly wings and leaves, but Arturo couldn't afford it. When Fausto stopped by the thrift store to replace his socks with holes, he found a toy medical kit. If Arturo Junior was disappointed on his birthday that he did not unwrap a microscope, Fausto never saw it. What he saw was a boy who looked much older than nine clamping the ends of the stethoscope over his ears and pressing the chest piece against Fausto's chest, listening to his heartbeat as if no other sound were more important in the world.

Fausto was even more indulgent with Rogelio. Once he'd paid all his bills for the month and sent money to his family in the Philippines, whatever cash was left over from his paycheck he spent on Rogelio. Luz insisted that he not spoil her son, though she was guilty of buying him so many toys that Rogelio lost interest in the old toy as soon as she came home from Porterville with a new one. When Luz went to the Philippines in February to adopt another baby boy, Fausto slipped into Rogelio's pockets sticks of gum, hard candy in brightly colored wrappers, and chocolate bars that never melted in his little hands because Rogelio ate them up so quickly.

Fausto no longer cared where Luz was adopting the baby or who was bearing the child. What was gone was gone. It was beginning to seem like four-and-a-half years was really ten years where Marina was concerned. He borrowed the Dodge Dart and took Rogelio out for car rides in the country, pointing out all the different kinds of orchards—peaches, plums, and apricots—and promising Rogelio that they'd return in the summer when the stone fruit was ripe. An early spring was in the air, in the fields. It made Fausto's heart dance as wildly as Rogelio's bare feet prancing across the backseat of the car. And when Rogelio laughed, Fausto wanted to cry.

―――――――――

Teddy came up every weekend in March. It reminded Fausto of the beginning of the strike when Teddy was a regular on the picket line. But in early April, Teddy told Fausto that his visit to Delano would likely be his last. After getting his master's degree, he had applied and was accepted to the Peace Corps to teach English at a government secondary school in Malaysia.

Fausto walked Teddy for the last time to his Volkswagen Beetle parked in the Filipino Hall's lot. "So this is it, eh? You are leaving for good."

"I hope not." Teddy pulled out his car key from a hole in his jeans pocket.

"Why Malaysia? It's too far away."

Teddy smiled, his lips barely visible amid the scraggly whiskers of his moustache and beard. "That's what Wendy said when I sent her a postcard. She asked me, 'Why go somewhere else when there are a lot needy people right here?'"

After graduating, Wendy got her teaching credential and moved to Seattle with her college sweetheart. While he earned his masters degree in business administration, she taught second grade in a poor neighborhood. After they got married, he tried to persuade her to teach in a better school district, but she refused. When she had twins, she quit to raise her sons.

"Wendy talked about going back after the boys are bigger, but she's loving motherhood so much she wants to have another baby." Teddy reached into his glove compartment to grab a pack of cigarettes.

"Another baby!" Fausto exclaimed. "Good for her."

Teddy lit a cigarette and took a drag. "Another one leaving not only the fields, but the whole fucking movement." He sighed, the cigarette dangling from his lips. "It's a new decade. I suppose change is to be expected."

"You always say change is good. Don't forget you are leaving too."

"For a good cause, but I'll be back in two years." Teddy dumped ashes from his car ashtray into his coffee mug and turned to Fausto. "Give me some skin, Manong Fausto!" he demanded. Instead of shaking his hand, he gave Fausto a bear hug.

Fausto swiped at his own eyes, which he didn't want to admit were tearing up, before he let go of Teddy. "Maybe you'll like Malaysia."

"Maybe, but my heart's in my work with the pinoys." Teddy started the engine of his car. It gave a great shudder. Teddy groaned. "We'll see if I even make it to LA."

"You'll go farther than LA."

"The tide is turning," Teddy said. "The growers are falling like dominoes. You're going to win this battle. You won't need me anymore, but I wish I could be here when UFWOC signs those bastards. Everything will be right in the fields, at least for now."

"For now." Fausto nodded. "For a while."

Teddy laughed. "You know that saying, 'never trust anyone over thirty'?" When Fausto shrugged, he said, "They're wrong, you know? They've never met you manongs."

The car jumped on its wheels as he put it in reverse. It rattled out of the parking lot and turned the corner. Soon, all Fausto was left with was the popping sound of the Beetle's engine and the smell of Teddy's cigarettes.

When Fausto heard the news, he shook his head. Either Teddy didn't tell Fausto everything or he could read the future. A few weeks after Teddy left Delano, in April 1970, UFWOC signed a grower who owned three of the biggest vineyards in Coachella Valley. Soon two other growers from Delano signed, including John Depolo, one of the union's bitterest opponents. With those victories secured, Chávez announced that the US Catholic Bishops' Committee on Farm Labor was directing its attention on the growers in the Delano and Bakersfield areas. Fausto kept reminding Prudencio, Ayong, and especially Benny that the end of the strike—nearly five years old—was near.

Late July was hot and dry as desert wind. Electricity hummed in the air. News leaked that Joseph Kostelic, the biggest grape grower in California with 10,000 acres, had worked through contract negotiations with Chávez at the nearby Stardust Motel. The union had met with twenty-eight other grape growers, including George Cuculich, on the campus of St. Mary's Catholic School. They agreed to sign the contracts at UFWOC's headquarters. By midmorning the road leading to Forty Acres was gridlocked with cars and buses filled with farm workers and volunteers. Fausto, Benny, Prudencio, and Ayong were among them, moving at a crawl on Garces Road, passing the transmitting towers of Voice of America. The line of cars made Fausto believe he was going on a pilgrimage to see a miracle—*it was a miracle*—growers and farm workers coming together.

Masses of people—many wearing buttons and armbands bearing the black thunderbird—were moving past the executive offices, newspaper office, and gas station. The four pinoys joined the wave of farm workers that swelled into the headquarters, a newly built concrete building. Fausto pushed his way as near to the front as he could, pulling his friends with him. Microphones and pens lay on a long table. Television and newspaper reporters jostled for position, adjusting camera equipment and testing tape recorders. One television cameraman aimed his lens at the long, cloth banners hanging on the wall behind the table. *Viva La Huelga, Viva La Causa,* the banners proclaimed. Other banners were inscribed with mottos, some in English, some in Spanish: "First Relieve the Needy, Then Ask Questions" and "For the Hungry, *Wait* Is a Hard Word." Off to the side stood a chipped statue of Our Lady of Guadalupe, the union's adopted patron saint.

A priest wearing glasses and another man led the singing of strike songs, which echoed throughout the hall. Fausto sang along. At the end of each song, people shouted, *"Viva la Huelga! Viva la Causa! Viva César Chávez!"* Fausto caught the look of discomfort Benny exchanged with Prudencio. Benny had never uttered the slogan.

The cameras started whirring when the twenty-six growers from Delano and their families stepped into the hall. Shouts of *"Huelga!"* erupted, and then another strike song, *"De Colores,"* began in earnest. The clergy followed the growers, and then César Chávez and Larry Itliong entered, with the rest of the executive committee members, including Philip Vera Cruz, bringing up the rear. Fausto nudged Benny and Prudencio and pointed his chin in Larry and Philip's direction. The Filipinos are being represented—Larry is seated at the front table— Fausto was trying to tell them. And Chávez was wearing a white barong shirt!

Chávez spoke of the strength of nonviolence and thanked everyone who had supported the boycott. Thunderous applause rang out. Chávez's voice grew somber when he announced: "Ninety-five percent of the strikers lost their homes and they lost their cars. But I tell you I believe that in losing those worldly possessions, they found themselves."

"Ninety-five percent?" Benny raised an eyebrow.

"Chávez is exaggerating for the camera," Prudencio grumbled.

Fausto ignored them. He felt faint, though he didn't know if it was from the heat or the bodies pushing up around him. Maybe Chávez had his reasons for boosting the numbers. It didn't matter. Even if 5 percent of the strikers had lost their home and their cars, that number was very dear, each number a person.

Larry spoke next, recounting the hardscrabble story of the Filipino farm workers in America. "But today is a new era for the farm workers. We hope for better conditions and a better way of life for all of our people," he said.

Mr. Cuculich stood sullen faced in the middle of the pack of growers. Macario would have to abandon the Teamsters; under the terms of the union contract, everyone who worked on the farms had to be a member of UFWOC. With all the growers signing, Macario could not escape UFWOC. When the growers signed the papers, cameras flashed across the hall and volunteers and farm workers shouted, *"Viva la Causa!"*

Fausto spotted Arturo; they waved to one another in victory. He caught glimpses of Ahmed, Severo, and Fidel in the sea of faces. After the signing, he would seek them out and congratulate them. Maybe he would even splurge and call Teddy long distance to tell him the good news, describe every detail of the historic day. Prudencio, Ayong, and Fausto hugged one another. Fausto turned to give Benny a hug, but Benny pulled away.

"What is wrong?" he said in his cousin's ear.

"The contracts have finally been signed, but *no ania nga gastos?*" Benny said.

"Hah? What do you mean at what cost? Ai, you cannot measure such things!"

"I'm thinking of us, what we went through together."

They stood inches apart, but the space between them was growing enormous.

"I'm thinking of Marina," Benny said.

"It does not matter anymore!" Fausto said. He wanted to shake Benny and at the same time hug him and not let go, but he held back. "It's over! *Awanen!*"

People were elbowing them, trying to move to the front where the cameras had turned to the crowd, putting a face on the nameless farm workers for their viewers. The crowd, mostly Mexicans and Chicanos, had separated him and Benny. He was being pushed forward while Benny had fallen behind. Everyone, it seemed, was making some kind of festive noise—stomping feet, clapping, whistling, and chanting. The men near him cried out, *"Viva La Causa,"* but what rang in his ears were Benny's words. He thought of Chávez's words. *Had he found himself?* He spun around amid the bodies, suddenly feeling as if he were among strangers—with Benny lost to his sight.

CHAPTER 13

Down a long, dark valley

Delano, Spring 1973–Winter 1997

In black-and-white streaks across the television screen, sheriff's deputies in riot gear emerged from the vineyards in Coachella Valley, tearing protestors' shirt collars as they dragged them to a row of squad cars. Thin ribbons of blood trickled out of the ear of a Chicano man who was thumped on the side of his head with a billy club. Another farm worker, covered in dust, lay in a fetal position. A Chicana was handcuffed and shoved by a deputy who towered above her. Television cameras caught carloads of Teamsters union members swarming the edge of the field, swinging tire irons and clubs, striking flailing arms and the backs of fleeing picketers. When the attackers saw the cameras, they jumped into their Cadillacs and sped away. The screen blacked out and went silent for a moment.

A young reporter in a suit with short hair and sideburns stood by a road, gripping a microphone. The field around him was empty, the road vacant. "Three years ago, California table- and wine-grape growers sat down with César Chávez and inked a historic union contract guaranteeing farm workers pay raises, grievance procedures, a hiring hall, and pesticide safeguards," he said, and mopped his forehead and neck with a handkerchief. "With the contracts expiring this year and the vineyards ready to be harvested, it's clear the growers have no intention of re-signing with Chávez's union, now called the United Farm Workers. The growers are collectively siding with the International Brotherhood of Teamsters, a rival of the UFW."

Fausto and Benny exchanged glances in front of the television set. Benny looked away first, a pained expression on his face.

"The Teamsters are here in Coachella, trying to woo farm workers to sign up with their union, while at the same time courting growers," the reporter said as he walked down the middle of the road. "Their battle cry, 'Anyone but César,' is resonating with the growers. I spoke with farm workers who claim they're being harassed into joining the Teamsters. Some say they're afraid of being evicted from the camps for supporting Chávez and his union, while others worry they'll be replaced in the fields with scab workers. None, however, would go on camera for fear of retribution."

The radiator beneath Benny's living-room window hissed and banged. It was harvest time in Coachella Valley, though in Delano the late spring air was unseasonably cold. A laundry basket heaped with clean clothes sat by the sofa. Benedicto Junior—nicknamed BJ and adopted as a baby four years ago—slept on the loveseat. A herd of tiny plastic horses had tumbled into the valley of a knit blanket covering his bunched-up body. Rogelio, almost six and a half, sat on the rug halfway between the television set and the sofa. He had been playing with his set of yellow Tonka trucks, but now was staring at the television screen.

The reporter crossed property lines and pulled aside a canopy of leaves to reveal bunches of grapes. "Instead of blossoms in the spring-time, blood is spilling in the fields," he said. The camera panned the vineyards and then gave way to a scene filmed earlier in the day of sheriff's deputies chasing a group of UFW picketers.

"Ai sus!" Luz rushed in from the kitchen and stood in front of Rogelio to block his view. "He should not be watching this," she said, and turned off the television set.

"We need to know what's happening in Coachella," Benny said.

"Apay ngay?" She pulled Rogelio to his feet and handed him one of his trucks—a sign that meant he needed to stack his toys in the living-room corner. Luz anchored the laundry basket to her hip. "Why should I care what happens in Coachella?"

"Whatever happens there will affect contract negotiations here," Fausto said.

Luz tapped Rogelio on the back to get him to go to his room. She gave Benny a severe look. "Whoever the growers favor, we will sign up with that union," she said, and kicked stray horses and Tonka trucks into the corner before leaving the room.

Benny lifted his chin at the television set. *"Patinayon to la nga agapapatan? I cannot fight anymore. This is too much for me."*

"We'll not always be fighting," Fausto said, though he knew better.

"Maybe we can get Larry to come back and help fix this mess," Benny said.

Fausto shook his head. Larry Itliong had tried to quit many times in the past over the treatment of the Filipinos within the union but was talked out of it. His countrymen knew it was only a matter of time, and finally two years earlier he resigned from the UFW over political disagreements with Chávez and a dispute over his monthly stipend. When an unfounded rumor spread that he was working with the Teamsters, the UFW faithful—even many of the pinoys—kept their distance from him.

"Larry can't help us," Fausto said. "We'll fight again. After a few contracts—"

"Ai, I'm getting too old for such talk!" Benny massaged his lower back. "I want to enjoy my family, not worry about the next strike. BJ's fourth birthday is coming soon. We have to start thinking about retirement."

"Retirement?" Fausto laughed. "You are not even sixty-one."

Benny touched his temple, dusted with gray roots. "We are going to retire one of these days, and I need a job to retire from!"

Fausto pulled the blanket over BJ's ears, careful not to wake him. "You have to wait until BJ is finished with college, eh?"

Benny crouched beside the loveseat and brushed BJ's bangs away from his eyelashes. Fausto counted in his head. Eighteen, maybe nineteen, more years before Benny could retire. That was a long time to be pruning and picking grapes.

"I cannot work in the fields forever," Benny whispered, as if he'd followed Fausto's thoughts, though it seemed as if he was talking to his sleeping son. He turned his hands over and traced the calluses on his palms. *"Saan nga kastoy,* not like this," he said, stroking BJ's cheek with his fingertips.

———————

By July, violence had fanned out from Coachella Valley to Bakersfield like fire in a field of dry grass. At the farm owned by grower Tony Sabich, police officers sprayed Mace in picketers' eyes and stunned them with batons before packing them into patrol cars to be deposited in the county jail. The incident happened in Bakersfield, but the scene was replayed over and over again on the news. Both Fausto and Benny knew that once the UFW contracts expired in Delano at the end of July the fields would once again be filled with picketers, Teamster thugs, and policemen and deputies in riot gear.

Throughout the summer a growing uneasiness spread across the vineyards in Delano. Fausto had been working for Jack Dragovich since the contracts were signed in 1970. He couldn't bring himself to go back to work for Mr. Cuculich, though he and Macario had been speaking to one another since that summer. Now that the Teamsters were muscling their way onto the fields again, Fausto knew Mr. Cuculich and Macario were waiting for the UFW contracts to expire. Just as in the Coachella Valley, the Delano growers, including Dragovich, cut off negotiations with the UFW and were signing up with the Teamsters. Benny, who also worked on the Dragovich farms, was reluctant to participate in union activities. Fausto persuaded him to pass out leaflets in the fields encouraging workers to remain loyal to the UFW, but he worried that others might be as uncertain as Benny about enduring another costly strike.

One early August day, several picketers in Delano, including Arturo's friends Raúl and Fernando, were arrested and jailed. Word got out at Forty Acres that Chávez was considering not striking but scattering members across the country to encourage a larger boycott of table grapes. Fausto and Benny were relieved by the news. More good news emerged when they left the fields the next day: the county had released all the picketers in its jails without forcing them to post bail. Perhaps, Fausto told Benny as they headed home, no blood would be spilled at all in Delano.

But the morning following the release, Fausto and Benny arrived at Forty Acres to Manong Flor's news that a group of picketers, including Ahmed, were celebrating last night at a west-side bar. The group was gathered outside the bar when a deputy in his patrol car demanded that they leave the premises. When they refused, the deputy leapt out and threatened them. The group scattered, but the deputy ran after one of the men, a Yemeni picket captain. As soon as he caught up to him, the deputy struck him with his flashlight and dragged him to his patrol car. Now the Yemeni, whose head was slammed into the sidewalk for several blocks, was near death at a local hospital. Fausto asked Manong Flor if the injured man was Ahmed, who had signed up as a UFW picket captain. No, Manong Flor told him. His name was Fahmi Abdo Sallal. Ahmed's friend.

"Thirty-five years old!" Manong Flor said, wiping greasy tears from his leathery cheeks. *"Ai sus!* Who is gonna tell his mother back home he is dying?"

The hospital parking lot and lobby swelled with people, with heads bowed or faces offered up in prayer, their lips silently moving. Fausto pushed his way to Ahmed, who stood in the thick of the vigil. Ahmed shook his head at Fausto, mouthing—*he is gone*—and nothing more. Fausto hugged his friend, whose clothes were steeped in the heady scent of khat. Fausto breathed deeply, imagining that he was with Ahmed and his countrymen, chewing the leaves not so much for their dulling effect but for the occasion to mourn together.

"I will help carry Fahmi's coffin through the vineyards and streets of Delano. Then I will accompany his body back to his family." Ahmed stared at the gleaming floor as nurses and doctors hurried past without a glance. "He came here eighteen years ago, but we are from the same town, Mukalla."

"Brother, I hope your Allah leads you safely back home," Fausto said.

Ahmed's eyes flickered. "What is home, Fausto? Where is it for people like us?"

Fausto put his hand over his heart. "All our family and friends are here. They are one and the same, eh?"

"Then I will take you with me."

"And you will stay here too," Fausto said.

Ahmed pointed to the clock on the wall and said, "Fahmi's parents have just woken up." He looked up at the ceiling and murmured, "Allah, give me strength," before walking away. Tunic flowing, a blaze of white under the fluorescent lights, he seemed to float down the hallway, despite footfalls that plodded across the waxed floor.

All Fausto could see was Fahmi shaking dust from his close-cropped hair, his filmy eyes betraying flashes of helplessness; Fahmi thought he would be stuck in the fields forever.

––––––––

Benny dropped Fausto off at the Forty Acres meeting hall. The entire ride, his face seemed to demand, "What now? Who is next? Will it be *me?* Will it be *you?*"

"Tomorrow I'm going on the picket line," Fausto said, as he stepped out the car.

"I thought they would stop picketing by now," Benny said. "Another lie! I'm staying home. You should too. Look what is happening!"

"That is why we cannot stay home," Fausto said, but Benny only revved up the engine. *"Ania ngarud iti maipagteng mo, saan tayo nga pumanaw?"*

"People are dying now, Fausto. This is what another strike will cost us." Benny slammed his fist against the steering wheel. "What else are you willing to give up, eh? Are you willing to die now? Not me! I have two boys who need me!" His voice broke. Tears gathered on the wrinkles beneath his eyes. *"Nasapulak ida!* I need them!"

"Benny," Fausto said, gently, "we all need each other. Nobody else has to die."

Benny passed his hand over his face and sped away from Forty Acres.

A few days after Fahmi's death, when Fausto and Prudencio showed up at Forty Acres for picketing assignments, Fausto was surprised to see Georgina standing beside Arturo. He explained to Fausto that his wife had doubted Chávez's ability to win the last strike and now believed this strike would be over sooner if everybody took their support into the fields. She wore her Sunday outfit—a white blouse with pearly buttons down the front and lace-trimmed collar—and her hair pinned up in a bun. She was already waving her huelga sign, while Arturo watched with dark half-moons carved out beneath his eyes.

As they stood in line waiting for assignments, Fausto noticed a plastic bandage cutting into Arturo's fleshy wrist. His son, now twelve, was still playing with the doctor's medical kit that Fausto had given him for his ninth birthday. Arturo Junior had asked his father to let him pick grapes in the summers to help the family, but after one summer in the fields Arturo preferred that his son read science books and play doctor.

Fausto tapped the bandage. "What is your sickness today?"

Arturo held up his wrist. "Junior say I got another disease."

Arturo pulled off the bandage from his wrist, which left an indentation in his skin. "Junior say this time I suffer from pick-it-itis," Arturo said. "He tell me I need to stay in bed. He never push me so hard to stay before. So I tell him it important to picket. Our job at stake. So he give me 'medicine.'" Arturo stuffed the bandage in one jean pocket and took out a piece of hard candy wrapped in red cellophane to show Fausto before returning it to his other pocket. Arturo winked. "I take medicine before I go home. Plenny time."

Fausto, Prudencio, Arturo, and Georgina were dispatched to Arvin, south of Delano, near Bakersfield. Raúl, Arturo's friend, was their picket captain. When they arrived, picketers had already amassed along the property line of Joseph Kostelic's farm. Cars clogged the roads leading in and out of the vineyard. Georgina hurried after a group of women to target an all-female crew. Fausto, Arturo, and Prudencio headed in the opposite direction until they spotted scabs darting in and out among the rows of vines.

"Friends, come out of the fields! You are being treated like slaves!" Fausto yelled. When he saw that they were Mexicans, he signaled to Arturo, who called out to them in Spanish. The men looked up and hesitated before disappearing deeper into the fields. All was quiet. Fausto waited, smelling grapes that would be spoiled by month's end if they stayed on the vine. Soon he saw a dark-haired head, a work boot, a flash of a red bandana. He pointed south. "They are still there, Arturo."

But Arturo began coughing. His face turned red.

Prudencio patted him on the back. "You better take your son's medicine."

"I'll get you some water," Fausto offered, and headed toward Raúl's Ford Thunderbird parked along the road, where a cooler full of ice water was sweating on its hood.

Fausto placed his hand over his heart. It was thumping madly. He didn't want to be back on the picket line, of course, but he felt alive, even as he trembled. He hadn't felt this sense of purpose since the last strike. As he filled a tin cup with ice water, he saw the group of women raise their placards and shout at scabs farther down the road. Georgina was trying to wave two signs. She would be important this time around—people like her who supported the last strike but didn't come out, Fausto thought. The duration of the strike would be weeks, if not days, because of the flood of new supporters. He walked back, wondering what his life would have been like if Marina had found a way to endure the last strike. He shook his head. No more spilled milk. *Awanen.*

Fausto held out the cup to Arturo when a black Ford pickup truck stopped in the middle of the road, its motor still running. "All you wetbacks, start swimmin' back to Mexico!" shouted the driver, a young man with pale skin and a droopy moustache.

Angry shouts erupted ahead of Fausto where Raúl led a group of picketers. Now in his early thirties, Raúl was no longer gangly but packed with muscle. He still had the same showy haircut—slicked back and shiny with pomade—and the same fieriness. He raised his fist, and shouted, "I'm an American citizen! I was born in this country, in California."

The driver leaned out the window. "Did you fight in Vietnam for your country like a man? I'll bet you were hiding in the vineyards all those years!" The driver laughed, but his passenger, sitting back in the shadows, neither moved nor said anything.

A few people in the crowd tossed rocks at the pickup truck, though the rocks were slung low and skipped across the asphalt. The driver released a string of curses. He pointed to the untouched door before kicking it open and jumping out. "Who's going to pay for this damage?" he demanded, and punted the rocks into the crowd.

By now the picketers, at least three lines deep, surrounded the pickup truck.

The driver slammed the door. "Back off! Or I'll blow you all back to Mexico!"

The passenger in the cab, who was silent the whole time, poked the long barrel of a rifle out the window. The black muzzle stared down at Fausto.

Fausto's legs froze. Picketers scattered. He squeezed his eyes shut as if that would make the rifle go away. Two shots rang out, strangling his breath, making everything go silent. When he opened his eyes, Arturo pitched forward, his mouth gaping. Fausto caught his friend. Water spilled on their shirts. The tin cup was wedged between their ribs.

The pickup truck—a fuzzy, roiling black cloud—sped off.

Blood, not water, seeped across Arturo's chest, just below his heart. Fausto's knees gave out under the weight of his friend, but he did not fall. Somehow, he held onto Arturo, who was almost twice his weight and a foot taller. Fausto could hear again—muffled sounds at first and then screams that punched the air. Bodies crowded in, cutting off Fausto's view of vineyard and sky, even air. Raúl and Prudencio lifted Arturo and laid him on the ground. Georgina flitted across—a blur of black and white. Fausto dropped to his knees, his arms dangling, his hands sticky and warm. Georgina sat on her haunches next to Arturo, trying to raise him up. She pulled on his sleeves, but her wet fingers could not hold onto his damp shirt. She grabbed his wrists, but they lay on the ground as if anchored.

Raúl peeled back Arturo's shirt. The near-perfect hole was burrowed in Arturo's thatch of hair. With each staggered breath, blood oozed out. Raúl tore off his red bandana from his neck and pressed it against the wound. Wide-eyed, Arturo gasped and gurgled. Fausto passed his hand over Arturo's eyes, leaving smears on Arturo's lids. Mute, Georgina opened Arturo's mouth and leaned forward, as if to give him her breath.

But she fell back hard on the ground and covered her face. Arturo's lips were wet with blood.

A car drove up close to the crowd, and for a moment Fausto thought the truck had returned. But it was Arturo's friend Fernando in his brown Chevy Chevelle. Four men lifted Arturo and lay him across the cramped backseat. His hand rested on the floor, his knees pointed at the ceiling, his feet turned inward. He looked like he had fallen asleep, too tired from picketing to make himself comfortable. Raúl crouched in the backseat, the wet bandana between his hand and Arturo's chest. The women shuttled Georgina to the front passenger seat, where she kept reaching for her husband. Her hair, no longer pinned up, flowed like a mournful river. One pearly button on her blouse was still white. She turned to the window, as if searching for someone, and then the car bolted like a spooked horse.

"Does anyone know who was in the pickup?" one of the white volunteers said.

A Chicano, a black bandana tied around his neck, came forward, stepping over the fallen placards. "I have seen that truck before," he offered.

"I saw his face," a young Chicana said. "He had a mustache—*el diablo.*"

"He'll pay with his life," one of the black picketers roared.

"*Sí, sí,*" the picketers yelled out.

"*Viva* Arturo!" the Chicana shouted, even as her placard trembled in her hands.

Fausto walked away. He couldn't breathe amid the dust that their stomping boots had drawn from the hot earth. His shirt stuck to his skin, but he didn't have the strength to take it off. Something crackled and popped beneath his work boot. It was a piece of hard candy, smashed into crystals and powder, trapped inside its red plastic wrapper. As he tucked Arturo's medicine in his trouser pocket, bits of powder stuck to his fingers.

"Fausto!" Prudencio caught up with him, panting. "What now?"

Fausto thought of Arturo Junior. Who was going to tell him? He wished he were as brave as Ahmed. Maybe it wasn't his place to go to the boy, but he asked, "Can you take me back to the apartment? Let me clean up. Then we'll go to Arturo's house."

"Are you sure?" Prudencio's face was as ragged as his breath.

"Maybe I'll not say anything." Fausto looked away. "Maybe I'll just watch over him until someone else can tell him, eh?"

"He's a big, strong boy," Prudencio said, but his voice was full of doubt.

There were no cars at Arturo's house. Fausto and Prudencio slipped past the chainlink fence surrounding the yard. The front door was wide open. Through the screen door, they could see Arturo Junior on the sofa. The toy stethoscope was slung around his neck as he moved the chest piece across the curve of his grandfather's back. He saw them before Fausto could say anything. Arturo Junior waved at them to come inside. Arturo Junior's grandfather moved to the end of the sofa so their two guests could sit between them. But Prudencio kept his head down and stood by the open door.

"My *abuelo* says I'm too old to play with these toys." Arturo Junior removed the stethoscope and tucked it into his medical kit.

Fausto sank in the middle of the sofa whose upholstery looked as if feral cats in the neighborhood had used it as a scratching post. "You are practicing!" he said with more force than he meant. "When you get to medical school, you'll know a lot."

"I'm not smart enough to go to college to be a doctor," Arturo Junior murmured.

Fausto grabbed his hand. "Who said?"

"My teacher says I'm strong, I have the body of a farm worker, just like my father." He turned out his feet, already longer than his father's. He spread his hands on his thighs—hands his teacher might have argued were too bulky to perform surgeries.

"*Maestra estúpida!*" Fausto pounded his fist on the white batting that sprouted from a hole in the upholstery. "She should not be a teacher!"

A car pulled into the driveway. Arturo Junior sprang from the sofa and looked out the window. "It's just Fernando," he said, disappointed.

Fernando swung the screen door wide open, nearly tearing it off the door frame. Fausto stood up and Prudencio stepped aside. Arturo Junior's grandfather, who had dozed off on the sofa, jerked himself awake. Fernando didn't look at Fausto or Prudencio. He pulled Arturo Junior down to the sofa next to his grandfather.

"*Junior, Señor Esperanza, te traigo noticias malas,*" he said in a rush of words.

"Speak in English!" Arturo Junior moved away from Fernando.

"I was speaking in Spanish for your abuelo's sake," Fernando said.

"I will tell him." Arturo Junior crossed his arms.

"Your father was picketing in Arvin. Two men in a pickup truck started an argument with the picketers." Fernando mopped his forehead with a balled-up handkerchief. "One of the men in the truck fired two shots with a rifle. Your father is in a hospital in Arvin. Your mother is with him."

Arturo Junior stared at Fausto. "You didn't tell me," he accused.

"I did not know if it was my place to tell you. I came here to be with you." Fausto shoved his hands in his trouser pockets and felt the candy wrapper crackle in his fingers.

Arturo Junior whispered in his grandfather's ear. Tears flowed down the old man's cheeks. Arturo Junior looked over his shoulder. "I'm afraid for my abuelo. He has a bad heart. But he wants to see my father," he said in a calm voice. He cupped his grandfather's silver-whiskered chin and whispered, *"Entiendo, entiendo."* Arturo Junior held him by the arm as they both rose. "My *abuela* is in her room asleep. She's in frail health too. Please help me take them to my mother." When Fernando just stood there, Arturo Junior barked at him, *"Apúrate!* Hurry up! Are you deaf? I said my abuela is in her bedroom!"

Fernando hurried down the hallway. Fausto rushed to the other side of Arturo Junior's grandfather. "Tell me what you need, if you need me. Do you want me to help?"

Arturo Junior met Fausto's gaze with shiny eyes. "Yes," he said, his voice part-boy, part-man. "Be here for me when I need you. *Por favor.*"

Fausto and Prudencio returned to their apartment, where Benny was waiting for them, his hands behind his head like a prisoner of war.

"I heard what happened to Arturo," Benny said in a low voice, even as Prudencio went to check on Ayong. "First that Arab boy and now Arturo! What will happen next?"

Fausto sat down in a chair whose legs were as wobbly as his felt. "The other side is getting desperate."

"You cannot control what the growers will do when they become desperate!" Benny crouched in front of Fausto. "The UFW has already lost! We don't have money or supporters or contracts. Nobody out there cares anymore. *Kapilitan nga agsardeng tayon!"*

"Stop? Why do we have to stop now?"

"I'm joining the Teamsters." Benny got up and retreated to the other side of the room. As Fausto shook his head, Benny said, "I did not come to this decision easily. If we all join the Teamsters, if there is only one union for all the farm workers, the violence will stop. The Teamsters have the backing of the growers. They have money to take care of us. The hiring problems for the pinoys will go away."

"You know the Teamsters are not for the farm workers!" Fausto said. "You are doing what Macario and Luz are telling you to do!"

Benny pounded the wall. Paint chips fell from old fissures in the plaster. "I made the decision. You are afraid to admit I can think for myself." He leaned into the wall, slump shouldered. "I don't want to argue with you. I don't want to leave us like this."

"Just leave, then! *Inkan!* Go on!" Fausto said. "How can it be any other way when you tell me you are betraying the union and abandoning me?"

"I don't want blood on my hands." Benny headed for the door. "This is not a war. We pick grapes. Yet two people—one a good friend—have been killed in the name of the UFW—"

"Two?" Fausto stood up.

"*Impagarup ko nga ammom.*" Benny held on to the doorknob. "I thought you knew. Arturo passed away before they got to the hospital." He bowed his head and made the sign of the cross. "I'm sorry, I'm sorry."

―――――――

Within a week Fausto prepared for two funerals. He put on his barong shirt and joined Fahmi's funeral procession. The coffin was draped with two flags—the UFW flag with its black thunderbird on one end and the red-white-and-black stripes of the Yemen flag on the other end. Ahmed carried the rear of the coffin. Two Yemenis led the procession displaying a picture of Gamal Abdel-Nasser, the late leader of Egypt, as hundreds of Arabs fell in line. Fausto shook his head in disgust. No union leaders were in sight, though a congressman supposedly was somewhere in their midst. Farm workers and union supporters—ten thousand, Fausto read later in the *Delano Record*—walked the four miles through the vineyards and streets of Delano, in hundred-degree heat. The procession ended at Forty Acres, where a Catholic and Muslim service was held. Afterward, Fausto, Prudencio, and Ayong returned to the apartment. Fausto peeled off his barong shirt and chiseled off his dress shoes. He fell asleep in the bathtub. When he awoke an hour later, the blisters on his feet had opened up and his skin was as shriveled as raisin grapes.

The day after the funeral, Fausto and hundreds of Arab farm workers followed Ahmed to the airport in Bakersfield. Ahmed tried to thank everyone who came, even as his flight was being called, but once he saw Fausto in the sea of faces he waded through the crowd to reach him.

"Good-bye, Brother." The serious look never left Ahmed's face—in the hospital, at the funeral procession, as they stood before one another.

Fausto took Ahmed's extended hand and stared at their entwined fingers. Four decades under the Central Valley sun had turned their skin the same shade of brown. It was as if Fausto were holding his own hand. "Good-bye, Brother," he answered.

Ahmed's eyes pored over Fausto's face as if trying to memorize the shape of his eyes, the droop of his mouth. Then he turned away and strode down the covered walkway that would take him to his plane, to his destination of Yemen worlds away, to the brilliant blue waters of the Gulf of Aden, the ancient city of Mukallah, to a mother's wail.

Three nights later, Fausto donned his barong shirt and joined the candlelight procession that wove through the streets of Delano. Arturo's body was displayed in the recreation hall of one of the local parks for mourners to offer their last respects. Fausto sat in the back of the converted memorial chapel until his votive candle melted down and he could no longer keep his eyes open. It was past midnight when he left. Arturo Junior remained seated in front of the casket, his back straight against his chair.

The day of Arturo's funeral marked the sixth straight day of hundred-plus temperatures. The sun burned through to their scalps. Dust in the air forced many to squint. Arturo Junior, as tall as any of the other pallbearers, including Raúl and Fernando, insisted on carrying the front of his father's coffin for the five-mile procession, with Fausto and César Chávez by his side. At the graveside, with a column of cypress trees in the background, Georgina broke down and Arturo Junior's grandmother had to be revived with smelling salts. Arturo Junior whispered in his mother's and grandmother's ears through their lacy mantillas and glanced at his grandfather, as if keeping watch. Only when César Chávez spoke, did he lower his head.

"Arturo is a martyr in a just cause in the fields," César said in a quiet voice. "All of our actions these many months will give purpose and memory to his life. The more we sacrifice and the harder we work for the cause, the more life we give to the spirit of our brother Arturo Esperanza."

Arturo Junior followed his mother and scattered soil across his father's coffin. Dirt rained down on the draped UFW flag and a spray of white lilies. At the end of the service, Fausto made the sign of the cross, though he wanted to shake his fist at the cloudless sky, at God. He should have taken the bullet. Fausto waited until he was one of the last to leave the cemetery. Arturo Junior gave him an awkward hug. When he thanked Fausto for coming, Fausto wasn't surprised that within days the boy's voice had deepened.

Fausto showed up at Arturo's house a few days after the funeral with two bags full of food that he bought from the local Mexican grocery store and an envelope with money at the bottom of one of the bags. Georgina answered the door in all black, with a black scarf covering her hair. She stepped outside and shut the door behind her.

"I would like to help you and Arturo Junior," Fausto began.

Georgina kept blinking her eyes as if dust still floated in the air.

"Me *ayudar,*" he said.

"*Gracias.*" She tried to smile, but her lips flatlined instead. "*Ésto no es un buen momento,*" she whispered, and half-turned her head toward the front door. "You come," she said, looking off into space as if searching for the right word. "Christmas!" she blurted out. "Okay?" She took the bags from Fausto as he stood dumbly and watched her deposit them just inside the house by the door. "*Gracias, gracias!*" she said over and over.

"Christmas?" Fausto asked, as if she had misspoken. He craned his neck, hoping to see if Arturo Jr. was inside.

"*Sí, sí!*" she insisted and turned her back on him to retreat into the house. "*Por favor, por favor. Gracias!*"

Fausto stood outside for several moments, not hearing a sound. *Christmas.* When he finally walked to his car, he used his bare arm to wipe the sweat from his face.

Benny knew the way to force peace between him and Fausto was to use Rogelio. Fausto wouldn't have admitted it to his cousin, but it was true: he would stay angry, but he could not stay away. He refused to give up

Rogelio a second time. The day Benny signed up with the Teamsters, he came to the apartment to tell Fausto that he and Luz were returning to work for Jack Dragovich. They had no babysitters for the summer.

"I thought maybe you might want to watch the boys during the week while the strike is going on. You can still picket on weekends," Benny said, with one foot on the porch and the other on the porch step below, as if he wasn't sure he would be welcomed. The crossing signal bell rang, warning of an approaching train, and Benny waited until the thunder of its engine and long row of boxcars faded. "Listen, we need someone to take care of the boys," he said. "Rozelle's uncle offered to watch them, but Luz does not trust him. His eyesight is bad and he runs errands with the boys in his car."

"And Luz will trust *me?*" Fausto laughed. *"Saan ko nga panunot dayta."*

"I trust you. Or does a traitor's trust not matter to you?"

"I will do it for Rogelio," Fausto answered, then rushed to add, "And for BJ too."

Fausto liked watching the boys during the week without Luz hovering over him. He was spending all his change taking them to the nearby convenience store to buy comic books and candy. When they returned one afternoon from their outing, Rogelio dashed off to his room to hide his Cracker Jack box. BJ waited for Fausto to remove his street shoes and put on his house slippers, and then took Fausto's shoes and set them by the front door.

"Uncle Fausto," the boy said. "Do you like Rogelio better than me?"

"No, no!" Fausto swept the boy up in his arms. "Why do you say such a thing?"

BJ pouted, exposing the raw pink of his lower lip. "Rogelio told me so. He said you give him more candy and toys and spend more time with him because he is more special to you than I am."

"That is not true," Fausto insisted. "Rogelio is bigger and older than you. When you are taller and your stomach gets bigger, you will get more of everything." He set BJ down.

BJ looked at him with doubt. He stood on tiptoes and drew a line across Fausto's chest with his finger. "When I am this tall, I will get more toys too. Okay?"

Fausto fingered the button on his shirt, the milestone. "Next week, you might grow three inches."

As BJ dashed off to the bedroom he shared with Rogelio, Fausto vowed to give more attention to him, even though in his heart he favored Rogelio. BJ was fussy with the meals Fausto served, but Rogelio ate everything, including bowls of rice mixed with raw egg yolk. He watched Rogelio wash his hands, fingers that he taught the boy to eat with because that was the Filipino way—no matter what Luz said. Sometimes he fed Rogelio with his own hand. When he did, Fausto wondered if Rogelio would ever learn the truth.

———

One afternoon, when both boys were supposed to be taking their naps, Rogelio slunk into the living room as Fausto read the newspaper. Eyes red from crying, Rogelio bunched himself up in the corner of the sofa.

"*Apay ngay?* What happened?" Fausto demanded.

Rogelio smeared snot and tears on his face with his arm. "BJ said my real Daddy was going to take me away!"

Fausto sat down next to Rogelio and massaged the boy's foot. He had long toes, just like Fausto's own. "Why did BJ say that?"

Rogelio lifted himself off the pillow with his elbows, a defiant look on his face. "He was mad because I told him I was more special."

Fausto tried to smooth down the cowlick on Rogelio's head. "You should not say things like that. You hurt his feelings first."

"What he said was worse." Rogelio plopped back down on the pillow. "He said Mommy and Daddy can't stop my real Daddy from taking me away. BJ said he's coming any day now." The boy gave a start when the house creaked. "Uncle Fausto, can you stop my real Daddy from taking me? I don't want to leave home. I don't want to leave *you!*"

"I don't want you to leave me, either," Fausto said. "Maybe it's not such a bad thing for your real Daddy to want you back. It was not his choice for you to be taken away. Other people made that decision for him. If he wants you back, it means he loves you very much."

Rogelio drew back. "But he's not really my Daddy. He doesn't deserve to be called Daddy. How can he love someone he doesn't even know?"

"Maybe he is not a stranger." Fausto's heart began to race. "Maybe you have been with him the whole time, and you and your Daddy have loved each other all this time."

Rogelio's mouth hung open. "I don't know what you mean."

Fausto didn't expect the time to come so soon. Rogelio was barely seven years old, but everything seemed to be leading to this moment, like a dream. A flash of red caught his attention. Luz was standing in the kitchen doorway, a bandana pulled down around her neck, straw hat bunched in her fist. How long had she been listening to them? Her face was streaked with sweat and dirt, her eyes clear and cold. She threw down her straw hat and reprimanded Rogelio for not taking his nap.

"But Uncle Fausto was telling me a story," he said in a high-pitched voice.

"He was telling you a fairytale!" Luz lunged and clipped Rogelio on the leg with the back of her hand. *"Inkan!* Go to your room and take your nap."

When he shook his head, Luz pinched his bare thigh. Rogelio let out a yelp and rubbed at the red marks on his skin. Fausto pulled her arm away without thinking.

"Don't talk back to me!" She shook her finger at Rogelio. Then she whirled around and yanked her arm away from Fausto. "Don't you poison him with your talk—in my house. And don't you tell me how to discipline my son—*my* son!"

"You should not hit him, Luz. He's just a little boy."

She snorted. "But it's okay to throw your pregnant wife out? It's okay to ruin my niece's life for good?" Her voice broke. "Why should your life not be just as bad?"

"What do you mean?" Fausto grabbed at her sleeve—the cloth still warm from ten hours in the fields.

Luz jerked away from him and clapped her hand over her mouth. Rogelio peeked out from the hallway, tears sheeting his face. Fausto wanted to flee with him, just as he had wanted to do after Rogelio's baptism. Now, he decided, was the time for the truth. But Rogelio ran down the hallway as the front door opened and Benny padded into the living room in dirt-stained socks, drying his face with a towel.

"Fausto is leaving our house—for good," Luz announced to Benny.

"Luz, *nag kari ka kaniyak*—" The towel hung limp in Benny's hand.

"I don't care what I promised you! He was trying to tell Rogelio—" she swallowed hard "—who his real father is."

Benny gave Fausto a pained look. *"Agpayso daytoy?"*

"Of course, it's true. Why should I lie?" Luz said.

"Why should Benny trust what you say?" Fausto said to Luz. "You kept secrets from him and me. You are keeping my wife from me. And my child too!"

"Your selfishness is making you blind, Fausto!" Luz held her head in her hands. "I am protecting everyone and I cannot do it anymore!"

"You are only protecting yourself!" Fausto spat out.

Benny raised his hand to quiet them, but it was the sound of screeching tires in front of the house that broke up their fight. Bam!

Luz's head jerked in the direction of the hallway. "Where is Rogelio?"

Fausto raced out the front door first, with Benny at his heels. A white pickup truck blocked the middle of the street at an angle, yards from where Rogelio lay on his back. Rogelio pushed himself up, sobbing, his legs sprawled out. Fausto reached Rogelio first, though somehow Luz had gotten past Benny.

A middle-aged Anglo man jumped out of his cab. "I didn't even see him," he said, swiping off his cowboy hat. "He just darted across the road like a squirrel."

"*An-nay!*" Luz dropped to her knees, as if she were the one in pain. She cupped Rogelio's face and gently picked off the grit pressed into his cheeks and bloodied lip.

Fausto tried to reach past Luz to comb out Rogelio's tangled hair, but she pushed him away. "Call the ambulance. Call the police," she shouted at Fausto, though it was Benny who retreated to the house. Luz tried to slip her arm beneath Rogelio's knees.

"Don't move him," Fausto said. "You might hurt him more. Wait for the ambulance."

Luz gently released Rogelio. "*I* might hurt him more? *You* did this!" She pounded her fists into Fausto's gut, trying to push him down to the ground but only managing to stir up a cloud of dust. "I'll not let you touch him! I'll not let you ruin another life!"

"Hey lady!" The driver dropped his hat and tried to separate them. Luz stumbled back when he yelled, "Ma'am, we gotta get this kid to the hospital!"

Fausto examined Rogelio's legs, the odd angle of his leg to his hip. There were scratches and deep gashes on his shins. Black gravel was embedded in his cut skin.

"Tell me where you feel pain," Fausto said.

Rogelio pointed to his left leg. When he shifted his weight to his right hip, he cried out in pain. "Please take me away, Uncle Fausto."

"We cannot move you," Fausto told him. "We have to wait for the ambulance to take you to the hospital. The doctors will fix your legs."

He wiped Rogelio's face with his handkerchief. How cool to the touch were the boy's forehead and cheeks, despite the blistering heat. He expected Luz to pound his back, but she was kneeling where the driver had deposited her, crying, with her arms wrapped around her stomach.

When the ambulance arrived, Luz climbed into the back with her hand clenched to the steel bar of Rogelio's stretcher as if soldered there. At Benny's request, Fausto stayed behind with the driver of the pick-up truck to talk with the police officer who came to the scene. Benny carried a sleepy BJ in his arms to a neighbor's house and then followed the ambulance in his car. Some of the neighbors ventured to the edges of their lawns and fences, pretending to retrieve the afternoon newspaper or water their plants, but nobody crossed the street.

It seemed like hours passed before Fausto was finished with the police report and Prudencio was able to pick him up and drive him to the hospital in Porterville. He found Benny in the emergency-room waiting area, talking with a doctor. Rogelio was being transferred to a hospital in Fresno for surgery that night. The X-rays showed that Rogelio had broken his left femur in two places near his hip, which meant he would be in a leg and hip cast for several months. At some point, he would be able to get around on crutches, but once the cast came off, he would require extensive physical therapy because his leg was going to be very weak. The doctor talked of inserting steel pins and performing multiple surgeries through the years. He lowered his voice when he said Rogelio's left leg might be shorter than his right leg as time wore on. The difference in length between the two legs was going to depend upon the success of each surgery. Rogelio had vomited several times but was resting now after the nurse had given him pain medication.

When Luz emerged from the restroom and saw Fausto next to Benny, she refused to let Fausto see him. "Get out!" she said. Her eyes were red and puffy, her nostrils rimmed with mucus. "You don't belong here."

"*Husto daytan*—enough, Luz!" Benny's voice was sharp, though his face was lined with weariness. "Fausto belongs here. *Ammom dayta!*"

Benny's words struck Fausto in the heart. What could he mean other than what sounded so obvious? Fausto longed to rush past the double doors, where Rogelio lay on the other side alone. He was at the hospital when Rogelio's appendix was taken out last year. He wanted to be here for Rogelio now.

"Let me help pay for the hospital." Fausto took out his wallet and pretended to thumb through bills, but Benny waved him off.

"You help by staying away!" Luz jutted out her chin.

A gray-haired nurse interrupted her. "Mr. and Mrs. Benedicto Edralin, your son, Rogelio, has been asking for his mother and father ever since he woke up. Please follow me, one at a time." She walked noiselessly across the floor in her thick-soled shoes.

"I'll see Rogelio first," Luz told Benny. "When I come back, you better be alone."

When she disappeared behind the swinging doors, Fausto asked about Rogelio.

"He's much better." Benny stared down the hallway. "They gave him medicine. Luz said he was screaming in the ambulance, but she couldn't do anything for him. She said his cries sounded like his real mother, when he was born. But he'll be all right. He's a strong boy." He turned his back on the double doors. "You should go home now and rest."

"I cannot leave him," Fausto said. *How could he leave his son?* "It's my fault."

"Fausto, it's not your fault—it's *our* fault." Benny shook his head.

When Fausto finally left, he didn't imagine the doubt that flickered in Benny's eyes.

––––––––––

For several weeks, Benny's voice echoed in his head until he had twisted Benny's words into outright condemnation; it was easy to do when he couldn't go to sleep or woke up in a cold sweat. He decided to stay away from Terra Bella even before Fidel told him that Luz announced to the community that Fausto was barred from their home. Mostly everyone sided with Luz. First Marina and now Rogelio. Not fit for marriage or fatherhood. Luz was surely telling Rogelio that he wouldn't have run out of the house if Fausto hadn't scared him with his harmful words, if he hadn't fought with her.

With his days freed up, Fausto went on the picket line or found work here and there picking plums or apricots. He told himself to visit Georgina and Arturo Junior more, that it would make him feel better, but it was hard enough getting out of bed every morning. Sometimes he caught himself not caring what happened in the fields, whether the UFW was making progress negotiating its expired contracts or being stonewalled by the growers, just as he was being stonewalled by Luz.

One evening in October, Benny was waiting for Fausto in front of his apartment, wearing a heavy coat to ward off the fall chill, the early frost. Two months had passed since the accident. It was pitch black outside the circle of faint light thrown out by the entryway lantern. Benny straightened up. "I should have come sooner. *Pakawanen nak.*"

"*Apay ngay?* Why do I need to forgive you? You are not the one at fault."

"*Bay-amon!* Let it be! I don't want to talk about blame," Benny said, and stamped his feet on the concrete. "*Ai sus!* It's cold tonight!"

Fausto pulled out his key. "You want to come inside?"

"No, I cannot stay long."

"Is everything okay? Is Rogelio okay?"

"Rogelio is good. You know that," Benny said. "Nothing like that."

"Then what? Why are you here this time of night?"

Benny massaged his temple. "We are moving to Chicago."

The words slowly sank in. "If it's not my fault, why are you abandoning me? Why are you taking Rogelio away from me?"

"We are not taking him away from you." Benny turned into the shadows. "Luz has been talking about moving to Chicago for many months now."

"*Apay ngay?* Why now?"

"You know one of Luz's cousins is married to a doctor. He knows the best surgeons over there for Rogelio. We want the best for Rogelio." Benny stepped into the circle of light and looked Fausto in the eye. "Do you not want the best for him too?"

"Of course! Yes!"

"Macario is throwing us a going-away party on Saturday. You'll come, eh?" Benny blew on his fingers. "You can visit us whenever you like."

Did it matter how far away Rogelio would be from him? Terra Bella, Chicago—it was all the same. Luz would do everything in her power to keep him away.

Benny stepped down from the porch. "It's all for the best. I cannot stand between you and Luz forever or watch you hurt yourself more. I don't blame you. I blame *me.*"

"Hurt myself more? *Ania iti kayatmo nga sawen?*"

"You know what I mean!" Benny said. "All these years—almost seven years now—I know what you have been thinking!" His eyes were glassy and sharp like hard frost. "Stop it now, eh? You stop thinking you know something. *Stop!*"

Benny cut across the white lawn to his car, ice crystals crunching beneath his work boots. Fausto stood in the entryway, every muscle tense, as Benny's car pulled away from the curb. The lantern light barely outlined the steps below him. Darkness was creeping in. His world had grown smaller. It was just Delano now.

In the fall of 1973, Chávez called an end to the grape strike when it didn't force the growers to the negotiation table. The violence stopped immediately. Fausto began a letter telling Benny that the fields were peaceful now, but when he heard Benny got a job as a bellhop, with good tips, at a fancy hotel, he threw the letter away.

The UFW expanded its boycott of table grapes and wine across the country, hoping that tactic would be more effective in hurting the growers' profits and bringing the two sides together to talk. The boycotts were successful; grocers were throwing away spoiled grapes. But the growers held their ground, and as time passed union membership dwindled even more. Fausto read in the *Delano Record* that while millions of Americans refused to buy grapes, the boycott was useless in its goal to overthrow the Teamsters, which had cemented its relationship with the growers. He tried to remain hopeful, but it looked as if the Teamsters would be the main union in the fields for many years.

When the UFW began lobbying for labor laws to guarantee workers the right to unionize, Fausto joined Prudencio and Ayong picking citrus fruit in the wintertime and stone fruit in the spring and summer. They kept their apartment in Delano and spent weekends at the Forty Acres compound and the People's Café. Whenever Manong Flor saw them in the corner of the dimly lit bar, nursing glasses of warm Dos Equis, he laughed through the gaps in his rotted teeth, and said, "There go the three manongs."

In 1974, the UFW was getting ready to open a retirement home for the elderly strikers, particularly the pinoy strikers who had no family to take care of them. The UFW board had accepted Chávez's earlier proposal of building a retirement home and approved the preliminary plans drawn up by Larry Itliong before he had left the union. Construction had commenced on the east side of Forty Acres in 1972. Now two years later, Fausto, Ayong, and Prudencio were helping to finish up the buildings in time for the opening ceremony. Prudencio was pleased that the housing project was going to be named in honor of the union's first casualty—Paulo Agbayani. It was the least the UFW could do for the Filipinos, who were now a minority group within the union. The union newspaper, *El Malcriado,* had run an article condemning the Filipinos' hobby of cockfighting as immoral, which Prudencio railed about for weeks. With Larry Itliong long gone—though Philip Vera Cruz and Pete Velasco were still on the board—the union was finally exposing its true feelings for the Filipinos.

Many pinoys were grumbling not only about the UFW but Chávez himself. Though they were Catholic too, the veteran pinoys didn't believe the Church should be involved at all. Prudencio reminded them of what Larry's longtime friend from Stockton, Ernesto Mabalon, had once said of Chávez and his march from Delano to Sacramento six months after the farm workers first walked out of the vineyards: "Marching 366 miles behind a statue of the Virgin Mary is not a strike."

"I'm too old to argue about that again!" Ayong dug his bony knuckles into the hollows of his cheeks, as if scratching at peat dirt still lodged in his pores. "Maybe I will quit for good and move into the retirement home—1974 is a good year to retire."

"If I retire, then I'm going to die." Fausto held out his palms, crusted with layers of yellowed skin. "What will I do with these hands if I no longer work?"

"There's plenty of room for a garden and pens to raise goats, pigs, and rabbits." Ayong pointed at a level area, away from the union offices, health clinic, gas station and main building, which housed fifty-nine units, a kitchen, dining hall, and recreation room. Ayong's eyes were as hazy as the distant foothills to the east in the morning light. "I never had my own room here in the States. Never lived in a place that had central air-con, either."

"Central air-con!" Fausto whistled. "You will get soft!"

Prudencio snorted. "We never had such luxuries before; why now?"

"We earned it!" Ayong said.

Fausto sat on his haunches and scooped up a handful of dirt. "And we helped build it."

For the past six months, every weekend the three of them worked side by side with hundreds of people who came to Delano from across the country to contribute their time and skills at Forty Acres. At lunch, Fausto met foreigners who had traveled from as far away as Europe and Japan. He asked many questions, and as he listened to them describe their customs and food, it reminded him of the long afternoons hearing about Miss Arnold's travels. Fausto was grateful that so many strangers cared about old-timer Filipino farm workers whose faces were invisible in and out of the fields and whose lives had not improved much, even though they came to America decades ago to change their luck.

Weeks before the ribbon-cutting ceremony, Arturo Junior made his way around the stacked bricks and saltillo tiles to greet Fausto. How tall he had grown! He bent down to give Fausto a hug. Despite his height and bulk, he was soft and gentle looking.

"I should have come to visit you and your mother," Fausto said, but even as he spoke, the words felt lame. "I was not there for you."

"My mami wanted us to be alone. I lost track of time, taking care of her and my abuelos," Arturo Junior said, his voice even deeper than when Fausto remembered from the funeral. "I wanted to find out what happened to my papi, but my mami wouldn't let me. She was afraid she'd lose me too."

"Ai, Junior," Fausto said, cupping Arturo Junior's cheek. Tiny whiteheads were sprinkled across his forehead and nose. Peach-like fuzz darkened his upper lip. "She was trying to protect you. It would have been too dangerous. The police were not even helping."

"They covered it up. I know it. One day I'm going to find out—when I'm older and they can't push me aside." Arturo Junior pulled away. "Call me Arturo now. I'm almost fourteen."

Fausto smiled as the boy tugged at his jeans, which were too short on him. "Arturo," he said slowly, testing the sound of the boy's name—his father's name, his good friend's name—as it passed through his lips. "Your father died for a good cause."

"Maybe that will mean something to me later," Arturo said, not caring that some volunteers had stopped loading sacks of cement onto a wheelbarrow to eavesdrop. "All I know is: they shot him in cold blood, and they're walking free. Mami said you were right next to him. She said you could've been shot too."

"It should have been me. Your father had a family and a home."

Arturo shook his head. "Remember the night you came to our house drunk after Marina left? You were so sad. Papi put you in my bed and we let you sleep in. I was scared for you. That night, Papi told me to take care of you. He said there would come a time when he would be too old or he wouldn't be around to do it, and I would be the one to look after you. That's why I wanted to sleep on the floor that night."

Fausto's cheeks burned with the memory. "When I woke up, you came to my side right away and held my hand."

"That's what good nurses do," Arturo said. "I'm gonna be a nurse and take care of my mami, my abuelos, and you."

"The world is bigger than Delano, Arturo." Fausto chuckled, though the thought made him both wistful and sad. "My teacher Miss Arnold and my four older cousins taught me my world was bigger than San Esteban. When you graduate from high school, you'll want to leave this little town." He stamped his foot on the ground. Topsoil billowed up and settled on his work boots.

"As long as my family and you are here, I'll be here." Arturo thrust a brush flecked with dried white paint into Fausto's hand. "I'm painting rooms. Wanna help?"

As Fausto walked with Arturo, he heard his name being called out. Teddy Enebrad came bounding over building materials like a hurdler, carrying two cans of paint. Fausto hadn't seen him in more than two years. Teddy's hair was shorn at the ears; he was clean shaven. He wore a fringed suede vest, though he still sported torn-up jeans and a familiar T-shirt. Arturo pointed out which building he was working in and left the two to catch up. Teddy gave him a bear hug.

Fausto held onto him tightly. "I thought maybe you had stayed in that Malaysia!" he teased.

"Nah. A bout with dysentery convinced me I'm not cut out for the Third World over the long haul." He pulled on the back of his hair, as if he hadn't gotten used to his short haircut. "I started my PhD program at UCLA last fall."

"Are you married yet, Teddy?" Fausto glanced at his left hand.

"I go by Ted now, and no, I'm not married." He laughed. "I'm too busy. UCLA started an Asian American Studies Center while I was gone, but I'm helping to shape the program now. One day, Manong Fausto, Asian American Studies will be a department in the UC system. Marriage and kids will come later."

"Not too much later," Fausto advised. "You don't want to wait as long as I did."

"Don't worry about me." Ted steered Fausto in the opposite direction of the building where Arturo was painting. "I've got a surprise for you. When I heard about the retirement home being built, I got in touch with someone from your past, and we made plans to meet here this weekend. She has her heart set on seeing you again."

Fausto caught his breath. For one foolish moment, he thought Ted was talking about Marina. He searched the grounds, certain he could recognize her in the crowd. Ted whistled two times. A woman emerged from behind a parked pickup truck, carrying a baby in her arms. Wendy! Fausto was happy to see her, even as disappointment washed over him. Gone were the bouffant hairstyle and twiggy figure. She wore her long hair in a ponytail, with a center part. Pregnancy had given her curves and more flesh. She wore a peasant skirt and platform shoes, fashionable, as usual, and not practical for volunteer work. Teary eyed, she gave Fausto a hug and kissed him on both cheeks. She pointed out two little boys, who had abandoned a tall blond man as he stacked saltillo tiles into a wheelbarrow. The boys were playing tug-of-war with a piece of rope they'd found on the ground.

"Look how big they are now!" Fausto clapped his hand to his forehead. The boys' sandy-colored hair and identical faces mirrored their mother's features more than their father's. "And a baby." Fausto peeked at the baby's smooth-skinned face, the web of teeny blue veins on its eyelids. It kept sleeping despite hammers banging, the roar of trucks coming and going, and the shouts of directions given to the lay volunteers by plumbers, carpenters, and bricklayers. He fingered the baby's hair, soft and weightless as dandelion threads.

"Kimberly—our New Year's baby—is five and a half months," she said, and kissed the crown of her daughter's head. "William and Jackson—they go by Will and Jack—are five. So now you know why I haven't written or sent out cards all those years! Just a busy mom in Seattle."

"You came all the way from Seattle?" His voice was full of wonder.

"I wouldn't have missed this for the world. I still keep up with what's going on with the UFW. I've taught my boys not to eat table grapes," she said, grinning, her lips shiny with pink gloss. "And Steve and I don't drink Gallo wine."

Ted wrinkled his nose. "Awful stuff anyway. Easy to boycott."

Wendy laughed. She turned to Fausto and rubbed his back. "I know the UFW's been taking a beating, but it'll survive. How have *you* been?"

Fausto's eyes stung. How could such a simple question catch him off guard, have the power to strip away years and layers of thick skin down to the wound? He fumbled for the handkerchief in his pant pocket. Ted threw his arm around Fausto.

Wendy wiped his tears with a corner of her daughter's pink blanket, and whispered in his ear, "I heard about your wife and the house. I'm so sorry."

"She was going to have our baby," Fausto said, without shame. He didn't tell them about the car accident and how Rogelio had been taken far away from him to Chicago.

The baby stirred. Wendy nuzzled her cheek in her baby's wispy curls—so blond they were hard to see. Fausto resisted the urge to trace his finger along the whorl of the baby's hair and find the soft spot on her head that pulsed as if her heart were just beneath the thin layer of skin and bone. Nida had shown him the spot with her firstborn. *If you put your finger right on top of it, you can feel the pulse.* He had found Rogelio's. The pulse had surged up his finger, into his own heart.

Fausto mopped his face with his handkerchief, lingering to pinch the bridge of his nose just in case more tears sprang without warning. "Don't worry about me. I can take care of myself."

"It's been tougher for you guys on the front lines," Ted said. "Nothing would have been gained without all of your sacrifices. Right?" He looked at Fausto the way a child waits for the hoped-for approval of the parent—*wen, wen.*

"There were many sacrifices," Fausto said slowly, his words above a whisper. His mouth hung open.

"You don't have to say anything more." Wendy brushed the rims of her eyes with her fingertips, the cotton-candy color of her nails turning glossy. "Everyone has regrets, Manong Fausto. You just hope they're the right ones."

"The right regrets." He turned the words over. "Maybe," he said, but he wasn't sure.

It was quiet for a moment, before Wendy asked, "Is that Manong Prudencio?"

Prudencio was pushing a wheelbarrow full of dusty cement sacks;

Ayong trailed him, lugging a water hose over his stooped shoulders. Several feet away, Severo Laigo directed a group of young pinoys who were carrying poles that would support the wooden canopy over the saltillo-tiled walkway. Severo's twig-like arms waved with authority, his silver hair glinting in the sun. There was still so much to do and so little time before the ribbon-cutting ceremony! Manong Flor couldn't keep up with them. He stopped often, glancing about. He cleaned the thick lens of his glasses with his shirttail and started walking in the wrong direction. Behind him, two burly men unloaded tubs of Chinese pistache, blackwood acacia, carob, and camphor trees.

"Will you retire here, Manong Fausto?" Ted's voice was cheery.

"If I retire, I'll die. What will I do with my time? Think of more regrets?"

"Retirement is a time to enjoy yourself," Wendy said. "You could go back home and see your family."

He had trained himself not to think about Marina all these years. The sting of remembrance made him hold onto forgetfulness with such fierceness. He could never afford to go back now, and even if he could, he didn't belong there anymore. "Once the contracts are signed, I'll work until it is time to bury me and my union card six feet under Kern County soil!" Fausto said.

"At least you haven't lost your stubbornness!" Ted picked up the cans of paint at his feet. "My crew is probably wondering where I went. Do you want to join me?"

Wendy tugged at Fausto's sleeve. "We're planting rosebushes."

Fausto patted Ted's arm. "I'll paint with you and Arturo Junior tomorrow." He turned to Wendy and smiled. "I like to garden," he said shyly. "I like roses."

Ted shrugged in exaggerated defeat and started walking away. "I don't take rejection kindly," he called out, "so tonight's dinner is on me—your choice of restaurant."

"We're treating you to breakfast in the morning," Wendy informed Fausto, as they walked to where her husband and sons were waiting for her by a pickup truck full of rosebushes. The boys' arms were wrapped around their father's long legs.

Her husband towered over Fausto as they shook hands. "I'm honored to meet you. Wendy speaks of you with great fondness and respect," he said, his voice serious.

The twin boys gazed up at him in awe. "Is this your home?"

"This is a home for old people," Fausto said, bending down. "Do I look old to you?" He winked at Wendy and Steve.

One of the boys examined Fausto's face with startling blue eyes. "You don't look as old as my great grandma. She lives with lots of old people."

Wendy massaged the slack skin that once stretched tight across Fausto's biceps. "He still picks grapes in the summertime. You know how heavy those crates of grapes are? Well, Manong Fausto can carry them in and out of the fields."

"Then you can help us plant roses," the other boy said. They each took one of his hands and pulled him forward.

How soft their skin felt against his, how little their fingers were in his hand—just like Rogelio's once were! He hadn't forgotten. *Ai sus,* he hadn't forgotten!

Wendy put the baby in a sling, and everyone carried gallon-size pots of roses across what was going to be the front lawn. "Watch Manong Fausto first!" she told her boys, and handed Fausto a shovel. "He once had a big garden and knows all about plants."

One boy kneeled beside him and the other stood before him, solemn-faced. Fausto took pleasure in their attention. He speared the tip of the shovel into the ground with his work boot and twisted the handle, feeling great satisfaction when the earth gave way easily.

At the end of the weekend, the hundreds of volunteer workers gathered for a group photograph. Fausto had just finished painting a room with Arturo when they were summoned to the front of the building. He was heartened when Ted and Wendy sought him out. They argued over who would stand on his left side after Arturo claimed the right side, by virtue of having known him the longest. Wendy, with the baby slung in front of her, won out, with Ted pressing in from behind. Fausto kissed the baby's soft spot. The twin boys pushed up against him, trampling on his feet to get closer. Fausto winced, but it was a good kind of pain. So many people—young and old, local and foreign, of all different colors—huddled close together. He touched strands of his hair, stiff with dried paint, with fingers still smelling of wet earth. But he stood tall in his coveralls, as if he were all cleaned up, wearing his barong shirt.

When Governor Jerry Brown signed into law the Agricultural Labor Relations Act in August 1975, nearly a year after Agbayani Village opened, Ted sent Fausto flowers with a congratulations card. All the political lobbying by Chávez and the UFW had finally paid off. Fausto bought the *Delano Record* and the newspapers of all the major cities, and over beer at the People's Café, he, Prudencio, Ayong, and Severo savored the various accounts of the UFW's victory. Fausto tried to understand the legal wording—it was a foreign language to him. But Prudencio pointed to a line in one newspaper account that simply said the law was enacted to "ensure peace in the agricultural fields by guaranteeing justice for all agricultural workers and stability in labor relations." Farm workers could now engage in union activity and select whomever they wished to represent them during contract negotiations with the growers, without the interference of either employers or unions.

"We have rights! We are legal!" Ayong said, giddy with good news and drink.

Severo folded his hands on the table, hands that Fausto noticed had begun to tremble more and more in the past year. "There will be peace in the fields now."

The familiar crash of billiard balls erupted from the pool tables behind them. A nickel clinked into the corner jukebox and a brash Mexican song made the speakers and Fausto's ears vibrate. Through the storefront window, Fausto spied a telephone booth across the street. He could call Benny to relay the news. He squinted at his watch. What time was it in Chicago? Would Benny be home now after carrying the luggage of wealthy guests to their hotel rooms? Fausto swished the flattened beer in his glass.

"What is the matter with you, eh?" Ayong shook the newspaper beneath Fausto's elbow.

"I know what you're thinking," Prudencio said gently. "Put your losses behind you, Fausto. Listen to me: all our years here we were slaves in the fields. Nobody knew. Like ghosts in the vineyards." He slapped at the headline of a front-page newspaper. "Now everybody out there knows who we are, what we went through, how we fought back. We changed our lives and the lives of all the farm workers behind us. We have something to be proud of, finally." He wagged his finger at Fausto and gave him a severe look. "This is what you should be saying. This is what you would be telling us!"

Fausto could hear himself saying such things with fervor to disbelievers and worshippers alike. To Marina, Benny, Mr. Cuculich and all the growers, Manong Magno, Ted, Wendy's twin boys, and those who had looked at him and his dirty work clothes through the years with scorn or indifference. But he needed more time. How could he tell this to his friends when they wanted to celebrate? He lifted his glass and forced a smile and the words to come out: "To peace in the fields forever!"

In 1977, the Teamsters' national leaders determined that the few gains made in farm organization weren't worth all the resources they had invested. Fausto gloated over the newspaper articles on the federal investigation of the union's alleged violation of racketeering laws and internal clashes that threatened to destroy its existence. But Forty Acres responded to the Teamsters' departure with relief, not excitement. The UFW was locked in other battles—farm-labor abuses and attacks on the Agricultural Labor Relations Board by state legislators whom the growers had befriended. Despite the existence of the farm-labor law, little had changed. Growers disrupted elections, barred organizers from their farms, fired pro-UFW workers, and refused to bargain. Regulators were not verifying months-old union elections held on the farms. Fausto wasn't surprised to hear that Macario and others in Terra Bella decided not to be represented by a union. Macario quit working for George Cuculich to work as Frank Radic's foreman when his former boss declared that he wanted peace with the UFW.

It shouldn't have been a surprise, then, when one evening Mr. Cuculich passed through the doors of the People's Café, removing his hat as if he were in a church. He strode across the room, avoiding the stares of farm workers, and sat across from Fausto.

"Seems like years since I last saw you, Fausto," he boomed, as they shook hands.

"It *has* been years, Mr. Cuculich."

The grower slapped the table and laughed deep from his gut. "Now don't go adding years to my life! I'm already old, and Lord knows all this unionizing's pushed me past middle age." He threaded his fingers through his thinning hair, all gray now.

Fausto tipped his glass of beer in Mr. Cuculich's direction. "Do you want a beer?"

"No, thanks." Mr. Cuculich rubbed his slimmed-down stomach. "I lost a lot of weight over this union trouble. It's the only good thing that came out of all this. I figure I might as well keep it off." He stole a glance at the room cramped with long dining tables and pool tables with shredded felt tops.

"Did you come here to play pool?" Fausto took a sip of beer. "There is not much exercise in playing pool."

Mr. Cuculich threw back his head and laughed again. Even the hair in his nostrils was gray. "Well, you gained a sense of humor—and a sure voice, Fausto Empleo, and I mean that as a compliment." When he leaned forward, the table suddenly became smaller. "To tell the truth, I was looking for you." He glared at the competing noise of the jukebox. "I don't get my feelings hurt very often, but you hurt my feelings when the contracts were signed and you didn't come back to work for me. I know you're going to say I was forced to sign those contracts, but times have changed. I've changed. I'm all for equality—for you and for me." The grower turned over his squared hands on the table as if revealing all his cards. "I miss my number-one pruner. I'm asking you to come back to work for me."

Fausto sat back, stunned.

"I don't know if you'll believe me, but I never set out to take advantage of anybody," Mr. Cuculich said, as he picked at the napkin in front of him. "You probably heard Macario and Nick went to work for Frank Radic. They like that Frank's still putting up a fight. Frank's stubborn. Macario's stubborn. Hell, we're all stubborn! But at least I figured it out. If I'd known how costly the fight was going to be, I would've let Itliong and Chávez unionize on my ranch from the get-go. I would've raised wages to keep everybody happy. I would've thrown up portable toilets in the field. It's a small price to pay for all the crops that were wasted." He tore up the napkin into bits and then stared at the mess he'd made. "But hindsight is twenty-twenty, right?" A sad smile crept up on his creased, sunburnt face as he looked out the window. "I kept a loaded shotgun on the fireplace mantel to protect my family after Jimmy's bike and our house were vandalized. That's not a way to live, now is it? Those days are over." He cleaned the table with a sweep of his hand. "But let's not talk about that anymore. Let's mend fences. It's what the good Lord wants us to do in the end, right? What do you say, Fausto? Come back to my ranch."

Fausto couldn't imagine mending fences with Macario or anyone else in Terra Bella, but as he stared back at Mr. Cuculich, who sat before him with his hand extended, who sought him out in a place he never would have set foot in before, something moved deep inside him. He grasped the grower's hand.

"I'll come back, but only if you let Prudencio and Ayong return with me too."

"Of course!" Mr. Cuculich shook Fausto's hand. "We're building a bathroom with indoor plumbing in the newer camps."

"We cannot stay in the camps anymore," Fausto said. "Our apartment is close to stores and our recreation in town." In truth, the long walk from the fields to the camp would be too hard on them.

"Once you're back in my fields, you'll feel ten years younger." Ignoring the bar crowd that was watching them, Mr. Cuculich came over to Fausto's side of the table and gave him a quick hug. The grower's hand, as leathery as Fausto's own, lingered on his arm. "Welcome back, Fausto! I'll see you Monday morning." There was a spring in Mr. Cuculich's step as he walked out the door.

Maybe, Fausto thought to himself, he would be just as light-footed when he returned to his old boss's fields.

One hot afternoon in late August 1980, after they had worked for Mr. Cuculich for nearly three years and put in ten-plus hours that day, Ayong passed out cold bottles of Dos Equis to Prudencio and Fausto. He clinked his bottle against theirs and raised it in the air. "It is time for me to retire," he announced, and took a swig of beer.

Prudencio and Fausto exchanged surprised looks. "You make more money than me with your per-box bonuses!" Fausto declared, though it wasn't true.

Prudencio rubbed Ayong's curved back. "Now that you're closer to the ground, maybe you should pick strawberries."

Ayong swatted Prudencio away. "I am eighty years old! I am done!"

Prudencio roared with laughter, spilling his beer on the floor. "You're like Fausto, maybe sixty-eight. But you're not older than me. You're not seventy yet."

Ayong soaked up the pool of beer with a soiled dishrag. "Ho, I lied then! I lied to labor contractors and foremen because I knew they would turn me away for being too old." He straightened up and pushed the long sleeve of his shirt to flex his bicep, which was more loose skin than muscle. "I can work for another ten, even twenny, years, but why should I? When the harvest is done, I will move to the Village."

"What about your roommates, eh?" Prudencio demanded. "*Ket, dakamen ngay?*"

"You both will join me," Ayong said, surprised, as if they ought to know better.

There were many benefits to retiring to Agbayani Village, he insisted. They would have a cook preparing their meals again. Although Manong Flor had retired to Abgayani Village and helped in the kitchen, he had collapsed and died, fittingly, after washing the evening's last pot. His passing was the first death at the retirement home. Ayong pointed out that with two acres set aside for gardening they could stake out their own vegetable plot. They could raise roosters in spite of the fact that the union board didn't like that the Filipinos raised them for cockfights. The old-timers didn't care.

Fausto couldn't imagine retiring; he was sure to live past a hundred. But when Ayong moved to the Village, Prudencio and Fausto joined him. When Arturo, a nursing student at Bakersfield College, heard that Fausto had retired, he said Fausto would be his first patient after graduation. Arturo teased Fausto, saying that retirement was making him shrink, and began calling him "*hombrecito.*"

At the Village, each set of bedrooms shared a bathroom, which connected the two rooms. Because the building wasn't filled to capacity, some residents had their own bedroom, like Prudencio and Fausto, who shared a bathroom. It was strange to wake up in a larger room and not have anything to do, but Fausto soon established a routine. He avoided the cockfights, but he and Severo won the most pennies and nickels from the other rummy players on Friday and Saturday evenings. Sometimes, instead of money, Fausto accepted services, such as weeding his vegetable plot and shoe polishing, though there were no fancy places to wear shiny shoes. In the spring, they grew tomatoes, string beans, okra, squash, watermelon, and cantaloupe. Fausto and Prudencio helped the new groundskeeper, Stanley, prune the rosebushes along the walkway. Parties were thrown on weekends when the weather grew warm. It seemed every week during the summer they were butchering goats and pigs, raised in pens in the back, and making *kaldereta* out of goat meat and roasting pork on the brick barbecue that the volunteers had built. One evening, Fausto returned to his room after a party, and as he prepared for bed he thought how the parties at Agbayani Village reminded him of the San Esteban Circle Labor Day weekend festivities. When he lay in bed, lights turned off, the sounds of the dance echoed in his head: the band playing "Night and Day," feet shuffling on the polished floor, laughter and shouts of joy as relatives reunited. And Macario's confident voice serenading, entreating everyone to dance: *For all the members of the San Esteban Circle!*

The following spring, when the orange groves exploded with blossoms, Fidel visited Fausto and informed him that after months of battling with lung cancer, Domingo had passed away in the hospital. Fidel urged Fausto to attend his cousin's funeral, but Fausto was afraid to face his relatives, and then he heard that Benny couldn't come because he had hurt his back. Although he promised Fidel he'd come, Fausto tended to his garden the day of Domingo's funeral. He bought a yellow rosebush and planted it at the end of one row—the row he, Wendy, and her family had planted—in his cousin's memory.

He checked often for insects and disease on the young leaves of the rosebush. One late spring morning, as he bent down to examine a crinkly leaf, a first sign of powdery mildew, he became lightheaded and had to sit down. He removed his gardening gloves and rested. When he stood up, he bent over with his hands on his knees and stayed there for several moments. A tear landed on his work boot. The cracked soil swallowed up the next two, and he blinked back the rest. A warm breeze passed through, calling upon him to straighten up. Someone had brushed their fingers across his shoulders. He whirled around, wiping his face with his hands. The breeze made the air around him hazy, making him doubt his vision of the ruffled hem of a white nightgown, flowing and disappearing behind the brick building. He took a step, but something made him turn to the roses. Domingo hovered over the yellow rosebush. His face was calm yet tired. He moved his lips, but Fausto could only hear the gentle wind weaving through the leaves of the nearby Chinese pistache trees, a hushing. Fausto thought Domingo mouthed, *"Hustoon, hustoon. Hush, it's okay."* Fausto faced the cloudless sky and counted in his head. Today was the fortieth day of Domingo's passing.

Aside from sending a Christmas card every year, Ted Enebrad visited Fausto at the Village from time to time when he conducted research and interviews with the manongs. Fausto was especially excited when

Ted came in the summer of 1983 with good news. He had traded in his Volkswagen Beetle for a Toyota four-door sedan and proposed to his girlfriend in the spring, following the announcement that they had been granted associate professorships at UCLA. As Fausto and Ted walked the Village grounds, Ted showed him his favorite picture of his fiancée in her navy gown and hood at graduation.

"She teaches in the history department. I'm split between the history department and the Asian American Studies Center," he said, hitching up loose jeans. He was still thin—too busy to eat, he claimed—and wore his hair short, though he had grown back his beard.

Fausto returned the picture to Ted, nodding his approval of the petite pinay who clutched a diploma in one hand and Ted's arm in the other. "When is the wedding?"

"We haven't set a date." Ted stopped in the courtyard to replace the picture in his beat-up wallet. "There's a battle brewing over our efforts to develop AAS from an ethnic studies program into a department. We'll get more respect and funding from the university if we're a department. In the meantime, I've been honing my curriculum." He rested his hand on Fausto's shoulder. "You know I'm teaching my students about the Filipinos' contribution to the farm workers' union. I've held off asking you until now, but I'd like you to talk to my students about the Filipino farm workers' struggle. They'd appreciate hearing your story in your own words. I'll bring you there and back, and you'll stay with me at my place, of course."

Fausto pulled away from Ted. "I don't want to talk about the strike."

"Just the strike, Manong Fausto. Nothing more," he said quietly.

"Nothing more?" Fausto repeated. He knew Ted didn't mean everything outside of the strike was easily pushed aside, but he shook with anger just the same. "I cannot talk about the strike without revealing what I lost. They are the same thing. Ai, you should know!"

The courtyard seemed to cave in on him—the bricks, the oily poles, the saltillo tiles. He pulled at the top button of his shirt. Why couldn't he find his way to his room? "My cousin Domingo died of cancer," he blurted out. He turned his back on Ted and walked quickly to his room, careless of the retired farm workers who stared at him.

Ted caught up with him. "I didn't know."

"How could you know?" Fausto said. "I did not know!"

"I'm sorry."

"No, *I'm* sorry." Fausto focused on the tiled walkway, its crooked line of grout as his map to his room. "I did not see him when he was sick. I did not go to his funeral. I got a lot of time to think, a lot of things to be sorry for." He made it to his room and leaned against the brick wall, feeling winded. "I have many regrets. All the wrong ones."

Ted was short of breath too. "Are you saying you regret everything you did?"

"Wen, wen!" Fausto groped for the doorknob, but it wasn't within his reach.

"I don't believe you." Ted wedged himself between the door and Fausto. "Did you think there would be victory in the fields without pain or sacrifice? There's no such thing." His voice and eyes were fierce, as fierce as when he confronted the townspeople in the supermarket parking lots, the scabs hiding in the fields, and the Teamster members who got in his face. "Manong Fausto, you chose something greater than yourself."

"I don't want it! I want peace in my heart." Fausto slapped his chest. He would have slapped the side of his head, but Ted grabbed his hand.

"There are different kinds of peace, Manong Fausto." The fierceness was in Ted's grip as well, though his voice was softening.

Fausto shut his eyes tight. He couldn't look at Ted's face. "Then I have the wrong peace! I made the wrong choices all my life. I did not have to lose Marina. I accepted losing her too easily. I should have asked for help—not for money but to save her, us, but I was ashamed. I did not fight hard enough for her. That's why she never came back. Because I was a coward, because I did not believe."

Fausto wriggled free and spit on the sidewalk outside his door. "Goddamn growers! Goddamn unions! I hear what's going on in the fields. The growers are still bullying the workers. The UFW is not a union anymore. It's a business, making money under the name of a union! They bully their own members. Larry is dead, Ben is gone, Pete is gone, Philip is gone. Many Filipinos have left the union. The union has changed, but what have we changed in the fields? You come back in ten years and tell me if our sacrifices still make a difference, huh? Then maybe I won't regret everything!"

"You're right about all that, but the fight had to start in the first place— do you understand what I mean? And the pinoys had the conviction and the courage to do it." Ted's eyes grew moist. He shook his head. "I don't believe you at all when you say the fight in the fields all those years didn't matter!"

Fausto's face was burning from his tirade, from his shame over disrespecting Ted, who had made sacrifices as well, who was still fighting for Fausto and the rest of the pinoy farm workers, though it was a different kind of fight—a fight to be remembered, a fight to not be forgotten. He knew they were two different things. It was best not to say anything anymore. It was best if he went to his room alone and shut the door behind him. But Fausto stayed and offered his handkerchief to Ted, who took it from him and wiped his eyes.

"It's so damn hot here," Ted murmured, turning away. "I never got used to this heat."

In the fifteen years since Ayong, Prudencio, and Fausto moved to Agbayani Village, it seemed whenever someone caught a cold or the flu, Fausto was felled by the illness too. He insisted that the cause was retirement; in the first seventy years of his life he could count on one hand the number of times he got sick. Prudencio and Ayong teased him that he was just growing old, like the rest of them. Fausto didn't want to admit it. Fifteen years had gone by quickly, though in the last few years, his quiet existence among the manongs was rocked time and again. Some of the manongs returned to the Philippines when relatives responded to their letters and opened their homes to them. Some moved in with relatives in nearby towns—Ducor, Earlimart, Porterville, Pixley. Others passed away in the Village; most of them, like Severo, went peacefully in their sleep to the other side. Whenever ambulance sirens awoke Fausto, he bolted up in bed and pulled the sheets to his sagging chest, wondering who had left them this time. By the close of 1995, Fausto, Prudencio, and Ayong were the only manongs left.

Prudencio was getting more forgetful. He forgot to prune the roses back and their branches grew out wildly. Once, he pruned the yellow rosebush too much, and Fausto scolded him harshly. Prudencio mumbled an apology, but the next month he pruned it so far back that the rosebush's canes withered and never recovered. Another morning, Prudencio cut himself shaving. Fausto rushed into the bathroom when he heard Prudencio make gurgling sounds. Prudencio, his face drained of color, told him he forgot what he was doing and then didn't recognize who was bleeding in the mirror or what was dripping on his hands and into the sink. Arturo had already been checking on Fausto every other day for years. When Fausto told Arturo about the growing incidents, Arturo began checking on Prudencio, as well. Prudencio's sheets needed to be washed several times a week until Arturo stocked their bathroom with diaper-like underwear. Fausto had to remind Prudencio to change out of his soiled underwear every day and even changed the sheets when his friend forgot to do it himself.

One winter evening, Fausto found Prudencio sitting on his haunches in his long johns in front of a blanket he had dragged out from his closet.

"Ania? Ania dayta?" Fausto said, peering over Prudencio's shoulder.

"I don't know. I found it in my closet." Prudencio yanked on the corner of the blanket and four asparagus knives clattered to the floor. He drew his hands to his face.

Fausto laughed. "Did Ayong give these to you when we moved in?"

"I don't know." Prudencio stood up and kicked at the knives with his bare foot as if they were garter snakes to be killed. He inched his way to the bathroom.

"We used to cut 'gras with these." Fausto recognized his knife. It felt strange and yet familiar in his grasp. Decades after he had carved it, his calluses still fit in the indentations of the worn handle. He gave a shaky swipe of the blade. He would have ruined asparagus spears with such a motion! He held up Benny's knife—not one spot of rust spoiled it—and laid it down on the blanket. "Do you want me to put them back in your closet?" he asked.

"Saan!" Prudencio said. "You take it away! I'll not sleep with those *bunengs* here. By and by, someone might kill me with them!"

Fausto wrapped the knives in the blanket. When he stood up, Prudencio was gone, his door left open. But Fausto didn't have far to go to find him. Prudencio was clinging to an olive tree in the courtyard, his knobby arms and hands part of the ancient trunk.

In August 1996, for fifteen consecutive days temperatures spiked above a hundred degrees, breaking decades-old records. Plants withered. Pigs and goats languished in their pens. The rabbits had to be moved to the shade. Nobody ventured outdoors past noon. After lunch, Ayong, in a long-sleeved work shirt, donned his straw hat and picked up a hoe in the tool shed. "Stanley is not here today," he announced to Fausto. "I will spray water on the animals. *Ai sus!* They will die of heat stroke."

"Forget the animals," Fausto warned. "Ai, *you* will get heat stroke this time of day!"

Ayong laughed, only three teeth left in his mouth. "After all those years in the fields, do you think a little heat will bother me? I am ninety-six years old! Walking around with Ben-Gay all over my body! I will not even feel the sun."

Ayong shouldered the hoe and marched to the garden and pens, raising dust in his wake. Fausto returned to his room to grab a work hat, but a heavy lunch made him drowsy and slow. And then the air conditioner kicked in. He lay down and closed his eyes. He would take a short nap—just fifteen minutes—and then join Ayong.

Something startled Fausto awake. When he looked at his clock, he discovered he'd been asleep for three hours! Though the air conditioner was still humming, he was shaking and perspiring. He hurried to the garden in his house slippers. Several goats, huddled in a corner of their pen, began bleating. When Fausto approached the fence, they fled in different directions. Through the chicken wire, he saw the tip of a hoe, Ayong's work boots, his legs curled up. He shooed the goats away to get to his friend. They had nibbled on the straw hat, which lay across Ayong's face. Fausto didn't dare lift the hat. He felt for Ayong's pulse beneath his seared skin.

Fausto sat crouched under the hot sun, breathing through his mouth. He heard clucking sounds nearby. Prudencio was spearing tomatoes with a branch and clicking his tongue against the roof of his mouth. Fausto rose to his feet and limped to the gate. Prudencio didn't even notice him until Fausto grabbed his arm. He waved the branch at Fausto, then a shadow crossed his face.

"How long have you been out here?" Fausto demanded.

Prudencio held his wristwatch up to his face. "Maybe since two. Maybe earlier."

"What have you been doing here all that time?"

Prudencio looked astonished. "I've been watching the garden grow." He shook the dried stalks of corn. The pale-yellow kernels had shriveled to sharp pebbles.

"You did not see what happened in the goats' pen?"

Prudencio entered the pen. "Ai, how did that scarecrow get here? Let's put it back before the crows get the corn!" He tossed the branch to the ground and grabbed Ayong's ankles.

Horrified, Fausto pulled him off by the shoulders. *"Ammon no siasinno daytoy?"*

Prudencio cowered by the fence. *"Saan!"* He turned defiant, his lip curling down.

"It's Ayong. He's dead."

Prudencio stared at Ayong's body and then at Fausto.

"Dead!" Prudencio shouted. "Dead!" A nearby blackwood acacia shook as sparrows shot out from the leafy branches and into the washed-out sky. They shrank to pinpoints and disappeared in the air. Prudencio backed up against the fence, groping for the top rail. "Dead," he whispered, and inched his way out of the pen, holding on as if in darkness.

At Our Lady of Guadalupe Church, Fausto stood by Ayong's open casket, studying his friend's features—the way his mouth seemed to cave in because he had lost so many teeth and the wrinkles bunched up all over his face, even on his lips. He had never really retired; he was always in motion at the Village. But now, Ayong looked peaceful, finally resting. At the gravesite, as Ayong's coffin was lowered into the ground, Fausto glanced around him and shook his head. Only a handful had come to pay their last respects.

"He was a good man and a good friend, eh?" Prudencio said, as he climbed into the backseat of Arturo's Camaro.

Fausto nodded. He rolled down the window, but the heat outside, like a thick wall, kept the hot air trapped inside. Prudencio pushed himself up against the opposite window.

"Ai, what was his name again?" Prudencio whispered.

"Ayong." Fausto kept his voice even. "Ayong Ordona, from Saoang."

After Arturo settled Prudencio down for a nap, he stopped by Fausto's room and sat next to Fausto on his bed. "It's time for Prudencio to go to a nursing home," Arturo finally said. "Hombrecito, he needs someone to look after him full time."

"I don't have anything to do around here. I'll take care of him," Fausto said.

"You can't carry him if he hurts himself. He could wander outside of the Village." Beads of perspiration had formed on Arturo's face. "What if he gets hit by a car? You're gonna blame yourself—I know you too well. Do you want that?"

"Shhh!" Fausto hissed, his eyes darting from the bathroom door to his front door to the window. Did any evil spirit hear Arturo? Should he close the window and shut the doors? "Don't talk about bad things like that! Do you want them to come true?"

"No! That's why I'm telling you: Prudencio needs to go to a place where he'll get better care." Arturo put his head in his hands and let out a long sigh.

"If Prudencio leaves, I'm all alone."

Arturo lifted his head, stunned. "You won't be alone, hombrecito. I'm taking care of you."

"You cannot be here all the time, not like Prudencio! I won't let you take him!"

But Arturo arranged for Prudencio to be put in a nursing home in town. Against Arturo's wishes, Fausto told Prudencio that he was going on vacation. Prudencio packed his bag, flush with excitement over what he called a "change of place," though every day now some part of his room and the grounds were becoming foreign to him.

As they waited for Arturo to take Prudencio away, Fausto sat with his friend in the recreation room in matching stuffed chairs that faced the stone fireplace, two suitcases at their feet. Prudencio closed his eyes and fell asleep. Fausto leaned his head back and fell asleep too. When he woke up, Prudencio was hovering over him, as if he were afraid Fausto had left him. His eyes were as clear as a winter morning without fog.

"Did we do good with our lives?" Prudencio wanted to know.

"Huh?" Fausto sat up, kicking the suitcase with his foot.

"I hear the migrant workers talking—what's going on in the fields." Prudencio clapped his hands over his ears. "Sometimes I think we are getting ready to strike again. Ai, I get confused! Did we not make a difference?"

Fausto brought Prudencio's hands to his lap and held them tight. *"Wen, wen,"* he said, fighting doubt in his heart. "We made a *big* difference."

"That's good." Prudencio nodded, his lips trembling into a smile. He made the sign of the cross. "When I die, I want my mass at Our Lady of Guadalupe Church."

Fausto wagged his finger at Prudencio. "You stop talking like that! If you die, I'll be mad at you and God!"

"St. Mary's is for the growers, the rich people," Prudencio said. "Our Lady of Guadalupe is for us farm workers. That's how it was when we were striking."

Fausto smiled at his friend. *"Malagip mo dayta?"*

"Sure, I remember. Why not?"

Fausto laughed. Prudencio joined him. Remember this moment, Fausto told himself. God willing, they would both remember this moment years from now.

Fausto visited Prudencio in a bedroom without a window, which made them both feel restless. Prudencio complained that the food tasted like medicine. He was losing weight. The sheets pooled in his lap, but he twisted Fausto's arm hard. Fear had kept him strong.

"I want to go back to the Village. Will you help me?" Prudencio dug his fingers into Fausto's skin with long, yellowed nails that needed trimming.

Fausto smoothed back the greasy strands of gray hair from Prudencio's temple. "You go to sleep now. I'll be back in the morning to get you."

Prudencio wouldn't let go. "Stay here with me! We'll escape together *tonight*." He looked over his shoulder and chuckled. "We'll outwit that Chinese woman and the pinoy contractor, eh? We'll leave Seattle and go find your cousins in LA!"

Fausto didn't know whether to be astonished or heartbroken. He patted Prudencio's hand. "We have to pretend to be asleep, remember? She stands by the door and listens to us breathe, so go to sleep and I will wake you when she leaves, okay?" he whispered. Fausto sat next to the bed and waited for Prudencio to sleep. Even as Prudencio began snoring, Fausto couldn't bring himself to leave. He would stay the night and worry in the morning how to leave, knowing that this was a difficult routine he would have to master. He didn't know how long he had slept until a nurse informed him that visiting hours were over. Fausto stood up, lightheaded. Everything was white. It made him lose his way for a moment. He imagined it was the same for Prudencio all the time. But then the nurse showed him the door and hurried him out before he could say good-bye.

Fausto never went back, afraid that the last image of Prudencio would be the drooling fingers he kept poking in his gaping mouth. When Arturo told him of his old friend's passing, Fausto said that Prudencio's soul flew out the window his friend imagined was there. What was left, even before he was gone, was no longer the same man who was the best pruner on the farm—even though Mr. Cuculich would never admit to it because he was partial to Fausto. Prudencio could gird canes with expert fingers even in the numbing cold and worked so quickly that he left Fausto a row behind.

As the winter sun set, casting a cold glow across the frosted fields, Fausto sat in his own room. No matter how difficult the day in the fields had been, Prudencio would always look at him with a ready smile and squinty eyes surrounded by leathery skin, as if he were welcoming, not cursing, the searing, unforgivable sun.

CHAPTER 14

Reunion

With Rogelio beside him and Rogelio's hand resting on his back, Fausto walked out of his room and into the courtyard. The sun branded his head and shoulders the moment they lost the shade of the Chinese pistache tree. Heat seeped through the weave of his cotton shirt and into his skin like a menthol ointment. The hundred-degree heat would have sapped him, but he felt refreshed, sharing silence in the open spaces. They walked in a wide arc in the cleared field. Rogelio marveled at the hardiness of the plants and weeds that took root in the sandy soil. It made Fausto look at the land with appreciative eyes, though dust dulled everything in their path—the once-shiny leaves of nutsedge and patches of yellow-flowered sow-thistle. Dust coated the starry seed heads of Bermuda grass. All the while, the almond scent of pink-and-white oleander blooms simmered in the heat.

Rogelio steered Fausto toward the building. "Let's get some water and go back to your room. I don't want you to get heat stroke," he said, but it was Rogelio who was wilting. He blotted his face with Fausto's handkerchief as beads of perspiration formed on his upper lip. "Are you okay?"

Fausto nodded. He gazed at the tips of the cypress trees above the tiled roof. He wanted to put a hand over his heart—it was racing again—yet he didn't want Rogelio to worry or the day to end. But now that he was done talking, he felt empty. Though he was grateful to be with Rogelio, he was still waiting. They went to the dining hall to get a pitcher of ice water. Even though Fausto had done most of the talking—his mouth was cottony and his lips cracked like the grounds of Agbayani Village—Rogelio drank most of the water and then refilled it before returning to Fausto's room. Ignoring the urge to pee, Fausto felt as if he had drunk all the water.

"I didn't want to distract you while you were talking," Rogelio began, as they settled in their places—Fausto on his bed and Rogelio in the chair. "But I know Professor Enebrad."

It wasn't what Fausto expected to hear, but the news stunned him.

Five years after they moved to Chicago, the hotel workers union and the corporation owning the hotel that Benny worked for clashed over raises. Luz was furious; he never told her he had joined the union. But the strike lasted only ten days. Benny retired when he turned seventy-two, less than a year before a contract standoff triggered a strike that lasted for months. Housekeepers, banquet servers, and bellhops who had served for decades were replaced with temporary workers who were forced to do the work of many. Benny wanted to support his former co-workers, but Luz refused to let him. His health was not so good. His knees would not hold up on the picket lines, especially in the Chicago winters.

Rogelio was a freshman at the University of Illinois, living at home, commuting to the Chicago campus—and following the strike closely. To Luz's horror, he switched his major from pre-medicine to history and earned a minor in Asian American Studies, where he first heard about the Delano grape strikes. He asked Benny about his involvement in the strikes, but both Benny and Luz stonewalled him. He learned more when he earned his master's degree in history at Wayne State University in Detroit, where he pored over Larry Itliong's papers, which were held at the university's Walter Reuther Library. He finally heard Benny's story after the first stroke.

Fausto's cheeks prickled with heat. "Why did you not tell me? Why did you not stop me from going on and on if you knew everything already?"

Rogelio laughed. "I know a lot about the grape strikes," he said, then turned serious. "But I didn't know your story. Dad told me I needed to hear it from you."

While in Detroit, Rogelio got in touch with Ted Enebrad, who had been named chair of UCLA's Asian American Studies department. They kept in contact, and Professor Enebrad advised Rogelio when he applied for the position of lecturer for the academic year. His appointment would begin next month for the fall semester, and he was going to meet Professor Enebrad and look for an apartment before flying back home.

Fausto thought of his neatly folded clothes in his drawer, his few possessions, the suitcase in his closet. "You are moving to Los Angeles?"

"My contract is just for the year, but I'm hoping I can work my way in," Rogelio said. "When I got the news, I wasn't sure about going because of Dad's health, but he was really proud of what I was doing."

"What does Luz think of this?"

Rogelio shrugged. "Happy I finally got a real job—though short term—but not happy I'm going so far away."

Luz and Benny had traveled farther than Rogelio was going, but she scolded him. There were no new worlds to discover, no reason to go away to change one's luck or one's destiny—that was what *they* did for their children. But she was wrong, Rogelio told Fausto. There is always the past to uncover. That is a journey too. In the uncovering, it seemed, one's life changes. Things were connected, Rogelio was convinced. If he hadn't gotten interested in the hotel and grape strikes, he wouldn't have asked Benny questions and learned things about him that he'd never known before. He wouldn't have looked up Professor Enebrad and wouldn't be moving to Los Angeles. Even Professor Enebrad wondered aloud if Rogelio was another reason—unknown at the time—why he didn't push Fausto to talk about the strike all these years. Perhaps that calling wasn't his, he speculated to Rogelio.

"Professor Enebrad couldn't stop talking about you," Rogelio went on.

Fausto still received Ted's Christmas card and annual letter. He knew about the big appointment. Ted finally married his pinay girlfriend, despite a delay. They were both doing so well at the university that they were still too busy to have children. What a shame, Fausto thought, when every holiday there was no news of babies. They could afford to have many children, and with his big heart, Ted would make a good father.

Ted never returned to Agbayani Village, even as he lectured and published articles through the years about the contributions Filipino Americans made to California's farm labor movement. In one Christmas card, he wrote to Fausto that his absence was not a result of being angry but of wanting to respect Fausto's wishes. Fausto felt bad about their last visit and wanted to write back, but still, after all those years, he couldn't say that in exchange for his losses something bigger was gained. Wasn't that what Ted wanted to hear? In last year's card, Ted added a postscript: "Hope to see you soon." He must have known then that Fausto's life would change. Maybe Ted thought Fausto's heart would change too.

"When you and the manongs walked out of the fields, you were fighting for better wages and basic working conditions in your lifetime," Rogelio said. "But you were also helping to put labor laws on the books to protect everyone who came after you."

Fausto sat up. Rogelio spoke with such confidence. He reminded him of Ted. But he couldn't nod in agreement. He watched the news on TV. He still read the *Delano Record*. Because of the victories in the fields, the farm workers he stood side by side with saved money for their children's college education and steered them away from the vineyards. When they retired, so did their legacy in the fields. The new immigrants, who had no connection to history, were no match for the battle-tested growers, whose families would continue on for generations. The growers had gained more wealth and power; they contributed money to political campaigns and made friends with legislators. Meanwhile, in the last thirty years, the UFW, its membership on the decline, took on other issues outside of organizing workers and negotiating contracts. Fausto was still getting solicitations in the mail to support farm workers' rights, but he heard talk in the dining hall about the lack of basic health and housing needs for the immigrants, how they struggled to live on low wages. Where were all the donations going? What were the union leaders doing, he wanted to know? But none of the migrant workers at the dining tables could answer.

"In the end, nothing has changed. The workers are still poor, and the union leaders are rich like the growers," Fausto declared. "*This* is what I lost everything for?"

"Forget about the UFW!" Rogelio was angry too. "I'm talking about what the Filipino farm workers and their leaders fought for, what they were pushed out for!"

Rogelio paced the room with the same uncontainable energy as Ted Enebrad. In his agitation, he favored his right leg, making Fausto's cheeks grow warm with guilt.

"Have you ever heard the phrase 'history repeats itself'?" Rogelio asked, stopping in the middle of the room. "The pendulum swings back and forth, left and right, right and wrong. Sometimes it takes decades or hundreds of years. Sometimes it's only a few years, depending on so many factors." Rogelio took a deep breath. "Sometimes bad situations never change. But change has to happen in order to make something right. You were part of that first wave of change in the vineyards. To be the first takes a hell of a lot of courage—and sacrifice. There is no other way! Do you understand?" Rogelio locked eyes with Fausto. "The UFW lost its focus. But the growers didn't, so it's inevitable that the pendulum shifted. So now we have to find the next wave of leaders to start something, to make things right again."

"Maybe this time it starts in the classroom," Fausto responded.

Rogelio smiled and nodded. "Professor Enebrad's trying to do that."

Fausto hesitated. "What does Ted say about me?"

"In the classroom and out, Professor Enebrad calls you his hero."

"What do *you* call me?" Fausto whispered above the whir of the oscillating fan.

"You're my hero too."

It's what sons tell their fathers, but he said it so casually it sounded insincere. It made Fausto uneasy, made him not want to go forward anymore. He wanted to retreat to the bathroom, but he was on the edge of not being able to hold himself together. All his bones, tissues, and organs seemed to be dissolving. Yet he stood on his feet, mumbling that he needed to pee again, which was true, but he meant it to be an excuse. With each step, the room grew bigger. He was halfway to the bathroom when his legs gave out. He fell on his left hip. The pain shot out from his bone, blinding him with a sharp whiteness.

"Nasakit, nasakit!" he moaned, squeezing his eyes shut, rolling on his back.

"Uncle Fausto, are you okay?" Rogelio's voice was feverish, pitched— and far away. "Do you want me to get Arturo?"

"No!" Fausto wouldn't open his eyes. *"No!"*

Rogelio carried him back to his bed, taking care as he lay him down on his right side. He removed Fausto's shoes and gently rested his hand below Fausto's left hip. "Tell me where it hurts."

"I'm not broken!" Fausto barked. He watched Rogelio arrange the pillows around him. "Why did you call me 'uncle'?" The word, like a thorn, kept pressing into his flesh.

Rogelio screwed up his face, as if berating himself. "I mean, Ninong Fausto."

His words rang false. There was still hope. Fausto glanced at the dresser drawer, where he kept the rosary in its sterling-silver box. "I'm not your ninong."

"Dad told me he asked you to be my ninong first."

"Macario is your ninong. You know who I am. Don't be afraid of me!"

"I'm not afraid of you," Rogelio began. He stopped and sat on the bed close to Fausto. "I'm afraid of hurting you."

"Hurting me?" Fausto laughed. "You see this thick skin?" He stabbed his finger into the calluses on his palms. He stabbed harder as his body went numb all over.

Rogelio looked as helpless sitting next to Fausto as he had been when he was seven, crying on the side of the road. "Uncle Fausto——"

Fausto slapped his own hand. "Stop calling me 'uncle'!"

"What do you want me to call you? Tata? Tiyong?"

"What did you come all the way from Chicago to say to me, eh? Say it! Ai, say it *now!*"

"You're making this hard." Rogelio reached out to him.

Fausto struck Rogelio's hands with his fists. *"Say it!"* he thundered.

Rogelio received Fausto's repeated blows with his palms, never flinching.

Fausto pulled back. Rogelio couldn't even say it. Hell, Fausto couldn't do it, either. In their silence, Fausto knew the truth. Now everything was empty—Rogelio's blank face, his small room. It was a new kind of emptiness, unlike the heaviness he carried with him after Marina and Benny had left, after losing Cary and Serapio, after Arturo, Domingo, Ayong, and Prudencio had died. This emptiness filled out his body, making him bloated. His head swelled, his joints and muscles could not feel pain, his fingers tingled, incapable of touch. Fausto took a deep breath. The force of it splintered something in his chest.

"I have lost everything!" The words escaped in the heat. Fausto covered his face. A wave pushed up from his chest and forced his mouth open, even as he clenched his teeth shut. Tears seeped between his fingers. And then, just as suddenly, his whole body shuddered and an ancient cry stung the air.

"Uncle Fausto." Rogelio kissed the crown of his head. "You haven't lost anything!"

Rogelio embraced him, his skin slowly warming Fausto's own, his muscles pressing against Fausto's bones. How strong his nephew was, yet how gentle was his touch! *Kaanakan.* Nephew. It was a foreign word on his tongue, once reserved for Macario's and Domingo's boys. It didn't belong to Rogelio, not even when he was a little boy. How on earth could he start calling him something else now?

"I lost my family back home: Marina, Benny, everyone in Terra Bella. Maybe I'll never see my child." Each word, every breath left Fausto emptier. "I have nothing now."

"Does the truth change your feelings for me?" Rogelio drew back, his face wet with Fausto's tears. "I never knew why you favored me, but I was grateful for your love, especially when I found out that my real parents kept their first four children but not their fifth. They made their decision without seeing what I looked like or how I'd turn out."

"You turned out good, Rogelio," Fausto said fiercely.

"When I was born, I was handed over just like that." Rogelio stared at the damp handkerchief. "Mom said that woman deserved our pity because her life would never improve. Mom said I should thank her because she made the decision to give me a better life. It was a gift to give me away rather than get rid of me or resent me if they had kept me. Dad kept reminding me that love made them my parents and me their son."

Fausto bowed his head. "You lost Benny. You lost your father. How selfish of me to think only of my losses! You must miss him so much."

"There were so many times I woke up late and panicked," Rogelio whispered. "I got dressed quickly so I could go to him at the hospital, so he would hear me—wake up to the sound of my voice—and I would be the one who brings him back. And then I remembered. And I stopped myself—before I left the house or at a stoplight. Once, I got as far as the hospital entrance. And then I remembered."

Fausto knew what it was like to wake up as if nothing had changed and then realize you're alone. Every morning, for months, the initial shock snatched his breath away. He lived for those fleeting moments when in his half-sleep he thought Marina was in the shower or the kitchen. He imagined water running, her singing, sometimes the hazy sight of her nightgown hem, her slippered feet as she stole out of the bedroom without a sound. At night, he pressed his face into her pillow and draped strands of hair—pulled from her brush—across her pillow.

Marina's face came to him at his window, her emerald-flecked eyes burning a hole in his heart. He wasn't startled or ashamed. Of course, she would be here with Rogelio and him, looking the same as she did the last time he saw her. Only now, instead of running away into the darkness, she was combing blades of grass that fell like green tears from her hair. *Mailiwak kenka unay unay! Ayayaten ka unay unay!* After all these years, he could not miss her or love her more than he did now.

"Did Luz tell you what happened to Marina?" An urgency rose in Fausto. "Is she happy? If she is happy, that is good enough for me." He looked back. Marina's hair, dripping wet, covered her face. He needed to see her eyes. But dusk washed her away. "Tell me," he said, to the empty window. "Tell me." He turned to Rogelio.

———

Marina didn't leave for the Philippines on the same day she flew from Bakersfield to Los Angeles. She went to a clinic to get her vaccinations. Luz didn't tell Benny about the delay, fearing that Fausto would go after her. With the money Luz had given her, Marina returned to Vigan. But neither her parents nor her brothers and their wives would take her back because she wanted to keep the baby. Her childless sister Trinidad took her in, with the hope of raising the baby. Marina answered Luz's letter, writing that she had no place to go. By her sixth month, Trinidad had complained of the extra mouth to feed until Marina promised she would work in a garment factory after the baby's birth. But now, she wrote, she was sorry for having made any promises to her sister. The pregnancy had weakened her. Each kick from the baby felt like a knife wound. Its weight made her back ache. Sleepless at night and wretched during the day, she vomited into her ninth month.

Luz timed her visit before Marina was due. She tried to convince Marina to return to the States with her and live with her and Benny. But Marina said she could never go back. When she was bedridden with early contractions, Luz offered to adopt the baby—the baby would have a better life in America, plenty of food and clothing, an education, a better future. Though the baby's well-being was Marina's only concern, she couldn't part with a child who was causing her so much pain, who was a part of her. Marina spit out the rag she was chewing on, her fingers writhing across her face like tiny watersnakes, and demanded to know what would be left of her if Luz took the baby.

Fausto winced at the thought of her suffering alone in Trinidad's house. Nothing was easy, not marriage or pregnancy—not even life itself. "She must hate me," he said.

Rogelio shook his head. Marina still loved him, which astounded Luz. Marina insisted that Fausto was kind and goodhearted. But when he marched out of the fields, he overturned their lives. She blamed the union for changing him, making him choose grand ideas instead of his wife, his child, their home. It almost changed her too, until she saw the cost. But he couldn't see that. If only he had turned his back on the movement, she fretted, they would still be together.

How could Marina have separated him into two beings and feel differently about both sides? Why not just hate all of him? He deserved it. And yet, Fausto was grateful to know that wherever she was, she still loved a part of him. It was just enough—this gift—for him to accept.

"Where is she now?" Fausto struggled to stand, ignoring the dull ache in his hip. "Did she let Trinidad raise our child? Do I have a son or a daughter? Where is our child?"

Rogelio settled Fausto back against the pillows. Marina, he said, endured a long and difficult labor. She passed out from the pressure of the baby's head on her tailbone, so they opened her belly to get the baby girl. They both suffered infections and stayed in the hospital for a week. Luz spent the whole time there too, still hoping to change Marina's mind. But Marina refused to let go. She was released from the hospital against her wishes and taken back to her sister's house, where, clearheaded and somber, she named the baby Lulu. Lulukisen.

All those months of working in the packing house—how she hated grading and packing oranges as they tumbled endlessly down the steel chutes, smashing her fingers—and still she kept the name. It meant she hadn't forgotten her life, *their* lives, back in Terra Bella. Fausto grinned, giddy as a new father.

"Do you have pictures of Lulu? She must be a mother now—and Marina a grandmother!" The thought stunned him. Thirty years have passed, he reminded himself, as he hid his hands—the wrinkles, the veins—by crossing his arms tightly against his chest, his fluttering heart. There were whole lives connected by blood he never knew existed.

A faraway voice came to him. "Uncle, there's more."

Trinidad was elated with the baby. While Marina was in the hospital, she found her sister a job as a seamstress in an American manufacturer's factory. But before Lulu was two weeks old, a typhoon struck the island of Luzon in November, near the end of the typhoon season. Manila was hit hard. Luz found refuge in a hotel with fortresslike walls, and she telephoned Trinidad before the power lines went down, insisting that they stay with her until the storm subsided. Later that afternoon Trinidad and her husband appeared at the hotel, looking as if the wind and rains had swept them across town and laid them at her door. But where were Marina and Lulu?

Wild-eyed, Trinidad told Luz the wind had ripped doors off their hinges and smashed windows. The walls of their house began to shift and collapse outward. Trinidad called out to Marina, but when Marina emerged with Lulu in her arms she bolted in the opposite direction, never looking back. It was hard to see in the silver rain that came slashing down like knives, amid the surrounding houses that were dancing violently. She caught sight of Marina's flowing white nightgown and then nothing more. She heard the baby's cries going downhill, lost in the wind as it howled across the black sky. Trinidad and her husband fled just before the roof fell to the floor with a boom that echoed in her ears all the way to the hotel. It was all her fault, Trinidad told Luz. She beat into Marina's head the fact that she and her husband had paid the hospital bill, making the baby—who would be renamed—belong to her.

Fausto's heart thumped as if the wind were in his chest. "Did they find them?"

Marina's body was discovered the next day under a sheet of metal from the house.

Fausto lowered his head, loose at the neck. "And Lulu?"

"They never found the baby." Rogelio locked his hand on Fausto's shoulder. "A lot of people went missing for good, Uncle."

Fausto pulled away from Rogelio. He could be angry with Trinidad—and he was—but what was the use? Marina would not have been in Manila had he not thrown her out. As he stared at Rogelio, his anger shifted. "Luz kept this from me all these years!"

"She was devastated, Uncle Fausto," Rogelio insisted. "She brought Marina to the States to take care of her. She felt responsible for what happened. It was years before she told Dad everything. And then how could she tell you, no matter what came between you and Dad? If she told you the truth, it would have killed you. But if she let you keep believing I was your son, then somehow you'd be spared and I'd be near you. She didn't think through that you'd want to take me back. It was one of the reasons we moved. It was tearing them apart inside. She and Dad didn't know how to undo what they'd done. Deceiving you was wrong, but how can I blame her or Dad for trying to protect you?"

"Maybe she was protecting me in the beginning, but her lie made it worse for everyone!" said Fausto. "It's better to have no hope at all!" Even as he spoke, he wasn't sure he believed his own words. Otherwise, it meant he would have let go a long time ago.

"Uncle Fausto, who can be rational in matters of the heart?"

"You think I'm judging Luz." Fausto pressed his lips together to keep them still. "I'm just trying to understand, that's all. It takes a big heart to understand and forgive. Maybe in the end, I'm not able."

"That's not true! I know how big your heart is."

Rogelio remembered the elementary school secretary calling home. Rogelio was feverish and complained of a stomachache. Both Benny and Luz were at work, but Fausto was at the house babysitting BJ. He didn't have a car, so he woke BJ from his nap and they hurried to school as fast as they could run. When nothing could stop Rogelio's cries, Fausto borrowed Truelino Orpilla's car and drove him to the hospital in Porterville, where Rogelio had his appendix removed. What mattered then—and what Rogelio remembered now—was not that Fausto had saved him from serious illness but that Fausto had carried him for a mile under the June sun. After they got home, Fausto mopped Rogelio's face with his handkerchief, though he was the one who was winded and drenched in sweat.

"Too much time gone by," Fausto said. "You don't know me anymore."

Rogelio's eyes flashed. Years ago, Fausto would have stubbornly, happily mistaken them for Marina's emerald flecks. But he saw them clearly now.

"I won't let you punish yourself." Rogelio said. "If Dad were here, he'd tell you to give in because I always win."

Fausto looked up at the cracks in the ceiling. He glanced out the window, half expecting a straw hat to peek in. "If I could see your Dad, I would give in," he said, the corners of his mouth growing heavy.

Rogelio sat beside Fausto and held him for several moments, letting silence wash over them. "I didn't mean for everything to come out like this," Rogelio said. He stood up, his hand lingering on Fausto's shoulder. "This is too much news. You need to rest."

Fausto was exhausted, but he didn't want to be left alone. "If I take a nap, it won't be for long," he said, reaching for Rogelio's other hand. "Will you be here when I wake up?"

"*Wen*, yes, of course, Uncle," he said. Rogelio massaged his fingers. "I'm going to get the stuff that Arturo left in the office for me. I went to a nursery in Porterville so I could bring you some potted geraniums. I got six red plants for you."

"You remember that!" A smile bloomed on Fausto's face.

"Being here these last few days brought back a lot of memories," Rogelio said. "I'll be waiting outside for you." He kissed Fausto on both cheeks and closed the door.

A stillness descended, even as the fan's blades whirred, its neck clicking from side to side. Fausto filled his lungs and exhaled, falling back onto his pillow, as if everything Rogelio had said now struck him in the face like the hacking wind and rain of a typhoon.

A road full of ruts lay before Fausto. Rows of orange trees, heavy with white starry blossoms, fanned out on either side. He was driving his old Bel Air on the country roads, with no destination in mind. Soon the orange groves gave way to fields of tilled soil. In the gathering dusk, he came upon a lone house surrounded by a chainlink fence. The exposed garage was lit up, though empty. He slowed the car down. A petite woman stepped into the garage and placed a long-handled shovel against the wall. A blanket was tucked under her arm. She laid the blanket on top of a table and began removing wet laundry from a washing machine. She shook each piece of laundry—a colorful patchwork quilt and baby clothes—before placing them in a basket. When it was full, she put the blanket on top, hitched the basket on her hip, and entered the house from an interior door. The light in the garage went out, and another light came on in one of the front rooms.

The woman looked like Marina—her size, the housecoat that hung down past her knees, even her rubber slippers. He turned off the engine. As if by sheer force of his desire, she came to the window. She kept staring out, her eyes locked onto something in the darkness. Was she looking for him? Lulu? She moved away from the window but passed a few times more, as if she couldn't make up her mind whether to look again or not, confront and be crushed by the truth or invite hope, its faint possibility. She returned, but to pull the curtains shut and turn out the light. He waited in vain for the curtains to part, finally giving up when his hunched shoulders began to ache. From the back seat, he fished up a sweatshirt smelling of musty grapes and rolled it into a ball. They would talk in the morning when they were both clearheaded, he told himself. He stretched across the car seat, his head against the makeshift pillow, and fell asleep.

His neck cramped up in the morning. When he saw the glove compartment inches from his face, he gave a start. Didn't he sell the old Bel Air years ago? His breath was sour as he licked his hands and, looking in the rearview mirror, smoothed the stray hairs on his head. He wasn't surprised that he had just a few gray hairs along his temple. "I'll tell her I'm sorry. We'll start over again. I promise," he told his reflection.

But when he stepped out, an abandoned house stood before him. Yellow weeds reclaimed the blackened soil. Tree trunks had turned to charcoal. The house was exposed, the frame charred. He crept to the fence. The front door was ajar, the windows smashed, with pieces of glass sticking up like sharp teeth. He circled the property. The backyard was leveled, with no trace of a garden having once thrived. There was no laundry basket, blanket, or shovel in what used to be the garage. No surrounding houses.

He ran back to the car and drove off. As he gripped the steering wheel, he noticed the veins on his hands. In the rearview mirror, he saw so many wrinkles etched on his face that he was sure any muscle twitch would cause his face to shatter into a million pieces.

Fausto jerked his head to the side, his cheek brushing against a feverish pillow. He expected to look out his window and see rows of orange trees sloping up the hills. Instead, Rogelio stood above him, the fan unplugged on the floor.

"You had a bad dream. You were shivering." Rogelio smoothed his temple.

"*Awanen!* Too late." Fausto eased himself to a sitting position, his whole body damp with sweat. "Nobody is living in the gray-brick house, eh?"

"Ninong Macario told me it's been abandoned for years," Rogelio admitted. "Somebody bought the land recently. What's left of the house will be razed this fall."

Their house. It was once their house. Fausto blinked at Rogelio as if he were looking at the sun. What else did time reclaim?

Fausto caught sight of the containers of velvety red geraniums on his desk. He exhaled slowly, as if afraid he wouldn't be able to take another breath. The gift made him realize that Rogelio was not going to take him with him. Maybe Rogelio could help him plant them near his room. Maybe that was the best he could hope for. He watched Rogelio set a bowl of rice, fried fish, and steaming pansit from the dining hall on a TV tray near his bed. His stomach growled, but he wasn't sure he had the appetite.

Fausto stared at the mound of rice on his plate. "It was not the strikes or the union that made me lose her."

Rogelio's knife and fork idled in his hands.

"Maybe everything happened because I did not believe in myself.

Because of my fear, I did not believe in us." Fausto's room felt drafty again.

Rogelio set his utensils down. He moved the TV tray to the side and squatted in front of Fausto. "Marina loved you. She didn't give her baby away like my biological mother did. She fought for her and named her Lulukisen. Don't you think she would have picked another name if she didn't love you, if she didn't want any memory of you at all?"

"I don't know anymore," Fausto whispered.

"You know, Uncle, deep down you *know.*"

"If she still loved me, then I did not deserve her at all."

Rogelio took Fausto's hands and kissed them, kissed his calluses, his ropey veins, his loose wrinkles. "Uncle Fausto, there were so many things in your life you didn't deserve, but her love was God's grace." He towered over Fausto. "You have to accept everything—good and bad, fair and unjust. You have to receive everything that comes into your life and embrace it. Then the bad things, well, they aren't as bad when you look back on your life."

Fausto nodded, for Rogelio's sake. Maybe he would come to that acceptance, that peace later. But he couldn't do it right now. Rogelio nodded back as if to say, *You will get there, Uncle, I have faith in you because I will be there with you in the end.*

Rogelio pulled up one of the chairs and pointed to the food. *"Mangan tayon!"*

Fausto devoured the mix of rice and fish, then moved on to his helping of pansit.

Rogelio picked at his food. "Uncle Fausto, I was planning on spending the night here, if that's okay with you. Arturo is letting me borrow his car in the morning since he brought me here. I'd like to take you to see Ninong Macario."

For a moment, Fausto sat unmoved, even as he saw out of the corner of his eye a duffel bag by the door. Then he resumed slurping on his noodles.

"Ninong Macario wants you to come," Rogelio continued. "Auntie Rozelle was asking for you too. They said everybody in Terra Bella wants to see you. Ninong Macario is having Uncle Cary's body taken back to San Esteban. He asked me to see what needs to be done when I'm in LA. He wants you to write the epitaph on the tombstone. He said you were the smart one, the one with the American education."

Fausto tore off the charred fin from another fish with such effort that it crumbled in his hand. He mashed the fish into his rice with his fork. Macario's sons were lawyers and surgeons, his grandsons and granddaughters bound for college. He just wants to brag in person. Fausto pushed aside his fork and scooped rice with his fingers, trying to imagine Macario as an old man, afraid to tell him about Benny. He thought of Cary finally going home. It made him lightheaded. It made him see inky blotches on his rice as he blinked.

Cary sat in a chair at the foot of his bed, leaning forward, twirling his fedora in his hands. His crisp wool suit—how itchy it must be in this heat—was pressed, his tie dangled from his neck. His hair, thinning but still wavy, brushed against his shoulders.

Fausto lifted his chin. *You want this too?*

Though his cheeks were hollow, Cary grinned, his teeth brilliant, like whitecaps on the South China Sea off of San Esteban on a sunny, cloudless day. He sat up straight and positioned his fedora with the brim casting a shadow across his eyes.

"Yes, I want this, Uncle Fausto," Rogelio said. "Will you do it for me?"

Fausto glanced at the foot of his bed. The chair was empty. He scratched his head. "It's what everybody wants," he said, in wonderment. Maybe he wanted it too.

"It's settled then. We'll go in the morning." Rogelio speared a piece of fish with his fork. "And then next weekend I'll take you to the San Esteban Dance."

Fausto scowled. "I did not agree to that! Ai! You are pushing me!"

"Remember, Uncle Fausto, I always win," Rogelio said, and ate the piece of fish.

Fausto tried to hide his smile by licking his greasy fingers. "Do you remember how I taught you to eat with your fingers? Luz scolded me: 'Use a fork.' I told her this was the Filipino way, but she didn't like, so I stopped."

"I remember the raw egg mixed with rice. To this day, I can't eat eggs."

"You ate it all," Fausto shot back. "Every time. Cleaned out the bowl."

Rogelio twirled noodles with his fork and said, "Because I wanted to please you." He pulled his chair closer to Fausto. "Your hands are shaking. Here, Uncle Fausto, let me feed you," Rogelio said.

"Eh?" Fausto said, pretending not to have heard.

"Let me feed you, Uncle." With his fingers, Rogelio scooped bits of his fried fish and mixed it with Fausto's rice. He formed it into a ball and held it up to Fausto's lips. Fausto hesitated before Rogelio placed the food on his tongue. Fausto took his time chewing and swallowed. A lump formed in his throat. Rogelio offered another scoop of fried fish and rice, and Fausto opened his mouth wide to receive it.

———————

When Fausto awoke, his bedroom walls were awash in pink light. It was another too-quiet early morning. The time—12:20—on his wind-up clock greeted him. As he got out of bed, a burst of energy ran up his legs like a shock of electricity. He put on a plain white shirt—a peace offering for Macario—and pulled out a blanket from his dresser and set it on top to remind him to bring it with them. He touched his chin, calluses catching stubble. As he entered the bathroom, he told himself he'd have to shave before leaving the Village.

Rogelio opened the door from Prudencio's room to the bathroom. He was wide awake, though his clothes were rumpled and his hair pushed up from the back. "Good morning, Uncle Fausto. How are you feeling?"

"I feel good. I'll shave and then we eat breakfast before we go, eh?" He set his shaving cream and razor by his sink, and cleared his throat. "Before we see Macario, I would like to go to the house in Terra Bella."

Rogelio stared at Fausto's reflection in the mirror. "I'm not so sure, Uncle."

"My baby is there," Fausto said, unashamed of talking of such things at his age.

Somebody hushed him. In the mirror his mother was rocking back and forth on her heels. One end of her shawl was over her shoulder. She clutched it as if it were a baby, patting her hand against her chest. Years of sun had wrinkled the skin around her eyes and mouth. Hard labor had bent her fingers. She brushed back strands of white hair near her forehead and gazed at Fausto as if he were still her boy, the teenager who left her for good, the old man who would always be her son. He waited as long as he could stand it, watching her as he used to do in the outdoor backyard kitchen when she tossed cut-up meat and offal into the gravy of pig's blood, garlic, chili, and vinegar. She blew kisses into the pot as she stirred with a big wooden spoon, the secret ingredient that made her *dinardaraan* flavorful.

Fausto knew he shouldn't turn around, expecting to find her there, but he did. Rogelio turned around too, following his gaze. Fausto was surprised he wasn't disappointed that there were just the two of them in his room. Rather, he was filled with gratitude.

Rogelio shrugged. "I understand, Uncle, but I think it would be too hard on you."

"I have nothing to remind me of Lulu, except for the story you told," Fausto said.

He wished he and Marina had given the first baby a name, even if they didn't know if it was a boy or a girl. "The baby is in the melon patch," he said. He meant the handkerchief, the shoebox—things he could hold in his hands.

"Are you sure you know where? And you know what you want to do?" Fausto nodded.

In his dream, though Fausto swore it was real, Marina had dug up the baby's grave and wrapped something from it in a blanket. He kept Ayong's gardening tools, along with their asparagus knives, in his closet. Now that it was settled, he would get the shovel and put it next to the blanket. He was ready. He nodded again, this time with the same energy that had coursed through his body when he awoke in the morning. He filled the sink with warm water. He wasn't used to someone watching him shave. When he splashed his face, his hands shook. With one stroke of the razor, he slashed his cheek.

"Son-of-a-gun!" He threw the razor into the sink as if it were to blame.

"Let me help." Rogelio wadded toilet paper and pressed it against Fausto's skin.

"If I was picking grapes, I would have cut myself with the clippers." Fausto laughed.

"Hold still," Rogelio commanded, and swabbed the cut with rubbing alcohol he had found under the sink.

The medicine smell and cold sting made his eyes water. Long after the blood had dried and Rogelio insisted on shaving the rest of his face, wiping cream with a hot towel, Fausto could not stop his eyes from watering. When they were done, Rogelio put his arm around Fausto's shoulder and led him to the dining room. The faint citrus scent of Rogelio's aftershave reminded him of orange blossoms, but Fausto couldn't find his voice to tell him.

———

They were the only diners at this hour, so Fausto gave Rogelio a tour of the big room, with its stone fireplace, built with local river rock. He was pleased that Rogelio pored over every element in the room with silent reverence as if each was a sacred object in a sacred place. Fausto kicked the soda machine that used to eat up his quarters. He walked across the saltillo tile floors—tiles Ted had helped to lay. As he ran his hand along the picnic-style tables, the feeling that he would not return to this place came over him again. Rogelio promised he would visit him often, but now Fausto—bolstered by this feeling—imagined Rogelio insisting that Fausto live with him once he found a suitable place for the two of them and was settled in Los Angeles.

Rogelio shook a bottle of ketchup over his hash browns, but before he could unscrew the cap and squeeze the bottle, Fausto spanked Rogelio's hand. He was sure the condiments were the same ones put on the tables when the Village opened twenty-three years ago. Rogelio laughed, replacing the bottle in its dust-ringed spot in the Lazy Susan. Fausto crossed his arms, satisfied. He could get used to helping Rogelio in this way.

Before they left, Fausto pointed out a plaque on the wall and Rogelio read the words out loud: "We came to help patiently, you helped us grow. We came to build lovingly, you taught us strength and courage. Your spirit and conviction inspired us to struggle and to fight for fairness and equality. Our lives are changed forever. You became friends, brothers, mentors, and Manongs to us all, and we are eternally grateful—the Agbayani Village crew and volunteers."

Fausto hadn't read the plaque in years. It made him think of Ted in his youth—the torn jeans and T-shirts, the long hair and beat-up Volkswagen Beetle. It made him think of sitting with Prudencio and his suitcase, waiting for Arturo to take Prudencio away.

"We should go, eh?" Fausto glanced at his watch. He sniffed hard—his nose had begun to run. *Mapan tayon!* Let's go!" he said, surprised at his urgency.

Arturo came looking for them as they left the dining hall. He gave Rogelio his car keys, explaining the temperamental nature of his Camaro. Sometimes it was hard to start in the heat, so it was good that they were going midmorning. But Arturo went through his routine: gently pump the gas pedal, then turn the ignition key over for a count of ten seconds.

When Rogelio told him they were going to see the gray-brick house in Terra Bella, Arturo turned to Fausto with one eyebrow raised.

Fausto laughed. "You think I'll stay in Terra Bella? Maybe I'll go back to Los Angeles." He didn't care what Rogelio was thinking; his whole body hummed like a power line and tingled as if all his fluids were surging and washing over him in a baptism.

Arturo cupped Fausto's face with his enormous hands and looked him in the eye. "Wherever you go, I'll be waiting for you right here, hombrecito." He drew an "X" in the ground between them, the topsoil parting easily to reveal the hard earth.

"When I come back, you better be here then, eh?" Fausto pulled away, commanding himself not to cry. "*Ai sus*, you stirred up all that dust!"

Arturo insisted on strapping Fausto in his car seat, just as his co-worker drove up and honked her horn. He made her wait as he stood at the entrance of the Village and waved good-bye. Fausto waved back, craning his neck, sure that Arturo was still standing in the driveway long after the row of tall, slender cypress trees and oleander bushes swallowed him up.

———————

Fausto proposed seeing the Cuculich camp first, though he knew the old bunkhouses had been razed and new structures built a long time ago. The detour, however, would also give him more time to prepare himself for the house in Terra Bella. It didn't matter that the gray-brick house was abandoned or perhaps burned to the ground. He was more afraid of setting foot in the garden. Never mind that he likely wouldn't be able to locate the exact spot after all these years. Maybe in the end he would just take a handful of soil.

He stole a glance at Rogelio, who was checking the symbols on the dashboard. *Fausto wanted more time!* Mr. Cuculich once told him to be thankful for what he had. It was enough to be with Rogelio now, though he felt time hurtling them forward. He gave Rogelio directions to the camp, staring out the window at the vineyards that seemed to fade before him. Rogelio asked for more details, but Fausto went blank. After remembering so much the last few days, the numbers on the signposts at the intersections confused him.

"It's okay. We'll find it. We aren't in any hurry," Rogelio said.

Though he went to the bathroom before they left, Fausto needed to pee. He tried to ignore it, pressing his thighs together, but the urge only grew stronger. He leaned over, yanking on Rogelio's sleeve. "I have to pee," he said.

Rogelio parked the car on the shoulder of the road. Rows of fat Emperor grapes on leafy vines stood on either side of the empty road. Rogelio led him in a few rows deep. Fausto apologized as he fumbled with his zipper. As if to make him feel better, Rogelio unzipped his pants and peed alongside him, his stream direct and forceful. But not much came out of Fausto, though he shook his penis to coax it. When he was in the car, it seemed as if he could have filled a dry lakebed. As they got back on the road, Rogelio asked Fausto who owned these fields, but Fausto didn't know where they were at all. He told Rogelio to keep driving; he would find their way back. A few miles passed when the urge to pee returned. He thought he had told Rogelio to stop, but Rogelio kept driving. Fausto unbuckled his seatbelt and unlocked the car door. As he reached for the handle, Rogelio let out a gasp and swerved the car off the road, kicking up dust.

"I need to pee!" Fausto said in a loud voice, and stumbled out the car. Rogelio's face was stripped of color as he helped Fausto into the fields. Not a single drop came out.

"We're going back to Agbayani Village," Rogelio said when they emerged from the fields.

Rogelio tightened Fausto's seatbelt. Fausto opened his mouth and drool bubbled out. His nose began to run. When he squeezed his eyes shut, tears flowed from the corners. He wiped his eyes, and his fingers were soon wet and milky-white. It was as if all the fluids in his body were being drained from every opening except his penis! He lurched forward, struggling to breathe. And then he started babbling, not recognizing his sounds as words.

"I'm going to take you to the hospital instead, Uncle Fausto." Rogelio stuck his head out the window. The road was still empty. He gripped the steering wheel. "We'll find a house or a crew working somewhere. They'll tell us where to go." He started the car, but the engine sputtered and died. He turned over the ignition, counting ten seconds, and pumped the gas pedal several times with great restraint. The engine kicked a few times and then died. Rogelio yanked his portable phone from his shirt pocket and pushed buttons.

Fausto heard Rogelio's frantic voice talking on the phone, but it was fading. Who was he calling? Arturo? Macario? His head lolled to one side, facing the fields. How ripe the grapes were for harvesting! Surely a bumper crop! But where were the farm workers, their cars parked on the shoulder of the road, the packing cart, the stacks of crates? Was it Sunday morning? He'd lost track of time. Fausto's fingers stiffened. An iciness gripped his hands and pushed up into his arms. It was a shock to feel Rogelio's fingers rub his skin, trying to warm him up. In the Delano heat? He wanted to laugh. Instead, he leaned back. He could not keep his eyes open.

How much time had passed before he first heard the siren, a faint echo? He didn't know. It grew louder. Its wail pierced his ears, shook him awake. He heard men's voices that didn't belong to Rogelio, and then Rogelio's voice breaking. By now his legs and arms were as brittle as icicles, rattling at the joints, ready to break off. He didn't want to move. But two strangers lifted him out of the car. The sun struck his face as his head bobbed back and forth. When he opened his eyes, Rogelio's face swung in and out of view above him. The two men lowered him onto a stretcher that was hard on his bones. His cheek brushed up against stiff baby-blue paper, crinkling in his ears, roaring like an ocean. He felt himself being glided into a big box, the sun disappearing behind a white horizon with gray padded sides and small windows that captured the cloudless sky. *It is very beautiful over there.*

Doors slammed shut, an engine revved up. Two rows of bright lights forced his eyes shut. Buttons popped as his white shirt—his peace offering to Macario—was pulled apart. Scissors nipped at his undershirt. A rush of cold air pummeled his chest when his undershirt was ripped off as if rotted. Strips of paper were being torn. The strangers pressed sticky dots on his chest. *We are on our way to the camp where I used to live, to the fields where I used to pick grapes for thirty years. We are going to see my first baby. Then I'm going to Los Angeles with Rogelio.* Nobody seemed to be listening to him. *Today is a good day.* His body shook with the revelation, with the force it took to yell the words at the top of his lungs.

One of the men stuck him with a needle. Fausto's mouth stiffened. Metal clinked on one side of him, and then high-pitched beeps rang in his ears. He felt as if his heart had been removed and was floating, beating, to his right—where Domingo and Serapio were hunched, solemn faced, Domingo clutching his wool fedora, Serapio holding his combat helmet on his lap. The beeps were slowing down, the moments between them lengthening like the shadows of a late fall afternoon. When he gasped, a rubber cup was snapped over his mouth. *Breathe.* With every breath, cold air forced its way into his lungs.

"I want you to know I'm so lucky we got this chance to be together again."

Fausto squinted his eyes as Rogelio's face, upside down, appeared above him. Rogelio's fingers brushed his cheeks in between the elastic straps with the softness of feathers. Rogelio's hands cupped his chin, fluttering against his skin like anxious wings. Fausto gave a start, realizing that Rogelio was with him, that he had remained with him the whole time when Fausto thought he had been left with strangers and greeted by spirits.

Fausto wanted to tell him that *he* was the lucky one. He tried to reach for his throat, but every movement he made was slow and heavy. The air around him, once plentiful, coming from the rubber cup, now became a deep ocean. His lids were thickening. All his senses seemed to fade, except for his hearing. The men talking in low voices, Rogelio reciting prayers, *Hail Mary, full of grace, the Lord is with you.*

Like a swimmer bursting up from the water, Fausto opened his eyes with all his might. He blinked several times. He had risen above them all. How could that be? Instead of looking up at Rogelio's face, he saw the top of Rogelio's head leaning over his body. Domingo and Serapio were gone. Rogelio's fingers were entwined with his, but he could not feel a thing! And then another blink and he was no longer in the ambulance. The white roof was below him for a moment. The ambulance soon sped ahead of him, down the road, as straight as a spine, the rows of vines on either side like ribs. It headed toward Delano until it became a white speck of dust.

The air was still. Fausto looked around him. Hard sunlight struck the silver and red Mylar flags along the edges of the vineyard. The flags glittered, whipping in a wind he could not feel. Hundreds of pale yellow butterflies, light as confetti, fluttered across the asphalt road. Crows cawed, throaty as trombones, one after the other, and landed on bowed telephone lines bordering the road, their oily black heads glinting in the sun. He rose above the acres and acres of vineyards, the even rows of vines. The flags below winked in waves like so many tiny flashbulbs going off.

All sound was muffled now, except for the wind siphoning dust from the earth below. A dark funnel swirled at his toes and ankles, spun up and swallowed his legs, chest, arms, and finally his face. Dust entered his mouth when he licked his caked lips, sucking his throat and lungs dry. It corked his nostrils. It clouded his vision. When he could no longer see below, he looked above him. The sky was lit up, bathing him, warming him. He saw flashes of yellow straw, a ringlet of jet-black hair, a baby's fist—pink and translucent, its fingers uncurling, blooming. He thrust his arms upward as the dust pulled him toward the light.

ACKNOWLEDGMENTS

A writer is only as good as the community and books that nurture her.

The following books gave my novel its depth: *America Is in the Heart* by Carlos Bulosan; *Delano: The Story of the California Grape Strike* by John Gregory Dunne; *The Fight in the Fields: Cesar Chavez and the Farmworkers Movement* by Susan Ferriss and Ricardo Sandoval; *Filipinos: Forgotten Asian Americans* by Fred Cordova; *Forty Acres: Cesar Chavez and the Farm Workers* by Mark Day; *Huelga: The First Hundred Days of the Great Delano Grape Strike* by Eugene Nelson; *Long Road To Delano* by Sam Kushner; *Philip Vera Cruz: A Personal History of Filipino Immigrants and the Farmworkers Movement* by Craig Scharlin and Lilia V. Villanueva; and *The Philippines Reader: A History of Colonialism, Neocolonialism, Dictatorship, and Resistance* edited by Daniel B. Schirmer and Stephen Rosskamm Shalom.

Listening to the recollections of a number of people helped me see history through their eyes. Among those are Anita Navalta Bautista, the late Frank Perez, Leatrice Perez, Angelina Magael, Virginia Zambra-Melera, Hub Segur, the late Don Watson, the late Andy Imutan, Sid Valledor, the late Jack Pandol Sr., the late Benny Ordiz, Jimmy Mar, and Kelly Padula. Thanks to Diana Pickworth for her help with Yemen culture and history. I am grateful also to my late mother, Conchita Enrado; my sister Heidi Enrado; and my relatives the late Benny Agustin, the late Fausto Ayson, Annie Esperanza, Fred Eala, and Daniel Toleran, who all helped me navigate through our community history.

I received assistance in finding articles, books, and information about time periods that were not mine from the staff of the Filipino American National Historical Society (Stockton chapter), the *Delano Record*, the University of California at Los Angeles Asian-American Studies Center, Bolerium Books in San Francisco, the San Francisco Maritime Museum Library, the California Military Museum, and the Museum of History and Industry in Seattle.

Thanks to Angelina Candelario Noveloza, Samuel Orpilla Jr., Marc Barcelona, Nelia Barcelona, Lea Barcelona, Jasmin Lucas, Art Lucas, Narcissa Labasan, and Finely Agbayani Pusag, Jr. for the Ilocano translations, and to Monica Alvarez-Selles for the Spanish translations.

With heartfelt gratitude, I thank Sands Hall, Kimi Ynigues, Frances Badgett, Paul Calandrino, Jack Beaudoin, Dan Chaon, Kathy Brackett Verschoor, and the Squaw Valley Community of Writers for careful readings of drafts and/or discussions on the craft of fiction, and for long-distance writerly comfort and community through the years. I am especially indebted to Laurel Kallenbach, whose editing has enriched my novel and made it so much better than I could ever have imagined. Thank you, Laurel, for more than a quarter-century of your friendship.

For helping me with the last leg of the journey, I thank Lori Merish-Rose, Eugene Rose, Evangeline (Vangie) Buell, and Harvey Dong at Eastwind Books of Berkeley.

I respectfully acknowledge Bienvenido N. Santos, who wrote about the manongs in his book, *Scent of Apples: A Collection of Stories*, which was given to me by my sister Heidi many years ago.

Lastly, I am deeply grateful to my family, David, Jacob, and Isabella, who allowed me to spend time with my other family and community for the past eighteen years. Thank you for your love, support, and patience.

NOTES

It was necessary to make a few historical deviations in my novel. Although the timelines vary according to different sources, the pensionado program ran from 1903 to 1928, resuming in some form after my 1929 scene on the ship until the outbreak of World War II; Yemen formed a pact with Egypt and Syria in 1958, not in 1955; Paulo Agbayani died in April 1966, not August 1966; a typhoon did not strike the island of Luzon in November 1966; a killing frost did not shut down the Central Valley's citrus crops during the winter of 1966; a hotel strike did not occur in Chicago in the 1970s; and although efforts began in 1991, the Asian American Studies Program at the University of Illinois in Chicago was not formalized and a minor not offered until the fall of 2010.

Chapter 13's title, "Down a long, dark valley," comes from a quote by Jack T. Conway, executive director of the Industrial Union Department, AFL-CIO, in a February 1966 newspaper article. Conway testified on behalf of Walter D. Reuther, president of IUD, and said, "Exploring the problems of our nation's agricultural workers is like groping painfully and slowly down a long dark valley where sunlight seldom penetrates and there are very few resting places."

ABOUT THE AUTHOR

Patty Enrado was born in Los Angeles and raised in Terra Bella, California. She has a bachelor's degree in English from the University of California at Davis and a master's degree from Syracuse University's Creative Writing Program. She writes about healthcare information technology and lives in the San Francisco Bay Area with her husband and two children.